W9-BUT-923

When We Found Home

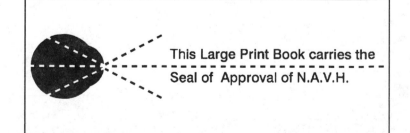

This Large Print Book carries the
Seal of Approval of N.A.V.H.

WHEN WE FOUND HOME

SUSAN MALLERY

THORNDIKE PRESS
A part of Gale, a Cengage Company

Farmington Hills, Mich • San Francisco • New York • Waterville, Maine
Meriden, Conn • Mason, Ohio • Chicago

Copyright © 2018 by Susan Mallery, Inc.
Thorndike Press, a part of Gale, a Cengage Company.

ALL RIGHTS RESERVED
This is a work of fiction. Names, characters, places, and incidents are either the product of the author's imagination or are used fictitiously, and any resemblance to actual persons, living or dead, business establishments, events, or locales is entirely coincidental.
Thorndike Press® Large Print Basic.
The text of this Large Print edition is unabridged.
Other aspects of the book may vary from the original edition.
Set in 16 pt. Plantin.

LIBRARY OF CONGRESS CIP DATA ON FILE.
CATALOGUING IN PUBLICATION FOR THIS BOOK
IS AVAILABLE FROM THE LIBRARY OF CONGRESS.

ISBN-13: 978-1-4328-5326-6 (hardcover)

Published in 2018 by arrangement with Harlequin Books S.A.

Printed in the United States of America
1 2 3 4 5 6 7 22 21 20 19 18

I've always been a big believer that while we can't control the family we are born into, we can certainly create the family of our heart. It's something I've done all my life: finding amazing mentors, loving friends and advocates who wouldn't give up on me, even when I wanted to give up on myself. There's an old saying about blooming where you are planted. I would say, first find a garden that makes you really happy and then go ahead and bloom there.

This book is for those of you who have chosen your family — heart by loving heart. May you always be loved and treasured for the beautiful bloom that you are.

CHAPTER ONE

As Delaney Holbrook watched the man in the suit approach, she did her best to remind herself she'd given up on men in suits — in fact all men and most suits, when it came to that. She was a different person, with new and improved goals, although she could still admire excellent tailoring. And nice blue eyes. And a firm jaw. And his walk. He had a very purposeful walk that was incredibly appealing. She sighed. So much for giving up on men in suits.

She waited until he was directly in front of her before giving in to temptation and saying, "It's been six weeks and this is getting pretty serious. Don't you think I should know your name?"

She had no idea how he was going to respond. She half expected him to give her an icy stare and turn away, because this particular man in a suit had an impressive icy stare. She'd seen it more than once, albeit directed at others. But he didn't glare. Instead he smiled. No, that was wrong. He didn't just *smile,* he gave her a slow, sexy grin that kicked her in the gut and left her feeling all fluttery and stupid and just a little hopeful.

Talk about opening Pandora's box.

"I'm Malcolm."

His voice was low and masculine, with just enough gravel to give her a happy shiver along her spine.

"Good morning, Malcolm." She pointed at her name tag. "Delaney, although you already knew that."

"I did."

"Your usual?"

Malcolm was a double shot, extra hot, large latte. Although he arrived every morning at exactly seven forty, he bypassed the busy coffee stand in the middle of the building's lobby, instead making his way to the special bank of elevators that required a cardkey or a security escort to reach their lofty levels. But sometime midmorning, he would wander down for a morning latte.

Her shift ended at ten and more than once she'd found herself lingering, oh so foolishly, so she could take his order. A ridiculous truth that should have embarrassed her, but didn't. Instead of telling herself that at twenty-nine she was too old to be crushing on a handsome stranger, she went with a kinder, gentler message. Time did heal and as she'd suspected, she was more than ready to return to normal life . . . whatever that turned out to be.

"My usual," he confirmed as he handed over a reloadable gift card to pay for his coffee, along with a tall white mug. She ran the card through the cash register, then walked over to start his drink.

Luzia, her teammate, untied her apron. "I'm going to go to the storeroom for more supplies," she said. "You going to be okay by yourself?"

"I will."

Luzia smiled politely at Malcolm before stepping out from behind the counter and walking across the lobby.

Alone at last, Delaney thought, careful not to laugh. No way she wanted to explain what was so funny.

Malcolm slid the coffee card back into his wallet, then returned his attention to her. "You're new."

"Relatively. I've been here nearly two months." She tipped the small metal pitcher of milk so she could insert the steamer. The familiar hissing, gurgling sound began. She poured four shots of espresso into the mug

9

he'd brought.

"You're with Alberto's Alfresco." She nodded at the logo on his mug. "Your company owns the building and our little coffee stand is a renter. Hmm, does that make you my boss?"

He grinned. "Don't go there."

"Why not? I suspect you like being a boss."

"Not all the time."

"Most of the time," she teased. "Your suit is too nice for that not to be true."

"What is your experience with people in suits?"

"I used to be one."

"Unexpected." One eyebrow rose. "Not anymore?"

"No. I've decided to go in a different direction." She poured the steamed milk into his mug. "I know what you're wondering, so to answer the question, it was my choice."

In a manner of speaking, she thought. The decision to change careers had been hers — the circumstances leading to that decision had not.

"What direction is that?" he asked.

"I'm going to be a naturopath." She waited for the look of confusion before adding, "It's a —"

"I know what naturopathic medicine is. It

10

emphasizes using the body's own systems for healing through a combination of Western medicine and natural cures." One corner of his mouth turned up. "My grandfather's housekeeper has a niece who graduated from Bastyr University with a degree in acupuncture or something like that. Are you a student there?"

She ignored the bit about his grandfather having a housekeeper — the suit already implied money, so she shouldn't be surprised. "That's my plan. I have to meet certain prerequisites in science and math but my business degree didn't require them so I'm going back to college to make them up." She shook her head. "It's been a while since I've had to go to class and study. My brain is still unamused and crabby about the whole thing."

He sipped his coffee. "What classes did you start with?"

"Biology and algebra."

He winced. "Good luck with that."

"Thanks. At first I had to read every chapter three or four times to remember anything. Now I'm down to only having to read it twice. The lab work has been interesting, though. In three weeks, we have to dissect things. I'm dreading that."

"There shouldn't be blood. Whatever it is

has been dead awhile."

"Still. Knives, cutting, organs." She shuddered.

His blue eyes brightened with amusement. "Is this where I remind you that you're basically studying to be a doctor?"

"Yeah, I get the irony. I try not to think about it, but I get it."

They looked at each other. She felt . . . *something.* Tension maybe, or awareness. Whatever it was, she appreciated the confirmation that she was alive, relatively healthy and moving on with her life. The world kept turning and dragging her along with it.

"I need to get back to work," Malcolm told her.

She wanted to believe there was a hint of reluctance in his voice, but she couldn't be sure. Still, it was nice to think about.

"Me, too." She glanced at her watch. "Or rather, head home and study for a few hours before class. Enjoy the rest of your day, Malcolm."

"You, too, Delaney."

He hesitated a second before turning toward the elevators. She watched him walk away and let herself imagine that he would spin back and ask her to lunch. Or dinner. Yes, dinner on his yacht. Or maybe they could helicopter to somewhere nice, although she wasn't sure where a helicopter ride from Seattle would get them. Portland? Vancouver. Oooh, an international destination!

Regardless, he would ask her to dinner and they would . . .

She laughed as she rinsed out the milk pitcher and made sure everything was in order for Luzia and the next shift. She and Malcolm would what? Go to dinner? Kiss? Fall in love?

Hardly. They had nothing in common. Years ago, maybe, when she'd been on the fast track in finance. Only then she'd been engaged to Tim. She wouldn't have noticed Malcolm at all.

"It doesn't matter," she told herself as she slipped off her apron. She had plans and dreams and hopes for the future. Not anything she would have imagined, but now, after everything she'd been through, they felt right. She would learn to heal others and if she got through that, she might have the chance to heal herself, as well.

Alberto's Alfresco corporate offices occupied the top three stories of the twenty-story building. The company leased out the rest to tenants that ranged from a dentist, three law firms and Amazon. The latter had

13

six floors where people came and went at all hours of the night and didn't talk to anyone who didn't work for their company. Malcolm Carlesso hoped they were building drones with artificial intelligence. He enjoyed sci-fi movies. Seeing one lived out in real time would be fun. Or not, he thought as he headed up to the top floor of the building. He didn't want to go out in a hail of angry drone gunfire.

Malcolm stepped out of the elevator. It was the middle of the workday and people were everywhere — walking in the halls, having meetings, taking calls in their offices. Alberto's Alfresco was a vibrant, multi-national, multibillion-dollar enterprise.

While the company had always been successful, until a few years ago, it had been much smaller. Malcolm had come on board right after he'd graduated from college. He'd been determined to grow the firm and make his grandfather — the Alberto in Alberto's Alfresco — proud. Two years ago, Malcolm's mission had taken on an urgency he couldn't seem to shake.

He passed his own office and went into that of the chief financial officer. Santiago Trejo had joined Alberto's Alfresco eighteen months ago when Malcolm had stolen him from a successful hedge fund. Together they made a formidable team.

Malcolm nodded a greeting at Santiago's assistant, sitting guard outside the open door, then entered the large corner office and took a seat. Santiago was on the phone. He smiled when he saw Malcolm and quickly wrapped up his call.

"Quarterly numbers from the East Coast are messed up," Santiago said cheerfully. "Our friends down in accounting are scrambling. I had to explain our 'fool me once' philosophy here at the company. It won't happen again." He paused. "What?"

Malcolm pulled his gaze from the view of the vast Seattle skyline and Puget Sound and looked at his friend.

"What do you mean what?"

"There's something. What happened? You look . . ." Santiago frowned, as if trying to figure something out. "Different. What's happened? Did you discover some new truffle oil vendor?"

"Nothing happened," Malcolm told him, then held out his mug. "I just went for coffee."

"And?"

"And nothing."

He'd talked to an attractive woman about something other than business. While un-

15

usual for him these days, it was hardly noteworthy.

Okay, maybe it was a little noteworthy, but not anything he was going to discuss with Santiago.

His friend was a "get back on the horse" kind of guy. Should a woman ever break Santiago's heart, a very unlikely event considering how many women came and went in his life, he would simply find one who was smarter, prettier or both, and make them both very happy. Malcolm had chosen another way to deal with his ex-fiancée's betrayal, and that had been to withdraw into work.

Still, he'd enjoyed talking with Delaney. And looking at her. He'd never had a type before, but as of today, he was definitely into redheads. Maybe he should —

Santiago's phone buzzed, then his assistant's voice came over the speaker. "Alberto is in the building. Repeat, Alberto is in the building."

Santiago looked at Malcolm. "Did you know he was coming? Do we have a meeting? It's not on my calendar."

"No meeting." Malcolm tried to figure out why his grandfather would show up with no warning, then reminded himself the exercise was futile. He would never guess. Alberto didn't like talking on the phone — if he felt he had something important to discuss during the workday, he would simply drive himself to the office and find the person he wanted to talk to.

The fact that he was here and not at their warehouse in the SoDo — south of downtown — district meant it wasn't about packaging or food, and wasn't that lucky. Malcolm still remembered the rotini-fusilli incident from three years ago when Alberto had discovered packaging that had used the two pasta names interchangeably, which might be fine for some but not for a company that prided itself on selling *authentic* Italian food.

The entire marketing department had been forced to listen to a twenty-minute lecture on the importance of knowing the different types of pasta as they prepared their campaigns. Information they needed to have, but perhaps not delivered by a man in his eighties who still occasionally broke into passionate Italian.

Malcolm set down his mug, then made his way to the elevator bank to wait for his grandfather. Alberto Carlesso had been born in Italy and brought to America when his parents immigrated in the 1930s. During the Second World War the then teenager had put his cooking skills and family recipes to good use in their Seattle neighborhood. Food was scarce and Alberto's ability to create delicious meals out of whatever was on hand had made him popular. Every summer, he'd made his own marinara sauce with the fresh ingredients grown on neighboring farms. Some of the bottles had made their way to New York where a few Italian grocery store owners had sold them at a tidy profit.

The elevator doors opened. Malcolm smiled at the slightly bent, white-haired man in a suit and tie who walked toward him.

"Hello, Grandfather."

"Malcolm, they still warn you when I'm coming, eh? What is everyone so afraid of? I'm an old man who no longer runs the company. I'm a pussycat without claws."

"I think you're more bobcat than house cat."

His grandfather grinned. "A bobcat? I like that."

Even though they'd seen each other at breakfast that morning, they hugged. Alberto was a toucher. Thank goodness he'd retired before the new standards for sexual harassment had come into law, Malcolm thought. Not that his straight-as-an-arrow grandfather would ever make a pass at anyone, but he would hug and occasionally clasp hands with whomever he was talking to — regardless of gender. While most of the employees understood that was just his way, a few were less accommodating.

"I saw the new catalog," Alberto said as they walked toward Malcolm's office.

Malcolm held in a groan. Catalog releases were always stressful. Would the customers respond favorably? Would the new products be successful? Would his grandfather want to know why they were offering a line of gluten-free pasta?

"Very nice," his grandfather continued. "I don't agree with the macarons but I understand they're very popular and have an excellent profit margin. You have to keep up with the times."

"We do."

They walked into Malcolm's office. The huge space had been Alberto's, before the old man had retired. Malcolm had replaced the old-fashioned wood paneling and the carpeting but otherwise had kept the room much the same. The desk and credenza, monstrosities from the 1970s, were a reminder of the heritage inherent in the company and Malcolm liked that.

They passed by the desk and made their way to the seating area at the far end of his office. Malcolm preferred to use a conference room when he had a meeting, but he kept the sofas for the same reason he kept the desk — because they belonged.

Malcolm's assistant walked in with a tray. She smiled at them both, set the tray on the coffee table and left. His grandfather picked up one of the two mugs of steaming black coffee, along with a piece of biscotti. After dipping the latter in his mug, he said, "I found her."

Resignation, irritation and inevitability battled for dominance. Malcolm realized it didn't much matter which won — it wasn't as if he was going to change his grandfather's mind about any of it. To Alberto, family was everything. A trait to be admired, even if it occasionally made everyone's life more complicated.

About the time Alberto had decided to cut out the middleman and sell his food directly to the public, through a mail-order catalog, he'd met, fallen in love with and married the pretty Irish girl who lived next door and they'd had one son — Jerry.

Alberto's Alfresco had been successful, with steady but modest growth. Jerry had little interest in managing the company, a disappointment to both his parents. Instead he'd taken over corporate sales, traveling all over the country. He'd never married, but he had managed to father a few children. Three, to be precise, all by different mothers.

When Malcolm had been twelve, his mother had brought him from Portland, Oregon, to Seattle and had demanded to speak with Alberto. She'd presented Malcolm as Jerry's son. Alberto had taken one look at Malcolm and had smiled, even as tears had filled his eyes. Malcolm was, he declared, the exact image of his late wife.

Jerry had been more reticent, insisting on a DNA test, which had proved positive. Within the week, both Malcolm and his mother were living in Alberto's huge house.

Malcolm remembered how confused he'd been at the time. He'd been ripped from the only home he'd ever known and moved to Seattle. His grandfather had been adoring, his father indifferent, and Malcolm had taken a long time to accept that the large house by the lake was his home. Back then he'd been unable to figure out why his mother had suddenly decided to change everything and for the longest time she wouldn't say. When she finally confessed she was sick and dying, he'd been forced to accept there was no going back. It would never be just him and his mom ever again.

When she'd died, Alberto had stepped in to take care of him. Jerry had remained indifferent — something Malcolm had come to terms with eventually.

Then two years ago, Jerry had died leaving — everyone had presumed — only one child. A few months ago, Alberto had finally brought himself to go through his son's belongings. There he'd found proof of two additional children — daughters. Keira, a twelve-year-old living in foster care in Los Angeles, had been easily located and moved into the house six weeks before, but an older daughter, Callie, had been more difficult to find. Until now, apparently.

Malcolm gave in to the inevitable and asked, "Where is she?"

"Texas. Houston. She's twenty-six."

Eight years younger than him and fourteen years older than Keira.

"She's living off the grid, as you young people like to say," Alberto told him. "That's why it took so long. The private detective had to trace her from Oklahoma. The lawyer will speak to her and confirm everything using DNA."

"Do you want me to go meet her and bring her home?"

Because like Keira, Callie would be invited to come live with her paternal grandfather.

While the twelve-year-old hadn't had much choice — Alberto and Malcolm were her only living family — Callie was an adult. She could tell her grandfather to go pound sand. Malcolm honestly had no idea what she would do. But the promise of inheriting a piece of Alberto's Alfresco would be difficult to resist.

"I'm sending a lawyer," Alberto said. "That makes it more official."

Malcolm wondered if that was the only reason.

He wasn't sure how he felt about the sudden influx of siblings. Keira confused him — he knew nothing about twelve-year-old girls. After enrolling her in a quality private school that was conveniently across the street from the office building, he'd asked Carmen, their housekeeper, to keep tabs on her. Every now and then he suffered guilt, wondering if he should be more involved in her life, but how? Take her shopping and listen to teen music? He held in a shudder.

"I'm hoping she'll move here," Alberto told him. "We'll be a family."

Before Malcolm could respond, his grandfather shifted in his seat. The late morning light caught the side of his face, illuminating the deep wrinkles. Alberto wasn't a young man. Yes, he was in good health, but at his age, anything could happen. Malcolm didn't want to think about what it would mean to lose him and he sure didn't want his last years to be unhappy.

"I hope she does, too," he said, wondering if he was lying, then telling himself it didn't much matter. When it came to his grandfather, he would do what Alberto wanted. He owed him that for everything that had happened . . . and everything he'd done.

CHAPTER TWO

At six thirty on an unexpectedly sunny Saturday morning, the condo building's impressive gym was practically a ghost town. Santiago Trejo split his attention between the display on his treadmill and the small, built-in TV screen tuned to ESPN and a list of games scheduled for the first Saturday of the year's baseball season.

Santiago enjoyed sports as much as the next guy, but the thrill of baseball eluded him. Seriously — could it move slower? Give him a sport where something happened. Even if the score was low in hockey or soccer, the players were always doing something. But in baseball entire innings could pass with literally absolutely no action.

The show went to commercial just as the treadmill program ended. Timing, he thought with a grin. He gave the machine a quick disinfectant wipe-down before grabbing his towel and water bottle and heading to the elevators.

His condo was on an upper floor with a view of Puget Sound and the peninsula beyond. He could watch the ferries and cargo ships making their way to port, have a front-row seat to Fourth of July celebrations and admire the storms as they blew through. When the weather was clear — not something that happened all that often in Seattle — he could see the Olympic Mountains. The gorgeous views and accompanying sunsets were very helpful when it came to the ladies — not that he needed props, but a man should have plenty of options in his arsenal.

After showering and dressing in jeans and a Yale Law School sweatshirt, he went down to his two parking spaces in the underground garage. A sleek, midnight blue Mercedes SL convertible sat next to a massive black Cadillac Escalade.

"Not today," he said, patting the Mercedes. "I have the munchkins." Not only would their mother not approve of them riding in a convertible, there wasn't any back seat.

Santiago made his way to his favorite bakery. Unlike the gym, the bakery was jammed with people out on a Saturday morning. He took a small paper number from the machine up front, then waited his turn. When seventy-eight was called, he walked up and grinned at the short, plump woman wearing a hairnet.

"Good morning, Brandi. Is your mother here? You know how I enjoy saying hello to her."

The fiftysomething woman behind the counter rolled her eyes. "You know it's me, Santiago. No one is fooled by this game you play."

He clutched his chest and feigned surprise. "Valia? Is that really you? You're so beautiful this morning, even more so than usual and I didn't think that was possible." He held open his arms. "Come on. You need a hug and so do I."

She groaned, as if the imposition was too much, but made her way around the counter. Santiago picked her up and spun her around until she shrieked.

"Put me down, you fool! You'll break your back."

He set her back on her feet and kissed her cheek. "It would be worth it," he whispered.

She laughed and slapped his arm. "You're incorrigible."

"That's why I'm your favorite."

"You're not my favorite."

"Liar."

She chuckled. "How's your mama?"

"Well. I'm going to see her right now, then take the rug rats to the zoo." He'd promised them a trip on the first sunny Saturday. Both of them had texted him yesterday with links to the weather report.

"They're good children." She eyed him. "You should be married."

"Maybe."

"You need a wife."

"No one *needs* a wife."

"You do. You're getting old."

"Hey, I'm thirty-four."

"Practically an old man. Get married soon or no one will want you."

He held his hands palm up and winked. "Really? Because hey, it's me."

Her lips twitched. "You're not all that."

"Now who's lying?"

She handed over a box with his name scrawled on the top. He'd placed his pastry order online after hearing from his niece and nephew.

"My cousin has a daughter," she began.

He passed her twenty dollars. "Uh-huh. So you've mentioned before. I love you, Valia, but no. I'll find my own girl."

"You keep saying that, but you never do. What's wrong with you?"

"Nothing," he called as he headed for the door. "I'll know when I know. Of that I'm sure."

He crossed the street and got two grande lattes from Starbucks before driving just north of the city to a quiet neighborhood of older homes. Most were either remodeled or in the process of being upgraded, but there were still a few with the original windows and tiny, one-car garages.

He wove through narrow streets until he reached his destination and pulled into the long driveway.

The lot was oversize and had two houses on it. The front one was large — about three thousand square feet, including the basement, with a nice backyard and plenty of light. Behind it was a smaller house — with just a single bedroom — but it was comfortable, private and quiet.

Santiago would never admit it to anyone but every time he came to visit, he felt a flush of pride. He'd been able to do this for his family. Him — some farm worker's kid from the Yakima Valley. The property was paid for and in a family trust. His brother Paulo and his family lived in the front house and Santiago's mother lived in the smaller one.

He parked by the latter and walked up the

front steps. His mother answered before he could knock.

"All your cars are loud," she said with a laugh. "You were never one for subtle, were you?"

"Never."

He gave her a hug and kiss before following her into the bright kitchen decorated in various shades of yellow. As usual, it was scary clean, with nothing out of place. His condo was clean, too, but only because he was rarely there and he had a cleaning service. He handed his mom one of the lattes before opening the pastry box. He got in a single bite before it began.

"How's work?"

"Good. Busy."

"Are you eating right? Do you get enough water? You've never liked to drink water, but it's good for your kidneys and keeps you regular."

"Mom," he began, not knowing why he bothered. What was it about women over fifty? They just said what they wanted. He tried to summon a little indignation, but he couldn't. Not about his mom. She'd earned whatever attitude she had now through years of pain, sacrifice and hard work.

She sipped her coffee and leaned against the counter. "Are you losing weight?"

"I weigh exactly the same as I did last time you saw me and last year and the year before."

"Are you getting sleep? You stay out too late with those women. And why don't I get to meet any of them? You never bring a girl home."

"You told me not to unless I was serious."

"That's because you go through them like you're in a revolving door. Look at Paulo. He's your younger brother and he's been married twelve years."

Santiago took another bite of his cinnamon roll, thereby avoiding answering the question. He loved his brother, and his sister-in-law was one of his favorite people on the planet, but there was no way he wanted his brother to be his role model. Paulo had gotten his girlfriend pregnant when they'd both been seniors in high school. They'd married quickly, had their kid and another one two years later.

Paulo had gotten a job on the assembly line at Alberto's Alfresco and never left. Santiago had tried to talk to him about going to college, or learning a skill but Paulo said he preferred to work the line. He'd moved up to supervisor and that was enough for him.

Hanna, Paulo's wife, had stayed home

with the kids until their youngest was five and then had gone to community college. Now she was in her final year of her nursing program and would graduate in a few months.

"We each have our own path, Mom."

"You don't have a path," his mother grumbled.

He winced. "Please don't say I have to get married. Valia already lectured me when I stopped by the bakery."

"Good for her. I worry about you."

He stood and crossed to her, then kissed the top of her head. "Don't worry, Mom. I'm fine."

The sound of running feet on the walkway offered salvation. Santiago released his mother just as the front door flew open and his niece and nephew raced toward him.

"The zoo opens at nine thirty," twelve-year-old Emma said. "I have a list of all the baby animals we have to visit. I'm monitoring their development."

"Of course you are."

Noah, her ten-year-old brother, scoffed, "She thinks she's so smart."

"I am smart," Emma told him. "I'm going to be a veterinarian. What are you going to be?"

"I'm going to play football!"

Santiago eyed his skinny frame. From what he could tell, Noah took after his mother in build, but maybe the kid would blossom. Or learn to be a kicker. He grabbed them both and squeezed tight enough to make them squeal.

"We'll look at the baby animals and the bears and the lions," he said. "Maybe one of you will misbehave and the lion can have you for dinner."

"Oh, Santiago." Emma shook her head. "You always threaten to throw us in but you'd never do that. You love us."

He walked back to the table and sank into his seat. "How can you know that? You're growing up so fast. It's depressing."

"I'll be thirteen in ten months."

He looked at his mom. "I don't like this. Make it stop."

"Children grow up, Santiago. Sometimes they grow up and get married and have children of their own."

He faked a smile and thought about banging his head against the table. What was going on today with the women in his life? With his luck, Emma would want to fix him up with one of her teachers. He was happily single. He dated plenty. Some would say too much. He liked his life. One day he would meet the right one and then everything would change but until then, why mess with perfection?

Noah grabbed a jelly donut then slid onto Santiago's lap. "Can we go to the Lego store after the zoo?"

"Of course."

Emma perked up. "And the bookstore?"

"Definitely."

"You spoil them," his mother murmured.

He looked at her. "And?"

She smiled. "You're a very good uncle."

He winked. "Thanks, Mom."

Blowing ten grand on a five-year-old's birthday party was beyond the definition of insane, Callie Smith thought as she positioned the car-shaped cookie cutter over the sandwich and pressed down as evenly as she could. When she carefully peeled away the excess bread, she was left with a perfect car-shaped PB&J sandwich — sans crust, of course.

The menu for the event was fairly simple, and all based on the Disney movie *Cars*. Small cups contained carrot, celery and cucumber sticks — aka dipsticks. Two kinds of organic punch along with organic apple juice were at the refueling station. The catering firm's famous mac and cheese had been remade with pasta in the shape of wheels, and there were car-inspired mini hot dogs ready to go. Callie had already put half a cherry tomato and slice of cucumber to simulate wheels onto one hundred tooth-picks, ready to be shoved into place when the mini hot dogs were heated and put in the buns.

The cake was an incredible work of art — a stylized twelve-inch-high modified layer cake shaped to look like a mountain with a road circling up to the top where a small car sat, along with a banner reading *Happy Birthday Jonathan.*

The previous afternoon Callie had filled the loot bags with *Cars*-related toys, and had carefully rolled all twenty-five Pit Crew T-shirts with the names facing up. Yes, each boy would get a personalized T-shirt to wear for the party and then take home with him.

Janice, her boss and the owner of the catering company, hurried into the kitchen. "I already have a knot in my stomach. The rest of the staff has a pool going on how long it takes the first kid to throw up, but I'm hoping we can get through this one without any disasters. How are you doing?"

Callie pointed to the tray with the PB&J sandwiches. "All ready. I'll cover them with plastic wrap to keep them fresh. The hot dog wheels are done. Just have someone stick them on before putting in the hot dogs. Veggies are finished, the cake is in place and I've put out the loot bags. Oh, and the T-shirts are by the front door to be handed out as the guests arrive. Just so you know, there are three Brandons."

Janice groaned. "Of course there are." She looked around their client's massive kitchen. "You've done it again, Callie. You took this idea and ran with it. I would still be trying to figure out how to pull it all together."

Callie did her best to offer a sincere smile — one without a hint of bitterness. What was going to happen next wasn't Janice's fault. Instead, the blame lay squarely on Callie's shoulders. She could whine and stomp her feet all she wanted. She could point to her ex-boyfriend, but in the end, the decision had been hers and so were the consequences.

Rather than make Janice say it, Callie untied her apron. "I need to get going. The first guests will be arriving and I shouldn't be here."

Janice's mouth twisted as guilt flashed in her eyes. "I'm sorry. I just can't risk it."

Callie nodded. "Do you want me back at the shop to help with cleanup later?"

"Why don't you take the rest of the day off? We have to prep for the Gilman wedding Tuesday morning. I'll see you then."

Callie nodded, doing her best not to calculate how much she would have made if she'd been able to stay and work the party. Being an hourly employee meant every penny mattered, but there was no way. She got that . . . sort of.

"Have fun today."

Janice gave a strangled laugh. "With twenty-five little boys? I don't think so."

Callie got her backpack from the utility room closet, then walked out the back door. She dug out her phone, opened her Uber app and requested a car.

Normally she would just take the bus back home but this part of River Oaks didn't have a whole lot of public transportation — especially not on a Sunday morning. So she would splurge.

Ten minutes later she was in the silver Ford Focus and heading for her more modest neighborhood. It wasn't close to work, but it was inexpensive and safe — two priorities for her.

She had the Uber driver drop her off at the H-E-B grocery store so she could get a few things. Only what she could carry home and consume in the next couple of days. The room she rented came with kitchen privileges, but Callie preferred to use the small refrigerator and microwave she kept in her room. She'd learned that storing anything in the main kitchen was a risky proposition. House rules were clear — don't take food belonging to someone else. Unfortunately enforcement was haphazard and Callie didn't want to chance someone taking her food.

She heated soup — the dented can had been 50 percent off! — then got out a four-month-old copy of *Vogue* that she'd fished out of a recycling bin to read while she ate. Janice only took day jobs on Sundays and the caterer was closed on Monday, giving Callie almost thirty-four hours off. At ten on Monday night she would start her other job, cleaning offices in the financial district.

She finished her lunch, then loaded her biggest tote with clothes, sheets and towels before heading to the local Laundromat. The afternoon had warmed up and gotten more humid — fairly typical for Houston in early spring, or any time of year.

The temperature inside the Laundromat had to be in the upper nineties. The crowded, noisy space was filled with families completing chores before the grind of the new week began again.

Callie found two free washers together, loaded her belongings and inserted a ridiculous number of quarters. She was lucky — she had to take care of only herself. Her bed was a twin, so the sheets were small. She could get away with two loads every two weeks, but how did people with kids make ends meet when it was three dollars to wash a load of clothes?

She went over to one of the empty chairs by the window and pretended to read her library book, all the while secretly watching everyone else.

There was a young couple who couldn't stop smiling at each other. Newlyweds, she decided, noting the modest diamond ring on the woman's left hand. They were probably saving for their first house. There was a family in the corner. The kids were running around while the parents carefully avoided looking at each other.

Uh-oh. They were fighting big-time. Neither of them wanted to back down. That was never good. One thing she'd learned over the years was the power of saying *I'm sorry.* People didn't say it nearly enough.

"Can you read to me?"

Callie looked at the pretty little girl standing in front of her. She was maybe three or four and held a big picture book in her hands. Callie'd seen her mom come in with two other kids and more laundry than she could manage. In the flurry of finding empty washers and loading clothes, the toddler had been forgotten.

"I can," Callie said. "Is this a good story?"

The girl — with dark hair and eyes — nodded solemnly. "It's about a mouse who gets lost."

"Oh, no. Not a lost mouse. Now I have to know if he finds his way home."

The girl gave her a smile. "It's okay. He does."

"Thank you for telling me that. I was really worried." She slid to the front of her chair and held out her hand for the book. "Would you like me to start?"

The girl nodded and handed over her precious book. Callie opened it and began to read.

" 'Alistair Mouse loved his house. He loved the tall doors and big windows. He loved how soft the carpet was under his mouse feet. He liked the kitchen and the bathroom, but most of all, Alistair loved his bed.' "

Callie pointed to the picture of a very fancy mouse bed. "That's really nice. I like all the colors in the bedspread."

The girl inched closer. "Me, too."

Callie continued to read the story. Just as she was finishing, the girl's mother walked over and sank down into a nearby chair. She was in her midtwenties and looked as if she had spent the last couple of years exhausted. She waited until Callie was done to say, "Thanks for reading to her. I didn't mean to dump her like that. It's just the boys are hyper and there's so much laundry and damn, it's so hot in here."

"It *is* hot," Callie said. "No problem. I enjoyed reading about Alistair and his troubles."

"Again," the little girl said, gently tapping the book.

"Ryder, no. Leave the nice lady alone."

"It's fine," Callie told her. She flipped back to the front of the book and began again. " 'Alistair Mouse loved his house.' "

This was nice, she thought as she continued with the story. A few minutes of normal with people she would never see again. A chance to be like everyone else.

She read the story two more times, then had to go move her laundry into a dryer. By then Ryder, her brothers and her mother had gone outside where it was slightly cooler and the boys could run on the grass. Callie watched and wondered about them. Where did they come from and why were they here now? Ryder's mother must have gotten pregnant pretty young — her oldest looked to be seven or eight. So she'd been, what, seventeen?

Unexpected tears burned in Callie's eyes. Force of habit had her blinking them away before they could be spotted. Tears were a weakness she wasn't allowed. She'd learned that lesson pretty quick. Only the strong survived.

She and Ryder's mother were probably the same age or at least within a year of each other, yet Callie felt decades older. Once she'd wanted normal things — to have a good man in her life, get married, have kids, some kind of a career. It had all been so vague back when she'd been eighteen, but it had never occurred to her it wouldn't happen. That in a single, stupid night she would destroy her future and set herself up for a life of having to explain herself over and over again.

She got her clothes out of the dryer and quickly folded them into her tote before starting the walk back to her small room. Each step on the sidewalk sounded like a never-ending refrain. *Convicted felon. Convicted felon.* She'd served her time, had, in theory, paid her debt to society, but she was marked forever.

She couldn't rent a decent apartment because no one wanted a convicted felon in their building. She couldn't work at a kid's party as part of the serving staff because no one wanted a convicted felon near their children. She couldn't get a job in a restaurant, despite having learned all about the food service industry while serving her time, because no one wanted a convicted felon near their customers. She'd earned her GED and had started on her associates degree while behind bars and that didn't matter, either.

One stupid, foolish, thoughtless act — robbing a liquor store with her loser boyfriend — and her eighteen-year-old self had destroyed her future.

Callie gave herself the entire walk home to mentally beat up on herself but once she walked into her room, she drew in a breath and changed the subject. She'd learned that, too. That a downward spiral was nearly impossible to stop, so she had to make sure she stayed positive as much as she could. She had a plan. It was going to take a while, but she had a plan.

She was saving every penny she could while working two jobs. When she had the money, she would buy a small condo that would be hers — no matter what. Right now having a home was priority one. She hadn't figured out exactly what she wanted to do, career wise, but she was open to possibilities. As for the great guy and a couple of kids, well, that was unlikely. She was wary of men and not very trusting of anyone who was willing to accept her past, so she was mostly alone, which was fine. One day it would all be better. It had to be. It just had to be.

CHAPTER THREE

Mornings at the coffee stand were crazy busy, with only occasional lulls. Delaney worked efficiently, her gaze drawn again and again to the building's large glass doors. Okay, yes, she and Malcolm had flirted on Friday. Big whoop. There was no reason to think he would acknowledge her in any way when he arrived this morning. There'd been an entire weekend between then and now. He could have totally forgotten her or gotten engaged. For all she knew, he was married.

No, she thought. He wasn't an icky guy. She had a feeling he was single — he just didn't strike her as the type to two-time. Although she could be totally wrong about that. From when she was sixteen until two years ago, there had only been one man in her life, so she was hardly anything close to a good judge of male character, but still. She didn't think Malcolm was involved with anyone or —

She glanced up from her place at the cash register and saw him walking through the building's large lobby. For a second she thought he wasn't going to acknowledge her, but then he turned in her direction and winked. A silly gesture that took a nanosecond and meant nothing yet had happiness and anticipation and bubbly excitement flooding through her. Oh, man, she had it bad, and for someone she barely knew.

She smiled at him before returning her attention to the next customer. Three people back, she spotted one of her favorite customers.

"Luzia," she called and nodded toward the preteen in a school uniform.

Luzia took Delaney's place at the cash register. "Is she your sister or something?"

"No. Just a friend."

"You take your break with her every day."

"I know. It's fun."

Two months ago Keira had walked up to the counter and demanded a double espresso. Delaney had laughed and offered hot chocolate instead. There had been a few minutes of quiet so they'd talked. Delaney had learned that Keira was twelve, new to the area, starting at the exclusive private school across the street and didn't have any family, save a brother and grandfather.

Over the past few weeks, she and Keira had formed a friendship of sorts. Keira opened up about her disdain for the school uniforms: "Seriously? Plaid? What? Are we in a porn movie?" and her dislike of her, as she called him, "asshole brother."

Delaney couldn't help thinking that underneath all that attitude was a scared little girl desperate to be loved. Not that she had any kids of her own, so maybe she was totally off base. Still, she couldn't shake the feeling that despite having family, Keira was way too alone in the world.

Delaney finished making a large hot chocolate with extra whipped cream, grabbed a black coffee for herself, then went around to one of the small tables at the side of the coffee stand where Keira was already seated.

"Thank you," Keira said, taking the drink from her. "How was your weekend?"

"Good. I mostly studied. What did you do?"

"Nothing. I stayed in my room and read and watched movies."

Which is pretty much what Keira did every weekend, Delaney thought anxiously. The preteen needed more in her life.

"What about friends? You're making them at school. You told me. Didn't you want to do anything with them?"

Keira, a pretty girl with big blue eyes and freckles, looked at her. "You do realize that would mean someone driving me somewhere. It's not going to happen. I'm not sure if my grandfather is still allowed to drive. Don't they take away your license when you get to be really, really old? I guess I could ask Carmen. She might help me."

"The housekeeper?"

Keira nodded. "She's nice and she cooks great. As for my ass —"

Delaney cleared her throat. "We agreed you weren't going to call him that anymore."

"But he really is one. I can prove it."

Delaney looked at her without speaking.

Keira groaned. "Fine. Fine. Can I call him my A-brother?"

"As in A+?"

Keira laughed. "Not that. Never that. A+. That's funny. How's biology?"

"Good. Scary, but good. I got a B on my first test."

"That's great! You were afraid you wouldn't even pass."

"I know. College is harder than I remember from the first time."

"You'll get it."

Keira was a sweet kid, Delaney thought. Funny, smart and, despite her feelings about her brother, kind. She always asked about Delaney's life and remembered what they'd talked about.

From what Delaney had pieced together, Keira had moved to Seattle from Los Angeles where she'd been living in foster care. But after that, the details got fuzzy. Apparently she lived in a big house with her grandfather, her older half brother and a housekeeper. Why the older brother wasn't on his own but instead lived with his grandfather was something of a mystery. Delaney wondered if maybe there were mental or emotional issues, which might explain his inability to connect with his sister.

"About your friends," Delaney began. "Are you hanging out with different people every day, like we talked about?"

"I am. Sometimes they just ignore me, but a few are talking back." She sighed. "It's hard. I'm not charming. Angelina was charming."

"Angelina is . . ."

"The drag queen who took me in when my mom took off. He was born Carl, but in his heart he was always meant to be an Angelina. After Angelina Jolie. He, I mean, she totally respects Angelina's life choices." She lowered her voice. "Not counting Brad Pitt, of course. Because I mean really. Why?

But all those children and the work she does around the world? That's why she took me in. I didn't have anybody."

"You have family now," Delaney said, not sure how much of the Carl/Angelina story was true. She wished she could talk to the asshole brother and tell him to step up and take some responsibility. Keira was desperately lonely. Why wasn't anyone looking out for her beyond paying for private school and giving her a roof over her head?

Keira ignored the family comment and said, "Angelina wants to transition. Carl/Angelina, I mean, not the actress. She's saving for the surgery, then wants to move to Hawaii because everything is beautiful there and she loves beautiful things."

Keira opened her mouth to say something else, only instead of speaking she jumped to her feet, screamed "No!" at the top of her lungs, then raced out of the lobby.

Delaney was so stunned it took her a full second before she could move. She ran after Keira who was barreling out the doors and into the busy street. Before Delaney could figure out what was happening, she saw Keira bend down and pick up something from the street, then turn back toward the safety of the sidewalk. But before she could make it, there was a hideous screech of brakes followed by a horrible thud as a Prius struck Keira, sending her into the air, then back onto the street where she lay lifeless, a tiny kitten cradled in her small hands.

The world went silent. All Delaney heard was the beating of her own heart. Everything moved in slow motion as the driver flung open the car door and ran toward the fallen girl. People emerged from everywhere to surround her. Phones were pulled out as dozens called 9-1-1.

Shock later, action now, Delaney thought, willing her limbs to move. She stumbled to Keira's side and fell to her knees next to her. Keira's eyes fluttered open.

"Take care of the kitten," she murmured, passing the small animal to Delaney before groaning. "I hurt."

"Just stay still, Keira. It's okay. An ambulance is coming. I'll take the kitten." The tiny creature trembled in her hands. "I'll stay right here."

"You know her?" a woman asked.

"She's a friend of mine. She, ah, goes to the private school. Keira . . ." Delaney swore. "I don't know her last name. She has a brother and a grandfather."

Her brother! Delaney had to call him. Only where was Keira's phone?

She looked around and realized the girl's

backpack was still next to her chair in the lobby eating area. Before Delaney could figure out what to do, Luzia ran out with Delaney's purse in one hand and Keira's backpack in the other.

"Are you going with her to the hospital?"

Delaney hesitated for only a second before nodding. "I'm going to call her brother to meet us there."

Delaney dug for the phone while a man yelled he would go tell someone at the school that one of their students had been injured. Delaney found the phone just as an ambulance pulled up.

She scrolled through the short contact list, then, despite everything, smiled. Right under the As — Asshole Brother.

As the EMTs began to work on Keira, the girl called out. "Delaney, don't leave me." She looked at the guy helping her. "She's my sister and she has to come with me."

"Sure. No problem. Now tell me where it hurts. Can you move your toes? Not your legs, just your toes. We're going to stabilize you, then get you to the hospital."

"I can move my toes and it hurts everywhere." Tears seeped out of the corners of Keira's eyes. "Delaney!"

"I'm right here. I'm calling your brother to let him know what happened."

"Don't bother. He won't care."

The tears came faster now and she started to sob. "It hurts. It hurts. Make it stop." The sobs turned into screams.

Delaney's own eyes burned as she pushed the button on the phone. *Pick up, pick up,* she thought frantically. The kitten stayed perfectly still, huddled against her chest.

"Hello?"

"Are you Keira's brother?"

"What? Yes. Who is this?"

"A friend of hers. Look, she's been hit by a car. She's conscious but I don't know how badly she's hurt. They're taking her to the hospital. Hold on." She turned to the EMTs who were loading Keira on a stretcher. "Which hospital?"

She repeated the information to Keira's brother. "I'm going with her so she won't be by herself. I have the kitten, too."

"Kitten. What are you talking about? Who are you?"

"Delaney, don't leave me!"

She saw that Keira was in the ambulance. She ran toward it. "I have to go. I'll meet you at the hospital. Hurry." She ended the call and started to climb in the back. One of the EMTs protested, but Delaney stared him down.

"She's a kid who was just hit by a car.

Give us both a break, okay?"

He nodded and helped her inside. Delaney sat close to Keira.

"It's going to be okay," she told the still-crying girl. "I'm right here."

She shrugged out of her sweater, folded it up and put it in her tote, then settled the kitten on top of it. "Once I know you're taken care of, I'll see to our little friend here. Do you trust me to do that?"

Keira nodded, even as she cried. "It hurts so much."

"I know, sweetie. I'm here."

The EMT in the back started an IV, then the sirens came on and they were moving. Delaney knew what was next — the hospital, where the sounds and smells would bring everything back. She mentally braced herself for the onslaught, even as she hung on to Keira's hand. For all she knew, she was all Keira had.

Malcolm barely glanced in his rearview mirror before performing an illegal U-turn. He'd been on his way to the company's SoDo warehouse when he'd gotten the call about Keira. As he calculated the best way to get from here to the hospital in morning rush hour traffic, he pushed the button to activate his Mercedes's voice control.

"Call home."

"Calling home. Landline. Dialing."

Seconds later he heard ringing. Carmen picked up. "Hello, Carlesso residence."

"Carmen, it's Malcolm. Someone just phoned to tell me Keira was in an accident." He hesitated before saying she'd been hit by a car. He had no idea how bad things were or what was going to happen. "I'm on my way to the hospital right now. Please call the school and find out what they know. And don't tell my grandfather until I get to the hospital and figure out what's going on. He'll get upset."

"Keira? At the hospital?" Carmen's voice was thick with tears. "No. Not that little girl. Is she all right? What happened? She was fine this morning."

"I'll call you as soon as I find out what has happened. Can you call the school for me?"

"Yes, of course." Her voice broke. "I will pray for her. She's so small. She must be afraid. When you see her, tell her I love her. Tell her I'm praying for her."

"I will," he said, wondering if it was physically possible to repeat that Carmen loved her. He'd managed to avoid that particular word for years now. "I'll call as soon as I know anything."

"Yes and I'll let you know what the school says."

"Thank you."

He hung up. What had happened? How on earth had Keira been hit by a car? She went over to the building's coffee stand every morning, but she knew enough to use the crosswalk, didn't she? They'd never talked about it. He'd just assumed . . .

Of course she knew, he told himself. She was twelve, practically thirteen. Kids were mature these days. They knew things and understood how the world worked. She would be fine. She always was. She took care of herself and —

He gripped the steering wheel harder, as he silently swore. Powerful, ugly guilt swamped him. He recognized the symptoms because he had a lot to be guilty about. His grandfather and now Keira. She was a kid and while he wanted to be there for her, he honest to God didn't know what to do with her. So he made sure she had what she needed and did his best to avoid her. Carmen seemed to pick up the slack, but was that enough?

He'd meant to do more, had wanted to get to know her, only he hadn't known how and he was still so angry with their father. Jerry's betrayal haunted him like a taunting ghost and in the end it was easier to avoid anyone who looked the least bit like him. It was easier to avoid his half sister, to tell himself she was doing just fine in her room at the opposite end of the hall.

He pushed the thoughts away. They weren't helpful right now. Later he could indulge in a little self-loathing but until then he had to focus on the problem at hand.

He arrived at the hospital in record time and found parking by the emergency entrance. At the information desk, he gave his name, Keira's and said he was her brother. The receptionist entered the information into her computer.

"She's here," the woman said. "Room 47. Through those doors, then follow the signs. They've taken her to get some X-rays, so she might not be there."

He pushed open one of the swinging double doors and was assaulted by the smells and sounds of a busy hospital. There were dozens of exam rooms, each filled with patients and families. Medical personnel hurried from place to place, patient charts in their hands as a calm voice requested Dr. Herron call extension five-two-three. Orderlies moved equipment and in the distance, someone was screaming.

Malcolm felt his gut tighten as he followed

the signs to Keira's room. He hoped to hell she hadn't been left alone. She was too young, and she had to be terrified, assuming she was conscious. He came to a stop as he realized he didn't know how badly she was injured.

Guilt later, he reminded himself and started walking again. He turned another corner and saw room numbers in the forties, then found forty-seven. The door was open and the bed was empty. He started to leave only to realize there was someone else in the room. Someone who —

The woman turned and stared at him. Her green eyes were wide, her face pale. Under any other circumstances, her expression of surprise would have been comical.

"Delaney? What are you doing here?"

"I could ask the same thing. Oh God! *You're* the asshole brother? No. It's you? Keira's your sister?"

Half sister. Only he didn't say that. "How do you know her?"

"She gets a hot chocolate every morning. We're friends. I take my break and we talk." She shook her head. "I don't understand. You're her brother? But you never talk to her. You walk into the building at the same time, but it's like you're a stranger. I never imagined you even knew her. What's with that? She's your sister and you don't say goodbye." Tears filled her eyes. "She's a little girl. You're supposed to say goodbye."

He reached for her instinctively. Tears turned into sobs. He wrapped his arms around her and held her for a few seconds, only to feel something odd between them. Something moving.

He stepped back as a small black-and-white kitten crawled out of her tote and mewed.

Too much was happening at once, he thought, struggling to make sense of the input.

A nurse stuck her head in the room. "Delaney, hon, just wanted to let you know, she's doing great. She'll be back in a second." She lowered her voice. "Nothing's broken that we can see. She's banged up pretty bad, but so far so good. There's still her head to worry about, but we'll get those tests done in a little bit." She offered a sympathetic smile. "I thought you'd want to know."

The woman left without acknowledging Malcolm. He turned to Delaney, who was petting the kitten and easing it back into her tote.

"Why is she telling you that? How come she knows you?"

Delaney sucked in a breath. "My dad was a cop. A couple of years ago he was shot and brought here. He was in the hospital over a month. I pretty much know everyone who works here."

"Is your father all right?"

"Yeah. He's in a wheelchair, but he's doing fine. He got engaged a few months ago." She shook her head. "I'm sorry. I'm having trouble concentrating. Everything happened so fast and there was no way to stop her. She just ran into the street."

"Why?"

Delaney stared at him. "The kitten. She saw the kitten and didn't want it to be run over."

Instead she'd been hit by a car.

Before he could ask any more questions, Keira was wheeled back into the room. She looked impossibly small in the bed. Her skin was a pale contrast to angry scrapes and bruises. She wasn't moving — he couldn't even tell if she was breathing.

Guilt merged with panic. Shouldn't someone do something?

Delaney took one of Keira's hands. "Hey, you," she whispered. "Your brother is here. You should have told me his name was Malcolm. Not knowing that made for a very awkward call."

Keira's eyes fluttered, then stayed closed.

"You're going to be okay, Keira," Delaney continued. "You're going to be okay."

They couldn't know that for sure, he thought grimly. Why wasn't she awake? Wasn't a brain injury more significant than any broken bones?

A doctor walked in. She was about five-four, with gray hair and a kind expression. "You two are the siblings?" she asked.

Delaney smiled. "Hi, Dr. Newport. This is Malcolm. He's Keira's brother. I'm a friend."

Dr. Newport smiled. "You're assuming I'll make an exception and allow you to stay."

"I kind of am."

"Then I will." The doctor turned to Malcolm and offered her hand. "Mr. . . ."

"Carlesso. Call me Malcolm. How is she?"

"Bruised and sore, but otherwise intact." She went on to detail the injuries Keira had sustained when she'd been hit by the car. "She's incredibly lucky. All her vitals are normal and her concussion is very mild. Still, we'll want to keep her overnight for observation. Just to be safe. She'll need to stay quiet for a few days, until the worst of the pain passes. She's going to be stiff and sore for a while."

He glanced at Keira who still had her eyes

closed. "Why is she unconscious?"

"She's asleep. We gave her something for the pain. Even without serious injuries, her body suffered major trauma. She'll wake up in a bit and you'll be able to talk to her."

Dr. Newport promised to look in on Keira before she was taken up to the pediatric floor. Malcolm excused himself to phone Carmen with an update. When he returned to the room, there was yet another nurse there, chatting with Delaney. When the nurse saw Malcolm, she hugged Delaney, then walked over to him.

"Hi. I need to get Keira's medical history. She was pretty out of it when she came in and Delaney didn't have any info." She opened her tablet and looked at him. "We'll start with the big stuff and work back. Any allergies or sensitivities?"

"Not that I know of."

"What about major surgeries?"

"I don't know." He looked at the bed, then back at the nurse. "I don't know. She's my half sister. She moved here from Los Angeles a couple of months ago. My grandfather arranged it. Let me call home and find out if he knows anything or if she came with medical records."

"Any medical information would be helpful. As an FYI, you're going to need her vaccination information for school and sports. Oh, wait." The nurse smiled reassuringly. "She's in school, right?"

"Yes. Puget Sound Preparatory Academy."

The nurse and Delaney exchanged a look. "Someone would have had to fill out a medical history to get her enrolled," the nurse told him. "So there is some information."

"I'll call Carmen," he muttered, feeling more and more out of his element.

"Great. Just buzz when you have the information and I'll come back." She smiled and left.

Malcolm stared after her. "It's not as bad as it sounds," he said, knowing his tone was defensive. "My grandfather enrolled her in the school. It's only been two months." How could he be expected to know very much about her?

Except she was his sister, a small voice in his head whispered.

"So it's all true," Delaney said. "I thought she was making it up."

"Making what up?"

"All of it. Moving from Los Angeles, that she's only been here a couple of months. Carl and Angelina."

"Who are Carl and Angelina?"

"It's really not important." She touched

63

his arm. "She's going to be okay. That's what's important, Malcolm. Focus on that and let the rest take care of itself over time."

He nodded at her tote. "That's the kitten?"

"Uh-huh. I'll take care of it until Keira's better."

He got the implied message. That of course his sister would be keeping the damned kitten that nearly got her killed, although at this point, the kitten was the least of it.

"I need to call Carmen and get her medical records," he said.

"The housekeeper?"

"Yes. Thank you for staying with her." He felt like he should say more, but couldn't think what.

"It's fine. She's sweet and I was glad to do it. She shouldn't be alone."

Malcolm thought of Keira's large suite of rooms at the far end of the hall. If she wasn't at school, she was alone most of the time. Sometimes she even ate dinner by herself. He should do better, he told himself. She was only a kid. It was just . . .

"Why did you call me the asshole brother?" he asked, suddenly remembering what she'd said when he'd first arrived. She couldn't possibly know enough to judge him.

Delaney flushed. "Sorry about that. I was surprised to see you." She looked away then back at him before digging in her tote and handing him a phone.

"It's Keira's," she said. "She never refers to you by name." She pointed to the phone. "It's, uh, in the contacts."

He pressed a couple of buttons, then scrolled through the info. Sure enough, under the *A*s — Asshole Brother. So much for having to guess how she felt about him.

"I need to call Carmen," he repeated.

"Go ahead. I'll stay here in case she wakes up."

He nodded and walked out of the room. Delaney would stay for now, but then what? At some point he was going to have to deal with Keira himself. He glanced at the phone. Apparently that day of reckoning had just arrived.

CHAPTER FOUR

Monday mornings were Callie's favorite time of the week. From eight until eleven, she could be anyone she wanted. A princess, an astronaut, or just some housewife filling a few empty hours. The cats at the shelter didn't care about anything but the fact that Callie changed out their litter boxes then spent time brushing them.

There was no way she could have a pet herself, but working at the shelter allowed her to get a little feline love in her life. There were plenty of head butts and purrs, as if the cats were thanking her for what she'd done.

When she'd first applied to volunteer, she'd been delighted not to find the ever-present felon question on the application. She'd taken the orientation class and had offered to clean out litter boxes. Not glamorous work, but satisfying all the same.

She liked coming in and finding out one

of the older cats had finally found a good home. She was happy to work with the more crabby residents, taking extra time with them. On the first Monday of every month, she carefully slipped a twenty-dollar bill into the volunteer collection can by the locker room. It wasn't much, but it was a significant part of her weekly spending money and the most she could do.

When Callie finished her shift, her T-shirt was covered in cat hair and she had an impressive scratch on her arm from a new kitty. He might be upset now, she thought as she washed her hands before leaving, but if he was still around next week, she would win him over.

She signed out, then started for the bus stop. She'd barely made it halfway across the parking lot when she became aware of a sleek black car keeping pace with her.

The vehicle was too nice to belong to the kind of criminal who would want to steal her battered secondhand backpack and there were plenty of people around should she want to scream and run. Even if she got abducted, someone would probably capture it on video.

With that not-very-comforting thought uppermost in her mind, she stopped, turned to the vehicle, put her hands on her hips and yelled, "What do you want?"

The car came to a stop beside her and a woman in her midthirties rolled down the window. She was well dressed and looked concerned.

"Oh, crap. I scared you, didn't I? I'm sorry. I was on the phone with my kid who's trying to convince me he's sick enough that he can't take his history test and I totally wasn't paying attention. I'm the worst. I'm sorry. Are you Callie Smith?"

Callie relaxed. "Who are you?"

"Shari Martin. I'm a lawyer." The dark-haired woman grinned. "I stopped working to have kids and let me just say, getting back into the real world isn't easy. Word to the wise, don't do it. Children are not worth the trouble." She shook her head. "Look, there I go again. This conversation isn't about me at all."

Shari got out of her car and handed Callie a business card. "I really am who I said I am. I need to talk to you. Can I buy you a cup of coffee?"

Callie's radar went on alert, even as she told herself she'd done nothing wrong. She'd served her time, lived in the halfway house the exact number of days she was supposed to, filled out all the paperwork and didn't have so much as a jaywalking ticket.

"What is this about?"

Shari's friendly expression softened. "Your grandfather on your father's side. He's been looking for you, hon. I'm hoping he's found you."

Callie felt her legs go weak. "That's not possible. There is no . . ."

No father? Of course there was a father — she hadn't hatched — but what she knew about him was sketchy at best.

Her mother had met a charming salesman at a convention. She'd been one of the models, as much on display as the product she was selling. Jerry Carlesso had walked over, smiled and introduced himself. According to Callie's mother, that had been the end of it. She'd fallen wildly, madly in love. Three months later, she'd turned up pregnant and Jerry had taken off.

He hadn't wanted anything to do with his daughter. He'd sent child support on and off, had never visited. Callie knew next to nothing about him. As for a grandfather, there was no way.

"I don't know what you're talking about," she said firmly, raising her chin.

"So the name Jerry Carlesso doesn't mean anything to you?"

Callie had a bad feeling her expression gave her away.

Shari nodded toward her car. "There's a nice little place about three blocks from here. We'll have coffee and split a Danish. That way neither of us have to count the calories. I'll talk, you'll listen, then you can make up your mind about what you want to do."

Callie thought about how she finally had her life together. Okay, things weren't great, but she was doing fine. She was saving money, working her jobs and in time, she would figure out how to be more than what she was with the albatross of her conviction hanging around her neck. She didn't need anyone, ever. That had become her rule to survive. She was completely and totally on her own.

Only when Shari held open the passenger door, she found herself walking toward the car. Before she could get her scrambled thoughts together, they were pulling out on the street and then it seemed silly not to go in and get coffee and a Danish and hear Shari out.

It was still early for the lunch crowd. She and Shari found a quiet booth at the back of the small café. They ordered coffee and agreed to split a cheese Danish. When the coffee had been poured, Shari pulled a folder out of her Kate Spade tote.

"All right. Your mother is Annette Smith. You are Callie Smith and you were born in Norman, Oklahoma, September 27, 1991. Your father is Jerry Carlesso, who had an affair with your mother, denied paternity but paid child support." Shari flipped through her notes, then wrinkled her nose. "He wasn't very regular with the payments." She looked up. "Is that right?"

Callie could only shrug. Everything about the moment was far too surreal. She never thought about her father. She'd never met the man and her mother hadn't talked about him beyond saying their relationship hadn't worked out and it wasn't anyone's fault. Callie guessed he hadn't been the nicest guy on the planet and had often wondered if she got the dark parts of her personality from him.

"So here's the story," Shari said with a smile. "At least as much as I know. Your father passed away a couple years ago. His father, your paternal grandfather —" Shari slapped her hand over her mouth. "Oh my God! I'm so sorry. I shouldn't have blurted it out like that."

"Blurted out what?"

"That your dad's dead. I'm horrible.

71

Please forgive me."

"You're way more upset than me," Callie told her. "I never met the man and he abandoned my mom when he found out she was pregnant. I honestly never think of him, so there's no sense of loss. It's fine."

"Still. I have got to be more sensitive. I have three boys. I think they've worn me down." Shari drew in a breath. "Okay, back to your family. You still have a paternal grandfather, Alberto, along with a half brother and a half sister. They all live in Seattle. If you're who I think you are, then the family would like to meet you."

A brother and a sister? A grandfather? Callie hadn't had any family beyond her mother. Not ever. It had always been just the two of them. Since losing her mom five years ago, it had only been her, which was how she liked it.

Her stomach tightened and she found it a little tough to draw in a breath.

"So here's the thing," Shari said. "We have to confirm the family connection using a DNA test. I need to swab your cheek and overnight it to the lab. They'll get it tomorrow and we'll get a call on Wednesday." She grinned. "They can do the test in like twenty-four hours. It's pretty rad."

Callie managed a smile. "Rad?"

Shari groaned. "Damn kids. Anyway, that's where we are. Once the DNA test confirms you're part of the family, I have a ticket to Seattle for you."

Callie's chest tightened even more. "I'm not sure I want to meet them. I mean it's all happening so fast. I need to think."

Shari leaned toward her. "Oh, you'll want to meet them. They're very well-off and there's a trust fund set up for you, Jerry's oldest daughter. If they're your family, you should go. I've been looking for you for nearly two months. You were hard to find. Some of it is your last name is so common and some of it is you don't want to be found."

Callie shifted uncomfortably. She didn't exactly live off the grid, but she had very little contact with the digital world. Plus she'd moved frequently since getting out of prison. First to the halfway house, then to a series of rented rooms until she'd found the one she was in now.

"I wasn't hiding," she said defensively.

"I know, hon. This is a lot. Once the DNA test is confirmed, I have a bunch of information to give you, but until then, consider the possibility. It might be the second chance you've been hoping for."

Callie flushed. She shouldn't be surprised

that Shari knew about her past — it would have been the first thing to pop during an investigation. But still, it was humiliating. And something she was never going to be able to put behind her, she thought grimly.

"They know?" she asked.

"Your grandfather does. I don't know if he's told anyone else."

"We don't know he's my grandfather."

Shari hesitated, then pulled a photograph out of her tote. It was black-and-white and obviously taken at a professional shoot years and years ago. The woman in the picture was about Callie's age and looked enough like her that they could have been sisters. Their eyes had the same shape, as did their mouths and the slope of their shoulders.

"Your paternal grandmother," Shari said. "She's no longer with us, but when Alberto sent me this, I just knew I'd found you." She nodded at the picture. "You can keep that."

Callie touched the picture gingerly — half afraid of claiming it or the woman in the photograph. How could this be happening? She was twenty-six and she knew nothing about her father or his family. To have them show up now made no sense. She should get up and walk away. Even if someone was looking for her, she didn't want to be found.

Before she could bolt, she wrestled with the fact that she might have family. For so long, it had just been a word, a concept that described other people's lives, but not hers. If she wasn't alone . . .

No! She was the only person she could depend on. She didn't need anyone else, and even if she did, she knew the danger of hoping, of believing, of trusting. Yes, her mother had always been there for her, but no one else.

Indecision tugged at her. She thought of her small rented room and her meager savings account. The possibility of a trust fund was a real lure. Even a few thousand dollars would mean finishing college and helping her with her condo fund. As for belonging, what were the odds? She would do better to take whatever money there was and disappear. Getting involved would only mean breaking someone's heart. She should know.

She drew in a breath as she surrendered to the inevitable.

"Where do I take the DNA test?"

Shari grinned and pulled a long, narrow plastic bag out of her tote. "Right here." She waved the bag. "Like I said, technology is rad. Ready?"

No. No, she wasn't ready. She wasn't anything but scared and nauseous and fighting hope with every fiber of her being. But she wouldn't show any of that. Instead she squared her shoulders and leaned forward. "I'm ready. Let's do this and find out who I am."

Delaney drove the handful of miles between her small condo and her father's house. As she got closer to the house where she'd grown up, the streets became more and more familiar. She could point to restaurants, corner stores and the school and remember specific events. The park where she'd played softball. The movie theater where a boy had first held her hand. The deli where she and her dad had gone every Wednesday night to get takeout. Much of Seattle was changing but her old neighborhood had thus far been spared. She knew gentrification was coming but hoped it would hold off for a while. It was nice to know that some things didn't change.

As she pulled onto her street, she slowed. Between the two stop signs there were about thirty homes. When she'd been a kid, she'd known the names of every family, had hung out at most of their houses. Her mother had died during childbirth so Delaney had never known her but that didn't mean she'd grown up without maternal influence.

Instead she'd had about thirty moms all looking out for her. Screwing up and getting away with it hadn't been an option. There were too many watchful, caring sets of eyes.

She parked in front of her father's house, her BMW out of place in the working-class neighborhood. For the thousandth time Delaney thought she should sell it and replace it with something more . . . ordinary. The four-wheel-drive sedan was a reminder of her old life. She'd been so proud when she'd bought it with her own money. Tim had wanted her to get something sensible — like a small SUV. That was a car for a growing family. They'd compromised, with her promising to sell the BMW when they got married and started having kids. Something that had never happened, she thought, stepping out of the car.

A minivan pulled up next to her. Delaney smiled when she recognized her friend.

"Hey, you," she called, stepping close to the vehicle.

Chelsea, a pretty brunette with her hair pulled back in a ponytail, grinned at her. "You here to see your dad?"

"I am. How's it going with you?"

"Busy!" She nodded at the infant and toddler, both in their car seats behind her. "We have a doctor's appointment and I'm running late. I can't remember the last time I showered and the in-laws are coming over tonight. It's card night." She sighed. "We have to get together and catch up. Say yes like you mean it."

"I do mean it," Delaney told her.

Chelsea rolled up her window and waved as she headed down the street.

Delaney watched her go. A few years ago, she had assumed she would be living a life just like Chelsea's herself. Married with a couple of kids, in-laws dropping by on a regular basis. Tim had talked about it all the time — what they would name their kids, what kind of tent camper they would buy and where they would drive to on their vacations. His dreams had all been the kind most people could relate to — getting married, having a family, putting his kids through college and living in the same house until he was too old to manage the stairs.

She'd wanted those dreams, too. Had told herself she would be happy when it finally happened. Only she'd been the one to take a different path from everyone she knew. First getting her college degree in finance, then taking a job at Boeing. She'd moved up in the company, had moved away from the neighborhood — only a few miles, but still a world away. She'd been the one to buy a condo on her own, and the BMW. Her dreams had been bigger than Tim's. Now, nearly eighteen months after his death, she wondered if he'd realized that and, if he had, what he'd thought about it.

She circled her car and opened the passenger door. The tiny kitten was asleep in the cardboard carrier the veterinary office had given her. The vet had guessed the kitten to be nine or ten weeks old. Weaned, but still a baby. Underweight, female and uninjured. His guess had been that she'd been abandoned. The staff had fed her after they'd checked her out and now she was sleeping off her feast.

"You're going to need a name," Delaney murmured. Picking one out would be fun for Keira, and a distraction from the pain of her recovery. She might not have any serious injuries, but she was going to be sore for a while.

Delaney carried the sleeping kitten up to the front door. The house had been built back in the 1940s, but modernized over the years. A ramp led from the driveway to the front door. Delaney took the stairs, then glanced at the specially modified van parked by the ramp. Her dad had come a long way, she thought, grateful for his recovery. She

knocked once, then let herself in the un-
locked front door.

"Hi," she called. "It's me."

"Hi, pumpkin," her dad called. "We're
back here."

Back here meant the kitchen, Delaney
thought with a smile. Because that was
where everyone always was in this house.

The kitchen was large and open, more
great room than just a space to prepare
meals. There was a big table in the middle,
a wood-burning fireplace in the corner and
a couple of worn sofas by the back windows.
On the opposite wall were the cabinets, the
stove and a large island.

When her father saw her, he grinned and
wheeled toward her. "How's my best girl?"

Phil Holbrook was a broad-shouldered,
well-muscled man in his midfifties. Despite
his inability to walk, he kept himself in
shape and never let on that he found his
wheelchair a problem.

"I'm good, Dad." She leaned over to hug
him, then handed him the carrier. "This is
the unexpected little friend I mentioned."

Beryl, a petite blonde two years older than
Phil, came out from around the island and
took the carrier. "Oh, she's precious. How
old is she?"

"The vet thinks nine or ten weeks. She

was probably abandoned."

Beryl looked at Phil. "Oh, honey, a homeless kitten."

"No," Phil said mildly. "We're not getting a kitten. This one already has a home."

"But what about another homeless kitten?"

"We're going to start traveling. We've got that European cruise booked for September. What would we do with a cat?"

Beryl looked pleadingly at Delaney. "Maybe you could keep her."

"Oh, I'm so staying out of this," she said with a laugh.

"Travel," Phil said mildly. "Lots and lots of travel."

Beryl mock pouted. "I hate it when you're sensible."

"No, you don't."

She lightly kissed him. "No, I don't."

Delaney set the carrier on the floor by the sofa. Beryl and her family had always been a fixture in Delaney's life from the time she was born. When Phil had been unexpectedly widowed and left with a newborn to care for, the neighborhood women had stepped in to help. Each mom had taken a shift, allowing Phil to go back to work. Delaney had grown up with Beryl's three kids, including Tim who was four years older than she was. The families had been close with Tim following in Phil's footsteps, career wise. After getting his associates degree, he'd joined the Seattle Police Department.

Ten years ago, Beryl had lost her husband to cancer and the neighborhood had rallied again. When Phil had been shot in the same ambush that killed Tim, Beryl and Delaney had gotten each other through the initial shock and grief.

Delaney wasn't sure when friendship had turned to more between the neighbors, but she was glad her father had finally found someone to love. He was recovered enough to have a relatively normal life and now he had someone to share it with. A few months before, he'd proposed to Beryl and she'd accepted. They were getting married in a quiet ceremony in late August, then taking their first cruise together in September.

Beryl straightened. "Go ahead," she told Delaney. "Your kitten will be fine until you're back. And while you're gone, I'll put together some food for you to take home. You're not eating enough."

"I'm eating plenty."

Beryl didn't look convinced. "You're thinner every time I see you."

"I wish that were true," Delaney said with

a laugh. "All right, I'm off to the pet store. I won't be long."

She'd told Malcolm she would keep Keira's kitten until Keira was home and able to take care of it herself. She'd half expected him to protest, saying his sister couldn't keep the kitten, but he'd only thanked her for helping.

As she slid behind the wheel of her car and started the engine, she admitted she was having trouble reconciling the confident suit-wearing guy she knew from the office to the shell-shocked brother she'd met at the hospital. She still couldn't believe Malcolm was Keira's asshole brother.

From what Keira had told her, she'd been living in foster care in Los Angeles when she'd been found by her long-lost family. Malcolm had flown down to LA to bring her to Seattle. Once settled in her fancy digs, she'd been enrolled at the very upscale Puget Sound Preparatory Academy and pretty much left on her own.

Delaney hadn't known how much of Keira's story was true and how much of it wasn't. Now she was even less sure. Not that she thought anyone was starving the preteen or beating her, but benign neglect wasn't exactly nurturing.

Malcolm seemed like a decent guy so what

was going on at home? Was it possible he simply didn't know what to do with a twelve-year-old? And what about the grandfather? Where was he in all this?

Delaney sighed. Maybe she was exaggerating the problem. Maybe there wasn't a problem at all. She would have to scope things out when she returned the kitten and then . . . Well, she didn't know what, but she'd been raised to take care of anyone in need and if she thought Keira needed her, she would be there in a heartbeat.

CHAPTER FIVE

"I'm worried," grandfather Alberto said as he sipped his morning coffee. "Keira is so young, so small. What a terrible thing to have happened."

"She's recovering. The doctor said she's going to be fine. Carmen is taking her to her pediatrician tomorrow." Malcolm paused, not knowing what else to say to comfort the old man.

Carmen had kept the news about Keira's accident from Alberto until Malcolm had confirmed his granddaughter was going to be all right. Still, Alberto had gone pale and even two days after her accident, he was more frail than Malcolm had ever seen him. His breakfast — oatmeal, two poached eggs and a bowl of fresh fruit — sat untouched. More uncomfortable, it was after seven and he hadn't bothered to dress yet. This from a man who was up by five thirty and in a suit and tie well before breakfast.

"I sat with her yesterday." Alberto's gaze was fixed on the table. "She slept so much."

"They gave her painkillers. I'm sure they knocked her out. Plus she has to heal from the accident. She has bumps and bruises. She was lucky." It could have been a whole lot worse. Or deadly, Malcolm thought grimly.

The driver of the Prius had been interviewed by the police. He had no record of DUIs, had tested negative for alcohol and drugs, and hadn't had a speeding ticket in nearly a decade. Keira had run into the street without looking and the driver had done the best he could.

"What if we'd lost her?" Alberto asked, raising his troubled gaze to Malcolm's face. "I don't think I could take that."

And there it went — the knife of guilt sliding in over ribs, right to the heart. Malcolm knew the words weren't meant to be a stab, but he felt the slicing all the same.

"We didn't lose her." In a desperate attempt to raise his grandfather's spirits he said, "We'll get the DNA tests today."

Alberto brightened. "Yes, you're right. I look forward to knowing my other granddaughter will soon be on her way to join us." His tension eased as his shoulders squared. "You're right. We were lucky with

Keira. She could have been badly hurt and she wasn't. It's a sign. Now Callie will join us and our family will be complete." He smiled at Malcolm. "You're a good man. I trust you, Malcolm."

Words that should have made him feel better and didn't. "I'm going to stay home with Keira this morning, then head to the office in the afternoon."

Alberto smiled. "She'll enjoy spending time with you."

Malcolm had his doubts, but he was committed now. Besides, what had happened at the hospital had shown him how little he knew Keira. She'd been living in the house two months and he barely knew anything about her. Carmen had stepped in to take care of things and he'd let her.

He finished his coffee. As he rose, he gently squeezed his grandfather's shoulder before heading upstairs. When Malcolm and his mother had first arrived in Seattle, Jerry hadn't been the least bit interested in having a son, but Alberto had been thrilled to discover he had a grandson. He'd welcomed both into the family home. Jerry had lived elsewhere, something Malcolm later learned to appreciate.

With Alberto, everything was easy. There was plenty of conversation and laughter, warmth and safety. With Jerry — Malcolm shook his head. He couldn't remember ever spending even a single meal alone with his father. Jerry had been nearly as absent after Malcolm had become a fixture in his life as before. He had no interest in his son and little interest in Alberto.

In contrast, Alberto had wanted to be a part of everything Malcolm did. He'd taken him to the business each week, after school, introducing him to the wonder that was Alberto's Alfresco. He'd attended parent-teacher evenings and every game when Malcolm had signed up for the soccer team. When Malcolm had lost his mother, Alberto had been the one to hold him while he sobbed out his pain. Jerry hadn't even come to the funeral.

Years later, after Jerry had died, Malcolm had moved back into the big house on the lake. He knew his grandfather wasn't getting any younger and wanted to spend time with him while he could.

At the top of the stairs, the landing became a long hallway. To the left was his suite of rooms, to the right were two additional suites. Keira had the corner rooms at the far end, chosen for the big windows and amount of light they let in. Carmen had been worried that a child from sunny Los

Angeles would find winter in Seattle too dreary. Malcolm had thought nothing about Keira's personal space beyond the fact that it was mercifully far from his own.

He liked to think he was inexperienced when it came to children rather than the asshole brother Keira's phone had proclaimed, but he had a feeling she was more correct than him.

He walked down the hall, then knocked on the partially open door. "It's Malcolm. May I come in?"

There was a very long pause followed by a soft "Yes."

Keira lay in the middle of her full-size bed. She looked impossibly small and pale against the lavender linens, her freckles and eyes the only color on her face.

The bed was against the far wall, giving her a view out large windows. She had the corner room. On the second wall of windows were a built-in window seat and a desk. Opposite them were custom bookshelves and a large dresser for storage.

Her suite was the mirror image of his at the opposite end of the house. He knew there was a large second room that had been decorated as a playroom-hanging out space for her and a full bathroom. His second room had been converted into a home office.

Carmen had picked out the furniture and arranged for the remodel and installation. Malcolm had done little beyond nod when shown the color palette she'd chosen. Now he wondered if Keira liked the room or not, because God knew he'd never bothered to ask.

He pulled her desk chair over to the bed and sat down close to her. The untouched breakfast tray sat on her nightstand.

"Did you sleep okay?" he asked.

She nodded. "My head hurts but the painkillers help. I'm going to get up later and walk around. Carmen says I need to get my blood flowing."

"Makes sense. The plan is for you to stay home until Monday, unless your pediatrician changes things tomorrow. I've spoken with your counselor at school. Your assignments are posted online and I'll pick up the rest of your books later. Everyone agrees you can wait until you feel up to starting on your homework."

Her blue gaze was steady, her mouth a straight line. "So if I think I'm not ready, I don't have to do anything?"

"Not for now."

"Isn't that ridiculous? What if I say I'm

never ready to start studying? How do you know I won't take advantage? Maybe I'm perfectly fine and should go back to school today."

He swore silently, realizing once again he was the least equipped person to be dealing with a twelve-year-old kid. He had no idea of what to say or think or how to act. She was a mystery to him, and not a fun one. She looked like their maternal grandmother and enough like Jerry to make him wary, but her personality was all her own.

"Keira, you were hit by a car. I think you get a break for a day or two." He hesitated. "Do you want to go back to your classes today?"

Tears filled her eyes. For one horrifying second, he thought she was going to start crying, but then she blinked several times and shook her head. "No. I'll stay home until Monday. But I'll start doing my homework as soon as my headache goes away."

Was a headache normal? Should he offer her something? He gritted his teeth and reminded himself that Carmen was handling the medications. Better that it stay in the capable hands of one person.

"What about the kitten?"

At first he wasn't sure what she was referring to, then he remembered the scraggly-looking creature Delaney had carried into the ER.

Delaney — now there was a problem without a solution. He'd done his best to avoid thinking about her, although at some point they were going to have to talk. He owed her. He had no idea what she thought of him, but based on how she'd glared at him while they'd been discussing Keira, she no longer found him the least bit appealing. Not that he cared about her or her opinion, it was only —

"Malcolm!"

What? Oh, right. "The kitten."

"Yes. I've been saving my allowance. I don't know how much it costs to buy litter and stuff but maybe instead of giving me the money, you could use it to buy food and a scratchy post. Cats need to sharpen their claws." Her jaw tightened and her chin raised ever so slightly. "Because I'm keeping the kitten."

He was more taken aback by the gesture than the words. Not that it *looked* familiar, but because he knew what it felt like to do it, mostly because he did it himself when he was backed into a corner. The gesture was a combination of defiance and bravado — a message to himself and whoever had provoked the sensation of being trapped.

92

On the heels of that revelation, he was forced to deal with the reality of what her words meant. Keira was concerned about having to pay for a pet. The guilt knife turned a couple more times, reminding him that if there was a way to screw up relationships in his family, he'd probably done each at least twice.

"You're welcome to keep the kitten —" he began, only to have her interrupt.

"It's just a kitten. Even cats aren't that big and I'll totally take care of her. I'll put the litter box in the alcove in my playroom and keep her in my rooms. She'll be fine."

He smiled. "Like I said, you're welcome to keep the kitten."

Her fierceness faded a little. "Oh. Thank you."

"Tell Carmen what you need and she'll get it. We'll have to have it checked out by a vet."

"Delaney already took her in. She texted me and told me and that she's a girl and she's pretty skinny but healthy otherwise. Lizzy is nine or ten weeks old. They think she was just abandoned." Keira's mouth trembled. She paused for a second, as if to gather self-control, then continued. "She'll need vaccinations, though. Do you want my savings for that?"

He didn't know if he should swear, throw something or take off for Bali. Instead he leaned toward his sister and did his best to look friendly rather than frustrated. "Keira, I will pay for whatever your kitten needs. Food, scratching posts, toys, vaccinations. Just tell Carmen, all right?"

"What if she needs surgery?"

"It's covered."

"Good, because she'll need to be spayed when she's six months old. It's the responsible thing to do."

"I'm glad you know that."

"What if she needs a heart transplant? They're expensive. Will you do that?"

He was fairly confident there was no such thing as a feline heart transplant, but that wasn't the point.

He looked at Keira, meeting her wary gaze, and nodded. "Yes. I will pay for your cat to have a heart transplant."

She visibly relaxed. "Okay. Thanks. I'll take good care of Lizzy. I promise."

"Why Lizzy? Why not Muffin or Fluffy or whatever else it is people call cats?"

She rolled her eyes. "I'm twelve, Malcolm, not five. It's Lizzy for Elizabeth Taylor because she's beautiful. I know it's a cliché, but it reminds me of Angelina and I still miss her."

He was having trouble following the conversation. "Angelina is your friend from Los Angeles. The, ah, person who took you in after you lost your mom?"

"I didn't *lose* my mom. She took off and left me and then she overdosed."

Keira was nothing like the sweet kids who had populated the sitcoms he'd watched when he'd been growing up. "But Angelina is the person who took you in?"

"Yes."

"And he, ah, she is a transvestite?"

"Transgender. Do you know the difference?"

It was not his world, but he tried to stay relatively current. "Yes. He was born in the wrong body, so on the outside he's a man but on the inside, she's a woman."

Keira looked impressed. "That's right. Delaney is going to bring Lizzy by tomorrow. She wants to give me another day to rest."

"Be sure to thank her for her help," he said, thinking he would have to check with Delaney about the expenses she'd incurred taking care of the cat. "Do you know when she's coming by?"

"Why?"

"I want to talk to her when you two are finished." He thought about everything that had happened just over forty-eight hours ago. "She took care of you, went with you to the hospital. Without her, it might have been hours before anyone knew who you were. I want to thank her for all she did."

"Oh, that's okay then. She's coming about three. You'll still be at work."

"I'll come home early."

Keira looked skeptical but didn't say anything. Malcolm glanced at her tray.

"You're not hungry? Do you want Carmen to fix something else?"

Keira reached for a piece of toast. "I'm hungry now. I have to get better so I can take care of Lizzy."

"Then I'll leave you to it." He rose and returned the chair to the desk. "I'm working from home this morning. Let me know if you need anything."

"I'm totally fine, Malcolm. You don't have to worry about me."

He nodded and went to his own suite of rooms. Once there, he couldn't shake her words. She'd told him she was fine the first day he'd met her. He'd wanted to know about her time in foster care and what she needed before they flew up to Seattle. She'd repeated the sentiment when they'd arrived at the house and Carmen had shown her where she would sleep. Keira always said she was fine and except for Lizzy, never asked for anything. Until now, he'd always taken her at her word.

A prickling sensation along the back of his neck had him wondering if instead of assuming all was well, he should probe deeper and find out for himself. Which would mean getting more involved in her life, getting to know her, something that until now, he'd avoided. Not because he didn't want to care, but because he didn't want to disappoint. Unfortunately it seemed that was no longer an option.

Santiago waited for the last quarterly presentation to be finished before wrapping up the meeting. Alberto's Alfresco had grown 4 percent in the previous quarter, thanks to an increase in prepared dinners. Not just entrées, but curated four-course meals that required the barest of preparation and yielded something even the fussiest of mothers-in-law would appreciate. Every sector was up, except for dried soups and powdered beverages — their sales had been flat, something Santiago hadn't expected. He was going to have to do some research.

He left the conference room and headed to his corner office. April was still the rainy season in Seattle, but the skies had momentarily cleared, giving him a view of the city. His office faced east — not exactly the prime west, Sound-facing office that Malcolm had — but Santiago didn't care. He could see the Sound anytime he wanted from his condo and he liked the relative quiet of his corner when he needed to number crunch.

He sat down at his desk and paused for a second, thinking he'd come a long way from the farm worker's kid he'd been when he'd entered the University of Washington on a football scholarship. He'd barely gotten through high school with a C average — he'd known sports were his only way out and he'd done his best to excel. Football he understood. He didn't love it the way some of the guys did, but he respected the opportunities it provided and he'd worked the program. Academically, he'd been terrified.

He remembered the first day he'd shown up in his dorm room. His roommate, some skinny kid with a serious expression and expensive luggage, had greeted him with even less enthusiasm than Santiago had felt. Malcolm Carlesso had been quiet, studious and about as much fun as termites. Two days later Santiago had been in the process of requesting a room change when he'd come back from practice to find a bowl of ice sitting in their small freezer. When he'd asked about it, Malcolm had said it was for Santiago's ice pack for his knee. Malcolm had been going to the communal kitchen anyway and had brought some back.

That simple gesture had been the beginning of a friendship that had lasted over fifteen years so far. Malcolm had helped Santiago realize he was a whole lot smarter than anyone had known. Santiago had taught Malcolm to loosen up and get rid of the stick up his ass. They'd roomed together all through college, even getting an apartment together their senior year.

When Santiago's mother had lost her job in Yakima, Malcolm had arranged for her to get a job at Alberto's Alfresco, and the family had moved to Seattle. When Malcolm had wanted to expand the company, he'd hired Santiago away from the hedge fund where he'd been the finance VP. They were a team — no matter what, he had Malcolm's back and he knew his friend would say the same about him.

Now he sat in front of his computer and pulled up the numbers for the soup and drink division. Something was wrong and he was going to find out what.

But before he'd gotten much past the first

layer of numbers, Malcolm walked into his office.

"What did I miss?" his boss asked, taking the visitor's chair by his desk.

"Nothing much. The quarterly meeting went well. We're up 4 percent. I've emailed you the summary reports, just let me know if you want to get into more detail."

"Any surprises?"

"Soups and drinks are down. I'm looking into it."

Malcolm rubbed his forehead. "Thanks. I don't think I'd be much help right now."

"You have a lot going on. How's Keira?"

"Physically? Healing. She sees her doctor tomorrow. As for the rest of it, I have no idea."

Malcolm was gifted when it came to business and a hell of a good friend, but he was not equipped to deal with a twelve-year-old girl. He wasn't relaxed around kids and he didn't trust easily. Whatever progress had been made on that front had been undone by Rachel nearly two years ago, Santiago thought, mentally calling Malcolm's ex-fiancée every crappy name he could think of.

Malcolm looked at him. "There was a kitten. That's how she got hit by a car. She saw a kitten and ran into the street. Can you believe it?"

"Yes. It's something Emma would do in a heartbeat. She's a kid, Malcolm. It was a kitten. What did you expect? That she would look both ways? She reacted."

"She could have been killed."

"Yes, but she wasn't. She'll recover and hey, now you have a cat."

His friend grimaced. "Lucky me. I said she could keep it."

"Good move." He leaned forward. "You have to relax around her. Pretend she's a regular person."

"Thanks for nothing. She *is* a regular person."

"Not to you. You act like she's an unwelcome life force. Kids are tough. Just let her know you care and you're there for her."

"I do care about her. I'm just not sure how to make her believe that."

"Fake it until you make it."

Malcolm glared at him. "What does that mean?"

"Pretend interest in whatever floats the boat of a twelve-year-old girl. At first you'll feel awkward and stupid but over time it will get easier. She's your sister."

"There's another one."

"Another . . ."

"Sister."

Santiago stared at him. "You're kidding. Like *Star Wars*? There is another?"

"Not funny and yes. Alberto found out about her the same time he learned about Keira, but he couldn't locate her." Malcolm hesitated as if he were going to say something, then seemed to change his mind. "She's twenty-six and living in Houston. We get the DNA test back today."

Santiago whistled. "Two new sisters. Any others out there lurking?"

"Not that Jerry knew about. Those were the only two mentioned in his papers."

"If the DNA test is a match, then what?"

Malcolm looked at him. "Guess."

"Let's see. Alberto will fly her out here and move her into the house."

"Bingo."

"You're awash in sisters. That's nice. I would have liked a sister."

"Take one of mine."

Santiago chuckled. "I do great with kids."

"Yes, you do. It's annoying."

"I'm a people person."

"That you are."

"You're better-looking but no one notices because you're such a tight ass."

Instead of laughing, Malcolm turned away. "Do you know how Keira had me listed in her phone?"

"What do you mean? She had your name wrong?"

"No." Malcolm looked at him. "On her contact list, I'm her asshole brother."

Santiago winced. "I'm sorry, Malcolm. She's having a tough time making the transition. It's still all new to her."

"Yeah, I know." He rose. "You're in her contacts, too. Under your real name. Hell of a thing."

"It'll get better."

"You sure?" Malcolm shook his head. "Never mind. I'll figure it out. Thanks for covering the meetings for me."

"No problem."

He watched his friend walk away and wished he knew how to fix the problem, or at least mitigate it. Maybe if he talked to Keira or . . .

No, he told himself. Malcolm had to figure out Keira in his own way. Santiago stepping in to play hero wouldn't help anyone, or so his brothers had told him about five thousand times.

CHAPTER SIX

Delaney had lived in Seattle all her life and still wasn't the least bit familiar with the area where Keira and Malcolm lived — probably because if the world were separated into haves and have-nots, she would definitely find herself on the side of the latter.

The closer she got to Lake Washington, the larger the homes and lots got until she was pretty sure they were called *estates* rather than something as pedestrian as *houses.*

She checked street numbers on mostly closed security gates and was surprised to find herself turning onto a gate-free driveway. The house in front of her was huge — massively tall and wide, with dozens of windows and double front doors that were suited for a modern castle. As she drove along the curved driveway to park in front of the house, she caught sight of the lake beyond.

Lake Washington was a long narrow lake only a couple of miles wide but over twenty miles long. It was beautiful, offered plenty of lakefront living but created a traffic nightmare for the east side of the metropolitan area. Finding one's way *around* traffic jams could be challenging when there was a giant lake in the middle of the commute corridors.

Delaney parked by the front door and looked at the carrier in the passenger seat. "You, young lady, have hit the jackpot. This house is going to be quite the kitty playground. You could get lost for days and I mean that in a good way."

The kitten meowed in response.

Delaney got out of her car. Before she could circle to the trunk and start unloading supplies, the front door opened and an attractive brown-haired woman walked out. She was maybe in her fifties, wearing jeans and a dark green twinset on the cool, cloudy April day.

"You must be Delaney," the woman said, holding out her hand. "I'm Carmen. I'm Mr. Carlesso's housekeeper." Carmen smiled. "That would be the senior Mr. Carlesso. You might have heard Keira call him Grandfather Alberto."

"Yes, that is what she calls him. It's nice to meet you. I've brought Keira's kitten. How's she doing?"

"Much better. She's still stiff and sore, but she's moving around and eating." Carmen's mouth twisted. "When Malcolm called and told me there'd been an accident, I didn't know what to think. We were all so frightened. She's still a little girl and she hasn't been here very long. I didn't want anything to happen to her."

At the mention of Malcolm's name, Delaney felt her stomach tighten. She was still trying to reconcile the sexy, teasing man who bought coffee from her with the cold-eyed brother who knew next to nothing about his own sister. She told herself not to judge, but it was hard not to.

At least she didn't have to worry about running into him — it was just after three in the afternoon. Malcolm would be at the office. He didn't strike her as the type to work from home.

"I'm glad she's better," Delaney said. "I'm hoping her kitten will cheer her up."

Carmen laughed. "Lizzy is all she's talked about. Come on. Let's get her upstairs."

Delaney had gone a little crazy at the pet store. In addition to a litter box and some food, she'd bought a bed and plenty of toys.

Delaney stacked the bags of cat litter onto a small, collapsible hand truck Carmen got for her, then put the case of cat food on top of the bags. She slung her tote over her shoulder and grabbed the bed and the bag of toys while Carmen collected the carrier and they went inside.

The foyer was large, soaring up two stories. If she had to guess, she would say the house had been built around the turn of the last century. There was beautifully carved wood everywhere, high ceilings and comfortable furniture. Delaney had a brief impression of a huge living room, a formal dining room and a long hallway before they went into the kitchen. Behind the pantry was an old-fashioned dumbwaiter.

"I don't use it much," Carmen said as she opened the door and they loaded the cat litter and food inside. "But it has its moments."

After she pushed a button, the doors closed and the motor kicked in. Carmen led the way back to the main, curved staircase and they went up to the second floor.

The upstairs dumbwaiter access was in a large linen closet. They stacked the litter bags and cat food on the hand truck before Carmen led the way down a hallway to two sets of double doors. They went to the far set and Carmen knocked once before opening a door and stepping inside.

"Guess who?" she called, her tone cheerful.

Keira raced toward them. "You're here! Did you bring Lizzy? Is she all right? Does she know I'm going to take good care of her?"

Delaney had only ever seen Keira in her school uniform. Out of the plaid skirt and white shirt, the preteen looked happier and younger. The healing bruise on the side of her face was the only reminder of the accident.

Impulsively Delaney set down her tote and packages and held out her arms. "I'm so glad to see you."

Keira hesitated only a second before flinging herself at Delaney and hanging on so tight, it was difficult to breathe.

"You scared me," Delaney whispered. "I was so afraid you were really hurt. You can never do that again!"

"I promise."

"Good." Delaney released her and smoothed her hair off her forehead. "You look good. A little battered, but otherwise healthy. Are you feeling all right?"

"I'm fine. Where's Lizzy?"

Carmen handed over the carrier. "Here

you go, little one. I'll bring up some hot chocolate and cookies."

"Thank you," Keira said as she dropped to her knees and carefully opened the carrier. Her breath caught. "Lizzy, you're real. I wondered if I dreamed you."

She picked up the kitten who stretched and yawned before settling in Keira's arms and meeting her gaze. Delaney sat on the floor next to them.

"She's pretty friendly. A little skittish, but she's warmed up over the past couple of days. I don't think she was feral, but I'm not sure she had a lot of contact with people."

"Thank you for taking care of her for me."

"You're welcome."

"I'm going to be a really good pet mom. I've been looking up stuff online." She looked at Delaney, her expression serious. "Cats should only have canned food. They don't have a strong instinct to drink water and dry food gives them kidney problems." She gently petted Lizzy. "I'm going to clean the litter box twice a day. That's what the articles say cats like." Her voice lowered. "I know what it's like to get used to a strange place, so I'm going to be with her all the time through the weekend. I'm not going back to school until Monday."

There was so much information in those few sentences that Delaney didn't know where to begin.

"Why don't you show me where you want things set up?" she asked. "Have you decided where to put the litter box?"

"In the other room."

Delaney stood, finally taking her attention from the girl and looking around at her bedroom. It was large, with plenty of windows and lots of light. She pointed to the built-in window seat with a comfortable cushion and lots of pillows.

"Lizzy's going to love sitting there and watching birds."

"I know. She can also climb around on my desk if she wants."

The walls were a pale gray color, the trim was white. The furniture all looked new, which made sense. From what she'd been able to piece together, Keira had been a bit of a surprise.

They carried everything into the adjoining room. It had been decorated as a teen girl haven with two bright pink club chairs, a deep blue sofa and a multicolored upholstered ottoman that acted as a soft coffee table in between. There was an under-counter refrigerator, a big wall-mounted television and plenty of storage. A fun white shag rug sat on top of the more elegant Berber carpet.

Keira pointed to a small alcove near the corner. "There was a dresser here that got moved out. I'll feed Lizzy on the other side of the room. You're not supposed to have food and the litter box close together." She wrinkled her nose. "No one wants to eat in the bathroom."

It took only a few minutes to get everything set up. Once the litter box was filled and the water bowl put out, Keira set the kitten on the floor, then sat next to her while Lizzy began to sniff and explore.

Delaney split her attention between the girl and the cat. "How are you feeling?" she asked.

"Better. My headache is gone and it doesn't hurt to read." She held out her fingers for Lizzy to sniff. The black-and-white kitten rubbed against them and began to purr. "My teachers put my assignments online, so I've been keeping up."

"I have homework, too," Delaney said. "Biology is hard."

"Have you done your dissection yet?"

"No. It got postponed. I didn't ask why because I don't want to know."

Keira grinned. "Maybe it's an inventory issue."

"Don't go there. Talk about gross."

"How are you going to be a doctor if you can't dissect something that's been dead like forever?"

"I'm not sure. I'm still working on that problem."

Leaving the world of finance to become a naturopath had made sense three months ago, but she was starting to have her doubts. She wasn't sure she was passionate enough to dedicate the next four years of her life to full-time study.

Keira reached for one of the feather-on-a-stick toys and waved it in front of Lizzy. The kitten immediately attacked.

"Have any of your friends been by?" Delaney asked.

Keira looked at her. "No, but we've texted. They wanted to know I was okay. I didn't feel very good until yesterday and now I have Lizzy. I'm fine."

"I worry about you."

"I know." Keira ducked her head.

Delaney wished she could be more sure about her friend. Keira's home situation was unconventional at best. Not awful, but maybe not as nurturing as it could have been.

"Carmen seems nice."

"She's great. She's fussing over me even

more than usual and she's really excited about Lizzy."

At least Keira had someone watching over her.

"Okay, I'm going to let you and Lizzy get to know each other," she said as she stood. "You have my number. Text me if you need anything. Even if it's just more cat toys. I'm happy to bring them by."

"I will."

Keira carefully closed the door behind them so Lizzy wouldn't get out. Carmen met them on the landing.

"Malcolm would like to speak with you," she told Delaney. "If you have a minute."

Delaney's breath caught. He was home? Why hadn't someone warned her before now? Not that it mattered, she told herself. She wasn't sure how she felt about him. Annoyance and maybe a little outrage had replaced attraction.

"Of course," she said, trying to sound neutral. She hugged Keira goodbye and reminded her to text or call if she needed anything, then followed the housekeeper down the long second-floor hallway.

Carmen knocked once before entering the suite of rooms. Delaney followed and saw his living space was very similar to Keira's although instead of entering a bedroom, she found herself in a study/home office. There was a comfortable sofa, a good-sized desk and lots of bookcases. A door stood open and she caught sight of a king-size bed with a bathroom beyond. Malcolm looked up from his computer, smiled and rose when he saw her.

"Delaney, I'm glad you stopped by. I've wanted to talk to you."

Carmen excused herself and shut the door as she left. Malcolm motioned to the sofa.

"Please. Have a seat."

He looked different, she thought. Instead of a suit, he wore jeans and a long-sleeved shirt that emphasized his broad shoulders. His eyes were dark blue, his jaw firm. Dammit, he looked good and she did not want to be sucked in by that. She hadn't liked the way he'd been so clueless about his own sister. He wasn't charming, she reminded herself. She wasn't the least bit attracted to him.

But sitting only a few feet away on a very comfortable leather sofa, it was difficult not to notice how her chest seemed just a little tight and her nerves were slightly on edge. Annoyance, she reminded herself. With annoyance came energy.

He reached in his pocket and pulled out a hundred-dollar bill, then handed it to her.

"Before I forget," he said with a smile. "For the cat supplies."

"I didn't spend anywhere close to this."

One shoulder rose. "You also took care of Lizzy. That can't have been convenient." The smile faded as he leaned toward her. "I also want to thank you for being there for Keira. I'm not sure I did at the hospital. Things were happening too fast. We all appreciate that you stayed with Keira until she got to the hospital. She must have been terrified. You were a comforting presence. Thank you."

He seemed so genuine, so caring, she thought, more than a little perplexed. What had happened to the cold stranger who knew almost nothing about his sister?

"I'm confused," she admitted. "At the hospital you were so distant and, um, stern."

"The asshole brother?" he asked drily.

"Something like that."

He sighed. "Yeah, it's been hard with Keira."

"She's a good kid." Delaney had a feeling her tone sounded fairly defensive.

"She is. I was talking more about myself than her. I'm not exactly a kid person."

"She really just showed up two months ago?"

"Uh-huh. My father died a couple of years

ago." He hesitated. "There wasn't a will so everything went to my grandfather and me. Around the first of the year, Alberto decided to get Jerry's papers in order. He found information about two daughters no one knew about."

He looked at her. "I should backtrack a little. My father was a salesman for the company and traveled all over. Apparently he liked women and they liked him. The three of us are the result of various relationships he had. Jerry wasn't interested in his children or paying regular child support. I didn't meet him until my mother brought me here when I was twelve. Alberto welcomed me right away, but Jerry resisted the connection. He and I were never close. I didn't actually know him very well at all."

There was something about the way he said the words, she thought. As if there was more to the story.

"Where's the other sister?" she asked instead.

"Arriving tomorrow. That's going to be interesting. She's older — twenty-six. I don't know that much about her. Keira was easier to locate. As she told you, she'd been living in foster care. Once we established paternity, I went and got her. She's lived here ever since."

She couldn't imagine finding out about a sibling after so many years. Maybe Malcolm wasn't as awful as she'd feared. Maybe he was just unprepared.

"And now what?" she asked.

"Now we make it work." He raised a shoulder. "What I mean is I make it work. The accident showed me I haven't been involved enough in Keira's life. She seems to have it all together, but the truth is she's a kid. I was her age when my mom brought me here. I remember how lost I felt and I had my mother with me. She might feel as if she doesn't have anyone and that's not right."

Delaney relaxed a little more. "It's her air of competence. It's a great disguise, but you're right. She's just twelve. She needs to know people care about her and that this is her home. Having Lizzy will help."

"I know nothing about cats."

"Keira's been doing research on the internet. You can ask her all about it."

"I will."

They smiled at each other. Tension seemed to swirl between them — the boy-girl kind, which was kind of nice and strange, all at the same time. Or maybe not. Maybe she was the only one feeling it and wouldn't that be both awkward and pathetic?

What was wrong with her? He was just a guy. Except she knew the problem — there hadn't been anyone since Tim and before Tim, she'd been a kid. All she knew about men and love and dating had been learned with Tim. What if they'd done it all wrong?

"Delaney?"

"Huh? Oh, sorry. I got distracted by something. What were you saying?"

"That I owe you."

If only, she thought wistfully. "Not really. I like Keira. Helping out with her was easy."

"Still. I'd offer to buy you coffee but that wouldn't be very exciting for you. How about dinner?"

D-dinner? As in . . . dinner?

She felt herself flushing and hoped her light makeup kept him from being able to tell. "That would be nice," she said, trying to sound casual, as if this sort of thing happened all the time.

"How about Saturday night? If you're available."

"Saturday would be perfect."

They agreed on the Metropolitan Grill at seven. Malcolm said he would make reservations.

"I look forward to it," he told her as he walked out of his room and down the stairs. "Do you want me to pick you up or meet

118

you there?"

"I'll meet you there," she murmured, thinking it would be too uncomfortable to have him pick her up. Too much like a date. Not that it was a date. Or maybe it was, she wasn't sure. Nor would she ask. It was a step forward, she told herself. Right now that was enough.

At the front door, she turned and said, "Keira said she's going back to school on Monday. Please tell her I look forward to seeing her that morning."

"I will." He lightly touched her arm. "You were right at the hospital. I should tell her goodbye, because it's the little things, right?"

"It is. I'll see you Saturday."

He smiled. "You will. I'm looking forward to it."

"Me, too."

She managed to get to her car without stumbling or shrieking or grinning like a fool, then started the engine and sedately drove down the long driveway. It was only when she was on the main road heading for home that she allowed herself a small shriek and a little shimmy in her seat before settling in for a long internal discussion about what on earth she was going to wear.

CHAPTER SEVEN

Callie planned to work on not feeling terrified just as soon as she stopped shaking. She supposed she should give herself a break — so much had happened so fast. Monday she'd been approached by a lawyer about her late father and some mystery family that wanted to meet her. Wednesday she'd heard from Shari on the results of the DNA test. They'd met and Callie had gotten a plane ticket to Seattle. Here it was Friday morning and she was on her way to a city she'd never been to so she could meet a family she knew nothing about.

Shari had been great — taking plenty of time to talk through the details. The family wanted Callie to relocate to Seattle. Callie hadn't known what to do, but in the end she'd decided to quit both her jobs and pack up her meager belongings and fly west.

Disrupting her life had been uncomfortably simple. Janice had been sad but understanding. At her cleaning job, her supervisor had barely said anything beyond "Good luck." Callie rented her room furnished, so she didn't have to worry about getting rid of anything big and she paid month to month, so there wasn't even a lease. A quick trip to the local thrift store had produced a second battered suitcase. In a matter of an hour, she'd uprooted her life.

Now at the airport gate, she tried to look as if she knew what she was doing. She'd never flown before. Until a couple of years ago, she'd never been outside Oklahoma. She'd ridden the bus to Houston and hadn't ever taken a vacation anywhere. It wasn't as if being in prison came with field trips. She was so unprepared, she thought, wondering if it was too late to bolt.

The morning had started with a town car arriving to take her to the airport. Shari had said everything was paid for but had suggested Callie might want to tip the drivers on each end. She had no idea how much, so had handed the older guy ten dollars. She wasn't supposed to tip anyone on the plane, was she? She'd read a couple of articles online and none of them had mentioned that.

The gate agent started the boarding process. Callie checked the seat number on her boarding pass again. It hadn't changed. She was in seat 3A. According to what she'd found out from her research, that could mean she was in first class. But how was that possible? Who would be ridiculous enough to pay extra to get her to Seattle? She would arrive at exactly the same time flying in the back of the plane. Still, when the agent said first class was boarding, Callie slowly walked up and handed over her boarding pass.

"Welcome aboard, Ms. Smith," the young woman said with a smile. "Have a great flight."

Callie nodded without speaking and started down the long, sloping hallway. As she got closer to the plane, her shaking increased. She couldn't do this, she thought frantically. She could not get on that flying coffin. They were all going to die.

At least then you won't have to deal with meeting your family.

The voice and the words came so unexpectedly, she laughed out loud. Her tension eased and she stepped onto the plane.

She figured out the numbering system and found her seat, then watched everyone else get on board. Her seatmate was a well-dressed, middle-aged woman who gave her an absent smile before pulling out a stack of fashion and gossip magazines and starting to read. Callie tried not to notice how threadbare her long-sleeved T-shirt looked next to the other woman's expensive knit jacket. The woman's wedding band was a row of diamonds and the center stone on her engagement ring was huge.

Once the plane was loaded, the flight attendants started the safety announcements. Callie checked her seat belt about sixteen times, then listened to every word of the safety demonstration. Before she was ready, the plane was racing toward certain death only to unexpectedly take off into the air.

She gripped both armrests, digging in her fingers until her knuckles went white, but the plane didn't plummet. Instead it went higher and higher, causing her ears to pop a little and the earth to seem to fall away.

"What can I get you two ladies to drink?"

Callie turned and saw the flight attendant standing by their row. The woman next to her ordered a glass of white wine. Callie asked for water.

"We'll be serving lunch today. A chicken pasta salad. Would either of you like to join us?"

The other woman nodded. Callie said she would like lunch, then wondered if she had to pay for it. All the articles she'd read had sworn first class tickets got a free meal, but she wasn't sure. Still, she'd taken a hundred dollars out of the bank, so she had cash with her, and her ATM card. She didn't own a credit card. They'd always seemed too risky.

The flight attendant returned with their drinks. A few minutes later, the captain came on the loudspeaker and gave them the details of the flight. Callie couldn't believe they would get from Houston to Seattle in only four and a half hours. It took almost that long just to drive to Dallas!

The woman next to her finished her *In-Style* magazine and offered it to Callie. "If you haven't read this one . . ."

Callie looked from the magazine to her, then smiled. "Thank you. That's very nice of you."

She smoothed the front of the cover, trying to remember the last time she'd read a new magazine. In prison she'd spent her free time reading books and studying for her GED. Her conviction had interrupted her senior year. Once she was out, she hadn't had the extra money for something so frivolous. Now she leaned back in her seat and opened the magazine to the first page. It was an ad for hair color. She studied the glossy photograph, read all the text, and wondered if she would ever get to feel normal again and take things like magazines for granted.

Four hours and forty-two minutes after they had pushed back from the gate in Houston, their plane arrived in Seattle. Callie pulled her backpack from under the seat in front of her and waited to walk out into a scary and unknown future. In that brief moment as she stepped onto the Jetway, she felt the cool damp air and shivered slightly. Her light jacket was nowhere warm enough for whatever the temperature was outside.

She followed the signs to baggage claim and took a steep escalator down two floors. As she stepped off, she saw several men in suits holding paper signs or iPads with names on them. Shari had told her car service would be provided in Seattle, so Callie looked at several of them before spotting one that said C. Smith.

She walked over to the driver. "I'm Callie Smith."

The older man smiled at her. "Nice to meet you. I'm Hal. Do you have checked luggage?"

"Two bags."

He led the way to the carousel. "Coming home from a trip or visiting?" he asked.

"Visiting. My first time in the city."

"It's been raining, which is pretty typical for this time of year." He chuckled. "Or any time of the year, except for summer. Never come here in late July and think it's going to be that nice all the time. And when they say it's just a light misty rain, they're lying. It rains a lot."

The suitcases began to appear. Callie couldn't believe how quickly they moved on the conveyor belt, going in a huge oval. She spotted hers fairly quickly — mostly because they were so shabby. She pointed them out to Hal, who collected them. Then they took the escalator up one floor and started for the parking garage.

The second they stepped out of the airport, Callie began to shiver. It wasn't that it was all that cold — although it was — what she really noticed was the dampness. It was as if the chill could get right inside her body.

Hal walked briskly along a skybridge toward the parking garage. He bypassed a pay station and a bank of elevators, then they went down another escalator to where there were rows and rows of large black SUVs and town cars. Hal led her to an SUV and held open the back door. She slid inside.

They drove onto a freeway and headed for the city.

"I'll point out a few things as we drive," Hal told her. "You'll see the Seattle skyline in a few minutes. We're on the wrong side for you to see the Space Needle — that's north of downtown. See that tall, black high-rise?"

She peered out the front window. "Uh-huh."

"That's the Columbia Center. It's seventy stories high. People around here joke it's the box the Space Needle shipped in." He chuckled. "All right, little lady, there on your left is Safeco Field — home of the Seattle Mariners. Right next to it is Century-Link Field, where the Seahawks play. Go Hawks!"

Callie smiled. No point in mentioning she wasn't that into sports. She figured it was a guy thing.

After a few more minutes, they got off the freeway and entered a residential neighborhood. She was relieved to see average-looking homes with pretty yards. The rain had stopped, leaving gray skies. The car thermometer said it was forty-seven outside. How was that possible? It was April!

Hal turned and drove and turned some more. The houses got bigger and farther apart and Callie's nerves returned. They made another turn.

"Look out the passenger window," Hal told her. "You should catch a glimpse of Lake Washington. This is a real nice neighborhood. Who did you say you were visiting?"

"Some, ah, friends."

He winked at her. "Friends with money. The best kind."

Sooner than she would have liked, they turned down a long driveway. Hal stopped in front of a huge, three-story house that looked bigger than a hotel. Callie wanted to crawl under the seat and never be seen, but it was too late. Hal had already opened her door and was taking out her suitcases.

She grabbed her backpack and stepped onto the wet driveway. She pulled ten dollars from her front jeans pocket and offered it to him.

I can't do this. Please take me back to the airport. But what she said instead was, "Thank you, Hal."

"You're welcome, young lady."

The front doors opened and a brown-haired woman in her fifties smiled at her. "Callie? I'm Carmen, the family housekeeper. Welcome to Seattle."

Carmen insisted on carrying one of the suitcases. Callie had a brief impression of a giant foyer with a two-story ceiling and lots of rooms filled with expensive-looking furniture. She couldn't seem to focus on anything but the fact that she couldn't breathe or stop shaking. What had she been thinking? She didn't belong here. So what if they were family — she wasn't one of them.

Before she could bolt, Carmen grabbed her hand and squeezed her fingers. "Alberto is so happy you're here. He's been waiting to find you." She hesitated. "Your grandfather is a wonderful man. I hope you'll grow to love him."

Callie had no idea what to say to that.

"This way," Carmen said.

They left the suitcases by the front door and walked by the wide, curved staircase, then down a hall and another hall. There was a turn and maybe a couple of bridges and a mountain, or so it felt. Finally they arrived at a book-lined study. An old, old man in a gray suit looked up from his book.

"Oh, Carmen, she is as beautiful as I imagined." He stood and smiled. "Callie, at last. Welcome, child. Welcome to your home."

He was taller than she'd expected — close to six feet — and despite his age, still handsome. She could see traces of the younger man he had once been. He looked strong and healthy and way too excited to see her.

"Mr. Carlesso," she began, but he stopped her with a quick shake of his head.

"Grandfather Alberto," he told her. "Or just Alberto if you're not comfortable thinking of me as your grandfather just yet."

He motioned to the sofa. "Come. Sit. We'll get to know each other."

She moved closer and sat on the sofa, as far from him as she could. He sank down, then poured them each a cup of coffee from the tray in front of him. Carmen smiled and left.

He handed her coffee and held out a plate of cookies. "Biscotti," he said. "We make them here, in the city. It's an old family recipe. They're one of our best sellers."

She looked at the weird cookie, then watched as he dunked it in the coffee before taking a bite.

"Best seller?" she asked.

"Alberto's Alfresco. It's the family company. I started it many years ago. We sell food and drink all over the world."

She stared at him. "You mean the catalog company?" Of course she'd heard of them — probably on TV or something. Everyone had. They were an upscale company that sold delicious Italian food. "That's you? I mean you're *that* Alberto?"

"I am. You are, as well." His gaze settled

on her face. "You look just like my late wife. She was so beautiful. It's been thirty years and I still miss her." He smiled. "I'm so glad you're finally here. You were not easy to find."

Callie didn't know what to say to that. Too much was happening too fast. She sipped her coffee and ignored her biscotti, all the while trying to get her breathing under control.

"How was your trip?" Alberto asked.

"Good. I've never flown before. It was different than I thought it was going to be. Everyone was very nice."

Alberto's expression was kind. "So much to get used to. I must remember that. If I move too fast, as you young people say, tell me. The lawyer said she told you about your father."

"That he's, ah, no longer with us?"

Alberto nodded. "Yes. It's unfortunate. He was difficult at times, but still my son. And he gave me you and your siblings. Let's see, there's Malcolm. He's a few years older than you, and Keira who is only twelve. We only found out about you girls a few months ago."

"Shari, your lawyer, mentioned that." She didn't know much about her father but what she did know wasn't very promising.

Not that she was going to have to deal with him but still there were —

A man walked into the study. He was tall and looked enough like his grandfather for her to guess the relationship. Unlike Alberto, his eyes were not kind . . . or welcoming. If anything, he seemed resigned.

"Hello, Callie," he said as he approached. "I'm your half brother, Malcolm."

She didn't know what to do. Stand? Sit and smile tightly? Run?

"Hi," she said quietly. "Nice to meet you."

"You, too."

Like Alberto, he wore a suit and tie. If she'd seen him on the street, she would have assumed he was rich and successful and gone out of her way to avoid him.

Malcolm took a seat across from them and poured himself a cup of coffee. "I'm sure this is all overwhelming."

"A little."

"You can take as much time as you'd like to get settled. There's a lot to explore."

Alberto patted her hand. "Seattle is a beautiful city. You'll want to see it and we'll show you around the company, of course. The executive offices are very nice, but you should see the factory where we create our magic."

She smiled. "I'd like that."

"Keira is so excited to meet you," Alberto continued. "She's very happy to have a sister."

Malcolm surprised her by grinning. "Yes, she's made it clear that she would not welcome another brother. My fault, I'm afraid." His smile faded. "Did you leave anything behind in Houston?"

The question was so vague, she didn't know if he was referring to a job, a boyfriend, a dog or an apartment.

"I didn't know what was happening," she admitted. "I thought it was easier to make a clean break." She supposed that if things didn't work out here, she could always go somewhere else. There was nothing to return to in Texas.

"Good." Malcolm rose. "Why don't I show you to your room? Dinner is at six thirty and I'm sure you'll want to take a little time to settle before then."

She set down her coffee. Alberto rose, put his hands on her shoulders and kissed both her cheeks. "Welcome, my beautiful granddaughter. We are your family now. Always we will be here for you."

His words sounded genuine. She saw tears in his eyes and felt the ice wall around her heart melting just a little. Then she turned and met Malcolm's wary gaze. Maybe she

133

was wrong but it seemed to her not everyone was thrilled by her arrival. If she had to
guess, she would say Malcolm wasn't happy
to have a felon in the family. All things being equal, who could blame him? Certainly
not her.

Malcolm left Callie to get settled, then
walked the few feet to Keira's door. His
sister had been after him all day to let her
know the *second* Callie arrived.

Just before he knocked, he paused to
remember the awkward trip he'd taken
down to Los Angeles when he'd gone to get
Keira. He'd had no idea how to deal with a
twelve-year-old, nor had he known what she
would be like. He'd filled a backpack with
snacks, an iPad loaded with games and a
couple of Disney movies, headphones, and
an activity book with puzzles and easy cross-
words.

Keira had been waiting at her social
worker's office. Everything she owned had
fit into a battered old-fashioned hatbox
decorated with pictures of landmarks from
around the world. She'd been wide-eyed,
thin and silent as they'd been introduced.

He hadn't known what to say beyond
explaining he was her half brother, that she
had a grandfather and that he was taking

her to live with him in Seattle. He promised her her own room and a good school. At the end of his awkwardly stilted speech, she'd simply picked up her hatbox and looked at him as if waiting for whatever was going to happen next.

He should have done more, he thought nearly three months after the fact. He couldn't say what, but he should have tried harder. They'd barely spoken on the two-and-a-half-hour flight. Maybe she'd been scared or nervous or hungry. But he'd only asked if she needed anything and when she'd said no, he'd believed her.

He remembered taking her to the airport gift shop and buying her a sweatshirt so she wouldn't be cold, but he'd done little else to make her feel comfortable or safe. He swore silently — couldn't he have offered her a candy bar or some chips? Something to show she was more than a chore he had to finish?

He thought about her phone. *Asshole brother.* He didn't want to be that. Whether or not he'd gone looking for more family wasn't the point. She was a kid and totally alone in the world. The least he could do was suck it up and give her some attention. So what if he was bad at it — at least he had to try.

He knocked on her door. She flung it open instantly as if she'd been waiting for him.

"Is she here? Is she here? What is she like? Does she look like me? Is she nice? Will I like her?"

Malcolm smiled. "You've been saving up those questions, haven't you?"

Keira danced from foot to foot. "Yes, now tell meeeee!"

He studied his younger sister. According to her pediatrician, she was about average height, slightly underweight and perfectly healthy. Her hair was light brown, her eyes blue and Carmen had said more than once he and Keira shared the same smile.

"She has your freckles," he told Keira.

She laughed, then ran to the mirror and stared at herself. "Really? All of them? I can't decide if I like my freckles or not."

He almost pointed out her opinion on her freckles didn't matter — it wasn't as if they were going away — but stopped himself in time.

"They're cute," he told her. "On you and on Callie."

Keira spun to face him and beamed. "Really? I can't wait to meet her. And I want to see her room."

"Give her a couple of hours to get settled," he said, repeating what they'd discussed the previous night at dinner. "We don't want to overwhelm her. You'll meet her at dinner. As to her room, you saw it yesterday, when everything was delivered."

Keira gave him a look that implied he was incredibly stupid but she would indulge him this one time. She crossed to the bed and scooped up the kitten sitting there. "Maybe she's scared. Maybe she needs a friend."

"Maybe she's tired from her trip and would like a few minutes before she has to deal with the whole family."

"There's only three of us, plus Carmen. That's not a lot."

"It might be to her."

From what he'd read in the report on Callie, since getting out of prison, she'd lived a quiet life. She'd stayed in a halfway house for nearly nine months before moving to Houston. She worked her two jobs, volunteered at a cat shelter once a week and lived in a rented room. She didn't seem to have many friends or much of a social life. As for what had gotten her arrested in the first place, from how she'd lived the last five years, that had been a one-time thing.

Keira sighed heavily. "Fine. I'll wait until dinner."

"Good. You seem to be feeling better. You have a lot of energy."

"I'm excited. This is so fun. We have a new sister. I could barely sleep last night. Aren't you excited?"

"Very," he lied. He didn't care about the trust fund his grandfather would set up for Callie or the potential division of the business. He already had enough. It was more that all these years later, he was still dealing with his father's shit. When was it finally going to end?

"I'll see you in a couple of hours," he told Keira. "Until then, leave Callie alone."

Keira batted her eyes at him. "I wouldn't think of doing anything else."

CHAPTER EIGHT

Callie stood in the center of her two-room suite, not sure what to think about any of it. Her head hurt, the world seemed to be spinning and she honestly couldn't believe any of this was happening. Before she could catch her breath or figure out if she wanted to faint, Carmen appeared, a tray in her hands.

"You must be tired from your flight," she said with a gentle smile. "And maybe overwhelmed. I brought you a snack to tide you over until dinner."

She set the tray on the dark gray tufted ottoman at the foot of the queen-size bed. "Let me show you around the room, then I'll leave you to get settled."

Callie could only nod. Speaking seemed impossible, as did making sense of any of this.

"I only had a few days to get your room ready," Carmen said. "If you want to make changes, go ahead. I have no idea if you like my taste or not."

The bedroom was huge, maybe twenty by twenty, with big floor-to-ceiling windows. The walls were cream except for the dark gray wall behind the bed. The head and footboards were upholstered in cream, the bedspread was the same color with a woven gold pattern in the center. The cream-and-gold color theme continued with a fuzzy cream rug. Dark wood accents — the dresser, the legs of the ottoman and the chair in the corner — added contrast. The nightstands were mirrored with glass-based lamps.

Callie had never been in a five-star hotel in her life. Come to think of it, she'd only ever stayed at a Quality Inn, her first two nights in Houston, but if she had to guess, she would say this was what a five-star hotel room looked like.

Carmen showed her the big bathroom with a long vanity and a separate tub and walk-in shower. There was a closet nearly the size of her rented room and a second room attached to the first.

"Malcolm uses his spare room as an office," Carmen told her. "I set up Keira's as a living space." She smiled. "I went brighter with her colors. Again, if you want to change any of this, please let me know."

The color theme continued. There were two sofas and a chair, all upholstered in cream, another tufted ottoman, plenty of small tables, floor lamps and a fun faux-fur throw rug done in a gold-and-white zebra print.

"I'm overwhelmed," Callie admitted. "Thank you so much for all of this."

"You're welcome." Carmen pointed to her right. "Keira's room is next to yours." She waved toward the left. "Malcolm's room is beyond the staircase. Your grandfather sleeps on the first floor. The stairs are more difficult for him these days. I have a suite of rooms on the third floor. Please make yourself comfortable, explore the house. You're welcome in the kitchen anytime you'd like. I keep a running grocery list. Just tell me what you'd like and I'll get it."

"I'll do that," Callie promised as her head began to throb. She just wanted to be alone and try to figure out how to process all of it.

"Then I'll leave you to get settled. Dinner is at six thirty. Just come downstairs and turn right." She paused. "Your grandfather is very happy you're here."

Good to know, Callie thought, not sure how she felt about her new circumstances, but determined to be polite. She followed Carmen to the hallway and thanked her again before shutting the bedroom door. She felt her legs start to give way but forced herself to keep moving. She sat on the bed, then turned on the nightstand lamps before checking out the tray Carmen had brought only to be overwhelmed once again.

There was a large antipasto plate filled with slices of several kinds of cheese and meat. There were olives and almonds and walnuts, mushrooms and cherry tomatoes. Crusty rolls sat on a smaller plate next to a ramekin of butter. A third plate contained a half dozen different kinds of cookies. S-shaped and pinwheels, frosted lemon drop cookies and chocolate-dipped butter cookies.

Even as her stomach growled, she honestly wasn't sure she could eat a bite. Not with her whole body fighting the need to bolt.

She ignored the food but sipped the tea as she checked out the big closet and saw there were more drawers there, along with built-in shelves and racks for her shoes. Back in the bedroom she found the remote for the television on the dresser, then walked into the huge bathroom.

The towels were the softest, fluffiest she'd ever felt and the shower was stocked with several kinds of shampoo, conditioner and body wash. There was a blow-dryer tucked in one drawer, along with a flat iron and a curling iron.

The sitting room had another television, a small refrigerator and more built-in storage. She saw several boxes stacked on the ottoman and walked over to inspect them. There was an iPhone, an iPad, chargers, headphones and a note about which carrier the family used, along with the house's Wi-Fi code.

Callie left the boxes untouched as she moved around the room. One of the end tables had a stack of magazines along with a couple of hardcover books. She opened the front cover and was shocked when she realized these were new books, bought from a store. They hadn't been checked out of the library.

She didn't know if she should laugh or cry. She had a sudden urge to scream or run or hide. Before she could decide, there was a knock, followed by the sound of her bedroom door opening.

"Callie?"

The voice was unfamiliar and very young. Callie went back into the bedroom and saw a slightly gawky girl smiling at her, a black-and-white kitten in her arms. The other sister, she thought.

"Hi. I'm Keira and this is Lizzy." Keira sank onto the floor and released the kitten, who immediately began to explore. "She just used the litter box so you don't have to worry about her peeing or anything. She's really good. I'm really glad you're here. Malcolm said I wasn't supposed to bother you but I had to come see you. I mean dinner is *hours* away. Did you have a good flight? Have you flown before? I hadn't and I was so scared, but Malcolm was with me and I didn't want to say anything to him. He can be intimidating. Oh, wait!"

Keira jumped up and raced to the door. "I'll be right back."

Callie sat on the rug and offered her hand to the kitten. Lizzy sniffed her fingers before rubbing her head against her hand.

Keira returned and handed Callie two night-lights.

"It's hard being in a strange place," she said. "It can be dark at night. These might help. I have them in my room."

The unexpected and kind gesture hit Callie with the force of a semitruck. She had to swallow before speaking so she wouldn't burst into tears.

"Thank you. You're very sweet." She motioned to the room. "This is kind of a lot to take in."

"It's big, huh? When I lived with Angelina, my bedroom was an alcove off the dining room. When I saw my room, I freaked. In foster care, I had to share a room, which wasn't too bad, only my foster sister was older and she talked about really scary stuff." Keira reached for Lizzy and hugged her close.

"So here's what you have to know. Grandfather Alberto is really old. Like ninety or something. He likes to give hugs and they're nice, even though he smells strange. He's funny and he really cares, which is nice." She rolled her eyes. "He always wants to hear about how school is and stuff, but it's good. Carmen is our housekeeper. She'll get you anything you want."

Keira kept looking at her. Finally she blurted, "We have the same freckles. Malcolm said but I didn't know if I could believe him. Do you like yours? I can't decide. Sometimes I like mine and sometimes I think they're ugly."

Without considering the consequences of the action, Callie reached for Keira and pulled her close. Keira was still for a second, then hung on with her free arm. The kitten squirmed between them before settling down and starting to purr.

Tears burned. Callie willed them away. To cry was to show weakness, she reminded herself.

"Your freckles are adorable," Callie whispered. "Now that I've seen yours, I like mine better."

They drew back and Keira grinned at her. "Me, too." She handed over Lizzy. "I've only had her since Wednesday. Monday before school I was having hot chocolate with Delaney who never lets me get coffee, by the way, even though lots of kids drink coffee. Anyway, I saw this kitten in the street and ran out to save it and was hit by a car." She shifted her long hair back so Callie could see the fading bruise on her face. "Delaney kept Lizzy for a couple of days and now she's here. Do you like cats?"

"I've never had a pet, but yes, I like cats." She'd always hoped to have a dog or a cat one day, although that dream had seemed a long way off.

"She lives in my room for now. I mean she's small and the house is really big." Keira looked around. "You have suitcases. That's nice. I have a hatbox I used. When my mom died and social services came, Angelina said she didn't want me to carry my clothes around in a trash bag like some foster kids, so she gave me her favorite

146

hatbox." Her mouth trembled at the corners. "I still miss her, but it's been a long time since I lived with her. I tried texting her, but the number's changed."

Her expression brightened. "Did you see your new phone and tablet? Malcolm isn't exactly friendly but he buys the best electronics. I had to get a computer for school and he got me a MacBook Air. I love it." She wrinkled her nose. "I go to this very classy private school. We have to wear a uniform. The girls wear plaid. It's ridiculous."

Callie appreciated the chatter. It kept her from having to say too much. She still felt incredibly confused by everything that was happening, but Keira's friendly conversation was safe and grounding.

"Do you have a lot of friends?" Callie asked.

"Some. It's hard to make new friends."

"It can be." Callie petted Lizzy. "Try giving compliments. They have to be sincere, of course, but girls really like hearing you think their shoes are nice or their hair is pretty. Guys probably don't care what you think of their shoes."

Keira grinned. "Right? I don't get boys at all. A couple of girls I know want boyfriends, but why? Anyway, school's okay. I like what we're studying. At my old school the classes were really easy. Here I have to work harder, but that's okay."

She paused, then said, "I'm glad you're here. I hope you like it and stay."

"Me, too. The sister thing is . . ." She searched for the right word.

"Bizarre," Keira said, drawing out the syllables. "But nice." She scrambled to her feet and reached for Lizzy. "Okay, *now* I'm going to do what Malcolm said and leave you alone to get settled. Want me to come get you before dinner? We can walk down together."

"I'd like that very much."

"Good. See you then."

Keira ran out of the room, the kitten in her arms. Callie stayed where she was on the floor and looked around. The space seemed less intimidating now that she knew Keira was next door. She had no idea what was going to happen over the next few days, but the fear had mostly faded. She reached for a piece of cheese and took a bite, then got up and plugged in one of the nightlights.

First she would unpack, she told herself. Then she would shower and maybe after that she would check out her new phone. Not that she had anyone to call or text, but maybe that would change. With luck, she had been given a brand-new start. If that was the case, she was determined to take advantage of every opportunity. Screwing up had too high a price.

Delaney's small condo came with a few unexpected features. When the weather was nice, she had a peekaboo view of Mount Rainier from her balcony, the garden window in the kitchen had a built-in tray for herbs, and there were his and hers closets in the bedroom.

When Delaney had decided to totally change her life, turning her back on corporate America and returning to college to become a naturopath, she'd divided her wardrobe into a before and after configuration. Her *before* life clothes included her beautiful suits, silk blouses, expensive shoes and a handful of cocktail dresses she wore to various events. Her *after* wardrobe was much more simple. Yoga pants, T-shirts, a couple of pairs of jeans, sweaters, tennis shoes and boots. She had three hoodies in different weights of fabric, depending on the weather, and a leather moto jacket she'd bought at a consignment store. She kept the *before* closet door shut and rarely went inside. One day she would have to decide what to do with those clothes, but not today.

At four o'clock on Saturday afternoon, she put down her mug of tea and walked barefoot into the large bedroom and crossed to the closed door. She was meeting Malcolm for dinner and knew that however soft the fabric, yoga pants would not cut it.

She opened the door and flipped the switch on the light, then waited for the kick in the gut that was recent but nonetheless painful.

Maybe it was silly, but she loved these clothes. Loved them. They were stylish, well tailored and pretty. She'd always felt confident and successful in her suits.

She still remembered the summer between her freshman and sophomore years of college when she'd joined an on-campus organization for future women business leaders. One of the speakers had been an image consultant, and she'd explained the importance of looking the part. Delaney had not only taken her advice to heart, she'd worked extra hours at her summer job to pay for a shopping session.

Monique had taken her to the downtown Nordstrom where Delaney had discovered the difference between a $110 Anne Klein jacket and a $600 Boss jacket. She'd tried on every suit brand and had learned that

Classiques Entier clothes fit her perfectly and that no one made a Ponte pant better than Eileen Fisher.

Monique had then taken her to the designer department where Delaney had nearly thrown up when she'd seen the price of an Armani blazer. But when she'd put it on, she'd fallen completely and totally in love. She'd also discovered that the St. John collection had been made for her body type, especially their conservative but elegant dresses.

None of her friends back in the neighborhood had understood her obsession with the perfect interview suit. While they'd been saving for summer strappy sandals, Delaney had been putting away all the cash she could for the perfect silk shell. She'd made friends with one of the sales associates who worked the designer department at Nordstrom, haunting the aisles until the kind woman took pity and told her about an upcoming sale. Delaney had walked into her first job interview wearing Armani.

She remembered the feeling of confidence, of knowing she looked the part. She wanted to be successful and it showed.

Now she ran her hand along the sleeves of her suits before turning to the dresses hanging neatly together. Nothing too fancy, she thought. It was just dinner. She picked up a black sheath and put it back, then reached for a dress she'd bought but had never worn.

It was dark green, a Jason Wu textured jacquard fit-and-flare sleeveless dress. At the bottom of the full skirt was an unexpected touch of small gold-tone grommets. Given that it was still April and cool, she would top the dress with a black leather jacket. She had simple black heels and her go-to diamond studs.

As she collected the various pieces, she hesitated before opening the small jewelry box sitting on top of the built-in dresser. She'd bought the earrings herself after her second promotion. She'd gotten a sizable raise and after saving for several months, she'd walked into Tiffany & Co. and purchased the diamond studs.

Her dad had been proud, but Tim had been furious and they'd fought for days. He refused to see the earrings as a sign of her accomplishment. Instead, he'd felt they were a slap — something he couldn't afford to buy her. He told her that women weren't supposed to buy their own jewelry — not like that. It was emasculating.

All her friends from the neighborhood had sided with Tim. All her work friends had told her she was doing the right thing —

that she had every right to celebrate the good things in her life. She and Tim had agreed to disagree and had never discussed the studs again, but every time she'd worn them, she'd felt his disapproval.

As she stared at the earrings resting in the palm of her hand, she wondered if she should sell them. Maybe the bad memories were just too strong. Maybe she *had* been wrong to want tangible proof of what she'd achieved. Only she'd felt so good buying them and so proud when she wore them. Deep down inside, she'd always believed Tim was wrong to think the way he did. Now she chided herself for being disloyal.

Delaney showered and did her makeup, then dressed. She tried to remember the last time she'd been out to dinner with a man who wasn't Tim or her father. If she excluded work events, then the answer was simple: never. She shook her head. She was twenty-nine years old and about to have her first date since she was sixteen? Holy crap — how had that happened?

She knew the answer, of course. She'd fallen for Tim in high school, had dated him through college, then gotten engaged to him. If he hadn't died, they would be married by now and she'd probably be a mother or at least pregnant.

She finished getting ready, then opened her Uber app to get a car. Twenty minutes later, she walked into the Metropolitan Grill and saw Malcolm was already there.

In the second before he noticed her, she took in the clean line of his jaw and how confident and handsome he looked. He was a man who took control, who wasn't intimidated by much. She smiled — one exception to that might be his twelve-year-old sister.

He turned and spotted her. Appreciation and interest darkened his eyes as he approached.

"You made it," he said, bending down and kissing her cheek. "You look beautiful."

"Thank you."

He gave his name to the hostess who seated them at a quieter booth. The restaurant was a Seattle mainstay, serving excellent steaks and generous portions. Delaney was already planning to use her leftover fillet on a salad for lunch the following day.

They ordered cocktails — scotch for him and a lemon drop for her. When their server had left, she leaned toward him.

"Tell me everything. How is Keira? How's the new sister? I've been wondering what it must be like to have unexpected family suddenly appear and I honestly have no idea."

"Could we start with something simple, like how to solve climate change?"

"That tough?"

"That confusing. Keira is doing much better. She's caught up on her schoolwork, is taking great care of her kitten and playing music too loud."

Delaney laughed. "A typical twelve-year-old."

"Apparently. Callie arrived yesterday." He hesitated. "She's quiet. This is a big change for her. She and Keira have the same freckles. Keira says all three of us have the same smile, but to quote her from dinner last night I 'never smile, so it will take a while to see it.' "

"Ouch. For what it's worth, I think you smile the correct amount."

"There's a limit?"

"Sometimes. Keira is very honest in her appraisals."

"Tell me about it. I'm still dealing with being the asshole brother. Or rather trying not to be." He shook his head. "Okay, it's been five minutes and we've gotten way too serious and deep for a first date. Want to start over?"

"Not really. This is good. We're getting to know each other." She liked that he was troubled by his baby sister's assessments.

Some people would have brushed aside a twelve-year-old's opinion but Malcolm had taken her words to heart.

Their server returned with their drinks. Malcolm raised his glass.

"To not smiling too much."

She laughed. "Absolutely."

"Tell me about your dad being in the hospital," he said. "Is everything all right now?"

"It is. He was a Seattle PD cop who was shot in the line of duty. He's in a wheelchair now. It was a tough adjustment but he did great. The whole city rallied to help."

He frowned. "When was this?"

"About eighteen months ago."

"I remember when it happened. Wasn't there another police officer — one who was killed?"

She set down her glass. "There was. Tim and I grew up together. We started dating when I was in high school and we were four weeks from getting married when he died."

Malcolm stared at her. "I'm sorry."

"Thank you. It was really difficult. Dealing with the loss and worrying about my dad." Feelings swamped her — like familiar friends who reminded her of a time she wanted to forget. "Everyone on the street where Tim and I grew up rallied and that helped. I pretty much lived at the hospital for three months. That's how I know everyone."

She didn't tell him how the sense of comfort had morphed over the weeks — how by the time her dad was able to go home she'd felt trapped. As if everyone was allowed to move on but her. Everyone was allowed to heal and change, except her. She was supposed to mourn Tim forever, to never be whole without him.

"My dad's doing great," she continued. "He's healthy. He doesn't see the wheelchair as a handicap. It just is." She smiled. "He started dating Tim's mother and they're getting married. In fact they're taking their first cruise in the fall."

"That's great. You must be relieved to know he's happy."

"I am."

"What about you? Are you happy?"

An unexpected question. "Most of the time," she lied. "I spent about a year feeling lost and confused, then I decided to quit my job and go back to college."

"What did you used to do?"

"I worked in finance, at Boeing." She'd been on the fast track for senior management. She'd been tapped early and given challenging assignments. At first Tim had been proud, but then he'd worried that her job was too important to her.

Malcolm raised his eyebrows. "My best friend is a finance guy. Numbers rule."

She grinned. "You know it."

"You've made a one-eighty turn. Are you excited about your field of study?"

"At this point, I'm mostly nervous. I'm making up the classes I missed getting my business degree. Right now that means math and science."

"That's right, you're taking biology. How was the dissection?"

"Delayed. Keira grossed me out by mentioning it might have been an inventory problem somewhere."

"Not a supply chain we want to talk about." He studied her for a second. "You're impressive."

The compliment surprised her. "Why would you say that?"

"Look at all you've been through in the past couple of years. It would have immobilized most people, but here you are, moving in a completely different direction. You're fearless. I admire that, and maybe I'm a little envious."

"Why?"

He leaned toward her and lowered his voice. "Promise not to tell anyone?"

"Of course."

"I'm inheriting a family business, which means my future was set for me long ago. Don't get me wrong — I don't want to do anything else. I've been very lucky and I get that, but every now and then I daydream about what it would be like to have taken another path."

"Such as?"

He grinned. "No idea. Some days I think it would be nice to fly jets for the navy."

"Land on an aircraft carrier?"

"Biggest rush around. Or maybe captain a charter boat in the Caribbean."

"Those are not the same thing."

"Yeah, I know."

She smiled. "They are also both serious 'I'm in charge' positions, so whatever you daydream about, you're never a follower."

"You're right. Whatever it is, it's fun to think about, but at the end of the day, I'm where I'm supposed to be."

"A good feeling."

"It is."

She sipped her drink, all the while envying his sense of certainty. Ever since the shooting, she'd been lost. Nothing had felt right and it still didn't.

No, she thought, knowing it was stupid to lie to herself. Her sense of wrong place, wrong time had started long before the shooting. It had started when Tim had proposed. Although she'd known it was coming, she was still surprised. So surprised, she'd almost not said yes. Only it had been Tim and weren't they supposed to be together always?

Not questions to think about while with another man, she reminded herself. Especially a handsome, successful guy who worried about his new-to-him sister. Better for her to be happy about her good fortune and let the rest of it take care of itself.

"So," she said, her voice teasing. "I'm thinking of having fish."

Malcolm stared at her. "Is this you being funny, because do you know where we are?"

She grinned. "You are so easy."

"I can be, if that's interesting."

She laughed. "It just might be."

The evening flew by. Delaney had been prepared for awkward silences as they got to know each other, but conversation had flowed. Malcolm told her about growing up in Portland with a single mother until they moved to Seattle when he was twelve and how hard it had been to settle into a new life. She talked about what it was like living on a street where everyone knew everything about her and she had dozens of moms to fill in for the one she'd never known. She even mentioned how, at the end of the day, those fill-in moms had gone back to their own families, leaving her behind.

They discovered they both loved horror movies — the cheesier the better — jazz and dark chocolate. They had a few mutual acquaintances from her days in the corporate world and neither of them understood people who didn't like the Seattle winters.

"The cold rain is the best," Delaney said. "It's an excuse to sit by a fire, read and drink hot chocolate."

"Or something stronger, although I'm with you on the reading."

The busy restaurant had gotten a little more quiet. Delaney noticed that several of the booths around them were empty and realized it was much later than she'd thought. Malcolm had long since paid the bill and they were on their second cup of decaf.

"This has been great," she said with a smile. "Thank you for asking me out to dinner."

"Thank you for taking care of Keira."

They both stood and walked out front.

"How are you getting home?" he asked.

"Uber." Because no one drove in the city

if they didn't have to.

"Me, too. Want to share?"

"Sure."

He opened the app on his phone and entered her address, then requested the car.

"Three minutes," he said, sounding unhappy. "Sometimes they're too efficient."

"Why would you say —"

Before she could finish her sentence, he pulled her around the corner and took her in his arms. His mouth settled on hers. The kiss was warm, gentle and more arousing than she'd expected. Need exploded, wanting grew and the urge to press her body against his was overwhelming. Delaney had to grab control with both hands to keep from whimpering as he drew back.

"And there's our car." His voice was regretful.

She was shaking too hard to respond. What on earth had just happened? Was her reaction because she'd been alone for so long or was it more specifically about Malcolm? It had just been a very chaste kiss. There hadn't even been any tongue. Yet she was aroused to the point of pain. Her breasts ached and between her legs, the very center of her was damp and swollen.

She slid into the back seat as Malcolm confirmed there would be two stops. She wanted to protest, instead telling him to come home with her. She wanted his hands everywhere, his mouth on hers, and his penis filling her until she had no choice but to climax and maybe scream.

Her reaction confused her. Yes, she'd always enjoyed making love with Tim, but she'd never been frantic before. She'd never wanted to beg and plead and rip off her clothes and —

"I had a good time," he said quietly.

"Me, too."

"I'd like to see you again."

She managed a shaky smile. "I'd like to be seen."

He chuckled. "Good. I'll call you."

They arrived at her building. They both got out. He kissed her again, more quickly this time, but her reaction was still the same. Intensely powerful arousal left her weak and desperate.

"Good night, Delaney," he said.

Dammit, Malcolm, come upstairs and take me as hard as you can. Only she didn't say that. She never had and she wasn't sure she had the courage. So instead she murmured, "Night," and walked to the door leading to the lobby.

Once she was in her condo, she set down her bag, slipped out of her shoes, then leaned against the wall. Something had happened to her tonight and she had no idea what it meant. Time had passed — had she unexpectedly healed? Or was her mind simply playing tricks on her? It had to be the latter, she thought grimly. Moving on had never been allowed.

CHAPTER NINE

Malcolm walked into the kitchen for his second cup of coffee. Carmen had taken Callie and Keira to church and Alberto was in his study, watching his favorite political shows. The house was quiet, which gave him the perfect opportunity to think about his date with Delaney.

He'd barely gotten to them sitting down to dinner when his grandfather joined him at the kitchen table.

"How was your evening?" Alberto asked.

"Good."

"Delaney is the young woman who helped Keira at the hospital?"

"She is." Malcolm briefly explained how they all knew each other and a bit about Delaney's past.

"I remember when her father was shot. A sad time for the city." His grandfather cupped his mug in both hands. "It's nice to see you dating again. It's been a long time."

"It has." While he'd gone out a few times since breaking up with Rachel, he hadn't been all that enthused about the process . . . until now.

Malcolm braced himself for more questions but Alberto only smiled knowingly.

"I like having you all in the house," Alberto said. "My grandchildren all close to me. I'm an old man, Malcolm. Having family nearby makes me feel content."

"You're not that old."

"Old enough to know what's important. Callie and Keira can help each other. They've both been alone for too long."

An insight that surprised Malcolm. He wanted to point out that Callie was a grown-up and could have as many friends as she wanted, and that Keira was with them, so not alone. Only he knew that wasn't what his grandfather meant. He was talking about belonging — connection. A sense of place in the world.

Alberto put his hand on Malcolm's forearm. "You have to let go of Callie's past."

"What are you talking about? I haven't said anything about it."

"Still, it's there between you. She's a good girl who made a bad decision. Don't hold that against her."

His grandfather was assuming a lot. For

all they knew, Callie had been on the road to getting locked up long before it had actually happened. She seemed all right, but who knew if that was just a facade?

"I'm neutral on the subject," he said carefully.

"I know why you're slow to trust. But she's family, Malcolm. She should be welcomed with open arms."

"I leave that to you."

Alberto smiled. "I have every confidence she'll win you over. I'm usually right about these things."

"That you are."

Neither of them mentioned that Alberto had been completely wrong once. When it came to his family, he offered blind loyalty. A loyalty his own son had betrayed. Not that Malcolm could blame the old man — none of them had seen it coming.

Regardless, Alberto had offered his heart first to Keira and now to Callie and he expected Malcolm to do the same. The hell of it was, saying no wasn't an option. There was no one Malcolm loved more than his grandfather and he would do anything for him. Even trust when he knew he probably shouldn't.

Callie woke to the sound of screaming. For

what felt like forever, as her heart pounded and she found herself unable to catch her breath, she had no idea where she was. The dark room with its mystery shapes was unfamiliar. She knew she wasn't back in prison — those screams were very different, but the ones she heard now were just as real.

She sat up and turned on the light by her bed. The room came into focus and she remembered where she was. Relief eased the tightness in her chest and slowed her breathing, then the scream came again.

Keira!

Callie sprang to her feet and raced from her room. She ran into the preteen's bedroom and flipped on the overhead light only to see the bed was empty. She raced into the second room, but Keira wasn't there, either. Callie was about to return to the hallway when she remembered the closet and crossed to the closed door.

Keira lay curled up in a corner, huddled in her comforter, Lizzy snuggled against her. Keira's eyes were open and wide with fear, her mouth trembling.

Callie dropped to her knees and pulled her close. "What's wrong? Are you okay? Did you have a bad dream?"

Keira nodded without speaking. Her whole body shook like she'd just been plucked from an icy lake. She sniffed several times, as if trying not to cry. Callie continued to hang on.

"It's okay," she whispered, noting how small and delicate her sister felt through the thick comforter. "You're okay."

Callie shifted to get more comfortable and moved Lizzy out from between them. The kitten stretched and yawned before collapsing on the floor and closing her eyes. Callie wrapped her arms around her sister again and waited for the trembling to stop. After a few minutes, Keira was able to speak.

"I have bad dreams every few days," she admitted in a small voice. "It's different stuff. Sometimes it's like the walls are laughing at me and I just can't sleep in my bed. The room is so big."

Callie thought about how before going into foster care, Keira had slept in a dining room alcove. Nothing in the girl's life had prepared her for living in a palatial house with too many rooms. She thought about her terror the first few nights when she'd been incarcerated. How some of the inmates would cry or scream. It had taken a long time for the fear to go away.

She leaned back enough to smooth Keira's hair off her face. "Want to come sleep with me?"

Keira bit her lower lip. "Lizzy, too?"

Callie smiled. "Yes, Lizzy, too. My bed is huge. We could invite Grandfather Alberto and Carmen, as well, if you'd like, but I think that would be weird."

Keira managed a shaky smile. "Maybe next time."

"Sure. Come on, let's go get settled."

Callie stood and scooped up the kitten. Keira scrambled to her feet. They went next door and all got into the big bed. Callie left the lamp on, but put it on the floor so the light wasn't in their eyes. Keira pulled up the covers and sighed.

"Thanks, Callie. This is much better."

"No problem. I'm right here. If you get scared, just wake me, okay?"

Keira yawned and closed her eyes. "I will."

Seconds later, her breathing was slow and even. No doubt the kid was exhausted, Callie thought, shifting to get comfortable.

Lizzy lay between them. The kitten stretched before standing and walking closer to Callie. She sank onto the covers and curled up, her back against Callie's stomach. Even through the layers of sheet, blanket and comforter, Callie felt the rumble of her purring.

Hope for what the future could be battled with a haunting sense of loss. She missed her mom, who had died while Callie had been in prison. She missed who she could have been if she hadn't screwed up. She missed being just like everyone else. And while she wanted to believe she'd been given an amazing second chance, she couldn't help thinking there was a massive catch somewhere. One that she had yet to figure out.

Monday morning Delaney alternated between giddy and nervous. She told herself she was being ridiculous. She'd been on one date and it had been nice. Not amazing or life changing, but nice. Or maybe *promising* was a better word. She could go that far. So it had been promising and now she was going to see him again and big whoop. She would be fine. When he walked in with his baby sister, she would simply smile and continue working. Because she was at work. Plus she was nearly thirty so she really should be able to do a decent job *and* crush on a guy at the same time. It was all about focusing on the right thing.

Her resolve lasted right up until she saw him walk in the door, Keira at his side. Malcolm spoke briefly to his sister before smiling at Delaney, then he walked away. Keira watched him go, her expression full of longing and pain.

Turn back and hug her! Delaney willed the message to Malcolm but he didn't receive it. He used his ID card to access the elevator for the upper floors and then he was gone. She turned back to Keira, who had gotten in line, and shook off any sadness before smiling at her friend.

"I'm going on break," she called as she started steaming milk for a hot chocolate.

She met Keira at the tables around the side of the coffee stand.

"How are you feeling?" Delaney asked as they sat down. "You look good. The bruise is almost gone. Any headaches?"

"I'm fine." Keira smiled. "Thanks for the drink. You should let me pay for them. I have money."

"I like treating you." She narrowed her gaze and pretended to be mad. "No running into the street, okay? Next time I won't chase after you."

Keira rolled her eyes. "Oh, please. You would so chase after me, but I promise I won't do it again unless I see another kitten. Or a puppy."

"No one wants a little animal run over, but you have to be careful."

Keira picked up her drink. "Because you wouldn't run into the street either?"

"I'm not going to answer that," Delaney told her primly. "How are things with your new sister?"

Keira sipped her hot chocolate, then smiled. "Callie's great. She's pretty and we have the same freckles. She really likes Lizzy. It's nice having someone else who's new like me." She wrinkled her nose. "She didn't make fun of my uniform when she saw it, which she totally could have. Oh, yeah, she and Malcolm had a huge fight this morning."

That didn't sound good. "About what?"

"That's what's so strange. I don't get it. At breakfast, Malcolm was talking to Callie about the city and things she could go look at although why she would want to do that by herself doesn't make sense to me. Anyway, they're talking and all of a sudden he tells her she's going to need a car. Grandfather Alberto agrees and then Malcolm goes on about different cars and that he's happy to go with her to buy a car and she just totally blows up and screams she doesn't want a car, then she ran upstairs."

Keira lowered her voice. "I think she was crying and I don't know why."

"A lot has happened. The situation has to be stressful."

"I guess. I cried a lot at first, so that makes

sense. Still, if Malcolm wanted to buy me a car, I would say yes."

Delaney grinned. "Is this where I point out you can't drive for several years?"

"Who wants to drive? I'd sell it and keep the money. You know, in case I needed it for something."

Delaney was about to ask for what when the truth slammed into her. Keira would need the money if she ran away. No, she thought. Keira wasn't looking to escape — she wanted to belong. The money would be for if she was thrown out.

She wanted to pull the girl close and hang on as tight as she could. She wanted to promise her that no one was going to run out on her or discard her ever again, only she knew her words didn't matter. Malcolm's did, and he would never think to say that.

"Good to know," she said, careful to keep her voice light. "If your brother asks for birthday present suggestions, I'll be sure to mention a car."

Keira laughed. "I wish. Okay, my homework's done, what about you?"

"I'm completely caught up and dreading my dissection lab. Ugh."

"I'm not sure you're ready for the whole doctor program."

"I do think about that, believe me." Delaney glanced at her watch. "All right, kiddo. It's time."

Keira finished her hot chocolate and tossed the paper cup into the recycling bin. "I can't decide if the other kids are going to say I was a hero for saving the kitten or stupid."

"You're a hero and now you have a pet." Delaney hugged her, then kissed the top of her head. "Just don't do it again."

"You are so bossy."

"I hear that a lot. Have a good day."

"You, too."

Keira waved and left. Delaney returned to work and finished out her shift. She was hoping Malcolm would show up at his usual time so she didn't have to text him. One way or the other, she wanted to talk about what Keira had said, although she had no idea how to bring up the subject. Thankfully, a few minutes before ten, he stepped out of the elevator, coffee mug in hand.

She started his drink, then clocked out before handing it to him.

"Do you have a second?" she asked, motioning to the tables where she'd sat with his sister a couple of hours before.

"Sure." He flashed her a smile. "Want to tell me what a great time you had and how you can't wait to do it again?'"

Her subject matter was far more serious, but at the mention of their date, she felt herself flush. "I did have a good time and I would very much like to do it again."

"Good, me, too." They sat across from each other. He looked at her. "So what's up?"

"I talked to Keira this morning." She'd thought about what to say and now it all seemed wrong. "Please don't tell her I told you or take this wrong, it's just . . ."

His blue eyes darkened. "Delaney, it's all right. I'm not going to get mad. What did she say?"

"That you and Callie had a fight about you getting her a car."

He frowned. "Yeah, we did and it came from nowhere. I have no idea why she got so mad at me, but she was seriously pissed. It's Seattle. She's going to need a car. What's the big deal?"

"I have no idea, but Keira said that if you wanted to buy her a car, she would take it in a heartbeat so she could sell it for the money."

"Why does she need money?"

"I don't know exactly. I'm wondering if maybe she doesn't feel completely safe. I don't think she wants to run away. She has nowhere else to go. I think she's afraid of being abandoned."

Tension filled her body. Not only could she be totally wrong about Keira, she had no idea how Malcolm was going to react. He could be angry, defensive, tell her she was full of crap or any one of a thousand other scenarios, none of which ended well.

He looked at her for a long time. "Well, damn. You're probably right. Her mom just disappeared on her, leaving her with nothing. If it hadn't been for a neighbor taking her in, she would have been on the street. From there she went into foster care, then she came to live with us. The last couple of years have been completely unstable. She's got to be scared."

He drew in a breath. "She's one of us. We'd never get rid of her, but I'm not sure she sees it that way." He nodded. "Thanks for telling me. I need to figure something out. So far it's not been a good day when it comes to my sisters."

"I'm sorry."

"Thank you." He smiled. "Can I change the subject?"

"Of course."

"I'd like to see you again. Are you dating anyone else?"

That was incredibly direct, she thought,

both flattered and slightly disconcerted. "Um, no. I'm not seeing anyone."

"Me, either. I'm not good at playing the field, unlike my friend Santiago. He always has a revolving door of women in his life. Variety and all that. I prefer to get to know someone first. It's a flaw."

She laughed. "It's not a flaw and you know it."

"Sometimes it works against me. How about dinner?"

"I'd like that."

"Me, too." He glanced around. "I'm going to leave now because I have an overwhelming urge to kiss you and this is not the place."

"There's the coffee bar storeroom," she teased. "Want to go there?"

"Don't tempt me." He rose. "I'll text you and we'll figure out when and where."

"That works."

His humor faded. "Thank you for telling me about Keira. I appreciate it."

"I'm glad."

She watched him walk away, admiring the cut of his suit and the body that filled it. Malcolm was an appealing guy. Honest, caring and totally clueless when it came to Keira. With a little nudge in the right direction, he could turn out to be an excellent big brother. As for her and what she thought of him, well, she was a little tingly and wildly intrigued.

CHAPTER TEN

Alberto's Alfresco owned three warehouses in the SoDo district, close to the stadiums. Alberto had bought two of them back in the early 1970s when prices had been cheap. The company's growth had forced a third warehouse to be added around 2005 and that had cost more than double the other two combined, but had been worth it. The following year, there had been a major overhaul of production, moving departments into different buildings so that all the frozen foods were shipped from a single warehouse rather than all three. The dry goods were put together, as were the supplies for the gift baskets.

When Santiago joined the company, he'd gone over the production schedule and had suggested several changes — most of which involved modernizing equipment. He and Malcolm had come up with a five-year plan, then had self-funded the project. In this warehouse, the gift basket section was finished and the update of the dry goods division would start in a couple of months.

One day, Santiago thought as he walked into the warehouse. One day they would be bigger than Amazon. He laughed out loud. Okay, maybe not that big, but close.

He signed in with security, showed his badge, then went into the oldest of the three warehouses.

Alberto's Alfresco sold everything from cheese plates to pasta to decadent hand-made chocolates. There was a line of house-branded cookware and celebrity cookbooks, along with spices, rubs and salts. In addition to prepared soups, there were packages of dry soup mixes and seasonal drink mixes, including a proprietary hot chocolate mix that was only available at the holidays.

Huge vats with giant mixers blended the company's various recipes to create the perfect seasoning for minestrone soup or spicy sangria. The mixed ingredients were placed in bins that were later poured into a funnel where they were measured out and put into small plastic bags, then sealed — all by hand.

With the soup mixes, the flavor packet was only one element of the whole package. Some contained dried beans, pasta or rice, along with dehydrated vegetables. All those individual pieces had to be collected into one upscale package.

This part of production was the oldest and most in need of refurbishing. Soon, Santiago thought as he walked the line and greeted the employees he knew. Automation would replace aging manual processes. Employees would be shifted to other divisions — the company was growing so fast, even with new computer-assisted robotics, no one would be laid off.

He and Malcolm made it a point to visit each of the warehouses every quarter, visiting at least two of the departments. That way they got to each division at least twice a year. Everything that mattered happened on the factory floor, he thought. Alberto had taught them both that.

He grabbed an inventory sheet, then went to spot-check the storage area. Keeping track of what was in the process of being created versus what was finished and waiting to be sold was an ongoing nightmare. Cost accounting had been one of his least favorite classes in college and now he had to deal with it every day. Irony, he thought with a grin. Life had a sense of humor.

As he headed for the storage area, he saw one of the first-level supervisors talking to a couple of employees and slowed his step. No big deal, he told himself, only it felt like a big deal mostly because the supervisor in question was his brother Paulo and the previous weekend when Santiago had brought his niece and nephew back home after their day together, he'd overheard Hanna and Paulo fighting.

Santiago had made a lot of noise as he'd ushered the kids in the house so Hanna and Paulo would know they weren't alone anymore. The fight had stopped and Paulo had ducked out the back before Santiago could talk to him. From the little he'd heard, the fight was a familiar one — Hanna wanted more for her family and was working toward it. Paulo was happy right where he was and didn't see the need to try any harder. It was a hurdle they couldn't seem to get over.

Santiago had to admit, he was Team Hanna for this one. When Paulo had first been hired at Alberto's Alfresco, he'd been a go-getter. He'd worked hard to get promoted, but once he made supervisor, it was as if he was done trying. Hanna, on the other hand, was about ready to graduate and become an RN. She already had a job at Overlake Hospital. Santiago couldn't be more proud of her.

Paulo spotted him. For a half second, his

brother seemed just as reluctant to have a conversation, then Paulo smiled and sauntered toward him.

"Checking on the little people to make sure we stay in our place?" Paulo asked. He smiled as he spoke, but Santiago felt the sting in the words.

"Making my usual rounds," he said easily, refusing to engage. "Everything going okay?"

"This place runs like clockwork."

All three brothers had dark hair and eyes. Paulo was four years younger than Santiago and about three inches shorter. Both he and Luis had their mother's slighter build, while Santiago took after their more athletic father. Growing up, he'd been the biggest, the strongest and the fastest by far. He'd also been the oldest, giving him an unfair advantage on every level. He wondered if those were all things Paulo couldn't ever forgive.

Paulo slapped his clipboard against his thigh. "Targets are being met, bro. You'll get your executive bonus and be able to buy another fancy car."

Santiago was aware of the bustle of work all around them. This was not the time to get into a family argument, but he couldn't let his brother's words slide.

"In here," he said firmly, pointing to the storeroom.

For a second he thought Paulo would refuse but after muttering something under his breath, he followed Santiago into the relatively private area.

"What is your problem?" Santiago demanded. "These days you are nothing but attitude."

"I do my job."

"And?"

"And nothing." Paulo's gaze shifted. "Anything else?"

He was all bristle and bravado, Santiago thought. Just like he'd been as a kid. Paulo had wanted to be the brother good at sports, but he had neither the physical talent nor the mental toughness. He'd tried out for everything and when he hadn't made varsity in any sport, he'd walked away and proclaimed it all a waste of time. Santiago had the feeling that was happening again.

"What is up with you?" he asked, trying to sound more interested than annoyed.

Paulo stared at him, his chin raised. Santiago half expected him to take a swing, although he had no idea why. Then his brother relaxed.

"Nothing. Nothing," he repeated. "It's all

good here. Things are tough at home. There are bills to pay and Hanna's on me all the time."

"About?"

"Just stuff." His brother's gaze slipped to the side.

"Do you need money?"

Paulo glared at him. "No. I don't want your money. Stop with the money. You're rich, we all get it. Don't you think it's enough that you paid for my house and put my wife through college? Why don't you just cut off my dick? Then you can be the only man."

The venom in his brother's voice stunned him. "What are you talking about? I'm trying to help."

"I don't want your help. I never asked for your help."

"You're being unreasonable. This is a family thing. We take care of each other."

"No." Paulo's jaw tightened. "You take care of everyone else. You don't care what we want, it's all about you."

"That's not fair. Hanna wanted to go to college once the kids were in school. She always talked about it. Why is it wrong that I helped out?" He leaned close. "Don't point the finger at me, Paulo. You had plenty of opportunities. What about your job here?

You could be moving up but you won't do the work. If you think you're stuck, you only have yourself to blame."

"Right." His voice was bitter. "Let me guess. You'll pay for me to go to college, too. Always the damn hero. That's all you care about. As for me, I don't give a crap."

Paulo walked out of the storeroom. Santiago let him go. When his brother got in a mood like this, there was no arguing with him. As for being the hero, Santiago was willing to admit to that. He took care of his family, he made sure they were all looked after and he knew exactly when that had first started.

His dad had died when Santiago had been eight. At first the family had done okay, but after a couple of years, money had gotten tight. The spring Santiago turned twelve, he'd hurt himself cutting asparagus for a local farmer. The ER visit had cost a few thousand dollars and the family didn't have insurance. He remembered hearing his mother crying when she thought everyone was asleep. There was no way to raise the money.

A week later, he'd seen a receipt for the bill — it had been marked *Paid.* A week after that, the same farmer had stopped by to talk to his mother.

There had been something in his mother's voice — a controlled loathing and resentment that only Santiago had spotted. When the man had left, Santiago had tried to talk to his mother about the farmer. Why had he been there and what did he want?

Something he can't have again.

Her words hadn't made sense for a long time, but eventually Santiago had put the pieces together. His mother had slept with the much older man to pay the medical bill. She'd been forced to do that to take care of her son. It was all his fault.

At that moment, shame had brought him to his knees. He'd vowed he would do everything he could to take care of his own. He'd gotten serious about football and despite a minor learning disability, he'd done his best in school. He was his family's ticket out. It wasn't so much being a hero as making sure he never hurt his mother that way again.

These days everyone was taken care of. There was a family trust and good medical coverage and plenty of insurance. He'd been blessed and he was generous with those he loved. As for Paulo, he could see it however he wanted. Santiago knew the truth.

Callie couldn't believe how long the days

had become. She was used to working two jobs and having almost no time to herself. But since arriving in Seattle, she'd done exactly nothing. Saturday and Sunday hadn't been so bad. She'd hung out with Keira, explored the house and figured out how to use her new electronics, had lunch with her grandfather. Then it had gotten hard. Monday had been a nightmare of nothing to do. Yes, she could text anyone, but it wasn't as if she had a bunch of friends. She had nothing to look up online, nothing to *do,* which left her restless, confused and more than a little anxious. By Wednesday morning, she knew she had to figure out a game plan.

She'd explored the neighborhood as much as she could and had figured out the bus schedule. She'd caught a ride to Target with Carmen and had bought a decent jacket and boots, although the cost had nearly made her weep. Even so, she'd indulged in a pair of faux Uggs that had made her heart beat faster just to look at them. Her poor savings account, she thought grimly. It was gasping for air. She knew she would need more clothes, things like sweaters and jeans, but she couldn't think about that. Not when she had more pressing matters. She needed to get a job.

She went down to breakfast early enough to see Keira before she left for school. Unfortunately that meant dealing with Malcolm, but since their, ah, *discussion* Monday morning about her needing a car, things had been quiet between them.

She walked into the large dining room and smiled at Keira. Her sister grinned back.

"There are macadamia pancakes," Keira said happily, still in her bathrobe. "Have you had them before? They're delicious. Carmen is amazing."

Callie eyed the plate of pancakes in front of her sister. "They do look good." She helped herself to coffee and juice and sat down.

Carmen came in from the kitchen. "Pancakes, Callie?"

"Thank you. That would be very nice."

Carmen smiled and returned to the kitchen. Callie stared after her, still not comfortable ordering food from the family housekeeper. She kept wanting to say she could fix it herself.

But that wasn't how things were done here, she reminded herself. The rich really were different.

"Where's Malcolm?" Callie asked, trying to sound casual.

"He already ate. He's in his study, on a

conference call." Keira rolled her eyes. "It's international. He's *very* busy."

Callie grinned. "Is he?"

"Uh-huh. He's expanded the company to a lot of Europe. I don't know all the countries. Sometimes he travels there." She thought for a second. "I'd like to go to London, I think. They still have a royal family and that would be fun."

"Because you'd meet them?"

"No, but I could see a palace. And maybe Paris." Her expression was wistful. "Angelina talked about Paris a lot."

Paris. To Callie it was like talking about the moon. Did regular people really get to go places like that? She couldn't imagine.

Of course a month ago, she would never have imagined that she would be living in this huge house in Seattle. Thinking about it made her head spin. She had family — a concept she couldn't wrap her mind around. Keira was great and Grandfather Alberto couldn't be nicer. When they had lunch, he'd told her the history of the family and had mentioned maybe five times how happy he was to have her here. Yesterday he'd talked about the company and how he started it right after the Second World War. But Malcolm was another story.

It wasn't that he was mean, it was just

that . . . She thought for a second — to be honest, the man scared her. She couldn't say why, but he did. He was so stern and serious about everything. Keira had confessed she referred to him as her asshole brother. While Callie couldn't claim he'd behaved that way with her, she got the sentiment.

She didn't want to think about Malcolm, so asked Keira about her English project. From there the topic shifted to the reality dancing competition they'd watched the previous night.

"You're wrong," Keira told her. "Madison was totally the better dancer."

"You just think she's prettier. Anastasia knew the routine."

Carmen came in with Callie's breakfast. There were pancakes, bacon and a lovely little fruit garnish. "When you're done, Malcolm would like to see you in his study," Carmen said with a smile.

"Uh-oh," Keira whispered.

Callie wanted to say she wasn't worried, but she found she suddenly had a knot in her stomach.

"I'll be fine," she lied.

"Better you than me."

Fifteen minutes later, Callie gave up pretending she could eat and went up to talk to Malcolm. At the top of the stairs, she turned away from her room and toward his. She told herself that if she didn't like what he had to say, she would leave. She could find a room to rent and a job and just get on with her life, only the words sounded a lot like whistling in the dark.

She knocked once on his open door and walked into his study. She realized immediately that his floor plan was the reverse of Keira's, only he used the front room as his home office and the back one as his bedroom.

He sat at a large desk. He was already dressed in a suit and tie, his jacket hanging by the door. He looked up when she knocked and motioned for her to enter and take a seat.

"Thanks for coming to see me," he said. "I wanted to talk to you about how you're settling in. Is your room comfortable?"

Was he kidding? Her room was amazing — of course it was comfortable. What else could it be? Was this a trick? She didn't know him well enough to guess so only said, "It's very nice, thank you."

Emotions chased across his face, but she couldn't read them. She supposed that a disinterested bystander would say that her brother was handsome and he obviously looked successful, but none of that mattered to her.

"I want to make sure you're happy," he began, then stopped. "I'm saying this all wrong."

"Then let me talk," she said, perched on the edge of her chair. "I need a job."

"What?"

"I need to work. I have to be doing something with my day. I can't just sit around here. Carmen keeps the house spotless and while Grandfather Alberto is a fascinating guy, I can't expect him to entertain me."

"Okay." He drew out the word. "What would you like to do?"

Go back to college, she thought wistfully. No, she would like to be eighteen again, on the day of her birthday, and not screw up her whole life. That's what she would like.

"You know I'm a convicted felon, right?" she asked bluntly.

Malcolm stiffened slightly. "Yes, but I —"

"Don't," she told him. "Don't say it doesn't matter. Of course it matters. It's something I have to carry with me every second of every day. It will never be out of my life." She drew in a breath to get control. "I was in high school. I had fallen in with some bad kids who skipped school and did drugs. My boyfriend convinced me it would be fun to rob a liquor store. I was young and stupid and . . ." She paused. "That's all I have. I was young and stupid. I wasn't bad or evil, just foolish. I was scared, but I thought I had to do it to keep him, so I went along. What I didn't know was he would use a gun and when we got caught, because he was a selfish jerk, that he would tell the police it was all me. I didn't ask for a lawyer, I told them I did it and before I knew what was happening, I was convicted."

She met his gaze. "I was wrong. I'm not blaming anyone else. I take responsibility for what happened, just so you know. I served five years and I've been out for three. I lived in a halfway house and I did what I was supposed to do. In theory, I have paid my debt to society, only it's never over. While I was in prison, I learned to cook. I worked in the kitchen and it was interesting and I got good at it, but I can't get a job in a restaurant. I can't get much of a job anywhere because they all have that box you have to check — the one about being a convicted felon."

She inhaled. "I worked nights cleaning offices and during the day I worked under the table for a caterer. I'm a good worker. I show up, I do my job. I just want to be like everyone else."

She realized she'd said too much — certainly more than he would want to know, so she pressed her lips together and waited.

He studied her. "You do realize your grandfather started a business based on food. It must be in the blood."

"Like little tiny pie slices floating around?"

One corner of his mouth turned up. "I wouldn't have put it that way, but why not? You're welcome to come work at the company. Just say the word."

"You'd give me a job there? Knowing what you know?"

He hesitated just long enough for her to figure out he didn't trust her. "Of course. For what it's worth, Grandfather Alberto knows about your past, but we haven't told Carmen or Keira."

Something she could be grateful for, she thought. "Thank you. And I would like a job at the company." It would give her a local reference. If she had to take off, at least she would have that.

"You can start tomorrow if you'd like."

"I would. Thank you." She prepared to stand, but before she could duck out of the room, he spoke.

"We should talk about money."

"You mean what you're going to pay me?"

He frowned. "No. The family money. I was

waiting for you to get settled, but I probably should have told you sooner." He opened a desk drawer and pulled out several envelopes. Two were legal size.

"There's a family trust," he began. "Each of us — you, me and Keira — inherit a third of that. In addition, you own a part of the business and part of this house. There are restrictions — you can't sell any part of the business. If you choose to walk away, then you lose your share of the company. The trust is different. That is fully yours regardless. You can't touch the principal until you're thirty-five, but you will receive a quarterly stipend."

He opened one of the envelopes and pulled out a checkbook. "This quarter's payment has been made. I took the liberty of opening a checking account in your name. You need to go to the bank and sign some paperwork to activate it, but the money is already in the account." He held out the checkbook.

Her stomach turned over as unease settled over her. She didn't want this, she thought. Despite what the lawyer in Houston had said, she wasn't comfortable just being handed something for nothing. She didn't know Malcolm or Grandfather Alberto. Why were they doing this? So what if Jerry was her father — she was a stranger.

"Callie?"

She took the checkbook and opened it. The neat printing blurred, cleared, then made her gasp. The opening balance was ten thousand dollars.

"Are you kidding?" she asked before she could stop herself. "That's what I get every quarter?"

He nodded. "As I said, you can't touch the principal until you're thirty-five."

"H-how much is that?"

"Five million."

"Dollars?" No. It wasn't possible.

"You're allowed two additional withdrawals between now and your thirty-fifth birthday," he said. "Of a hundred thousand each. If you wanted to buy a car or a house or something." He passed over one of the large envelopes. "All the paperwork is in here, along with the name of our family lawyer. She can explain everything to you. Just call and say who you are, then make an appointment."

Right, because she always met with family lawyers. Yawn.

Callie didn't touch the envelope and she carefully put the checkbook back. "This is too much."

"I know it's a lot to take in, but give it

time. You'll get used to it." He put a small envelope on top of the larger one. "As part of locating you and determining if you were part of the family, we ran a credit check on you." One eyebrow rose. "You don't seem to exist in the credit world."

"I pay cash for everything."

His tone gentled. "You don't have to, Callie. Not anymore. You're going to need a credit history." He tapped the envelope. "There are a couple of credit cards in there. Start using them. Pay them off every month. If you're not sure how to build credit, we can talk about it or you can find some articles online."

Her head hurt and she felt sick to her stomach. If she'd eaten more than a single bite of the pancakes, she was pretty sure she would have thrown them up by now. No wonder he'd been so casual about buying her a car. He could afford to buy her three or three hundred.

"Why are you doing this?" she asked.

"You're family."

"You don't even *know* me."

"That doesn't matter. You're Jerry's daughter." He hesitated. "And my sister."

She stood. "I don't want it. Any of it. I just want a job."

"Be ready at seven fifteen tomorrow."

"I will. Thank you."

She put the checkbook back on his desk and walked out. As she got to her room, she had a bad feeling that not taking the paperwork didn't mean it wasn't hers. No doubt she would find it in her room later. Malcolm might not be warm and fuzzy but he was thorough. According to him, she was now part of the family. Escaping seemed very unlikely.

CHAPTER ELEVEN

"This is so fun," Keira said from the back seat of Malcolm's car. "You're going with us. The office building is really nice and Delaney works in the coffee stand in the lobby. I don't think you've met her yet. She's great. She looked after Lizzy while I was in hospital."

Malcolm appreciated his younger sister's conversation. He had a feeling if he and Callie were alone in the car, the chill between them would freeze the engine.

He had no idea what he'd done wrong. She'd blown up when he'd offered to buy her a car and she'd been visibly upset when he'd told her about her trust fund. He wasn't sure she'd even listened. Telling himself she needed time to adjust wasn't working. He just wanted to know what the hell was going on.

Keira talked the entire drive. Once he'd pulled into his reserved space in the parking garage, they took the elevator up to the street level, then walked through the large lobby. Keira made a beeline to the coffee stand, where Delaney was taking orders.

For a second he looked at the stunning redhead and allowed himself to breathe. Everything was going to be all right, he told himself. Just as soon as she looked up and smiled at him.

As if on cue, Delaney did exactly that. The humor in her green eyes was what he needed to help him relax. He smiled back before turning to his sister and motioning to the elevators. Callie followed him through the security gate and up to the top floor.

He took her to his office and closed the door behind them. "There will be some paperwork to fill out," he told her. "HR will come by later to take care of that."

He hesitated, not sure what else to tell her. He couldn't talk about her clothes, even though he wanted to. They were in an office and there was a dress code — one he hadn't told her about. So instead of tailored pants or a dress or a suit, Callie wore jeans and a long-sleeved T-shirt. Given what she'd told him about her previous employment, it was possible that was all she ever wore, which made this slightly awkward situation his fault.

"Stop looking at me like that," she said unexpectedly.

"Like what?"

"Like you expect me to blow up at you any second. I'm not mad."

"You weren't happy about the car."

Her lips pressed together. "That was different."

"Want to tell me how?"

"It just was."

"Well, that's clear."

She glared at him. "This isn't easy, okay? Just give me some time to figure it all out. I'm dealing with a lot."

"It was just a car."

"Maybe to you." She put her hands on her hips. "Maybe to you, but to the rest of us, it's a big deal."

He hesitated. "Is it because you're afraid you won't be able to get a license?"

Her gaze narrowed. "You mean because I was arrested and convicted and served my time but I will forevermore be a convicted felon?"

He didn't know how to answer that, so he avoided the question and instead said, "I checked on the Washington State website. You can get your license with no problem. With your trust fund, you can buy whatever car you want and —"

"I can't drive," she shouted, then lowered her voice and repeated. "I can't drive. I never learned before I was arrested and it's not like they teach driver's ed in prison. After I got out, I never had the money for lessons, let alone a car, so I haven't learned how. Are you happy? Any other humiliating secrets you want to know?"

She stood in front of him, her shoulders square, her chin raised. Color stained her cheeks, so he knew she was embarrassed, but she didn't back down. For one very confusing second, he wanted to hug her and tell her that it was going to be okay — that they might not know each other very well, but she was family and he had her back. Only he didn't know her, didn't trust her and, to be honest, he didn't have her back.

"Keira was not this complicated," he muttered.

Callie looked like she was going to say something, but instead she crossed to the window. "Nice view."

"Thank you." He cleared his throat. "I'll arrange for lessons," he told her. "I'm not sure of all the particulars but I believe you sign up with a state-approved company and they take you from getting your permit through getting your license."

She looked at him. "Thank you."

"You'll be more comfortable with that, I think."

"Rather than you teaching me?" Her brows rose. "I think we'll both be more comfortable with that."

He smiled. "Probably." He let the smile fade. "Callie, I don't want to fight with you."

"We're not fighting. Believe me, this is not fighting. It's not a fight until the guards show up."

"We don't have guards."

"I meant metaphorically." She looked around at his large office. "I really don't belong here."

"You're Grandfather Alberto's oldest granddaughter. This is exactly where you belong."

"Right. Okay, what about the job?"

He hesitated. He had no idea of her skill set, but she was family and . . .

Her gaze narrowed. "You made something up, didn't you? Or you're going to."

"You mentioned working in catering. We have a food development division. You could start there."

Her expression was unreadable. "As what? Do I have a title?"

"Ah, I was thinking maybe as a director."

She rolled her eyes. "Do I have an office like this one?"

"It's a little smaller, but yes."

She swore under her breath. "I don't want this. Not any of it. Not the money or the house or the business or the fake job. I just want —" She turned away for a second, then looked back at him. "I'm out of here."

"Stop," he said before she could even take a step. "You're not going anywhere. I don't know if you have a history of running when it gets hard, but you're not running from this. You are Alberto's oldest granddaughter and by God, you will suck it up and figure out how to make it work. He's an old man who has already lost his only child. Now that he's found you, he's not going to lose you, too."

Not on his watch, Malcolm thought grimly. He wasn't going to be responsible for that, as well.

"You can't make me stay," she taunted.

"No, I can't, but I will hunt you down and do everything in my power to make your life hell if you walk out."

"You're threatening me?"

"If I have to." He told himself this was not the way to make things work with Callie. He could feel it in his gut. He sucked in a breath.

"I'm sorry," he told her. "I shouldn't have said that. The truth is he wants you around and I love him and want him happy. He's the only family I have. Callie, please, give it a try. For him. You can hate my guts all you want, but don't hurt him."

"I don't hate you."

"We're not exactly getting along."

"That's because you have a stick up your ass. Loosen up and be human."

"You could try being less defensive. Not every slight is because you went to prison."

Her gaze narrowed. "You're a pompous jackass."

"You're a professional victim too scared to try."

"You need to spend more time with Keira."

The shift in subject caught him off guard. "Why would you say that?"

"Because it's true. She's not settling in well. She's scared and there's too much stuff going on. You should be there more." She folded her arms across her chest. "All right, enough with the name calling. I'm not going to be the senior vice president of something made up."

He was having trouble keeping up with her. "You were only going to be a director."

"Whatever. I have a GED I earned in prison and a few units of an AA. I'm not exactly executive material. When I had lunch with Grandfather Alberto, he told me about the company. Don't you, like, make food and ship it across the country?"

"Yes."

"So there's a factory. I could do that. Work on an assembly line or sweep floors. I want a real job, Malcolm. Not something fake."

His grandfather would have a fit, he thought, but it was better than her walking out on them. "Okay, if that's what makes you happy. The factory is in the SoDo district. I'll take you there."

"Great." She hesitated. "Can we do this without telling them who I am? I mean I already have a different last name. Do they have to know I'm your sister?"

He knew what she meant — being one of the family would make her different and he already knew Callie just wanted to be like everyone else.

"No one has to know," he told her. "About who you are or your past. I'll make sure no one knows anything."

She visibly relaxed. "Thank you."

"You're welcome. Do you promise not to take off without telling me first? And by that I mean in person while giving me a chance to change your mind."

She paused just long enough for him to know she was thinking about her answer.

Her shoulders slumped a little.

"Yes," she said softly. "No disappearing in the night. But because of our grandfather. There's no other reason."

"There doesn't have to be."

"I feel old," Malcolm whispered.

Delaney chuckled even as tiny shivers rippled down her spine. Maybe they were from his warm breath, or the fact that they were standing close together as they waited in line in front of Din Tai Fung in the University District. There were over a dozen couples or groups waiting for a table at the popular restaurant, but being so close to the University of Washington campus, the demographic was decidedly on the young side.

"Because of all the college students?" she asked, her voice teasing. "Hmm, when did you graduate from UW?"

"Looking at them, about a million years ago." He grinned. "Okay, it was twelve years ago."

She looked into his dark blue eyes. "Well, darn, we just missed each other. I graduated seven years ago so we weren't on campus at the same time."

"Too bad. I would have noticed you for sure."

She smiled even as she remembered Malcolm noticing her or not wouldn't have been an issue. She'd been dating Tim and had always been true to him.

When Malcolm had called and asked her to dinner, she'd regretfully told him she had a study group for her calculus class until six and that she had to be at work by five thirty in the morning.

"I'd rather not wait until the weekend," he'd told her. "Can I meet you by campus and we'll make it an early night?"

How was she supposed to resist that? Now, as he drew her against him, shielding her from the wind, she knew there was a lot about him to like.

The line moved quickly and they were soon seated at a small table.

"I love the wonton soup," she said. "You can pick the dumpling type. I like them all."

The restaurant specialized in soup dumplings and noodles and was always crowded. Considering how packed it was, the restaurant's noise level wasn't too bad.

They quickly made their selections. That out of the way, Malcolm asked Delaney about her classes.

"Our first test is coming up in calculus," she said. "I'm terrified."

"You got a degree in finance. Didn't you

have to take calculus?"

"Yes, but it was for business majors. Trust me, this one is way different. There are actual math people in my class. They're so smart."

"You're smart."

"Thank you but it's different. They are scary smart."

"You've made a big change in your life," he said. "Still okay with it?"

She winced. "Ask me after dissection."

He didn't say anything, instead he just took her hand in his and rubbed her fingers.

"Fine," she grumbled. "I know what you're thinking."

"I doubt that."

"Maybe I should have thought more about the naturopath thing. It's a huge change and being a doctor requires a level of passion I'm not totally sure I have. I'm exploring."

"You're trying an early second act."

"Exactly." Which sounded so cool and fun, but she was less sure that was how she would define things. "It's so strange. All my friends from when I was growing up are on different paths. They're married with kids. Sometimes I have trouble relating to them."

"Sure. You and Tim never had the chance to get married."

Mostly because she'd put off the wedding,

she thought. And now it was too late. Not that she wanted to marry Tim anymore. She'd moved on — sort of. At least she hoped she had. She wasn't sure about anything right now and it was definitely time to change the subject.

She sipped her tea. "How are things going with Callie? Is she settling in?"

His expression tightened and he leaned back in his chair. *Uh-oh,* she thought. She was not a body language expert, but even she could read those signs.

"We don't have to talk about it," she told him.

"Why would you say that?"

"You practically built a wall."

He exhaled and leaned toward her again, then shook his head. "I have no idea what's going on with her, but it's not good. We're fighting. I barely know her and we're fighting. I don't fight with people, although according to Callie, it's not actually a fight, which means I have even less of an idea about what's going on."

"Want to start at the beginning?"

He hesitated. "Callie grew up in Oklahoma and moved to Houston. She never had much as a kid and there just weren't a lot of advantages for her. She, ah, she's having trouble adjusting to everything that's happening."

Delaney stared at him. "Malcolm, that shouldn't be a surprise. Of course she's in shock — who wouldn't be? Does she have any other family, aside from you and Keira?"

"No. She never knew her dad and her mom died a few years ago."

"Then she's been on her own. She's in a new city, with a brand-new family and no support system. She gets to be crabby."

"You're right. I need to remember that." He hesitated. "She said I need to spend more time with Keira."

Delaney might not have met Callie yet, but she suddenly liked her very much. "That's a good idea. She needs you in her life."

"I don't know how to act around her or what to say."

"Just ask her questions and listen to the answers. That's all she needs. To know that you care."

His steady gaze settled on her face. "I do care about her. She's family."

"Then that's all she needs to know." She put her hand on his arm. "I'm an only child, but I grew up on a street with a ton of kids. There was practically every family dynamic imaginable and what I learned was at the end of the day, each kid needs to know she's important and loved. The rest of it takes care of itself."

"You make it sound easy."

"Maybe it can be."

He grinned. "If you're wrong, I'm going to say so."

She laughed. "Go ahead. I'm not. You just wait. In a few months, you'll look at your sisters and realize you can't imagine life without them. More important, you wouldn't want to."

"I hope you're right."

"I am."

He leaned close. "You're very confident. I find that sexy."

"Really? I need to remember that."

"No, you don't. It's just a part of who you are."

Their server appeared to take their order, bringing their suddenly fascinating conversation to a halt. Still, Delaney was determined to remember every word, or at least the part where he'd said she was sexy. Lately she'd been feeling more and more out of touch with who she really was, or maybe who she was becoming. Regardless, she'd been confused and lost. Hearing someone call her sexy was a nice distraction from all that. Having Malcolm say it was even better.

■ ■ ■ ■

By Callie's third day at work, she was starting to feel a little more relaxed. The huge
warehouse hummed with activity as dozens
of people worked in the various departments. The different divisions were clearly
marked and she was getting lost a little less
each day. Even more important, she'd met
some really nice people and no longer felt
like a complete outsider.

She'd started in baskets and would stay
there for a couple of weeks before rotating
to another section of the building. Her
supervisor had told her the goal was to have
her trained in several positions so if one area
was short on help, she could fill in.

From what she could tell so far, the employees were pretty happy with their jobs.
Everyone rotated to different positions every
few weeks, keeping boredom at a minimum.
The atmosphere was pleasant and conversation upbeat.

On the surface, her job was pretty simple
— fill baskets with items, seal the whole
thing with cellophane and send it on down
the line. In truth, it was just a little more
complicated than it sounded.

At Alberto's Alfresco, there were two kinds

of gift baskets — standard and custom. There were about forty different standard baskets ranging from meat and cheese to breakfast in bed to summer picnic. Standard baskets had clear instructions explaining how much to fill, where each item was placed and at what angle. Diagrams and pictures at each station kept all the baskets uniform.

The custom baskets required a higher skill level. Customers could order everything à la carte. Depending on the size and quantity of the items, the basket size varied, as did the product placement.

Robots collected all the individual items and placed them on trays. The trays moved along a conveyor belt to the basket assembly area where actual humans put the baskets together. Every item was scanned before being placed into the basket, ensuring tight inventory control.

Today Callie was working on standard sampler baskets. They came in three sizes and contained items like vinegar, olive oil, gourmet salts, sauces, dry soup mixes and kits, nuts, and handmade truffles. Frankie, her mentor for the first week, had shown her how to put the baskets together, then had watched Callie put together one of each of the three sizes before approving her to work on her own.

Callie quickly caught on to the rhythm of the work and found she enjoyed the sense of accomplishment when she completed a basket. The only difficulty was the lever on the machine that cut the cellophane that went around the basket. The handle was at a ridiculous angle that made it difficult to push and about tore out her shoulder.

Other than that, her station had plenty of room and all the supplies she needed. She would guess this part of the warehouse had been updated recently — everything looked new. She liked the built-in controls of scanning every item before she put it in a basket and the hum of the machines. Many of her coworkers wore earbuds connected to digital music players, but for now Callie was content to listen to the sounds of the factory. Probably because she had so much on her mind.

Yesterday, on her lunch break, she had taken a bus into downtown and had met with the family lawyer. The very nice man had gone over everything Malcolm had, explaining it in a little more detail. Callie hadn't wanted to talk about the house or the business. There was no way she could deal with either right now. So the lawyer had gone over the trust fund, confirmed the bank accounts and credit cards, and had encouraged Callie to call with any questions.

After work today Callie was heading to the bank to sign whatever she had to sign to activate her checking account. The amount sitting in there stunned her and she wasn't totally sure that someone wouldn't take it all away, but until then, she was going to do her best to believe it was real. Malcolm had texted her with the information on the driving school. She'd already started studying to get her permit. Once she was ready to take the test, she would schedule an appointment to do so. After she passed, she would start her lessons.

Everything was happening so fast, she thought. She still didn't understand why being Jerry's daughter and Grandfather Alberto's granddaughter mattered so much — regardless of blood, she was still a stranger. But no one else seemed to think like that. In their minds, she was family.

She filled another basket and cut the cellophane that would cover it. She would be moved to custom baskets in a few days and was looking forward to that. Not only the change in work, but seeing what people ordered and familiarizing herself with the different products. One thing she'd noticed was that all the various food items were geared toward adults. Except for the hot chocolate in the drink mix department, she hadn't seen anything that was aimed at children.

"Hey, girl, it's time for lunch."

Callie smiled as Frankie leaned against her station. "Already? The morning went by fast."

Frankie grinned. "Uh-huh. You're new and impressionable. Eventually it will slow down. Trust me."

Frankie was a tall, slim woman in her thirties. She had dark hair that she wore in tight curls that came nearly to her shoulders. Like everyone else's, her hair was captured in a tight-fitting net. Callie left her net in place, but shrugged out of her pale blue smock that covered her to midthigh. She placed it over her chair and went with Frankie to the exit.

From what Callie had learned, two of the company's warehouses were next to each other. A covered walkway connected them, allowing them to share office space and a cafeteria. Lunch was a perk of employment. All she had to do was scan in with her ID card and she could pretty much eat anything she wanted.

She followed Frankie through the line.

There were plenty of healthy choices — salad, grilled chicken and fish — along with more traditional burgers, fries and pizza. Callie took a small salad and a big slice of pizza. At the end of the line, she grabbed an apple. One of the things she was enjoying about her stay in Seattle was all the fresh fruit. When she'd been on her own, she'd found it really expensive unless it was at the height of the season and it went on sale. She'd had pineapple the day before. In April!

She joined Frankie at a table with several other women. They were all very welcoming, asking her how she liked her job and where she was from. Callie didn't want to have to remember too many lies, so she stayed as close to the truth as she could. She said she was from Texas and that she'd moved to Seattle to be close to family. Then she'd changed the subject.

"Salad and pizza," Beverly, a large woman in her fifties, said, eyeing Callie's tray. "That's balance. When I'm skinny, that's how I'm going to eat."

"If you could eat like that, you'd already be skinny," another woman said good-naturedly.

Everyone laughed. Conversation flowed easily. Callie mostly listened. She was interested in getting to know them without saying too much about herself. One of them looked at Frankie.

"How's Levi doing?"

Frankie's brown eyes filled with tears. "He's holding his own. These are the hard weeks." She turned to Callie and offered a shaky smile. "My son is eight and he has bone cancer. He's in the middle of a round of chemo. It's hard on him." One shoulder rose and lowered. "We're lucky — he's not in the hospital this time, so I can work. I'm out of vacation time and sick leave, and we sure need the money."

Callie's stomach dropped. "I'm so sorry. That must be so hard for you."

"It's harder for Levi, but he's a good boy and never complains."

"The angels will watch over him," Beverly said. "You're in all our prayers."

"Thank you. Now let's talk about something more interesting."

"I don't know about interesting so much as fine," Beverly said, her voice low. "But the boss men are in the house."

The women all looked at each other. Frankie nudged Callie. "You said you're single, right? Maybe you'll catch one of their eyes. I'm happily married and even I can see they're handsome men."

"Rich, too." Beverly winked. "I find a large bank account is nearly as appealing to me as a nice ass."

"Who are the —" Callie stopped herself a little too late as an uncomfortable thought occurred to her. It was very possible one of the boss men was her brother. Honestly, she'd never thought of Malcolm as anything but someone she wasn't sure she liked. He was so confident and smooth and in control. For some reason, that totally got on her nerves. Maybe it was a sibling thing and if so, it was weird. But good-looking?

She supposed it was possible someone would find him handsome. If she thought about him dispassionately she guessed she could see it. Maybe.

"Malcolm and Santiago," Frankie said, interrupting her musing. "Malcolm Carlesso, grandson of Alberto Carlesso, founder of the company. He runs the whole place. From what I hear, he's fair. Not that he mingles with the likes of us." She chuckled. "Then there's Santiago Trejo."

"Santiago," Beverly breathed. "I need to get me some of that."

"You're old enough to be his mother."

"I'm *experienced*. There's a difference."

"Old is old, Beverly. Face it. You're too much woman for him."

Beverly sighed. "That I am." She turned to Callie. "Santiago is our CFO. And honey, he can CFO me anytime he wants."

"Stop it," Franke laughed. "You'll scare Callie."

"I don't scare that easily," Callie murmured. "So, ah, Malcolm and Santiago work together?"

"They do." Frankie nodded. "They're friends, too. They met in college, I think."

"Santiago used to play pro football," one of the women offered.

"He did not." Beverly waved her fork. "That's part of the appeal. He walked away from a deal."

"How is that appealing?" another woman asked.

"It just is. He used his brain to get ahead." Beverly glared at her. "Don't you say anything bad about my man."

"Your man?" Frankie chuckled. "That'll be the day." She stood. "Come on, Callie, let's get you back to your station. This afternoon, you're working on big baskets."

"Lucky me," Callie said with a laugh.

She carried her tray toward the trash. Frankie stopped to talk with another group of women at a different table. As Callie waited by the exit, she felt a weird tingling on the back of her neck. Not a chill exactly, but odd prickling for sure. She turned and saw a man watching her.

No, she thought faintly. Not a man. Some kind of god.

He was tall — maybe six three — with dark hair and incredibly broad shoulders. His face was movie-star handsome, his features chiseled. He had on a suit she would bet was custom-tailored and shoes that probably cost more than she'd made the previous year. His skin was several shades darker than hers. Hispanic, she thought and wondered if this was Beverly's fantasy man.

His dark gaze settled on her face. Callie realized she'd been staring and quickly turned away. But before she could duck out of the cafeteria, he approached.

"Hello. I'm Santiago."

His voice was low and deep with just a hint of chocolate. Which was an incredibly dumb thing to think, but she couldn't help herself.

"Ah, Callie."

"You're new."

She nodded. He was a lot taller than she was. His hands were huge, which she tried not to notice. She felt out of place, awkward and more than a little nervous. His stare was intense, as if he could see inside of her. As if —

Dammit! Santiago wasn't staring at her because he thought she was attractive. The man worked with Malcolm — they were friends. Santiago was staring at her because he knew who she was. He knew about her prison record.

Humiliation washed through her. Was he going to say something and ruin everything? She had no idea and all she could think was she had to get away from him.

"If you'll excuse me," she murmured. "I have to get back to work."

"Wait," he called, but she ignored him and hurried away.

Once she was out of sight, she began to run. For a second she thought about bolting — taking the cash in her checking account and disappearing. The only thing that kept her from acting on that was her promise to Malcolm and the realization that in the whole wide world, she had absolutely nowhere to go.

CHAPTER TWELVE

Santiago stood in the cafeteria long past when he should have started moving, only he felt as if he needed a second to clear his head. What had just happened?

He managed to take a step then another before getting a little momentum but by the time he got out of the cafeteria and into the long warehouse hallway, she was gone.

Callie, he thought, committing her name to memory, along with her face and the sound of her voice. Everything about her had been perfect. Her mouth, her eyes, the way she'd moved. He couldn't believe it — lightning had struck right there in the warehouse and no one had noticed but him.

He had to find out more about her. She hadn't been wearing a wedding ring, but maybe she was independent. No, he thought. She couldn't be married. She couldn't. She hadn't met him yet. He didn't have her last name but he had connections with HR. He would find out who she was and —

"What?" Malcolm asked as he approached. "Something happened. I can see it on your face. Is there a problem? Did some equipment break down?"

"I met a girl." Santiago shook his head. "No. I met a woman. I barely spoke to her, but there's something about her. She's beautiful. Her voice . . ." He looked at Malcolm. "I've never seen her before. I'm going to have to talk to Miriam in HR when we get back and find out her last name. We don't have a dating policy in the company, do we?"

His friend rubbed his forehead. "Dammit, Santiago, no. Not another one of your women. Not at work. They last for a week and then you move on and they're upset. We have a good crew here. Don't mess with them."

"It's not like that. I mean it. This is different. Totally different. She had the most beautiful blue eyes. And freckles."

Malcolm's expression froze. "Is her name Callie?"

"Yeah. How did you know?"

"I'm psychic." Malcolm started toward the exit.

Santiago kept pace with him. "Come on,

tell me. Who is she? She's new, right? She has a bit of an accent, but not much. I can't trace it. Not the South but . . ."

"Oklahoma via Texas," Malcolm muttered.

They walked outside, then he turned to Santiago. "This is not a good idea. You have to let it go."

"I can't. Something happened back there." He looked at his friend. "I mean it, Malcolm. This is different."

Malcolm swore under his breath. "Callie Smith is my half sister."

Santiago let the information settle in his brain. He knew about Jerry being an asshole and that he'd never had anything to do with his son. He knew about Keira and a second sister, but he hadn't realized, hadn't known it was Callie.

Relief swamped him. She wasn't married. Malcolm would have mentioned a husband. In fact as far as Santiago knew, Callie was pretty much alone in the world. He could show her Seattle, help her get settled and make some friends. He could charm her and romance her and convince her he was the greatest guy ever. It was only when the plan came together that he realized Malcolm was still talking.

". . . wanted a job. I offered her something

in the office, but she wasn't interested. She wanted to work on the line. It wasn't me."

"You think I'm going to judge you for giving your sister a job in the warehouse?" Santiago asked. "My mom worked here. My brother still does."

"Yeah, but shouldn't I have convinced her to, you know, do something different?"

Santiago patted his shoulder. "You have been in upper management way too long, my man. Honest work is always honorable. So what's she like? She's funny, right? I'll bet she has a great sense of humor. Does she hang out with Keira? Is she into kids? Did she mention a boyfriend? Not that it matters — I'm here and he's not but it would be good to know."

Malcolm groaned. "Stop it. Just stop it. I don't know very much about her and what I do know I'm not going to tell you. My advice is to stay away from her."

Santiago grinned. "You're being protective of her. That's nice."

Malcolm shook his head. "I'm being protective of you. Trust me. You don't want to go there."

Santiago battled instant anger. "She's your sister. You're supposed to take care of her. Jesus, Malcolm, don't be a dick."

"Sorry. That's not how I meant it. There

are things that —" He threw up his hands. "Fine. Whatever. You want to ask her out, ask her out. Just don't do it here, in front of everyone. Keep the personal life private. But later, don't say I didn't warn you."

All Santiago heard was that he had his friend's permission to ask out his sister. The sooner the better, he thought. There wasn't much time — after all, the two of them only had the rest of their lives together.

Because finding out his best friend wanted to date his sister wasn't enough to suck the joy out of his day, Malcolm had returned to his office to find an urgent message from Keira's school counselor. The woman had insisted they meet as soon as possible and with the school literally across the street from the corporate offices, Malcolm had realized there was no avoiding the summons.

Shortly after two, he walked into the large brick building and asked to meet with Phoebe Rayfield. He was escorted through a maze of small offices, then shown into one.

Phoebe was an average-looking woman in her midthirties. She managed to appear both earnest and disapproving as they shook hands. Malcolm remembered he'd been just as uncomfortable when he'd met with her after enrolling Keira in the upscale private school. He'd been unable to answer the most basic of questions, such as did Keira make friends easily or enjoy school. When he'd tried to explain why he didn't know anything about his new-to-him sister, Phoebe had been less than sympathetic.

"She's a child, Mr. Carlesso. It's going to be up to you to bridge the gap."

He doubted she would consider his efforts since then to be the least bit adequate, he thought grimly as he took a chair by her desk.

Phoebe settled into her seat, then gave him a tight smile. "You'll be pleased to know that Keira shows no signs of any lingering effects from her accident," she began. "All her teachers have kept a close eye on her and she's doing well."

The statement was a not-so-subtle reminder that he probably should have called to ask about her earlier in the week. Or spoken with Phoebe himself. Or maybe the school nurse, assuming the school had one.

"However," Phoebe continued, her tone icy, "we are all concerned about her response to a recent assignment."

"Which assignment?"

"Do you review her homework with her, Mr. Carlesso? Do you spend any time with her in the evening?"

"Some," he said cautiously. "I ask Keira about her homework and she always says it's fine. She doesn't seem to need help academically."

"I see." Phoebe's look of disapproval shifted to downright dislike. "The students were asked to write an essay about their family dynamics. All essays at her level are expected to be at least a thousand words. This was Keira's first paper."

Phoebe pulled a single sheet of paper out of a folder. On it was one lonely sentence. *I don't have a family.*

Malcolm felt a sharp kick in his gut followed by a double dose of guilt.

"Her instructor insisted she complete the assignment," Phoebe continued, pulling out several pages and handing them to him. "I'll give you a moment to read her paper and then we can talk about it."

I don't think my mom meant to get pregnant. At least that's what she always told me when I was little. She blamed me for a lot of things that went wrong in her life. Like if she hadn't gotten pregnant, she would be a famous movie star or something.

I met my dad a few times, but he wasn't very interested in me. He only wanted to have sex with my mom. One day he stopped coming by and my mom was really mad and she said it was all my fault.

Bile rose in the back of Malcolm's throat as he continued to read. Keira detailed her mother's abandonment and explained how Carl/Angelina had taken her in until her mother had died and social services had caught up with them.

Angelina couldn't keep me because she's a convicted felon. She took some jewelry when she was a personal assistant and I know that's wrong, but she was always there for me and foster care isn't good for kids ever.

Keira explained about being "found" by her biological family and brought to Seattle.

Our family dynamics are really simple. Grandfather Alberto loves me but he's old and doesn't get involved in the day-to-day activities. Carmen is great, but she's not family, so it's all Malcolm. I can't figure out if he doesn't like me or just doesn't know if I'm real. Sometimes, it's like he's surprised I'm still living in the house.

Keira talked about Callie joining them and how she'd come to have Lizzy.

I worry Malcolm will tell me I can't have Lizzy anymore, even though I totally take care of her. I wish things were different. I don't want to run away. Kids who run away are stupid — nothing good happens when you have to live on the street. But I don't know how long they're going to keep me. I try to make plans in case they do throw me out, but it's hard.

Nothing he'd ever read had made him want to throw up before. He'd moved way past shame into deep remorse and an awareness that he had completely neglected his sister in ways he hadn't known existed.

"I see this is a surprise," Phoebe said, her voice stern. "To be honest, I find that heartening. At least you didn't know what was happening. Mr. Carlesso —"

"Malcolm."

"Whatever. Keira is a smart, caring young woman who is crying out for help. When you first enrolled her here, I told you that she wasn't going to be able to make the transition from her previous situation to living with you easily. I told you she would need love, support and professional help. Did you get her into counseling?"

He wanted to say they'd all been so busy and that the time had gone by so quickly and that the suggestion had slipped his mind, but what was the point? He thought about Keira's phone and how he was listed as the asshole brother. He deserved to be called a lot worse.

"I haven't gotten her into counseling," he said flatly. "I will find someone today and get her started."

Phoebe handed him yet more paper. The top sheet was a list of psychologists.

"These have all been vetted by the school to be credentialed. We don't recommend one over the other. The remaining pages have further resources, including books that might help, along with websites with information that will be useful. Please don't wait, Mr. Carlesso, not on any of it. Keira is desperate. She's starving for love and support and she's going to be turning thirteen shortly. The teenage years are significant in her development. You have the resources. Now make the time. She's your sister and I'm hoping somewhere deep inside that matters to you."

The verbal slap hit hard, but Malcolm didn't bother defending himself. What was there to say? Keira was a kid and he'd completely let her down.

She had no one but him and their grandfather and Carmen. She didn't have control over her life or any way to make herself feel safe. She was his sister and somehow he'd allowed himself to pretend she didn't matter.

"Thank you for showing me this," he said. He wanted to add that things would be different but knew there was no point. At the end of the day, what Phoebe thought of him was irrelevant. This was about Keira, and he was going to do his damnedest to remember that.

Callie walked the half mile from the bus stop to the house. The rain was light, the temperature in the low fifties. Practically a heat wave, she thought with a smile as she shifted her backpack.

She'd promised herself she would be careful with her money, that she wouldn't let herself get cocky, which meant until she got her license, she was going to take the bus everywhere. Unless the weather was totally hideous — then she might call for a ride on Uber or Lyft. She would be taking her written test for her driver's license the first part of next week. Then the actual lessons would begin. If all went well, in a matter of a few months, she would be able to drive. Until then, the bus was fine.

Malcolm had offered to drive her to work, but she had to be there long before Keira had to be at school and she knew her sister needed the ride, not to mention time with Malcolm, way more than she did.

She drew in a deep breath and exhaled slowly. The bus ride and the walk had allowed her to release the tension from earlier. As far as she could tell, Santiago hadn't said anything about her past to anyone. Callie knew she was going to have to suck it up and talk to Malcolm about the situation. She was enjoying her work and her new friends. She didn't want to lose that.

She used her key to open the front door. She knew Keira was staying at school later than usual to help with the digital yearbook. According to Keira she had a good eye for layout and her help was desperately needed. Callie was just happy to know she was making friends.

She was halfway across the massive foyer before she noticed Malcolm sitting in one of the chairs by the wall. She checked the time on the large grandfather clock, then realized not only was her brother home early, he'd already changed into jeans and a sweatshirt. Even more disconcerting was the expression on his face. Not sadness, she thought, confused and alarmed. Not despair, but something close.

"Is it Grandfather Alberto?" she asked.

"No. Everything is fine with him. When you have a moment, I need to speak to you, please. I . . ." He rose and shoved his hands in his front pockets. "I need some advice."

A shocking revelation that made her more than a little uncomfortable. "All right. I just need to put my things away in my room.

Your study in five minutes?"

He nodded.

She ran up the stairs to her room. After hanging up her jacket, she emptied her backpack before smoothing the front of her long-sleeved T-shirt. There wasn't a whole lot else to do so she told herself whatever happened, she would be fine, then walked down the hall to Malcolm's room.

He was seated at the sofa across from the desk. As she stepped into the room he said, "Would you please close the door?"

She wasn't afraid, exactly, more apprehensive. He'd said Grandfather Alberto was all right and if something had happened to Keira, she would have been notified. A couple of days ago, Keira had asked Callie to be her In Case of Emergency contact on her phone. When Keira had shown her the entry, she'd also admitted that she'd changed Malcolm from Asshole Brother to Jerky Brother. Callie supposed it was a step in the right direction.

She sat on a chair opposite the sofa. "What's going on?"

Malcolm grimaced. "A lot, but first, how are you settling in at the warehouse? Are you enjoying the work?"

Small talk because it was polite or small talk to give himself the courage to get to the point? Had it been anyone but Malcolm, she would have assumed the latter.

"I am. It's interesting." She smiled. "Frankie says it will get boring with time, but by then, I'll be moving to a new station. The people are really nice. The company has a lot of good policies like rotating employees and assigning new people a mentor."

She thought of what had happened to her in the cafeteria, with Santiago. "Does anyone at work know about my past?"

"What?" He frowned. "No. It's not something I would discuss. It's not even in your HR file. The only people who know are our grandfather and myself." He shifted to the edge of the sofa and rested his elbows on his thighs. "Callie, I won't betray your confidence."

Which was good to know but didn't explain Santiago's intense stare. If he hadn't been thinking about how she used to be in prison, then what? And why?

"Thank you," she said, knowing she couldn't ask Malcolm about him. "What did you want to talk about?"

His expression tightened into something she could only call anguish. Before she could ask what was wrong, he pulled several folded sheets of paper from his back pocket and handed them to her.

"An assignment Keira completed for one of her classes. It makes interesting reading."

She didn't understand why he would want her to read a school assignment. It wasn't as if —

The words sank in. She felt Keira's pain as if it were her own, then found herself in the uncomfortable position of being sympathetic toward Malcolm. He didn't come out as the hero in his sister's paper.

I can't figure out if he doesn't like me or just doesn't know if I'm real.

She finished the paper, then read it again. Tears burned, but she held them in. Crying was a sign of weakness and she never allowed herself the indulgence.

She looked up at him. "I'm sorry. You know there's a lot going on with her, right? She's young and scared and still adjusting."

"Don't try to make it better than it is," he told her. "I'm very clear on the fact that this is my fault. I'm the one who should have taken the time to help her adjust and I didn't. I provided her with plenty of things, but not my attention, not even after the accident. I never asked about her. I don't talk to her very much." He looked away, then back at Callie. "I don't think of her as invisible, but I have no idea what I'm supposed to say. I don't want her to feel like this and I have no idea what to do to make it better."

Callie thought about the nightmares. Keira had them every second or third night. When they happened, Callie went and got her, and Keira and Lizzy moved to her bed. Maybe this wasn't the time to mention all that. Malcolm seemed to be dealing with enough.

"She's twelve," she said instead. "Maybe it would help to remember that. I know she seems mature, but she's still a kid who has lost everyone she's ever known."

Malcolm startled her by swearing and standing. He circled the sofa, finally stopping behind it before saying, "My mother brought me here when I was twelve. I never put that together before her accident. I remember being scared. The house was so big and so different from where I'd grown up. Grandfather Alberto was friendly enough and excited to have me here, but I didn't know him. Carmen was Carmen and my, ah, our father . . ." He paused.

"Wasn't all that excited to have you show up?"

"No. Jerry wasn't interested. Grandfather Alberto took one look at me and was sure. Jerry insisted on a DNA test. I went through all that with my mother and I was still scared. Keira doesn't have anyone."

"You're wrong. She has us." She pointed to the sofa. "Sit. You make me nervous when you loom."

One corner of his mouth turned up. "I don't loom."

"You are the loom king."

"I always wanted to be royalty."

They looked at each other. Callie drew in a breath. "Malcolm, she's scared every minute of every day. That's what this essay tells us. She's not sure of her place in the world. She's not sure of her place in *your* world and for reasons that are totally not clear to me, you're the one who matters."

He grimaced. "I don't know what to do. The school counselor gave me a list of psychologists. I have a call in to three of them to get her started with that. I should have done it from the beginning. But what else? How do I make her feel safe?"

Callie wished she had the magic answer, but she didn't. "Start spending time with her. Don't get all scary and insist you hang out for the day, but try to find ten or fifteen minutes where you can just talk to her. Ask about school, show interest in Lizzy, regular stuff."

As she spoke she wondered how regular

Malcolm really was. He'd lived a fairly rarefied life for a while now, not to mention solitary. Yes, he had Grandfather Alberto and Carmen, but how much did he really interact with them? She didn't think there was a regular girlfriend, and Malcolm didn't strike her as the type to go from woman to woman.

"I'll help with Keira," she added. "We're already becoming friends. She's fun and smart and I really like her. Oh, and she's doing a great job with Lizzy."

He swore under his breath. "I never thought about that. I never checked on that damned cat. For all I knew, she could have been starving."

"She could have been but she isn't. As Maya Angelou said, 'I did then what I knew how to do. Now that I know better, I do better.' You need to think about that as you deal with Keira. If you spend all your time beating yourself up, then it's still about you rather than Keira."

"You have interesting taste in books."

"While I was incarcerated, I had a lot of time to read."

He looked at her. "I really screwed up."

"Yes, you did. Now you can fix it."

"You're not sympathetic."

"I actually am, but you don't need sympathy right now." She thought about all that he'd told her, then circled back to their mutual parent. "Tell me about Jerry."

Malcolm's face tightened and his body went stiff. "You should talk to your grandfather about him. You'll get a better story."

"What if I want the truth?"

"Go talk to Grandfather Alberto."

She wondered what had happened between Malcolm and his father. Whatever it was, Malcolm was still dealing with the damage.

"You don't want Keira to feel about you the way you feel about him," she said softly. "You have a chance to fix all of it. Don't blow it."

She thought he might get mad but instead he nodded. "I'm going to make it right."

"That's a great goal. Be consistent and take it slow. Otherwise, you'll scare the crap out of her."

"I promise to be measured."

"If you're not, I'm going to pull you aside and show you the error of your ways."

He surprised her by grinning. "Of that, I have no doubt."

CHAPTER THIRTEEN

Malcolm decided to give himself the night to process everything he'd learned. He heard back from two of the psychologists and based on a half hour phone call with each of them, had picked the one he wanted Keira to see. He'd set up a two-hour intro session where he would attend the first hour, then he'd scheduled her once a week for the foreseeable future.

He'd had the sense to check her online calendar so the appointments didn't conflict with any school activities. Now he just had to talk to her about all of it.

He waited until midmorning on Saturday before going to her room and knocking.

"Come in."

He found Keira and Lizzy in the playroom Carmen had decorated. They were both on the floor. Keira had her schoolbooks spread out on the ottoman and Lizzy was playing with a small fabric mouse.

"Hi," he said, dropping to the floor a few feet away. "How's it going?"

Keira's mouth tightened and she instantly looked wary. "Fine."

"I wanted to talk to you about —"

She jumped to her feet. "It's the essay, right? I'm sorry. I was mad. I didn't mean any of it. I'm fine. I'm happy to be here. Really, really happy. It's all good."

He'd heard the expression about a breaking heart dozens of times, but he'd never felt it before. The combination of fear and pain in his sister's voice shattered him and he felt his heart split into pieces that could never be made whole.

"Keira, it's okay," he said, his voice as gentle as he could make it. "I mean that. I'm not mad and no one is ever going to send you away. I swear."

Doubt lingered in her eyes, but she sat back down and pulled Lizzy close.

"Okay," she said slowly.

He thought about Callie's Maya Angelou quote and told himself he now knew better. "I'm sorry you don't think of this house as your home. It is." How to convince her? How to make her see that they wouldn't ever want her to leave?

A thought occurred — one that would make sense to the savvy almost-teen.

"You own a third of the house."

She blinked at him. "What?"

"Okay, not you, but your trust. Grandfather Alberto has deeded the house to all three of us. It's in a legal trust, which means there are restrictions, but those are about age. You can't do anything with it, like try to sell your third, until you're thirty-five, but it's still yours."

Her expression morphed from doubtful to wary. "For sure?"

"Yes. You can ask Callie. She'll confirm it. No one wants you to leave. You're part of this family." He thought about all she'd been through.

"I'm sorry I haven't made more time for you," he continued. "I should have realized all you were going through. You lost your mom and Carl and —"

"Angelina," she corrected. "She's transgender and wants to transition."

"Right. Angelina. Sorry."

"Imagine how they feel."

He chuckled. "Excellent point. What I'm trying to say is you have a lot going on and I'm sorry I haven't been there to help. I'm not very good with children."

"No, you're not."

He winced. "I don't get a break at all?"

"No way. I don't trust you."

A kick to the gut, but one he'd earned. "I'm sorry. I hope I can change that."

She held Lizzy more tightly and wouldn't meet his gaze.

"Would you be willing to speak to a therapist?" he asked. "I think it would help for you to have a safe place to talk to someone who is only on your side."

"Would you go, too?"

"To the first session. Then you'd be by yourself. I'll drive you, but you'll have total privacy with the therapist."

"If she wants you to do something, do you have to do it?"

He didn't like ceding control, but in this case, he didn't have a choice. "Yes."

"Just like that?"

He nodded. "Keira, you're my sister. I'm sorry I haven't acted like your brother, but that is going to change. You belong here. You and Lizzy are family. It's new and complicated, but we'll make it work. I want that." He hesitated. "I don't want to be the asshole brother anymore."

"You're not," she blurted, then flushed.

He knew better than to assume he'd moved up the food chain. For all he knew he was now worse than an asshole in her eyes. "What am I?"

"The jerky brother."

"Is a jerk better than an asshole?"

She rolled her eyes. "Duh. Everybody knows that."

"Just checking. And for the record, my next goal is to be the slightly annoying brother."

One corner of her mouth twitched. "That's a lot to put in my contact list."

"You could abbreviate."

"SAB?"

"See? It works."

She smiled. "I'll think about it."

"Thank you. So Tuesdays at six thirty we are going to see the psychologist. I would ask you to give it a couple of sessions before making a decision about whether you like her or not."

"You mean if I don't like her, I don't have to go?"

"I want you to see someone, but if you don't like this one, we'll find another one. You have to feel comfortable enough to talk about what's going on or there's no point in the sessions."

"You're giving me a lot of power."

"Can you handle it?"

"I'll try."

"Thank you." He stood and wondered how to leave her room in a nurturing "of course I care about you" way. Before he could figure it out, she stood and threw herself at him, hanging on in a tight hug.

He put his arms around her and was surprised by how small she felt. How fragile. He hugged her back.

"I'm sorry," he whispered. "About all of it."

"That's okay."

"It's not and I'm going to do better. I promise."

She pulled back and looked at him. "I want to believe you."

"Give me a couple of weeks and then we'll talk about this again. You make your decision then. How's that?"

"Good."

He nodded at her stack of books. "I'll leave you to manage all that. Unless you want me to go over your assignments with you. Maybe schedule what homework you should do in what order. I could make a flowchart."

"Oh. My. God! No flowchart. And don't hover. It's creepy."

He laughed as he headed for the door. "There are a lot of rules."

"Maybe I should put them in a flowchart."

"I'd really like that."

"Of course you would."

Malcolm walked back to his study hoping

progress had been made. He had a lot of work to do, but this time he was determined not to let it slide. He'd hurt Keira — not intentionally, but she'd still ended up wounded and that was all on him.

Not-so-benign neglect. Ironic that after all this time, it seemed he was a lot more like his father than he wanted to admit.

Santiago waited until midafternoon to show up at the house. He'd spent the morning figuring out a game plan, because with a woman like Callie, he was going to need one. She was amazing and he had to be worthy.

He wasn't just going to call or text to ask her out. No, he would do it in person, and he would take the time to tell her about himself so she would be comfortable with him. He was going to be honest — sharing the good and the bad — because she deserved that.

He stopped and got flowers — a really nice bouquet with lots of orchids and roses. It was huge, so he bought a vase, too, because what if she didn't have one? She'd just moved and why would she have brought a vase? Carmen would know where one was, but that was different. So he carefully placed the bouquet and the vase in the back seat of his Escalade, then drove out to Malcolm's house.

He sat in the driveway for several minutes, trying to figure out what he was going to say, only to have Carmen tap on his window. He rolled it down.

"What are you doing?" she asked. "Are you sick?"

"No, just thinking."

"Malcolm's not here."

"I came to see Callie."

Carmen's brown eyes crinkled with laughter. "So that's the way it is, is it? All right, you foolish man. You come in when you're ready."

"No, wait." He got out of the SUV. "Can you ask her to come downstairs?"

"Of course, but you could go up to her room, if you wanted."

"No. I couldn't do that." It wouldn't be right. "Ask her to come down, but don't tell her why." He hesitated. "Do you think you should tell her it's me? I met her yesterday, but only for a second and we didn't really talk. No, don't say it's me."

"You are loco in the head."

"Maybe."

"I'll ask her to come down and other than that, I'm not getting involved."

"That's good. I'll wait in the living room.

Is that okay? Do you think I should wait somewhere else?"

Carmen threw up her hands and walked back to the house. Santiago grabbed the flowers and the vase and hurried after her. When they were inside, she pointed toward the living room.

"Go in there. Sit down. Don't move until Callie shows up. Is that clear?"

He nodded. "Very. Yes. Thank you."

The large formal living room had three fabric-covered sofas forming a U, with smaller chairs scattered around. There was some kind of wallpaper and lots of little tables. He'd never spent any time in the room and now that he perched on the edge of a narrow sofa, he found he kind of liked the space. It was a little fussy for his taste, but still appealing.

He put the flowers on the sofa next to him, then moved them to the table. He set the vase by the flowers, before putting it on the carpet. He was about to move it again when he sensed movement and looked up.

Callie stood in the wide doorway, her expression two parts wary, one part confused.

She was so beautiful, he thought, coming to his feet. She wore a long-sleeved tunic top over leggings. She had on Uggs and her hair was pulled back in a simple ponytail. She wasn't wearing jewelry or makeup, not even lip gloss, he realized as his gaze locked on her curved, full lips.

"Can I help you?" she asked.

"Yes. I mean, no, I'm here to see you." He reached for the flowers and held them out in front of him, like a sword. "These are for you."

He held in a groan. Everything about this was wrong, he thought. Awkward and forced. What had happened to his easy charm with women? He'd known how to get his way with the ladies since he was fifteen. What the hell was wrong with him?

"You brought me flowers?" she asked, not moving closer.

"Yes, and a vase."

"Why?"

"I didn't know if you had a vase."

She smiled. "I meant why did you bring me flowers?"

"Because you should have them."

Carmen walked past her into the room. She carried a tray over to the coffee table in front of him and set it down. There was a pot of coffee, two mugs and a plate of Italian cookies.

"He's not as deranged as he sounds," she assured Callie. "Just a little weird, but we love him all the same." She poked him in the chest. "Ask her to sit down, you moron."

Still holding the flowers, he motioned to the sofa. "Would you like to sit down?"

"Okay."

She sounded cautious, which he guessed made sense. She didn't know him — yet. Carmen shook her head and left. Callie took a seat on one end of the sofa. He put the flowers on the coffee table in front of her, along with the vase, then perched on the opposite end of the couch. He immediately jumped up and poured them both coffee.

"Do you take anything in your coffee?" he asked.

"Black is fine."

He handed her the mug and then held out the plate of cookies. He noted there were shortbreads dipped in chocolate and mentally thanked Carmen for bringing something with chocolate. Women tended to like chocolate and he wanted Callie to be happy.

When he'd poured himself some coffee, he sat back down and smiled at her. "Malcolm tells me you're from Texas and before that Oklahoma."

She glanced at him. "Okay, sure."

"I've been to Dallas a few times. I've never been to Oklahoma. Did you like it?"

"It was fine."

There was a moment of silence. He cleared his throat. "So are you enjoying Seattle?"

"What I've seen of it. There's a lot of green. I didn't expect that. Houston, where I lived before, has lots of trees, but it's different. Flat, for one thing. I didn't know about all the mountains."

"Have you been hiking?" he asked. "Probably not, you haven't been here that long. Maybe when it stops raining, we can go. It can be really beautiful. There are a lot of trails, even locally. At some point I'd like to get a dog — a big one to take hiking."

"Not a little one you have to carry?" Her voice was teasing.

He smiled at her. "I'm not the little dog type."

"How would you know? Maybe you'd enjoy a Chihuahua or a dachshund."

"I don't think so. How are things going with Keira?"

She relaxed and settled back against the sofa. "Good. She's really sweet and fun to hang out with. It's strange to suddenly have a sister, but if I had to pick, I'd pick her. We're still getting to know each other but I'm hoping we'll be close."

"And with Malcolm?"

Callie glanced at him, then looked away.

"He's good, too."

The complete change in her voice had him chuckling. "You don't hide your feelings very well, do you?"

She nibbled at her cookie. "I have no idea what you're talking about."

"Uh-huh. Malcolm can be a little tough to know, but he's worth the trouble. I met him back in college. We were roommates and we hated each other instantly." He raised a shoulder. "He was quiet and studious and I was a jock."

"Obviously you worked things out."

"We did." He put down his coffee and angled toward her. "Growing up I always thought I was the dumbest kid in class. Reading was hard for me and I had trouble with the textbooks. But I was big and strong and fast, so I knew I had to do well enough to get through high school. From there, a football scholarship would be my ticket out for me and my family."

Her beautiful blue eyes widened slightly as if she were surprised by the information, but she didn't tell him to stop talking.

"I don't know if I had some kind of learning disability, or if my brain was just slower to develop," he continued. "By the time I got to college, teachers had stopped trying, but not Malcolm. He tutored me all through my freshman year. He was way more demanding than my coach, but it paid off. I was able to read better and learn. I started doing really well in my classes."

"That must have felt good."

"It did. I was more than great on the field." He inched closer. "Don't tell anyone, but football was never my thing. I mean I'm good at it, but it wasn't my passion. Still, I figured I didn't have a choice. My dad died when I was a kid and I was responsible for taking care of my family. Pro ball would solve a lot of problems, so I figured when I graduated, I'd be drafted and play until I blew out my knee or shoulder or something."

He remembered listening to his friends on the team. They would spend hours talking about the future. Where they'd go in the draft, what they'd do with all the money they made. He'd said the right things, but he'd never felt them. He'd found the endless practices tedious. He enjoyed being part of the team, but at the end of the day, he was happy to go do something else.

"Malcolm showed me there were other possibilities. My grades were good enough to get into graduate school. I aced my GRE. The admissions test," he added. "I was accepted into the UC Berkeley Haas School of Business and I walked away from the draft."

She stared at him. "But it was football. You could have been rich and famous."

"I wasn't interested in being famous and I do okay now." He flashed her a smile. "I was lucky. My mom supported my decision. She was proud that I'd found another way. Anyway, I wanted you to know about me and about Malcolm, too. He's a good guy."

"I'll take your word for it." She sighed. "I'm sorry. That's not fair. He and I seem to get on each other's nerves, but I know he's trying with Keira and he's really been very nice to me. I guess I'm reacting to all the changes."

He liked her honesty. "They would be hard on anyone." Now that they were having a conversation, he decided he should just get it all out on the table. He didn't want any lies or misunderstandings between them.

"There have been a lot of women."

She'd taken a sip of her coffee and nearly spit. As it was, she coughed a few times, then sucked in air. "Excuse me?"

"I've dated a lot. None of them have been serious, but it's a long list." He wasn't sure what else to say. "I can give you details, if you'd like."

"No, thank you. Why on earth would you say that? And while we're on the subject, what are you doing here and why are you telling me all this?"

"I thought you knew. We're getting to know each other."

She stared at him, obviously baffled. "Why?"

"Because we're going to be dating. I want to ask you out and —"

Callie slammed her half-full mug on the table, sprang to her feet and glared at him. "No," she said loudly. "No. That is never going to happen. Just no."

Before he could even stand, she was gone, bolting from the room and leaving him alone with the flowers and the vase and very little else.

CHAPTER FOURTEEN

"You're here, you're here!" Keira danced in the foyer, spinning and laughing. "You have to meet Callie. She's the best. You're going to really like her."

Delaney smiled as she walked into the house. "You're full of energy."

"I'm excited!"

Delaney had impulsively texted Keira late Sunday morning, asking if she wanted to do homework together. She wasn't sure what it said about her that she'd been more comfortable getting in touch with a twelve-year-old than one of her own friends, but there she was. And if she were totally honest with herself, she would admit that when she was done with her homework, she just might see if Malcolm were home. So yes, she was pathetic on several levels. It was just that lately, her condo wasn't the haven it had once been. She was restless, confused and while not *unhappy,* then certainly not happy and she had no idea why.

Keira grabbed her hand and pulled her upstairs. "I'm writing a paper for my sociology class. It's on mixed-race marriages."

"You're in seventh grade. Isn't that a little advanced?"

Keira paused halfway up the stairs to glance over her shoulder. "It's an exclusive and expensive private school. Parents want to know they're getting their money's worth."

"I guess. I didn't take sociology until I was in college. I feel as if I missed out."

Keira grinned. "You did academically but not socially."

"Wow, that's so judgmental."

Keira only laughed and led the way to her room. Once there, she raced over to a pretty blonde holding Lizzy.

"This is Callie, my sister! Callie, this is Delaney. I told you about her."

Delaney saw the physical similarities immediately. The freckles, the blue eyes. No one would be surprised to find out those two were related. She also saw a bit of Malcolm in Callie, mostly in her smile.

"Nice to meet you," Callie said. "Keira talks about you a lot."

"Back at you. Welcome to Seattle. I'm sorry about the rain. It generally stops around the Fourth of July."

"Then I'm going to need a better raincoat."

Keira led them all into her playroom. Books and her laptop were spread over one of the sofas. A huge tray filled with sandwiches, fruit, sodas and brownies sat on the ottoman.

The three of them dropped to the floor. Lizzy greeted Delaney with a couple of head butts and some purring.

"She's getting so big," Delaney said, picking up the black-and-white kitten. "Aren't you, sweetie?"

Lizzy reached for a strand of hair. Delaney set her down, then turned to Callie.

"How are you settling in? It must be very odd to find out you have siblings."

"It was hard to grasp," Callie admitted. "But now it's all good."

"I'm an excellent sister," Keira announced.

"You are," Callie told her. "And my favorite sister."

Keira rolled her eyes. "I'm your only one."

"Then you'll never not be my favorite."

"Or your least favorite," Keira added with a giggle. "Which means you're my least favorite sister, too."

Their obvious affection for each other was

good to see, Delaney thought. Malcolm might have trouble relating to Keira, but Callie obviously didn't. She'd jumped right into the relationship. Hopefully Malcolm could learn from her. And speaking of Malcolm . . .

She honestly couldn't think of a way to casually mention him, so she reached for a sandwich and took a bite.

"Callie's from Texas," Keira said.

"And Oklahoma," Callie added, reaching for a sandwich. "It was much hotter there and a lot more humid. Now I'm here."

"I've never lived anywhere but Seattle." Delaney looked at Keira. "You've lived in two different states. I'm the bumpkin."

"Not necessarily," Callie told her. "Having a hometown is nice."

"It is." Delaney smiled. "I grew up on a great street where everyone knew everyone else. I lost my mom when I was born, so all the moms looked out for me. It was very difficult to do anything wrong. Someone was always around to tell my dad."

"Delaney's dad was a police officer," Keira said. "He was shot in the line of duty and is now in a wheelchair."

"I'm sorry to hear that." Callie looked surprised. "How is he doing?"

"Great. He's newly engaged and about to

go on his first cruise." She smiled as she thought of her father. "He's the kind of man who always finds a way. I admire that about him. Keira tells me you've gone to work at Alberto's Alfresco. What's that like?"

"Good. I'm enjoying the work and making lots of friends."

Delaney didn't know much about the family's circumstances, but she knew there was plenty of money and Malcolm had mentioned each of his sisters had a trust fund. She suspected Callie didn't actually have to work if she didn't want to. Delaney knew it said something good about her character that she'd insisted on getting a job right away.

"I recently went back to college," Delaney admitted. "It's so much harder than it was when I was eighteen."

"You are old," Keira offered with a grin.

"Yes, twenty-nine. I'll be eligible for social security next year."

Everyone laughed.

After they'd finished the sandwiches and made a big dent in the pile of brownies, Delaney and Keira pulled out their schoolbooks and started to study. Callie had a book on the history of Seattle that she'd checked out of the library. While Delaney ran through her calculus homework, Keira typed on her laptop and Callie read. Lizzy found a comfortable cushion and curled up for a nap.

By two thirty, Delaney just couldn't take it anymore. Yes, she enjoyed Keira's company and Callie seemed very nice, and the kitten was adorable, but she really, truly wanted to see Malcolm. Just thinking about him made her feel restless and happy at the same time. It wasn't a combination suitable to deep study.

She searched for a casual way to bring him up, then just went for the simple question. "Keira, is Malcolm around?"

"I think so." The twelve-year-old didn't look up from her computer. "He was going to work in his office in the morning, then go for a run. He might be back. You could go see. His home office is down the hall."

Delaney collected her things and stood. Callie looked up at her.

"It was nice to meet you," Callie said. "I enjoyed putting a name with the face."

"Same here. We should hang out sometime."

"I'd like that a lot."

Delaney walked toward Malcolm's office, changed her mind and started downstairs only to head back up to the second floor. Keira had said he was in his office. It wasn't as if she were showing up unannounced in his bedroom. She would knock and if he didn't answer, she would text him. Maybe he was still out running or maybe he'd left to go do something with friends. Or maybe —

She was dithering, she thought with exasperation. Remember when she used to be decisive? She groaned before walking purposefully to his door, knocking once, then pushing it open.

"Malcolm, it's Delaney. I was visiting Keira and wanted to stop by and say hi."

She paused just inside what looked like a den or upscale home office. She had a brief impression of a large desk, bookshelves and a sofa before she heard Malcolm's voice.

"Delaney?"

"Yes, I was visiting Keira and I . . ."

The rest of her words got caught in her suddenly tight throat. Malcolm appeared in the doorway of his study, drying his hair with one towel while wearing another towel around his waist. The room he'd come from wasn't a neutral den or kitchen or hallway — it was his *bedroom.*

"Is everything okay?"

A reasonable question and one she would answer once she got past the sight of him, well, pretty much naked. Oh, and once she caught her breath.

He looked good. Better than good. He was muscled, sexy and just so calm, standing there looking quizzical.

She felt herself flush and half turned away. "Sorry. I didn't mean to intrude. I was just —" She closed her eyes as she fought against embarrassment.

She was twenty-nine and according to Keira, very old. Shouldn't she be able to handle situations like this better? Except she'd only ever been with Tim and by the time they'd become lovers, they'd been together for a couple of years and even so, she'd never walked in on him naked.

"Sorry to bother you," she mumbled, remembering when she'd had it all together and wishing she could be that woman again. "I should go."

"Or not."

Two simple words spoken in a very low voice. Involuntarily, she turned back toward him and saw he'd dropped the towel he'd been using to dry his hair. His intense gaze locked on hers and even she knew exactly what he was thinking.

She hadn't bothered him at all. He wasn't the least bit annoyed. If anything, he was very, very interested in having her in his room.

Oh, my.

Heat poured through her, unexpected in its intensity. Wanting exploded as an almost-forgotten hunger roared to life. Her backpack fell to the floor.

He smiled at her. "If that's a yes, may I suggest you close and lock the door?"

What an excellent idea, she thought as she did as he requested. After the lock was secure, she turned toward the bedroom, only to find him walking toward her. His stride was confident, purposeful and right before he reached her, he dropped the towel around his waist.

It took every ounce of self-control not to gasp. The man was naked. Totally and completely, and still moving toward her. She barely had time to open her arms before his mouth was on hers.

The kiss was hot and deep and reminded her that she was alive and female and that her body had been built for a pleasure she hadn't experienced in nearly two years. At the same time, she put her hands on his bare shoulders and felt the erotic warmth of his skin. Dear God, this was really happening!

Anticipation grew until she trembled against him. She felt his fingers moving up and down her spine, which was nice, but not nearly enough. She pulled back slightly to drop her jacket on the floor, then toe out of her boots. Before she could do anything else, he pulled off her sweater. As it flew across the room, he leaned in and pressed his mouth to her jaw. He trailed kisses to her ear where he sucked on her earlobe for a second. When she felt his teeth lightly graze her skin, she moaned.

Her body was on fire. Heat burned everywhere. Her breasts ached and between her legs she felt that telltale heaviness that told her she was more than ready. She wanted him kissing a lot more than her earlobe. She wanted his hands everywhere, seeking, stroking, rubbing until she had an orgasm, then she wanted him to do it again and again.

She reached for her bra and unfastened it. His hands immediately cupped her breasts. The feel of warm skin on her curves was perfection. When he gently squeezed her tight, sensitive nipples, she felt the sensation all the way down to her clit.

He kissed her again. She met him stroke for stroke, as they mimicked what was to come. She touched him everywhere she could reach. His shoulders, his chest, his belly, then lower. She took his erection into her hand and began moving from base to tip. He drew back and stared at her.

"Bed."

She smiled, not sure if the single word was a request or a command. She was good either way. Stopping only to unfasten her jeans and push them and her panties to the floor, she trailed after him. As he pulled back the covers, she realized she'd left on her socks. They came to midcalf and were covered with little pigs with wings, but she wasn't sure he would care and she suddenly didn't, either.

She slid onto the mattress and held out her arms. He joined her, running his hand up and down her body before lowering his head to take her left nipple in his mouth. He circled the tip with his tongue, then sucked deeply, making her breath come in pants.

So good, she thought as the delicious tugging made the rest of her hum with need. She was aroused, happy and alive. How long since she'd felt any of those?

He moved to her other breast and sucked again. All rational thought fled as the very core of her cried out. Without thinking, she pushed his hand between her legs and parted her thighs. Not the most subtle invitation but one that Malcolm didn't seem to mind.

He found her clitoris immediately. At the first brush of his fingers, she felt a deep pull low in her belly. By the third she was halfway along a nearly forgotten journey. He started circling her with a steady rhythm that stole any sense of control she might have thought she'd had. She opened her legs as wide as she could, arched her back and gave herself over to the feelings he created.

Every muscle tensed. Every nerve quivered. He pressed a little harder, moved a little faster and she was right there, on the edge, so close. So —

"Yes!"

She came with a scream that was ripped from the very heart of her. She exhaled as the pleasure came in rippling waves of wow-did-I-need-this. Her orgasm went on and on until she thought she should be embarrassed, but dammit, she was due. Then it slowed and she was able to breathe again.

Warm lips pressed against hers.

"Watching you come nearly made me lose it."

Delaney opened her eyes and saw Malcolm smiling at her. The confession — one that made him seem even sexier than before — created a tiny crack in the wall around her heart.

"I'll bet you say that to all the girls."

"I wish, but no."

He turned and opened a nightstand drawer, then pulled out a condom. Once it was in place, he shifted between her thighs. She exhaled.

"I'm so going to enjoy this," she whispered.

"Not more than me."

She laughed. "Want to bet?"

"Later. I'll do anything you want, as long as it's later."

"Deal."

He eased into her. He went slowly, which she appreciated. Her body had to stretch to accommodate him. Fortunately she was so aroused from what they'd already done that she quickly grew accustomed to him.

He withdrew and pushed in again. The friction was perfect — just intense enough to get her attention. She drew her knees back so he could go deeper, then wrapped her legs around his hips as she gave herself over to feelings rushing through her.

With every stroke she was more and more aroused. Her body was alive with sensation. Need grew so fast, she was caught off guard. She went from "This is nice" to "Holy crap" in about eight seconds. Her breathing increased as she was suddenly on the edge.

Unable to stop herself, she whispered,

"Faster, please!"

He complied, moving in and out at a pace designed to make them both lose control. He filled her once, twice and then she was lost, crying out as her body shattered. Seconds later, he pushed in and shuddered his release.

They held on to each other until their breathing slowed. When normalcy returned, Malcolm lightly kissed her and smiled.

"You should stop by more often."

She laughed. "You have no idea how much I agree with that."

"Delaney and Malcolm are dating," Keira said, still looking at her computer. "I don't know if they're having sex yet."

Callie did her best not to yelp. "Maybe you shouldn't think about stuff like that."

"I can't help it. That's what people who date do."

"There's actually more to the process," Callie told her, only to realize that she was hardly in a position to discuss that topic. The last date she'd been on had landed her in prison. It felt like eighteen lifetimes ago, which probably explained why she'd acted so incredibly stupid when Santiago had mentioned going out with her. Just thinking about how she'd run out on him made her want to hide under a bush somewhere and never be seen again.

Keira sighed. "I guess. Still, it's a gross thing to do. I don't like boys."

"That may change."

"I hope not." Keira closed her laptop. "Did you like Delaney?"

"I did."

"Good. I hope we can all be friends."

"I'd like that."

Callie thought about all that Malcolm had told her and wondered how they could talk about it. "How's school?"

Keira looked at her. "Malcolm told you about my essay, didn't he?"

Callie flopped back on the sofa and covered her face with her hands. "You're saying I'm not the least bit subtle."

"Not really. It's okay. We can talk about it."

Callie rolled over to face her. "I know you were mad and scared."

Keira picked at the faux fur rug. "It's hard sometimes. I want to be okay, but I'm not."

"Do you think Malcolm's going to throw you out?"

Keira looked at her. "I don't know. Less than I did, but I still get scared. Where would I go? I'm going to be thirteen in a few weeks, but so what? I'm still a kid. I can't get a job or take care of myself."

Callie felt her sister's pain. Keira was dealing with way too much. It wasn't right. And there weren't a lot of ways to convince her that she was safe and secure. But without that knowledge, how would Keira ever relax enough to be a happy, mentally healthy young woman?

Callie slid to the floor and held out her hand, fingers splayed. "If Malcolm throws you out, I'll take care of you until you tell me you're sick of me. We'll take Lizzy and find somewhere else to live. Just the three of us. I pinkie swear."

Keira rolled her eyes. "Don't you think the subject is a little too serious for a pinkie swear?"

"I don't know. Is it?"

Keira's gaze settled on hers. "You mean it? You'd do that?"

"I would." She gave her sister a gentle smile. "It's not a hard promise to make. I would do it in a heartbeat, but I don't think Malcolm would let you go. He doesn't act the way he does because he doesn't care, but because he doesn't know how to be a big brother. He's still learning. Regardless, I would take you away and keep you safe."

Keira worried her lower lip for a second

before nodding slowly. "Okay, we can pinkie swear."

They locked little fingers and squeezed tight.

"I pinkie swear that whatever happens, I'll take care of you," Callie whispered. "No matter what, I'll be here for you."

Keira's eyes filled with tears. "I believe you."

"Good."

"Now will you tell me the big secret?"

Callie dropped her hand to her lap as the back of her neck prickled. "What are you talking about?"

"Oh, there's something. Malcolm and Grandfather Alberto have stopped talking a couple of times when I came in the room. Everybody has secrets, I guess. You, Delaney, Malcolm."

"What's Delaney's secret?"

"I don't know, but she has one. Sometimes she gets this really sad look. Malcolm's secret makes him mad, so I'm sure not going to ask him. But you don't get mad about yours."

Callie did her best to keep her mouth from dropping open. "That's really insightful."

"It's not hard. People forget I'm in the room and they say stuff. Or not." She smiled. "Are you a spy? Are you married? Is your mom a movie star?"

"Nothing so grand." She hesitated, not sure what to say. Telling Keira made the most sense, but what if it changed everything?

"I won't tell," Keira told her, her blue eyes solemn. "I more than pinkie swear."

"It's not that. I'm afraid you won't like me anymore."

"As if."

Callie nodded. "Okay. When I was a senior in high school I had a very bad boyfriend. He convinced me it would be fun to rob a liquor store, so we did and we got caught."

Keira's mouth dropped open. "No way. That's awful. Oh, wait. You were convicted, huh? And you went to jail. That's the secret. You're a felon."

Now it was Callie's turn to be stunned. "How could you possibly know that?"

"Angelina went to jail for stealing jewelry when she was a personal assistant. After my mom died, I couldn't stay with her because of that. They don't like convicted felons taking care of kids. Not if they're not related to each other, or anything. I don't think they would take me away from you because you're my sister." She leaned against the sofa and sighed. "Angelina was great. She made everything fun. We'd sing karaoke together." She looked at Callie. "It's okay. I really won't say anything."

"Thank you. I thought you'd be more upset."

Keira flicked her wrist. "Honey, life happens."

Callie started laughing, then hugged her sister. "Yes, it does. To all of us."

Keira hugged her back. They held on to each other for a long time. Callie felt some of the weight she'd been carrying ease just a little. Acceptance was a powerful drug, she thought. One that might be very hard to walk away from.

CHAPTER FIFTEEN

Delaney couldn't remember the last time she'd felt so good. After spending the rest of the afternoon and evening with Malcolm, she'd headed for home. She'd make a quick stop at a drugstore to buy a morning-after pill. While Malcolm had used a condom, she wasn't on any birth control. After losing Tim, there hadn't been any reason. She'd made a note to call her doctor and get on the Pill, then had tried to go to sleep, all the while having delicious, shivery flashbacks of the afternoon.

Malcolm had texted her twice, asked her out for dinner later in the week, and had told her how much he'd enjoyed her visit and everything they'd done. He was so open and welcoming, she thought, more than a little surprised. More like the sexy-smile guy than the man who barely acknowledged his sister.

Everyone had different sides, she reminded herself as she steamed milk the next morning. She didn't care that it was Monday or that she had a biology test next week or that she couldn't stop smiling. She was happy and she honestly couldn't remember the last time she'd felt that way.

Before Tim, she realized. Things had gotten complicated as she'd started to wonder if marrying him was the right decision, but she hadn't known how to talk about that. Marrying Tim was what she was supposed to do, just like now she was supposed to live her life remembering him. That was what everyone had said — at least she thought that was what they said. Or meant, or something.

She wasn't sure anymore. Not about Tim or what she was doing back at college or any of it. All she knew for sure was last night had been great and when she'd seen Malcolm dropping off Keira that morning, she'd felt all tingly inside.

She continued working, occasionally glancing at the clock, knowing that Malcolm would be by very close to her shift ending at ten. Sure enough at 9:58, the elevator doors opened and he stepped out.

"You're looking especially lovely this morning," he said as he handed her his mug and card to pay.

"I'm feeling that way, so it's good to know I match."

She handed Malcolm back his card, then asked, "Do you have to head right back upstairs?"

"I've a few minutes, if you do."

She nodded, clocked out, then joined him at one of the small tables. He shifted his chair so his back blocked them from the view of the coffee stand, then reached across her lap to take her hand in his.

"Hi," he said, staring into her eyes.

"Hi, back."

"It's nice to see you again."

"I agree. Yesterday was fantastic."

He smiled. "I'm glad you think so. I'm good at work, but lately I haven't been good at very much else. It's nice to know I'm good at you."

His words caught her off guard. Her throat went tight and she had the strangest urge to cry. What on earth? She drew in a breath and struggled for control.

"You *are* very good at me," she said, trying to keep her voice light. "What's up with the rest of your day?"

"Company-running stuff. You?"

"I have class this afternoon." She leaned close and lowered her voice. "Do you think I was crazy to walk away from a great career

so I could go to medical school and be a naturopath?"

"What? No. You should follow your passion. So many people don't."

The right answer except she just wasn't sure she *was* following her passion. A doctor? Since when? She'd barely gotten through frog dissection. How was she supposed to treat a person?

"What brings this up?" he asked.

"I don't know. Just things I've been thinking about. After the shooting, nothing made sense. I was so impressed with how the doctors and nurses took care of people. I felt lost and they inspired me."

"Sure. Your dad nearly died, Tim was gone. That's more than most people deal with in a lifetime. You probably questioned everything around you. Change is good."

She bit her lower lip. "What if I'm making the wrong change?"

His fingers laced with hers. "Delaney, if you're not sure, you don't have to keep going on the path you've chosen. You can be a naturopath or go back into finance or start a tea shop."

"Shh. Don't say the *T* word so close to where I work."

He smiled. "Okay, then a pet store. I'm saying you have options. Do what makes you happy."

"Does your work make you happy?"

"Most of the time. I like being a part of a family business. I like that my grandfather started the business and that he's still around. There are a lot of good traditions, a few practices that make me crazy and everything in between. I'm Malcolm Carlesso. This is where I belong."

Maybe that was what was missing, she thought wistfully. She wasn't sure where she fit anymore. Not on the street where she grew up, not in the Boeing finance department, not with Tim, not here.

The sense of not belonging was like a remembered emotion, she thought, trying to place it. Then everything sharpened into focus. She'd been young — maybe six or seven — standing on her porch, crying as Beryl had left to go home.

"I need to go be their mommy now."

Delaney remembered the shocking realization that the mothers who came and went were all temporary. Not hers at all and at the end of the day, they left and she was alone.

She shook off the feeling and returned her attention to Malcolm.

"It's just I was so sure," she admitted. "I was determined. But it's only been half of one quarter back at college and I'm questioning myself. Maybe I don't want to do the work."

He smiled. "No, it's not that. You've always been a hard worker."

"You can't know that."

"Am I wrong?"

"No, but —"

"See? It's only been eighteen months since everything changed. Recovery takes time. You're finding your way back. That's a good thing."

She stared at him. "You're way too self-actualized and in touch with your feelings."

"I sit in a lot of human resource classes. It helps with my management style." His smile faded. "You'd think I'd do a better job with my sisters, but that's still a work in progress."

"How are things with Keira?"

"Better, I hope. We have our first therapy session tomorrow night. I have no idea what to expect."

"You'll do fine. Just answer the questions and remember it's all about Keira."

"That's good advice. Thank you."

She rubbed her thumb along the back of his hand. "This got way too deep for both of us. I was planning on a little flirting while we talked about how great the sex was."

"We can do both. And the sex was great."

"It was."

He leaned close and lightly kissed her. "I can't wait until I get to see you again. We're still on for dinner?"

"Yes."

"Good." He rose and pulled her to her feet. "If you want to talk about your future or your past or anything, I'm here."

An unexpected offer from a very sexy guy. "I'll keep that in mind. And now I'm going to study my biology chapters."

"I always was attracted to the smart girls."

She laughed and they parted ways. As Delaney walked to the storeroom to get her things out of her locker, she wondered about Malcolm's past. Who had he loved and why had it not worked out? He was what, thirty-four? Why wasn't he married? Had someone broken his heart? Had he, too, loved and lost? Whatever had happened, he'd moved on. She liked to think she had, too. She was happy to be with him, happy it was so easy. But in the back of her mind, she had a mild sense of dread and the thought that whatever was going to happen wasn't going to be good.

Callie didn't love her early morning starts — she had to be at work at six fifty so she was clocked in and at her place on the basket line by seven — but she did enjoy walking out of there at three in the afternoon. She was able to do other things while most people were still working, like take her driving lessons.

The school where she'd taken her written test had scheduled her for one lesson and two practice sessions a week. Depending on how well she did, she could have her license in a couple of months. The best part was the instructor came to her with the car so she'd arranged for her lessons and practice sessions to start at work at three fifteen.

Malcolm had selected the driving school and paid for the basic course. Callie had supplemented that with the additional practice sessions. She wanted to be confident behind the wheel when she finally got her license. She wrote the check for the difference, then had waited several days, terrified it was going to bounce. But three days later, she'd gone online and had seen it had cleared. Now she just had to get the courage to use her credit cards.

Ron, her instructor, looked over at her. "Ready to try that roundabout again?"

She nodded without speaking and tried not to clutch the steering wheel too tightly. Roundabouts in residential neighborhoods were no big deal but the busier ones terrified her. She could never figure out who was going where and how that would affect where she wanted to go.

"Why don't you go in from the west and then head for home?"

"It's going to be great," Callie lied, hoping to give herself a little shot of courage, then turned in the direction Ron had indicated.

Her instructor insisted on giving her directions using compass terms rather than saying "Turn right at the McDonald's." He'd told her that the Seattle metropolitan area was laid out on a grid and the sooner she figured out which way was what, the quicker she would be able to find her way around. It turned out there was a difference between NE 9th and 9th NE.

Callie tried to drive confidently as she approached the roundabout. There were three cars in it already, but she told herself that was all right. She yielded to one, realized the others weren't anywhere close to her, entered the roundabout, then signaled and eased into the lane she needed. About five seconds later, she was out and going in the right direction.

"Excellent," Ron said. "Do you know your way home from here?"

"I think so. Let me try to get there."

She drove straight for a couple of miles before turning right, then left. A couple of blocks later, everything looked familiar. She passed her usual bus stop and knew she was only a half mile or so from the house.

When she'd pulled into the long driveway, Ron grinned at her. "You're doing well. My adult students are my favorites. Everyone is motivated and there's no attitude."

"That's because we're all too terrified," she told him as she parked in front of the house. "Sunday for practice?"

"Two o'clock. I'll be here."

"Thanks, Ron."

Callie collected her backpack and got out of the car. She used her key to let herself in and paused to marvel at the size and beauty of the house.

She lived here, she thought in amazement. She still wasn't used to the soaring ceilings and huge rooms. Things were starting to get familiar, but this wasn't home. She wondered if it ever would be.

Before she made it to the stairs, she heard Grandfather Alberto call her name from the family room off the kitchen.

"Is that you?"

Callie smiled. "It is. I'm back from my driving lesson."

"Excellent. If you have a minute, come tell me all about it."

She headed for the back of the house. The family room had a large television on one wall and two huge sofas, along with chairs and end tables and a small reading area by one of the floor-to-ceiling windows. Beyond the manicured lawn and elegant gardens was a big dock and Lake Washington. Today the water was as gray as the sky. She wondered what the view would look like in summer.

Her grandfather sat on one of the sofas. There was a book on the cushion next to him and a tray with little sandwiches, scones, a teapot and two used teacups. A third clean one was still on the tray.

Until coming to live here, Callie hadn't realized people actually used trays in their day-to-day existence. Didn't you just carry your plate and glass wherever you needed them to be? But since moving into the Carlesso mansion, she'd seen trays used all the time. And not just the same one over and over. There were different trays for different uses. It was all very strange.

Alberto patted the sofa. "Come sit with me, Callie. Tell me how you're doing. Keira sat with me after school and now I want to spend time with my other granddaughter."

Callie impulsively hugged him before sitting down. As soon as her arms closed around him, she became aware of how delicate he was. Keira would say old, and that was probably true. Still, there was something kind about the old man, as if he'd been around long enough to know to treat all living things with respect and affection. He had nothing to prove, nowhere else to be. There was only the moment.

"Tell me about your day. You are happy, yes?" he asked as he poured her tea.

"I am. My day was good. I'm enjoying my driving lessons very much. They're scary but exciting. I'm settling in." Or at least trying to. At least she didn't wake up not knowing where she was. And Keira hadn't awakened her with screams in four or five nights.

"How's work?"

She smiled. "Good. I've graduated to loading custom baskets. It's more interesting work. People have unusual tastes."

Her grandfather chuckled. "Ours is not to judge what they buy but to cash the checks."

"You're right. The people I work with are great. I'm making friends."

"That makes me happy. I want you to be at home with us. This is where you belong." He touched her cheek. "You remind me of my late wife. She was so beautiful and always had a smile for everyone. When we first started the company and had to work late, she would bring supper for everyone. Now there are computers and robots. I couldn't begin to know how to run things anymore."

"Malcolm seems more than capable."

"He is. He makes me proud." He looked at her. "I wish I'd found you sooner. I only learned about you a few months ago." He swallowed. "After my son died, I couldn't bring myself to go through his things for nearly two years. I'm sorry about that."

"It's okay. You couldn't know."

"But your life would have been easier. And what about Keira? She could have come here instead of going into foster care."

She took his hand in hers. "Please don't spend time thinking about what could have been. We're here now."

"Thank you for being so kind. I knew you would be. The influence of your grandmother, I think. Or perhaps your mother."

Callie smiled. "She was wonderful. So loving and supportive. I wish you could have known her."

"I wish that, as well. As one gets older, there are more and more regrets. Try not to have them yourself. They're a bitter taste that never goes away."

He excused himself to rest before dinner. Callie went upstairs thinking that it really was too bad that her mother had never had the chance to get to know Jerry's family. She would have enjoyed Alberto and she would have loved the house.

As Callie walked into her room, she thought about all the times she and her mom had played dress up when they were young. They had a box of old clothes, gathered from thrift shops and garage sales. Princess dresses, her mother had always said. They had pretend balls and teas and had danced and laughed until they were exhausted.

Callie sank onto the floor in front of her dresser and opened the bottom drawer. Inside was a small box filled with letters.

When Callie had been convicted and sentenced, her mother had been devastated. Callie's strongest emotions had been shame and fear. How could she have let that happen? How could she have been so incredibly stupid? She'd ruined her life and for what? Some jerky guy who hadn't bothered to stick around?

But her mom had been there. She'd promised to visit every week and she had, at first. Not that she'd stopped visiting, but Callie, humiliated and ashamed, had refused to see her. Eventually her mother had stopped making the hours-long trip every Saturday. Instead she'd written letters — each one more loving and cheerful than the next. Letters Callie had read a thousand times as she fought the tears she never allowed herself.

A few months before she was due to be released, the letters had stopped. A neighbor had finally written that the cancer Callie had never known about had claimed her mother. Their small house had been sold to cover medical expenses and Callie was left without a home or anyone who loved her. By the time she'd been released, she'd been determined never to screw up again. Not like she had. She would figure out a way to make her mother proud of her.

Now she touched the stack of letters, but didn't bother reading any of them. There was no point — she knew them all by heart. Sweet words, motherly advice, charming stories about everyday life and promises to love Callie forever.

Tears burned in her eyes and for once, she didn't fight them. There was no one to see if she was weak. No one to take advantage, no one to hurt her.

Tears slipped down her cheeks, silent rivers of pain and remorse. If only, she thought, her chest aching. If only she'd had the courage to face her mother in prison. She could have seen her again, could have talked to her, laughed with her, told her she loved her. But she hadn't and there wouldn't be a second chance on that mistake, either.

Someone knocked. Callie slammed the drawer shut, then quickly brushed her cheeks before standing and walking to open the door. She expected to find Carmen or Keira, not that her baby sister ever knocked, or even Malcolm. Instead Santiago stood in the hallway.

Despite the emotions still swirling inside of her, she was immediately struck by his sheer size and male beauty. The man was big and strong, with broad shoulders and plenty of muscles. His eyes were dark and penetrating, his mouth, well, there was something very appealing about it. He was still dressed in a suit, so he'd probably come from work, but she had no idea why he was here.

"What happened?" he asked, taking a half step toward her. "Did someone hurt you? Do you need me to deal with them?"

"I have no idea what you're —" Crap! The tears. She wiped her face, tried to think of a plausible lie, then settled on the truth. "I'm fine. I was just missing my mom. I lost her a few years ago and I was thinking it's too bad she never got to meet Grandfather Alberto."

"You sure that's it?"

Despite everything, she smiled. "Yes. You don't need to defend my honor."

"I would. I mean that."

"I have no idea why you'd bother, but oddly enough, I believe you." She stepped back and held open the door. "You can come in."

He hesitated. "It's your bedroom."

"We're not going to have sex, so I don't see the problem." She pointed. "There's a living room area over there. I'll be sure to stay at least six feet away so you don't feel threatened."

He walked into her bedroom. "You don't threaten me, Callie. Just so we're clear."

There was something in his voice — a hint of masculine that had her shivering, which wasn't good news. There was no way she could do the boy-girl thing. Not with a guy like him. She'd been out of the dating pool in a serious way and had no experience with men as an adult. Not that she could be sure he was here for anything but idle chitchat. Except he had asked her out the last time she'd seen him, so it wasn't unreasonable to think —

She silently groaned. See? She was right — she was woefully unprepared to be a normal person.

They walked into her sitting area. He took a seat on the sofa and she settled into a chair.

"Do you want me to ask Carmen to bring us coffee or tea or something?" she asked.

"I'm fine." He looked at her. "You sure you're all right?"

"I am. It's just sometimes I miss her a lot."

"I get that. I lost my dad when I was a kid and it's still hard." He loosened his tie, a casual gesture she found unbelievably sexy. "He was poisoned."

She gasped. "What? How? Poisoned?"

He made a T with his hands. "Sorry. I should be more specific. I grew up in Eastern Washington. There are a lot of farms and he worked on one. The spray they use to kill pests is pretty toxic and he was accidentally poisoned. The guy who owned the farm said he would take care of us and my mom believed him and signed away her right to sue him when he promised her forty thousand dollars."

He grimaced. "I'm sure it seemed like more than enough money, but she had three little kids and worked for minimum wage herself. It didn't last and we grew up pretty desperate."

She remembered what he'd told her before. About the football scholarship and how he'd felt the need to rescue his family. She'd been surprised he'd chosen grad school over the NFL, but he was happy and successful. He'd obviously made the right choice.

"Where's your mom now?"

"Here. She and my brother and his wife have a couple of houses on a large lot." He smiled at her. "You'll meet Paulo. He works at the warehouse. He's one of the supervisors."

She wrinkled her nose. "Management? You know how those guys are."

"Is this where I remind you I'm in management?"

"Really? I'm shocked. Because the suit is so not a giveaway."

He smiled. "Have dinner with me, Callie."

There it was again — an invitation. On the one hand he was stunningly handsome, very charming and she could totally relate to his background. On the other hand, he was completely out of her league. Not only because he was successful and smart and a thousand other adjectives she couldn't think of at that moment, but because of what he'd said about the women he'd dated. He was experienced and she was not. While technically not a virgin, it had been so long that she was pretty sure she could be grand-fathered in to the condition.

"What are you scared of?" he asked softly.

"Too many things to list."

"Give me an example."

"I don't know, why me?" She tilted her head. "You barely know me, I'm not that pretty and I work in a factory. I'm not well educated or sophisticated. I have way more emotional baggage than you want to know about. You could have anyone. Why me?"

She hadn't planned on being that honest, but there was no calling back the words.

He leaned toward her. "You're right. You're not that pretty. You're beautiful. I don't care about you having a formal educa-tion because I'm more interested in who you are as a person. What I know is you just inherited a bunch of money. You could be spending your days figuring out how you're never going to work again but within what, a week, you had a job. You didn't take the fake position your brother was going to give you. You insisted on something real. Besides, when I first saw you, I just knew you were someone I had to get to know. I'm listening to my gut."

If she hadn't already been sitting, his hon-est answer would have knocked her on her butt. She was confused, flustered and scared beyond reason, so taking refuge in humor seemed like the safest solution. "Your gut is probably telling you to take an antacid and you're confusing the message."

"I don't think so." He raised an eyebrow. "What will it be, Callie? Have dinner with me?"

No. No! She couldn't. There was too much risk and not enough reward. He was saying all kinds of cool stuff, but what happened when he found out the truth? He would be gone so fast, he'd burn rubber on the way out and probably break her heart in the process. No, no, no.

He stood and crossed to her, then pulled her to her feet and cupped her face with his large, strong hands. His gaze was intense, his expression tender and oh, the warmth where he touched her.

"Take a chance on me," he whispered. "Please."

She thought of the last guy she'd dated and how she had literally ended up in prison. She thought of her mother who had loved her and died without seeing her only child. She thought of the crappy rooms she'd lived in and how hard it was to start over when no one was willing to let go of the past.

Yes, she should tell him about her past and no, she wasn't going to. There was a disaster coming, but just for now she was going to be who she would have been if not for a single mistake.

She drew in a breath. "I'll go out to dinner with you, Santiago."

He released her face only to grab her around the waist before swinging her in a circle. "That's great. Friday. No, Saturday. I want to take you out Saturday night."

"Okay. Text me when and where."

"I'll pick you up at seven."

She nodded because she was afraid if she tried to speak, she would throw up. Maybe she would regardless. Or maybe everything was going to be perfectly fine.

CHAPTER SIXTEEN

Malcolm looked over the report Santiago had prepared, then grimaced. "You're right. Most of the time I'm okay with that, but I really wanted you to be wrong this time."

"Me, too." Santiago sounded as dismayed as Malcolm felt. Lower numbers than expected in the dry soups and drink mix division had triggered an automatic internal audit. That had confirmed what he and his CFO already knew — someone was stealing product. A lot of product.

"It's coming from the inside," Santiago added. "There's no other way it could be happening undetected. Not at that volume. Someone breaking in to steal would show up as a one-time thing. This is ongoing."

"I know. Should we bring in someone from the outside?"

"What, like a corporate detective?"

Malcolm raised his hands. "I honestly don't know. I've never had to deal with anything like this before. I have to say, I'm more disappointed than mad." He groaned. "That makes me sound like your mother."

"There are worse people to sound like. Let me do some looking. I have a few people I trust. I want to see what I can find out before we bring in outside help. This company is like family. I don't want to believe anyone is screwing us like that."

"Family, huh?" Malcolm shook his head. "I know what that means. Whoever is doing this is going to be in way more trouble than he has bargained for."

"Or she."

"Hell of a time to remind me of equal opportunity, but yes. The thief could be a she."

They were in his office. Santiago had scheduled meeting time, which was unusual. Normally they talked to each other when they were available. But the seriousness of the subject matter had changed things.

"Anything else?" Malcolm asked.

"I'm good." His friend grinned. "How are things with your new girl?"

Malcolm felt himself smile. "Great. Delaney's amazing. She's smart and funny and beautiful."

"You sound like you're falling for her."

Malcolm looked at his friend. "You know me better than that."

"You are cautious."

More so now, Malcolm thought. Still, there was something about Delaney. "I like spending time with her, but I'm not assuming anything until I'm sure."

"That's romantic. You might want to keep your reservations to yourself."

"I'm asking her to the charity gala."

Alberto's Alfresco was a sponsor for a local children's charity. Once a year there was a fancy evening with dinner, dancing and a charity auction. Tickets were exclusive and sought after and the guests were expected to be generous.

"I look forward to spending some time with her," Santiago said, then offered a smug smile. "Callie and I are going to dinner tomorrow night."

"Good luck with that."

Santiago's expression hardened. "Was that sarcasm?"

"No," Malcolm told him sincerely. "I'll admit we didn't get along when she first arrived, but she's growing on me. She's been very helpful with Keira and our grandfather is completely smitten."

She'd gotten good reports from her supervisor and from what he'd heard she was well liked on the factory floor. He'd screwed up enough lately to admit that he might have been too quick to judge her.

Santiago picked up the folder in front of him, then put it back down. "As your friend, I want to say, I'll take good care of her. You have my word."

Malcolm swore. "Don't talk to me like that. Of course I trust you."

"It's different with family."

"You *are* family."

Santiago's expression turned knowing. "You say that now. Give it a few weeks. I have a feeling everything is going to change."

"Not for me."

Delaney waited outside Keira's school as a light, misty rain flirted with her automatic windshield wipers. She'd offered an afternoon of study and junk food and Keira had accepted. Now, as students poured out of the building, she found herself wondering where she would be if Tim hadn't been killed. Not going back to college, she thought. He'd mentioned more than once that they were waiting so long to get married that he wanted to start their family right away. Had all gone according to plan, they would have been married about eighteen months. Would she already be pregnant and if so, what about her job at Boeing?

Would she be planning to quit? She knew what Tim would have wanted, although how they would have survived on his salary alone, she had no idea. Seattle was an expensive city. Housing alone . . .

"Not my rock," she murmured as she spotted Keira. Tim was gone and whatever they might or might not have done wasn't her issue anymore. There was no point in trying to solve problems that didn't exist. If she was trying to work through the past, then she should work through the past. If she was looking to distract herself from her vague sense of dissatisfaction, then that was something she would wrestle with another time.

Keira opened the back door and tossed in her backpack, then slid in next to Delaney and grinned.

"We can't go anywhere until I get a chance to change my clothes. This uniform is the worst."

Delaney glanced at the red-and-navy-plaid skirt and navy blazer. "It's adorable and the coloring is great for you. But if you don't like the skirt, can't you wear pants?"

Keira rolled her eyes. "They're plaid, too. It's awful. The boys get to wear navy pants. Why don't we? I tried to start a petition, but no one was very interested."

"Advocacy can be hard," Delaney teased.

"You know it."

Delaney laughed. "Did you bring other clothes with you? We can go to my place first, you can change your clothes, then we'll walk to the store."

"I have jeans and a sweatshirt in my backpack. It meant leaving my Spanish textbook at home but it was worth it." She sighed. "Next year three of our textbooks are digital. I can't wait. So much less to carry. When I asked why we couldn't have digital books this year, my teacher told me that seventh graders aren't responsible enough. So what does that mean? Something magical happens when we all turn thirteen? Does the responsibility fairy visit us?"

"You're in a mood."

"I know. I'm sorry. Just sometimes adults say really stupid stuff."

"We do."

Delaney's cell phone rang, connecting with her car's Bluetooth. On her nav screen she saw *Dad* followed by a familiar number.

"I should take this," she said, pushing the talk button. "Hi, Dad. I'm in the car with my friend Keira."

"Hi, sweetie. Hi, Keira."

"Hi, Mr. Holbrook," Keira said with a

smile. "How are you?"

"Very well. Thank you for asking." He chuckled. "Well done, Delaney. I was going to chide you for not stopping by to see me in the past couple of weeks but with your friend right there, I really can't."

Delaney tried not to feel guilty. She hadn't been avoiding her father — not exactly. There had just been a lot going on. School, her job, Malcolm, the sudden need to question every decision she'd ever made.

"Sorry," she said automatically. "You know I love the company."

"I'm pretty sure I'm still a good time," her father teased. "How about dinner?"

"Sure."

"Bring your young man with you. Beryl said the last time she texted you, you mentioned you were getting ready for a date."

Delaney winced. Keira held in a laugh.

"It's a little soon to be meeting the parents, Dad." Not to mention disconcerting. She'd never brought a man home before. Her father had known Tim since the time she was a kid.

"Nonsense. It's no big deal. I assume he knows you have family."

"He does."

"Good. Then figure out a night that works

and let me know."

"I will. I promise."

"Good. Love you, sweetie."

"I love you, too. Bye."

Keira made kissing noises, then giggled. "Does Malcolm want to meet your dad?"

"I have no idea but I guess we're going to find out."

Tension had her tightening her grip on the steering wheel. She consciously relaxed. Malcolm had relatives who made demands. He would understand and be fine with it, she told herself, only to realize *he* wasn't the problem. She was.

Not anything she wanted to think about right now. "How's school?" she asked.

"Okay. I'm liking it more now." Keira sighed. "Except for, you know, the uniforms. I've made a few more friends and that makes things better. I *want* to say everything is getting better, but I won't."

"Why not?"

"Duh. Because it could all go away."

Delaney stopped at a red light and looked at Keira. "What do you mean?"

"I don't want to jinx anything. If I'm too happy, then something bad might happen."

"Oh, honey, no." Delaney touched her hand. "Life isn't like that. There's no big punishment waiting to thump you on the head if you're happy with your life. You're supposed to be happy — that's kind of the point."

"Easy to say," Keira muttered. "Don't you ever think that if things are too good, you'll be in trouble?"

"No."

The answer was automatic, but as Delaney uttered the single word, she heard another one in response. *Liar.*

She told herself she wasn't lying because her issue wasn't punishment, not exactly. It was more that she wasn't supposed to move on. Or she could move on, but only for the greater good. Like quitting her job to become a naturopath. That was okay. But nothing else.

Jeez, really? Nothing else? What did that mean? She wasn't supposed to be happy? Or she could be a little happy, but not too happy? She knew she wasn't making sense and this was all tied in to what had happened when she'd lost Tim and how she hadn't been sure even before then, but she couldn't not marry him and maybe she'd felt a little trapped and —

"Delaney?"

"What?"

Keira pointed at the green light.

"Sorry. Your question threw me. I guess

maybe sometimes I do worry about being too happy."

"Like you're supposed to be sad forever?"

"Maybe. I don't know."

"I worry that I only get so much good stuff and if I get more, something really bad is going to happen."

"Are you talking to your therapist about that?"

"Do you think I should?"

"Absolutely. There are things that you need to be afraid of, but so often we get caught up in irrational fears. They can get bigger than we can handle. The past is complicated. You've been through a lot. You need help processing all your feelings. If you don't deal with them now, you'll deal with them later and it's going to be much harder then."

"Wow, that's really smart." Keira sighed. "Okay, I'll talk to her on Tuesday. Maybe I'll make a list so I don't forget."

"Good idea. You can start it when we get to my place."

Delaney wondered if she should make her own list. Find out what her "shoulds" were and then figure out why they existed in the first place. She had a nagging feeling that she'd been so caught up in dealing with the logistics of her father's injury and canceling the wedding and handling her grief that she might have forgotten to process a few emotions herself. Or maybe all of them.

Was that why she felt so confused and lost? Was that why she didn't know what she wanted to do with her life even though she'd already set herself in motion? And if she hadn't dealt with her emotions before, how on earth was she supposed to process them now? And if she did, where would she find herself?

"I so need chocolate," she muttered. "And maybe wine."

Keira laughed. "Only if I can have a soda. Carmen is very antisoda and so is the school. I would love a Dr. Pepper."

"Chocolate, wine and Dr. Pepper," Delaney told her. "We are going to party tonight!"

By Saturday morning, Callie had worked herself into a frenzy that left her stomach writhing. Why, oh, why had she accepted Santiago's invitation? She didn't know how to date — even more pressing, she had nothing to wear. Worse, she had no real friends she could call for advice, which left her in the awkward position of going to see her twelve-year-old sister.

Keira was dragging a ribbon while Lizzy

pounced. She looked up at Callie. "What's up?"

"I have a date with Santiago tonight and I don't know what to wear."

Keira rolled her eyes. "There is way too much dating going on in this family. I just don't get it." She sighed heavily before scooping up Lizzy. "Okay, let's go pick something."

They went next door. Callie stayed back while Keira looked around her closet.

"You're not kidding," her sister said. "You have almost nothing." She flipped through a couple of pairs of jeans and pulled out the sweater Callie had bought at Target before turning to her. "Did you leave your other clothes in Houston?"

Callie felt herself flush. "No. These are all my clothes. I wore a uniform at both my jobs and it's not like I went a lot of different places." Or any, she thought, trying not to sound too defensive, but confident she had totally failed.

"It's okay," her sister told her. "I was just asking. But you know this means we have to go shopping."

"That's what I was afraid of."

Callie didn't want to spend money on anything as silly as date clothing, but she really didn't have a choice. It was that or back out of the dinner, and for some reason, she really didn't want to do that, either, which left her in a quandary.

"I don't want to spend a lot of money," she admitted. "Especially on a dress I might not wear again."

"Makes sense." Keira studied her for a second. "At least you're not still growing so you'll be able to wear whatever we buy forever. We should get something super classic. You can go fun with shoes or maybe a little jacket. Do you have a nice coat?"

"Just the parka I wear every day."

Keira shuddered. "That isn't going to work. We are so going to the outlet store. Carmen will drive us."

"I don't want to trouble her. Tell me where it is and we can take the bus."

Keira stared at her. "You know there's a trust fund, right?"

"Just because it exists doesn't mean I'm going to squander it."

"Can we at least use Uber or Lyft? I'll pay one way from my allowance."

Callie thought about how scared Keira was about being abandoned. She would bet her sister was saving every penny in case she ended up on the streets. Offering to pay for the ride was a big deal.

"The bus is actually really nice."

"It's not close to the house and we're going to be walking around all day shopping. We'll be exhausted and you have to be rested for tonight."

All excellent points, Callie thought. "Sometimes you sound like you're thirty instead of twelve."

"I'm very mature. Now let's get going."

One Uber ride later they were walking into Nordstrom Rack. The outlet store was huge and jammed with clothes and shoppers.

Callie started to say she wasn't sure she could afford even super sale prices, but didn't think Keira would let her get away with that. They fought their way to the dress section. It was there that Callie discovered her baby sister had an eye for what worked.

"Angelina always used to tell me to pay a little more for good quality. If it's a classic piece, it will be worth it. Trends should be inexpensive, because you can't wear them long. We're looking for a pretty dress that you can wear on more than a date." Keira eyed her. "Prints are usually a big no, but if we find the right one, it might work. Especially if we can find a solid blazer to put on top." She grinned. "Then you'd have something for the office."

Callie felt her head starting to spin. "I work in a factory."

"For now. Besides, you're part of the empire. What if there's an owner's meeting?"

"It will probably be held in Grandfather Alberto's study."

Keira held up her arm, palm out. "Talk to the hand. I have to work."

Sure enough Keira attacked the dress racks. She flipped through them at a speed that made Callie dizzy, pausing only to pull out possibilities before discarding them. In less time than Callie would have thought, she had six different dresses to try on. Four were solid colors, while two were prints. On the way to the dressing room, Keira insisted they look at a display of leather jackets.

"It's almost May," she said eagerly. "These are going to be super cheap, and if we can find a good one, you can wear it forever."

She held up several jackets in front of Callie before choosing three, then they waited in line for a dressing room. Once they were inside, Callie started taking off her shirt.

"I can leave if you want," Keira offered.

Callie dropped her T-shirt on top of her purse. "I don't care if you don't." She grinned. "I was in prison. There's not much modesty left." At least not around other women. When it came to a man, her attitude might be a little different, not that she planned to find out anytime soon.

"Then I'm in." Keira dropped to the floor and pulled her knees to her chest. "Let's get moving, you. We have miles to go before your date."

"You scare me a little."

Keira grinned.

But when Callie tried on the first dress, the preteen was all business. Callie had barely gotten the three-quarter sleeve dress pulled down before her sister shook her head.

"No. It's way too old for you. Next."

"But —"

"No. It looks terrible on you." She gestured for Callie to move things along. "We still have to buy you some basic makeup."

"Make —"

"Up. Yes. Stuff you put on your face. You don't wear any."

"Not since high school."

"Seriously? Where have you been? In a —" Keira put her hand over her mouth as her eyes filled with tears. "I'm sorry. I'm really sorry. I forgot and I was just playing around. I was going to say cave, not that it matters. I'm sorry."

Callie hadn't known what to make of her time in Seattle. She was still adjusting and trying to figure out if she believed the good stuff. But when it came to her little sister, she was all in. She dropped to her knees and hugged her tight.

"It's okay. I would never take offense. You're such a caring, sweet person."

Keira held on tight. When they separated, she brushed away her tears, then motioned to the dress. "Just no. Try on the next one."

Less than twenty minutes later, they had chosen not one but two dresses. The first, for tonight, was a flirty white dress with black trim at the top of the fitted, square bodice and at the hem. There was a black floral print scattered across the full skirt. It was sleeveless, with wide straps, and fit her perfectly.

The second dress was a long-sleeved navy wrap. Sleek, sensible and in the kind of material that lasted forever.

"In case you have a business meeting," Keira told her. "Trust me, you need a go-to dress. The navy makes it unexpected."

"But this means I have to get two pairs of shoes," Callie said, trying not to whimper at the cost. Yes, the dresses were both marked down a zillion times, but the black-and-white one had started at three hundred and fifty dollars. For a dress!

"You can wear black with navy," Keira

told her. "We'll go get you a pair of simple black pumps. You'll own them the rest of your life. Trust me."

Callie found she did. Angelina had taught her young friend well. Keira picked the leather jacket Callie bought.

"The moto style might get old in a few years," Keira said. "But it's so cute on you and it's the best quality for the price. So in three years, you get a different one, right?"

Callie was doubtful about needing more than one leather jacket, but nodded in agreement. She'd basically put her fate in the hands of a twelve-year-old and she felt good about it.

Keira led the way to the shoe department and quickly sorted through the boxes, finding several pairs of black pumps. Callie tried them all on and ended up with three that fit.

"These," Keira said firmly, pointing to the classically gorgeous midheel pumps.

Callie's stomach knotted and her palms began to sweat. "Are you insane? They're two hundred and twenty dollars. Dollars," she repeated, drawing out the word.

"They're 50 percent off and these are Stuart Weitzman shoes. They are well made and incredibly beautiful. If you take care of them, they will last you forever. Every woman needs a pair of black pumps."

"I'm not sure I like Angelina," Callie muttered. "And I really don't like it when you channel her. Besides, I don't have that much cash on me."

"You have a credit card, don't you? And money to pay off the bill?" She put her hands on her hips. "I'm aware of how the economy works. I don't think a credit card is magic, but I do know if you can afford to pay the bill, which you can, you should buy these shoes. For what it's worth, I didn't get all this information from Angelina. I read a lot of fashion magazines. I'm going to start giving them to you when I'm done with them."

"I'm going to throw up."

Callie tried on the pumps again, then walked around. She caught sight of the shoes in the low mirror and had to admit they looked really good on her.

"All right," she whispered, half expecting the heavens to open up and lightning to strike her dead.

In the end, she bought the two dresses, the jacket, the pumps, three bras and a half dozen pairs of briefs, bikinis along with two thongs.

"I'm never wearing the thongs," Callie told Keira as they waited in line to pay.

"You say that now, but you'll thank me later. Panty lines are the worst."

As they moved closer to a cashier, Callie started to sweat. Yes, she had a credit card. She'd activated it at the bank and everything, but she'd never used it. What if it didn't work? What if she didn't know how? What if everyone pointed and laughed and —

"Next."

Keira pushed her toward the open cash register. Callie handed over her clothing, then fumbled in her wallet for her credit card. Her hands were shaking as she started to pass it to the clerk.

Keira took it from her and pushed it in a little square machine. Callie waited in terror as the word *Authorizing* appeared. Seconds later the screen filled with a box.

"You sign there," Keira whispered.

Callie nodded, scrawled her signature, then jumped when the little box started beeping at her. She pulled out her card as Keira took the bag. They walked toward the exit.

"Your credit card has a chip," her sister said. "If the store has a chip reader, you shove it in, chip first. If they don't have a chip reader, you swipe it down the side."

"I have no idea what you're talking about."

She was still shaking but at least the credit card had worked. That was something. And when the bill came, she would pay it right away. She knew that much. Pay bills early and in full. That was her new motto.

"Where to now?" she asked. "Home?"

Keira groaned. "No. We have to go to the drugstore and get you some makeup along with a cleanser so you can take it all off. Then you can buy me lunch."

Callie put her arm around her sister. "Yes, I can buy you lunch. Anywhere you want."

"All right! I'm going to see if we can get in at the Fairmont Hotel. They have a high tea I've wanted to go to forever." She rolled her eyes. "Malcolm is not a high tea kind of guy."

"I would agree with that. High tea it is. And the drugstore. Then I'm going to throw up."

Keira grinned. "You're going to do just fine. Wait and see."

Callie hoped her sister's optimism was based on something other than her sunny nature because Callie was a whole lot less sure. As far as she was concerned there were a million things that could go wrong and plenty of time in which that could happen.

"I'm still going to throw up later."

Keira sighed. "I swear I'm never getting a

boyfriend. They are so not worth the trouble."

CHAPTER SEVENTEEN

By the time they reached the restaurant for dinner, Callie still hadn't thrown up. She considered that a good sign and hoped the trend would continue.

Santiago had shown up right on time, looking handsome and just a little dangerous in black jeans and a black shirt. He'd escorted her to a sleek dark blue Mercedes convertible and they'd driven to a quiet neighborhood Italian restaurant. The decor was simple, the menu limited but he'd promised everything was delicious.

They'd each ordered a glass of wine and put the menus aside to peruse later. Callie looked around at the other patrons, all normal-looking people, laughing and talking.

"This is nice," she said, trying to remember the last time she'd eaten in a restaurant where one sat down to order, then telling herself no good came from going there.

"The food is great. Malcolm and I discovered it when we were in college. We're about three miles from the U."

"The U?"

He grinned. "University of Washington. We call it the U, or U Dub. As in *W*. The area around the university is the U District."

"I'm still finding my way around. You stayed here after college. You didn't go back to where you grew up?"

"No. While I was in college, my mom lost her job. Malcolm helped her find work at his company. Luis, my youngest brother came with her. Paulo, the middle one, stayed in Yakima to finish high school." He made a face. "Unsupervised, he got his girlfriend pregnant and they both showed up here in June of that year."

"Yikes. That must have been a shock, but it worked out, didn't it? She's the one who's about to graduate as a registered nurse, isn't she?"

"That's her. Have you met Paulo yet?"

"I don't think so." She smiled. "I've told you before — I don't hang out with you management types."

He reached across the table and took one of her hands in his. "Yet here we are."

His touch was gentle and warm. When he moved his fingers across the back of her hand, she felt little jolts moving up her arm.

"I'm still not sure how I got here," she admitted.

He leaned close and lowered his voice. "We drove."

She laughed. "Thank you for clarifying."

"Anytime."

"Does your mom still work for the company?"

He shook his head. "She went to college herself and now manages a doctor's office."

Callie heard the pride in his voice. And the love. "Your family sounds wonderful."

"I like 'em. Now what about you? You never met your father, right?"

"No. I knew nothing about him at all. My mom said they went out for a while and when she told him she was pregnant, he disappeared. Every now and then he sent money, but not often." She thought about how her mother had worked so hard for the two of them.

"She never dated much that I knew about and never married. I don't know if that's because he broke her heart or she thought men weren't worth the trouble. We always had each other."

"What were you like as a kid?"

"Pretty normal. I broke a few rules, but nothing big. I stayed out late sometimes and she had to bug me to do my homework."

Callie felt bad about that now. She should have tried harder, been there for her mom. She didn't want to think about what had happened and she sure wasn't going to tell Santiago — not until she had to. She knew once she did, all this was over and for now, she liked having dinner with a handsome man who held her hand and stared into her eyes.

"You didn't go to college?" he asked.

Her senses went on alert as they treaded very close to dangerous ground. "No. It wasn't really an option for me. I messed around for a while and then decided to move to Houston."

Fortunately for her, their server returned and they ordered. When they were alone again, Santiago asked, "Favorite type of movie?"

She hoped she didn't look as relieved as she felt at the change of subject. "It's a tie. I love action movies and romantic comedies, and I love World War II movies, especially the old ones."

He chuckled and reached for her hand again. "Unexpected. I'm with you on the action movies and I can sit through a romantic comedy if it gets me what I want."

She stared at him in surprise. "That's honest. So *Sleepless in Seattle* for sex? It's good to know your price."

His expression turned sheepish. "It's not that much of a transaction and I phrased my statement badly. I'm willing to compromise and if it makes the lady happy to watch something like that, then I'm in."

"Too late. You told the truth the first time. What else will you do for sex?"

He turned her hand over and traced the lines on her palm. "I don't have a list. It's more of what works at the moment. To be clear, it was always one woman at a time. I've never cheated and I work very hard not to lie."

Somehow they'd gone from teasing to serious and she wasn't exactly sure how they'd gotten there. Plus, having him stroke her hand the way he was made it hard for her to think. She felt as if someone had cranked up the temperature in the room. She was warm and slightly uncomfortable. Parts of her body had started to tingle in ways that weren't normal. At least not for her.

If she gave herself a second to think, she would admit she was probably aroused. Not that she could be sure. Her last sexual experience had been when she was eighteen, and the quick coupling in the back of a car hadn't offered much in the way of inspiration, at least not for her. Now that she thought about it, she wasn't sure if they'd even used birth control and wasn't she lucky not to have turned up pregnant?

"Callie?"

"Hmm?"

"What are you thinking? I lost you somewhere."

"I was thinking that I was a really dumb kid in high school and I'm fortunate I didn't end up pregnant."

"You don't like kids?"

"I love kids but no one should have a baby at eighteen."

His expression tightened. Her stomach dropped and all the gooey, tingling feelings faded.

"You got someone pregnant in high school?" she asked, her tone sharper than she intended. Then she remembered. "Paulo and Hanna. Sorry. I didn't mean . . ."

"I know what you meant and I agree. On the bright side, I have a niece and nephew I love." He looked at her and smiled. "Emma is twelve and Noah is ten. They're great kids and I hang out with them as much as I can."

"You're probably the perfect uncle."

"I try to be. As for Paulo and Hanna —" He hesitated. "They've been fighting a lot lately and I don't know what to do about it. I'm pretty sure the kids know, but I don't want to bring it up in case I'm wrong, but if they do know, they should talk to someone."

Here it was again, she thought. Him telling her way too much, too soon. What was it with this man that he felt so comfortable sharing intimate pieces of his soul?

"It's not your rock," she told him. "Or your problem or however you want to phrase it. It's their marriage and their relationship. Be there for the kids and offer to listen but otherwise, it's not up to you to do anything."

One corner of his mouth turned up. "You sound like Luis, my youngest brother. He tells me I get too involved in everyone's life. It's that damned hero syndrome."

"There are worse flaws to have."

"You say that now," he joked. "Just wait until I try to rescue you from something you don't want to be rescued from."

She doubted that would ever be a problem and wondered if she could trust herself enough to believe Santiago was what he seemed — a genuinely nice guy who was handsome, rich and sexy to boot. Then she sighed. No way, she thought sadly. There had to be a flaw. Her luck had never been that good.

■ ■ ■ ■

But by the time dinner was over, Callie was no closer to figuring out Santiago's fatal flaw. They talked easily through the entire meal, laughed at each other's jokes and at least from her perspective, had a great time. It was still early when they left the restaurant. She was trying to figure out a way to extend the evening, when he said, "I want to show you something. Can you give me another hour before I take you home?"

"It depends on what the something is."

He held open the passenger door of his car. "Nothing untoward. You have my word."

She got in the car and waited until he joined her before saying, "Untoward? No one talks like that."

"I know. It slipped out before I could stop myself. Before I know it I'll be using words like perchance and hither."

He drove through the city and into a quiet neighborhood. Callie had no idea where they were going. Not to his place — she believed him about nothing *untoward*. So where?

A few minutes later they turned into a driveway next to a regular-looking two-story house. Okay, she'd thought maybe a club or a bar or she wasn't sure what.

"We're visiting someone?" she asked cautiously.

He unfastened his seat belt and angled toward her. "I want you to meet my family. My mom, my brother and sister-in-law. I thought it would be nice."

The words sank into her brain, swirled around, then made their meaning clear. Callie opened her mouth, realized she honest to God had nothing to say, closed it before shrieking.

"Are you insane? Your family? This is the first time we've gone out. I've been away from the whole boy-girl thing for a while now, but even I know you don't ask some woman you've just met to meet your *mother* on a first date!"

She wanted to hit him, but figured it would be like hitting a rock. Painful and pointless. His mother? His mother! She was about to tell him to take her home when the front door opened and someone peered out.

Great. They'd been spotted. Now she had to go inside and pretend this wasn't totally strange and uncomfortable.

"Why are you upset?" he asked.

"Because I am. Because I don't need the

pressure. Because there's something wrong with you."

His steady gaze never wavered. "I know it's a first date, Callie, but this is the start of something important. I want to do things right and I want you to meet my family. Will you do that for me?"

No. No and no and no. Only she couldn't say the word and the way he was looking at her made her feel, well, special. If it was a game, he was the master and she was no match for his skill level. His family, dammit. Why did it have to be family?

She unfastened her seat belt. "Sure. Let's go."

He gave her a smile that would have melted a frozen planet. She was still reveling in the beauty of it when he opened her door and helped her to her feet.

They made their way up the three stairs to the small porch. A slim, dark-haired woman stood just inside the family room. She looked to be in her forties, but considering how old Santiago was, Callie knew she had to be older. She was very attractive, with her son's eyes.

"Finally," she said with a smile and she greeted Callie. "Finally he brings a girl home. I banned them nearly ten years ago. Always a different one every other week. I forgot their names, they came and went so fast, so I told him no more until you're serious. Until you find one who's going to stick. I never thought I'd have to wait so long." She hugged Callie. "I'm Enriqua and I'm so happy to meet you."

Callie was still trying to absorb that mini info dump when she was introduced to Hanna and Paulo. They both shook her hand. Callie thought she recognized Paulo from work, but wasn't sure.

"It's nice to meet you all," she murmured as they were ushered into the kitchen. She had a brief impression of modern appliances with traditional cabinetry before she was seated at a large farm table. Santiago sat across from her.

"Doing okay?" he asked quietly.

"I'm the first date you've brought home in ten years?"

She got the single shoulder raise in response.

She lowered her voice. "They obviously don't know this is our first date."

"They don't need to know."

She glared at him. "Later, I'm going to find something heavy and bash you over the head."

He winked. "You can try . . ."

Callie groaned. She didn't need him to be

334

charming. What had he been thinking, bringing her here?

Enriqua handed her a plate with a large piece of chocolate cake. Hanna carried over coffee and mugs.

"Decaf," she promised.

Paulo walked in with a bottle of brandy and several glasses. "Also decaf," he said with a grin.

Everyone got cake and coffee and brandy and settled around the table. Santiago's mother smiled at Callie.

"I understand you're Malcolm's half sister, through his father."

"That's right. It was a shock to me."

"I can imagine. You never met Jerry?"

"No."

"He was an interesting man. I only saw him a few times. He traveled a lot. Malcolm would know about him better than me." Her expression softened. "Malcolm's a good boy. So kind and generous."

Callie was more caught up in someone referring to her brother as a boy than the other descriptors. She agreed with generous — he was that. As for kind, well, he was growing on her. Like the famous Seattle moss, she thought with a smile.

Callie asked Hanna about her kids. Both were at sleepovers but Callie was shown pictures, then conversation shifted to the start of baseball season and the different places Callie should visit now that she'd moved to the city. About an hour later, Santiago said they should go.

When they were back in his car, he asked, "Are you mad?"

"No. Confused, but not mad."

"Why confused?"

"It's been one date. One. Why on earth would you bring me home to meet your family? What if it doesn't work out? What if I'm secretly an alien from another planet?"

He drove out of the quiet neighborhood and back toward her place. "You're very fixated on this being our first date."

"Because it is."

"There's something about you, Callie. I can't explain it, but there is. This is different. That's why I took you home. I wanted them to meet you, but I also wanted you to meet them. So you would know more about me."

She leaned back in the seat and wondered what she was supposed to say to that. He was too perfect, she thought sadly, her eyes burning. Too everything any woman would want and when he found out the truth, he was going to run so far, she would never see him again.

"I'm not who you think," she whispered, knowing she should tell him now and get it over with. Just spit it out and be done with it.

He turned into her driveway and parked in front of the house. "Is it the alien thing? Because I'm happy to represent the human species." He angled toward her and touched her face. "I know you're scared, Callie. I don't know why, but I respect your feelings. We'll work through it, I promise."

She wanted to tell him he was wrong, that once he found out, everything would change. Before she could gather the courage to tell him the truth, he leaned in and kissed her.

His lips barely brushed hers before he straightened, but he might as well have branded her. She felt the heat all the way down to her toes. The sweet, gentle kiss got through to her far more than any tongue action would have.

He got out of the car and walked her to the door, then cupped her face in his hands and kissed her again. He lingered this time, for a single heartbeat, before drawing back.

"I want to see you again," he told her. "Say yes."

She shouldn't. She couldn't. She was setting them both up. It was only, how could

337

she resist?

She put her hands on his chest, raised herself up on tiptoe, then kissed him before opening the door.

"Yes," she whispered and closed the door behind her.

There would be a reckoning and it was going to be ugly. She was making a huge mistake handling things this way. But telling herself that didn't seem to do any good. Which was a shame — she would think she'd already learned the price of consequences.

"You're quiet. Are you nervous?" Delaney asked.

Malcolm considered the question. "No, more contemplative." He glanced at her as he drove down the street. "I'm looking forward to meeting your dad, if that's what you're asking. If I looked uncomfortable it's because I was thinking about the fact that my half sister is on a date with my best friend. That's a level of weird I'm not used to."

Delaney smiled. "At least you don't have to worry about Callie meeting Santiago's family. It's a first date."

"Good point."

He wasn't sure how he felt about his sister

and best friend going out. On the one hand, he knew Santiago could take care of himself. On the other hand, he was less sure about Callie. Yes, she was an adult and she'd had experiences most people couldn't begin to relate to, but had she dated much since getting out of prison? Should he have tried to talk to her?

He held in a groan at the thought. No way. That was not a conversation that would go well.

He followed Delaney's directions and pulled up in front of a modest house on a street of similar homes. There were bikes on porches and not a BMW in sight.

"Anything I should know before we go in?" he asked.

"They're going to totally adore you," she told him.

"And you?"

She smiled. "I kind of adore you, too."

Her words were like a jolt of electricity. They woke him up and got his attention in a big way. Things had happened so naturally with her, he hadn't noticed that they'd gotten serious. Well, damn.

He poked around for regret or apprehension or any kind of worry and found only a happy sense of possibility.

"Delaney," he began, then realized he had

no idea what he was going to say. Or wanted to say. Or should say. "The adoration is returned," he told her, taking the easy way out.

She laughed and got out of the car. Malcolm circled around to join her. As they walked up to the front door, he saw the ramp that would allow a wheelchair easy access.

She knocked once and then let them in. "We're here," she called.

"In the kitchen."

She smiled. "Where else?" she asked in a low voice.

They walked down a short hallway and went through a larger-than-normal doorway into a comfortable kitchen. Malcolm had a brief impression of slightly lower than usual cabinets, new appliances and an older couple smiling at them.

Delaney's father had her dark red hair and green eyes. He sat straight in his wheelchair, looking confident and in control. Beside him was a slight blonde woman with a warm smile.

"You must be Malcolm," she said, holding out her hand as she approached. "I'm Beryl and this is Delaney's father, Phil."

The two men shook hands, then Phil invited him to join him in the family room.

Malcolm followed the other man into an open, comfortable-looking room with a big TV, lots of windows and a brick fireplace. Malcolm would guess the house had been built in the 1950s when the city had been growing.

Malcolm took a seat on the sofa. Delaney appeared a few seconds later, a beer in each hand. She handed them each one before giving Malcolm a look of regret.

"Beryl needs my help in the kitchen," she said. "Call if you need anything."

"He'll be fine," Phil said easily.

Malcolm smiled. "I'll be fine."

When Delaney had left, Phil eyed him. "So, you're dating my little girl."

"I am."

"Tell me about yourself."

Malcolm thought about asking what the other man would like to know, then figured he could guess the basics.

"I'm single, never married. My family owns a company that offers mail-order food all over the country. We've been expanding into the international market, but slowly so we don't screw up. I'm the third generation in the business. I have two half sisters." He decided not to go into detail on that. There was no way to keep the story short.

Phil eyed him over his beer. "You're what?

Thirty-three or thirty-four. Why aren't you married? In my day, you got married or people knew why."

"I was engaged a few years back. She cheated and we broke up. I've been more careful since then."

"Any convictions?"

Malcolm chuckled. "No. No arrests, either."

Phil grinned. "All right then. She's my little girl. I have to be sure."

"I respect that."

Delaney appeared with a plate of stuffed mushrooms and set them on the coffee table. She sat down next to Malcolm.

"Everything all right?" she asked anxiously.

"It's fine," he told her. "Your dad's looking out for you. I like that."

She groaned. "Dad, what did you say? Or ask? You weren't inappropriate, were you?"

"It's all good," her father told her.

Beryl joined them and handed Delaney a glass of wine. She sat in the wing chair opposite the sofa and Phil moved his wheelchair next to her. The movements were familiar, Malcolm thought. Connected. They were obviously happy together.

"Delaney told you I was a cop?" Phil asked.

"Yes. She told me about the shooting, as well. I remember when it happened."

"That was a dark time," Beryl said with a sigh. "Phil in the hospital, my Tim taken from us." She reached for Phil's hand.

Malcolm felt Delaney tense, but she didn't speak.

"It was so hard," Beryl continued. "The funeral, the weeks of worry." She smiled sadly at Delaney. "Tim and Delaney were only four weeks from their wedding. Everything had to be canceled. She donated her beautiful wedding dress to a young woman in Kansas who lost everything in a tornado. We still have the pictures from her wedding."

She patted Phil's hand. "Then he started to get better and we began to heal." She looked at Delaney. "I think about Tim every day. I know you do, too. But he'd want us both to be happy."

Delaney sipped her wine without speaking. Malcolm wondered what she was thinking. If she was half as uncomfortable as she looked, she was desperate for a change in topic.

"I understand you two are taking a cruise later this year," Malcolm said. "Where to?"

Phil grinned. "It's a first for both of us. I have the itinerary in my desk."

"He doesn't want to see that," Beryl said with a laugh.

"I would like to very much," Malcolm told her. "I've never been on a cruise."

Phil went to get the information while Beryl excused herself to check on dinner. When they were alone, Delaney squeezed his hand.

"Thank you," she murmured.

"Anytime."

CHAPTER EIGHTEEN

While Delaney was grateful that everyone seemed to have a good time, to her the evening felt endless. Every topic brought them back to Tim. Baseball — Tim had always loved the Dodgers. The cruise — what places had Tim wanted to visit. Her former career at Boeing — Tim had been so proud of her but ready for her to be a stay-at-home mom.

As Malcolm drove the short distance to her place, she wondered if it was always like that and she no longer noticed or if all the Tim talk had another purpose. If it was the latter, she honestly didn't know how much of that was directed at her and how much was directed at Malcolm.

When he parked by her condo building, he turned off the engine and looked at her.

"You okay?"

"Not really. I'm sorry about tonight."

"What? Why? I had a great time. I like

them both very much."

She groaned. "And Tim. Did you like him, too?"

He touched her cheek. "Tim was a big part of your life before the shooting. Beryl's his mom. It's okay they wanted to talk about him."

"Really? Because I can't figure out if they always do this or if they're warning you off."

"I don't think they're warning me off. It's just something you all have in common. He was a big deal, Delaney. You were going to marry him."

"I know. It's just . . ." She looked out the window. "They make him sound like a saint and he wasn't. He was a regular person with good and bad sides. We fought sometimes, just like everyone else." She turned back to Malcolm. "I don't know how I feel about my past. Isn't that strange? But I really don't. Sometimes I think I will never get over Tim and other times I wonder if I really could have gone through with the wedding. We were so different and I wanted more than we were going to have, which he could never understand. But we'd been together for so long and everyone expected us to get married. I just don't know."

He leaned in and kissed her forehead. "You don't have to know. Life kicked you in the gut and you've had to move on. Of course you wonder about what could have been. That's normal."

He was so calm, she thought. Strong and solid. She could depend on him.

"Sometimes I don't know if I made the right decision quitting my job," she admitted. "I miss my corporate life. I don't know if I want to be a doctor. And if I don't, I ruined my future by walking away from a career I loved."

She squeezed her eyes shut. "I can't believe I said that out loud."

"It's probably good that you did because it sounds like you've been keeping it inside for a long time. Delaney, you're twenty-nine years old. Whatever you decide, you didn't screw up your future. You had a great job and a skill set you can take anywhere. If you want to get back into corporate life, you can. If you want to be a naturopath, you're going to do that. If you want to start making birdhouses from gourds, I know you'll be incredibly successful."

"Birdhouses from gourds?" she asked, so taken aback by the concept that she started to laugh. "Where did that come from?"

"I have no idea, but you get my point."

She giggled. "Gourds? Not wood or even cardboard?"

"Cardboard wouldn't survive in the rain."

"Oh, right. Well, gourds are waterproof." She continued laughing until the last of her tension eased. The confusion and pain were still there, as always, but somehow they seemed more manageable.

She turned to him. "You've given me perspective. Thank you."

"I live to serve."

"Good to know. Now did time with my family terrify you or would you like to come up to my place?"

He leaned in and kissed her. "I thought you'd never ask."

Callie arrived home from work to find Keira waiting for her in the foyer. Her sister had Lizzy with her and immediately jumped to her feet when Callie walked in.

"You'll never guess," Keira said, doing a little dance while holding on to her kitten. "Guess, but you never will. It's cool, I think. Better than last time. I mean the flowers and the vase. That was dumb. Boys are so weird."

Callie laughed even as her heart gave a little flutter. "My guess is that Santiago sent me something." More flowers? No, Keira had said it was better, which implied different.

Since their date the previous Saturday, he'd been in touch every day. Little texts and emails. Funny shares or just a few words. Simple, easy communication that let her know he was thinking of her.

"He did!"

Keira led the way upstairs. Callie walked into her bedroom and saw a bouquet of flowers sitting in a large metal can — like a half-gallon coffee can. Only they weren't flowers.

She approached the table and saw the beautiful pastel blossoms were made of something else. Something that looked amazingly like . . .

"Wood!" Keira spun in a circle. "I looked up the company online and that's what they do. Each flower is hand carved. Aren't they beautiful? They're so pretty and delicate and the metal can totally contrasts with the flowers, which is great because otherwise it would be too sweet and who wants that." She paused. "There's a card."

"What does it say?"

Keira put her free hand on her hip. "Excuse me. I didn't read it. Looking at flowers is one thing, but reading your card is something else."

Callie grinned. "If you say so."

She opened the card and saw a scrawled

message. *Because I want this to last.*

She wasn't sure if he meant them or the flowers or both, not that it mattered. If Santiago was trying to win her over, he was doing a very good job. She felt herself becoming more vulnerable by the day — but not in a scary I-have-to-run-now way. Being courted was actually really nice.

"I have to call him and thank him," she said, looking at Keira. "Give me two minutes to do that and then we'll hang out."

Keira rolled her eyes, then made kissing sounds as she scampered from the room. Callie got out her phone.

"What do you think?" Santiago said by way of greeting. "Too much?"

"They're beautiful. Thank you."

"You're welcome. I saw them and I thought of you."

"I'm glad."

"Good. So Sunday morning. Come to church with me and my family, then stay to lunch. Once we're done with that, we can spend the afternoon hanging out."

Church? The man wanted to take her to church for their second date and then spend time with his family? What was with that? She couldn't decide if he was the most amazing man on the planet or if he'd been hit in the head one too many times.

"Callie?"

"That sounds great," she said softly, taking an incredible leap of faith.

"I'll pick you up at nine thirty. Bring a change of clothes so once lunch is done we can walk around the city or something. The weather guy swears it's not going to rain."

"I didn't know it ever stopped raining in Seattle," she teased.

"Wait until summer. We have a sucky winter, but the summers are beautiful." He lowered his voice. "I'm really looking forward to Sunday."

"Me, too. I'll see you at nine thirty."

He chuckled. "Yes, but don't worry. We'll talk before then. Bye, Callie."

"Bye."

She hung up, then clutched the phone to her chest. She was excited and scared and nervous and wow, church with a guy. That was unexpected.

She dropped the phone on her bed, then went next door to Keira's room and hugged her sister.

"What's that for?"

Callie hugged her again. "Santiago asked me to go to church and thanks to you, I have something to wear. Thank you for making me buy that wrap dress. It will be perfect."

Keira stared at her. "Your date is church?"

"That's not all of it. We're having lunch with his family and then hanging out for the day." She wrinkled her nose. "I'll be gone all day. Will you be okay?"

Keira sighed. "I'm going to be thirteen soon. I'll be fine. Besides, I'm going out with friends." She arched her eyebrows. "Grace's mom is dropping us off at the movies, then we're going shopping. Bella and Layla will be there, too."

Callie stared at her. "You're making friends. That's so great. I'm so proud of you."

"Oh, please. It's no big deal."

"It's a huge deal. Do you need money for the mall or the movies or food?"

"I already asked Malcolm who grilled me for like five minutes on my plans. I think I liked it better when he was ignoring me."

"No, you didn't."

Keira grinned. "No, I didn't. Anyway, my Sunday is taken care of. Want to do something on Saturday?"

"In the morning, I'm going to make a cheesecake. Actually I'll make one for here and one to take with me for the lunch. The morning temperature should be cool enough that it's okay in the car during church and it's the kind of thing that travels pretty well. I'll have to get some springform pans and —"

She realized Keira was staring at her. "What?"

"You know how to make cheesecake?"

"Sure. It's not hard. Want me to teach you?"

"Yes. You never know when you're going to need a new skill."

Callie laughed. "You're on. Okay, let's take Lizzy downstairs and play with the laser pointer. Then we'll do homework."

Keira collected her kitten and kissed the top of her head. "We don't actually do homework. I do homework and you read."

"I'm with you in spirit."

"Maybe you could be with me on my English paper."

Callie grinned. "That will never happen."

"You're so mean."

"And proud of it."

Malcolm thanked the custodian, then stood and shook his hand. The older man smiled as he left.

A couple of times a year, Malcolm set up a temporary office in one of the warehouses and invited his employees to come talk to him about whatever was on their mind. The company was growing fast and he wanted to stay in touch with everything that was happening.

There was a sign-up sheet for appointments and he made sure to build in time so if he had to go view a workstation or tour a stockroom, he could.

He made notes about janitorial supplies then looked up as the next person entered. His welcoming smile changed to confusion when he saw Callie.

"You're my three thirty?" he asked. "Why would you bother?"

Her expression hardened slightly. "I need to talk to you about work and my understanding of the company policy is —"

"I know how this goes, but we live in the same house. You could have talked to me there."

"This is about business." Her tone was defensive. "I waited until after my shift."

Malcolm realized he was handling the situation all wrong. Callie hadn't even told him what she wanted and she was already upset.

He forced himself to relax as he offered her a smile. "Please, have a seat. Next time, feel free to talk to me whenever you'd like. During your shift is fine with me. Thank you for scheduling the meeting. Do you want coffee or a soda?"

She eyed him suspiciously as she sat on one of the chairs opposite his desk. "I'm fine."

She pulled a piece of paper out of her back pocket. As she held it, he realized her hands were shaking. He frowned.

"Are you okay?"

"I'm fine. Can we get through this?"

"Certainly. Go ahead."

Callie cleared her throat. "First, there's a woman I work with. Frankie. Her son, Levi, has cancer. It's been really hard on her. He has to go back in the hospital for treatment and he's only eight." Her gaze narrowed as she glared at him. "That's younger than Keira."

"I'm aware of that. What's the problem? We have family leave time for this sort of situation. She can simply apply for it."

Callie's expression didn't soften at all. "She's used it up, and her sick leave and her vacation time. She's a single mom and Levi is her only child. She can't lose her job because she needs the insurance to pay for the treatments. It sucks all around."

Malcolm had to agree. Before he could ask what he could do to help, Callie continued.

"Everyone in her department wants to donate a few vacation days to her but our manager says they can't and he told everyone not to take it to HR. That seems wrong to me. It's their vacation days. Why can't she have them? The work is still getting done. Frankie's been here over ten years. She's well liked and well respected. She's a mentor, Malcolm. This is a really crappy way to treat a valued employee."

"You're right," he told her. "It is and I in no way agree with what the manager told her. That is not at all what we intended when we set up the company policies. We wanted to make things easier for our people, not harder." He picked up the paper. "Tell me Frankie's last name. I'll get with HR as soon as we're done here. She can have as much time off as she needs. I'll make sure her manager understands the policy."

Some of her tension seemed to ease. "Thank you."

"You're welcome." He nodded at her list. "What else?"

She glanced at her notes. "I've been working on the line filling baskets for a few weeks now. The lever for the cellophane dispensing machine is horrible. It's hard to use and the angle is wrong. When someone has to do small baskets, they're stuck using that machine all day. It physically hurts. It needs to be fixed. Several people have complained but no one is listening."

Malcolm had a bad feeling that the "no one" in question was the same manager who had not helped Frankie. Yes, they were a for-profit company, but everyone in management was supposed to understand that their people were their greatest resource.

"Email me the machine number and I'll have maintenance look at it before the close of business today."

She relaxed in her chair and smiled at him. "Really?"

"Yes, really. Also, I would appreciate it if you didn't mention our conversation to your coworkers. People are going to get moved around and there might be some retraining. It would be easier if no one thought it was punishment."

Her smile faded. "You're not going to fire the supervisor?"

"Not if I don't have to. However, if the retraining and a new position don't improve things, then I'll revisit my decision. Next?"

She tilted her head. "I have trouble understanding you. In some ways you're just so nice and in others, you're a complete, a completely different person."

He had a feeling she'd self-edited that last bit, but didn't call her on it. Instead he waited while she glanced at her notes.

"Okay," she murmured. "Last is the baskets. I've been working on custom baskets for nearly a week now. One thing that keeps coming to mind is all the food is for adults."

He frowned. "Who else would it be for?"

"Kids." She grinned. "Hey, if someone can afford forty-dollar olive oil, then they can probably afford some upscale kid-friendly foods. When I was in Houston, I worked for a caterer. You'd be amazed how much parents spent on parties for their children. I'm just saying that there are a lot of opportunities. Maybe come up with one or two kid party baskets with different kinds of cookies and maybe some prizes. Or a 'make Mom breakfast in bed' basket."

He felt the beginnings of a headache. "While that's really interesting, Callie, we have a R&D department. Their entire job is product development. I'm sure they'd already been over this material and have decided it's not worth the trouble. I honestly can't see anyone buying their kid a food basket from a place like ours. We already sell cakes."

"Not for children. They're too fancy and focused wrong. What about cupcakes in a jar? Those are really popular and —" She pressed her lips together. "Never mind. You're not interested."

The tension was back. "It's not that. I appreciate the thoughts. You're a part of the family and a part of the company. Maybe it would help if you went to college and —" He realized a sentence too late how that was going to sound.

"Right," she said, coming to her feet. "Because God knows I couldn't possibly have a good idea without a four-year degree. I mean, who am I? Some hick with a few community college classes and a string of blue-collar jobs."

"Callie, no. That's not what I meant. You're new here and we've tried a lot of food items that didn't work. I'm sure we've visited the kid thing. It's not viable. I appreciate the enthusiasm. I'm sure that in time and with more training you'll learn that . . ."

He stopped as he realized he was digging the hole deeper.

"What? What will I learn? How much time? How much training?" She shook her head. "Forget it, Malcolm. You're right. I don't know what I'm talking about. I haven't gone to college and I haven't been here that long. Just take care of Frankie and the lever and screw the rest of it."

She was embarrassed. He could see it in the flush on her cheeks. He'd made her feel bad about coming to him, which wasn't at all what he wanted.

"Callie —"

She started for the door, then stopped and turned to him. "You know what's really interesting? There are a few people here who remember our father. They're not saying much, which leads me to believe he wasn't that great a guy. Something we'd already guessed by how he treated Keira and me. It's really too bad you had to take after him."

She walked out of his office and slammed the door. Malcolm leaned back against the sofa and wondered how everything had gone so wrong so fast.

Callie hurried toward the locker rooms. She had to get out of the warehouse as quickly as possible, before anyone saw her and figured out what had happened.

Malcolm had totally dismissed her and had treated her like an idiot.

"Stupid, asshole brother," she muttered. "You think you're better than the rest of us. You think you're such hot shit that you control the world. Well, you don't control —"

She rounded the corner only to come to a complete stop as she saw Paulo standing

360

there. He had a clipboard in his hand, but instead of studying it, he was looking at her. As if he'd heard everything she'd said.

Her mind replayed her mini-tirade and she had to hold in a groan. Worse, double worse, he knew who she was. Or rather he knew who her brother was. And if he told anyone, she was going to be in big trouble.

"I . . ." she began, only she didn't know what to say.

Paulo surprised her by winking. "It's okay, Callie. I have an older brother, too, and there are times when I feel exactly the same way."

Which was nice of him to say, except his older brother was Santiago and she couldn't imagine him ever acting as horrible as Malcolm.

"I won't repeat a word," he told her as he turned to walk away. "Your secret is safe with me."

Which probably should have made her feel better, but oddly enough, really didn't.

CHAPTER NINETEEN

"You know there's a baseball game on," Hanna said pointedly.

Santiago stayed where he was, leaning against the kitchen counter. "No, thanks."

His sister-in-law sighed. "You are getting in the way."

"Then put me to work."

Yes, there was a game on but no way he was going to go into the family room with Paulo. Not when Callie was helping out in the kitchen.

Their morning had started great with Callie more beautiful than ever in a pretty navy dress. They'd sat close to each other in church. She'd surprised him by listening attentively to every word, then thanking him for inviting her.

"Before moving to Seattle, I hadn't been to church in forever," she'd admitted on the drive back to his brother's house. "I want to go more often. I appreciate you reminding me how much I enjoyed having a spiritual life."

She was just getting better and better, he thought as Hanna pointed to a stack of potatoes. "Peel those," she instructed.

He washed his hands and reached for the first potato. Callie returned from the powder room and tied an apron around her waist as she smiled at him.

"Can you handle that without adult supervision?" she asked, her voice teasing.

"I'm giving it a go."

They were having a traditional Sunday lunch, with prime rib and mashed potatoes. Hanna had started slow roasting the prime rib early that morning so it would be ready on time. Callie had brought a cheesecake that she'd made herself. He'd never met a woman who could make cheesecake. Now she helped Hanna with the vegetables, dicing and measuring as they worked on some casserole dish.

"This is nice," Hanna said with a smile. "I'm usually in the kitchen by myself."

"Where are your kids?" Callie asked.

"Next door, with their grandmother. They spend the time from church to lunch with her, just hanging out and talking." Hanna sighed. "They're both getting so grown-up. I don't know how long we're going to have these traditions with them."

"They'll always have the memories," Callie told her. "Wait and see. I'll bet they keep the tradition for their kids."

"That would be so nice." Hanna laughed. "But maybe I'm not ready to think about my babies having babies just yet."

"Thinking about having more babies?" Santiago asked, his voice teasing.

Hanna threw a piece of red pepper at him. "Bite your tongue. That part of my life is long past."

Which was a shame, he thought, because he liked babies. They were always growing and changing. He liked how they smelled and how they fit in his arms. He'd always assumed he would have kids of his own someday.

His gaze slipped to Callie, then he forced himself to look away. Too soon, even for him.

"Besides," Hanna added, "I got my baby fix satisfied at work. The pediatric rotation was so fun and my friend Melody is having a baby in a couple of months." Hanna wrinkled her nose. "A couple of us are throwing her a shower. I really have to start working on that."

"Do you have a theme?" Callie asked. "Once you figure that out, the rest usually falls into place."

"I hadn't thought of a theme. Have you given a lot of baby showers?"

"I used to work for a caterer." Callie smiled. "We did more kids' parties than I want to think about. Baby showers can be really fun and it's an opportunity to be creative."

Paulo walked into the kitchen. "Who's throwing a baby shower?" he asked, staring pointedly at his wife.

Hanna's shoulders went back. "I am, with a couple of women in my class. I told you about it. Everyone is pitching in."

Paulo glowered. "How much is that going to cost?"

Santiago felt the tension between them and sensed this was not the first fight about the shower. What was the big deal? If it made Hanna happy, wasn't that good enough? He was about to say something only to remember that his brother had his own life to deal with and no one appreciated him butting in.

Paulo muttered something under his breath. He grabbed a beer and stalked out of the kitchen.

"Sorry," Hanna whispered.

Callie looked at Santiago as if asking if everything was okay. He could only shrug.

She turned to Hanna.

"Do you know if the baby is a boy or a girl?"

"A girl."

"Okay, so here's some ideas. You can do a tea party-themed shower. You can pick up kids' tea sets at thrift stores for practically nothing. Use those for your colors. You serve tea sandwiches and scones and fresh fruit. Honeybees are popular right now. You could do a honey-themed shower using yellow and black as the colors."

"Isn't that a bumblebee?" he asked.

Callie laughed. "Yes, but it's okay. Cartoon bees are cute. Books also work. If the mom-to-be has a favorite kid's book, use that as the theme and use the illustrations as a guide for colors and decorations. Let's see. What else? We did a really cute shower back in Houston. They were naming the baby Mavis." She sighed. "Don't ask. Anyway, the theme was based on the old *I Love Lucy* TV show, but instead it was I Love Mavis. Everything was '50s inspired. It was a big hit. Oh, and with the food, you can do things that pop. Popcorn, cake pops. You know, because the mom is ready to pop."

Hanna blinked several times. "Wow. Just wow. You gave me so many great ideas in like five seconds. How did you do that?"

"Like I said, I worked for a caterer. Besides, I really like kids' parties. Give me twenty dollars and an hour at a thrift store and I can dazzle." Callie laughed. "On the other hand, if I'm shopping for myself, I'm totally lost. I can give you my number, if you'd like. We could brainstorm a few things."

"That would be wonderful. Thank you."

Santiago went back to peeling potatoes. He told himself that the pride he felt had nothing to do with him. Of course Callie was brilliant. He shouldn't expect any less. Still, he was proud as hell and happy. Just stupid happy and it felt good.

Callie breathed in the salt air. After lunch, she and Santiago had changed clothes. He'd driven to the waterfront and they were making their way to Pike Place Market. She felt good — relaxed and happy. She'd enjoyed the church service, and the lunch had been so much fun. Everyone had talked all the time, there'd been plenty of laughter, and she'd felt totally welcomed and accepted.

Almost as exciting, she'd felt she fit in. Her dress had worked perfectly and now, in jeans, a sweater and her new leather jacket, she felt carefree and pretty.

They were probably normal emotions for

everyone else, but not for her. Not in a very long time. For once she wasn't defining herself by her past but by who she was that day.

"Thanks for making the cheesecake," Santiago told her, taking her hand in his. "You didn't have to do that, but it was delicious."

"It's not hard to do and I had a good time in the kitchen. Keira helped me. I always enjoy her company."

"You were terrific with Emma and Noah today. They both like you."

"They're great kids." She glanced at him. "Are Hanna and Paulo having problems?"

His mouth twisted. "I don't know. I think so. They're fighting a lot and Paulo belittles her. I don't think that's a good sign." He sighed. "My mom would tell me to stay out of it."

"I think your mom is right. People have to make their own way."

"Yeah, well, that's not *my* way. I prefer to wade in and rescue the world."

She laughed. "So I've heard. Maybe this would be a good time to look in another direction and hum the *Jeopardy!* theme until the need passes."

"I might have to take you up on that. So where did you get all those shower ideas?

From your previous job?"

"Uh-huh. The caterer I worked for specialized in a lot of family parties. Baby showers, wedding showers, kids' parties. We were always trying to come up with something new and different." She glanced at him. "There are communities where things like parties for children become a competition, which is kind of sad, but good for business."

She hesitated, then admitted, "I tried to talk to Malcolm about incorporating food items for kids' parties into the company's selection. I've been working on baskets for a while now and it seems to me that could be something that sells."

Santiago surprised her by pulling her close and lightly kissing her. "Beautiful and smart. Am I the luckiest guy or what?"

She felt herself flush even as squishy, gooey feelings started to overwhelm her. "Don't be too impressed. It's not that big a deal."

"Yeah, it is. What did Malcolm say?"

The squishy went away, leaving her uncomfortable. "He wasn't impressed."

Santiago touched her face. "That's not like him. Let me —"

She took a step back. "No. Don't bring this up. It's my thing and I'll deal with it myself."

"But —"

"No. You getting involved isn't heroic. I need to figure out my relationship with Malcolm myself. I mean it. You can't fix this, but you can make it worse."

"Okay," he said, his tone serious. "I will respect your wishes on this. You have my word."

Something she could trust, she thought with relief. She didn't understand why Santiago wanted to be with her — there had to be a million women out there who would fall all over themselves to be with him. Maybe she was due for some good luck, she thought wistfully. Maybe, just this one time, she was going to get a break.

"So how are you with heights?" he asked unexpectedly.

"They don't bother me. Why?"

He turned her around and pointed. In the distance she saw a huge Ferris wheel right on the edge of the sound.

"We have to do that," she breathed. "I'll bet you can see forever from the top."

He took her hand in his and grinned. "Let's go find out."

Delaney couldn't remember the last time she'd cooked dinner at home for more than just herself. Not since the shooting, she thought as she slid puff pastry appetizers into the oven and set the timer. But even before that, Tim had never been a fan of her condo and preferred that they went out or over to his mom's for meals.

She checked the set table in the dining room. From where she stood, with the big window behind her, she could survey much of her condo. It was a fairly standard one bedroom with a small den. The walls were white, the hardwood a medium brown and the carpeting neutral beige.

She'd liked the location and the building. The neighborhood was desirable and there was plenty of shopping within walking distance. Her plan had been to fix the place up with paint colors and a few throw rugs. She'd wanted to get nicer furniture instead of the hand-me-down pieces she'd picked up along the way.

But somehow that had never happened. While she'd been proud of herself for being able to buy the condo on her own, she'd been upset that Tim hadn't been supportive. He'd wanted them to save for a house instead and she'd never been able to explain her need to have a little pre-marriage independence. After he'd been killed, she hadn't had the energy or interest in doing anything to her place. Now, as she saw the lack of anything personal anywhere and the bare walls, she wondered if it was finally time to figure out what she wanted from her home.

She shook off her musings and returned her attention to the table. Everything was in place. She'd even bought a bottle of Malcolm's very expensive scotch for their cocktail time. She glanced at the clock, then smiled. It was exactly six. Malcolm was always prompt so she would expect . . .

He knocked on her door. She was still laughing when she opened it.

"Are you ever late?" she asked, pulling him inside.

"Only in extreme emergencies." He kissed her, then drew back. "Delaney, I'm not sure dinner is a good idea."

For a second she thought he was suggesting they make love first and was about to say everything but the appetizers could wait but then she saw the worry in his eyes.

"What is it?" she asked, leading him to the sofa. "What's wrong?"

"Nothing. Everything." Instead of sitting, he shoved his hands into his jeans pockets. "Lately I'm screwing up everything I touch and I don't want to screw up things with you. That's too important to me." He looked at her. "You're too important to me."

"Are we talking work? Personal life?"

"My family."

She moved close and put her hands on his shoulders. "Listen to me very closely. Every second with you doesn't have to be a party. We're involved. That means we deal with whatever's going on in each other's lives. I happen to like everyone in your family, so maybe I'm a good person to talk to about whatever's going wrong."

He shook his head. "You're not going to like me very much when I'm done."

She smiled. "Who says I like you now?"

The teasing comment earned her a slight smile. He sat down on the sofa and she curled up in the wing chair opposite. The timer would ding to let her know the appetizers were ready. Until then, she wanted to listen.

He leaned forward, his forearms resting on his thighs. He sucked in a breath.

"I saw Keira's therapist yesterday for an update," he began, his voice low. "The good news is Keira's doing better. The bad news is we have a fuller picture of where she started."

Delaney waited quietly. This was his story to tell.

"She's not sleeping well. Apparently she sometimes thinks her bedroom is too big and she sleeps in her closet. Even then she has nightmares and Callie comes and gets her."

He raised his head and stared at her. "I had no idea. I thought everything was fine. I was barely paying attention to her and I didn't get her into therapy when I should have."

"You've changed all that," she said gently.

"Now. What about before? She's a kid and I let her be scared. She's still hoarding money even though I've tried to tell her she'll never be asked to leave. I thought explaining she owned a third of the house would help, but that doesn't seem to have made any difference. When I talk to her, she seems fine, but then I listen to her therapist and wonder how Keira makes it through the day."

"How's she doing in school?"

"Good. Her grades are coming up and she's making friends." He smiled at her. "She likes you a lot."

"I like her, too."

"She likes Callie."

"That's something."

He lowered his gaze to the floor. "Callie's really been there for her, which I appreciate. But . . ." He swore quietly, then looked at her.

"I blew it with Callie."

The timer went off just then. Delaney laughed.

"Literally saved by the bell."

They both stood and walked into the small kitchen. She took the cookie sheet out of the oven and put the little puff pastries onto a small tray. She'd already pulled out the ingredients for her cosmo. Malcolm quickly made her drink, then poured himself a scotch. They took everything back to the sofa where she sat next to him.

"Tell me about Callie," she said.

"I didn't like her at first," he admitted, then sighed. "No, I didn't know her well enough to like or dislike her, but I didn't trust her." He glanced at Delaney. "It's complicated."

"I believe you. And now?"

"She's great with Keira, she's doing well at work, everyone likes her."

"And?"

"And we keep butting heads."

"Maybe you're too much alike. You're siblings, so you probably have some personality traits in common. When we don't like something in someone else, a lot of the time it's because we don't like it in ourselves. Maybe Callie reminds you of you."

He stared at her. "I never thought of that.

Maybe. She came to me to ask about some stuff for work. HR issues and a lever on a machine. I took care of all of it, but then she wanted to talk about adding products to our catalog. Items geared toward children."

"Why not?" Delaney asked. "Anyone who can afford to shop regularly from the catalog can afford to indulge their children."

"You're saying we're expensive?" he asked with a grin.

"High-end."

"That's part of the appeal."

"So I've heard. Anyway, Callie had an idea and . . ."

"I basically told her she should go to college and figure out what she was doing first. Not in those words, but close enough."

Delaney winced. "She didn't take it well."

"No. I apologized, but it was too late. She said she'd never met our father, but from what she'd heard, I was just like him." He glanced at her again. "It wasn't a compliment."

"I got that. Have you talked to her about it?"

"Not yet. I don't know what to say."

He put down his drink and stood, then walked to the window and faced her.

"I was engaged before."

Something she hadn't known, but wasn't surprising. "What happened?"

"A couple of months before the wedding, I caught her in bed with my father."

Delaney gasped. "No! That's not possible. I mean of course it happened, but oh my God. Malcolm. I'm so sorry."

He looked out the window. "I couldn't believe it. I knew he was a womanizer, but Rachel was my fiancée. Plus it never occurred to me she would cheat. Obviously that ended things."

"What happened with your father?"

He faced her again. "I knew I couldn't stay in the company or be around my father. I was packing to leave town when my grandfather came to see me. I told him I had to go." His jaw tightened. "He begged me not to. He said he would throw my father out, but he wanted me to stay. So I agreed and the next day Jerry was gone. I don't know what my grandfather said, but Jerry left Seattle and I never spoke to him again."

Delaney could barely breathe. She'd had no idea there was this much pain in Malcolm's past.

"Alberto never said anything but I know he missed his only son. As far as I can tell, they never saw each other again, either, and then Jerry died."

He looked at her. "Jerry was never much of a father to me. We rarely spoke and he wasn't interested in me at all. I never got to know him. When I was a kid, I tried to get his attention but he made it clear he didn't have time for me so after a while, I stopped trying. I moved on and after what happened with Rachel, I was grateful he was gone. I suppose I hated him for what he'd done. But it wasn't like that for Alberto. I took Jerry away from my grandfather. I broke his heart."

"No." She came to her feet and crossed to him. "No, you didn't. He slept with your fiancée. He fathered children all around the country and never bothered to take care of them. He's the bad guy, Malcolm. Not you."

"I broke my grandfather's heart," he repeated.

"No, you didn't. Alberto adores you. You and your sisters are the reason he gets up every morning. He loves you."

"He loved his son."

"That doesn't mean you did anything wrong."

"You don't get it," he told her. "I'm good at work. I'm not good at anything else."

She wrapped her arms around him. "You're good at me and you're getting better at the other stuff. Just keep trying."

He hugged her back, holding her tightly. "What do you see in me?"

"You're very good in bed."

He chuckled. "Thanks. I guess that's something."

"It's a start."

"It's not anything I would have printed on a business card."

She looked at him. "Oh, I don't know. It would sure be a conversation starter." She released him and smoothed the front of his shirt. "Malcolm, you're a good guy. Trust yourself and take care of your family. The rest will fall into place. I've been through a lot of crap, so I know what I'm talking about."

"Thanks for listening."

"You're welcome. Now eat some of the appetizers. I took them out of the freezer and put them on a cookie sheet with my own delicate hands."

"I'm impressed."

"You should be."

They returned to the sofa. Delaney was mentally reeling from what he'd told her, but she would have to process it all later. For now Malcolm needed her full attention. He'd shown her what he thought was the darkest, worst part of himself. It was up to

her to let him know she hadn't been scared
away.

CHAPTER TWENTY

Callie stood in the hall outside of her brother's home study. She really didn't want to talk to him, but she knew she didn't have a choice. Despite how he'd not been interested in her ideas for offering child-specific foods and packages, he'd totally come through on everything else.

The annoying lever on the cellophane machine had been fixed and HR had issued a statement revising the vacation policy to allow employees to donate their days off to someone else. Both of the issues were far more important than her ideas about cupcakes in a jar, she told herself. She would thank Malcolm and move on.

She knocked on the door and waited for his "Come in." She mentally braced herself before walking inside and faking a smile.

"Do you have a second?" she asked.

"Sure. What's up?"

He motioned to the chair opposite his

desk but she figured she wouldn't be there long enough to bother sitting down.

"I wanted to thank you for following through at work," she said. "The lever is much better now and Frankie can take off three days next week to be with Levi when he has his next round of treatments."

Malcolm's gaze was steady. "You're welcome. Thank you for bringing the problems to my attention. The lever should have been fixed immediately. As for the HR policy, that misunderstanding has been taken care of."

"I noticed my supervisor has been out for a couple of days."

"He's getting retrained."

She couldn't help smiling. "If this were a science fiction movie or an action thriller, *retrained* could have ominous consequences."

"Hopefully it won't come to that."

He stood and walked around the desk until he was in front of her. "Callie, I'm sorry I didn't give you a chance to tell me your ideas before. I know how you feel about separating work from home so I won't ask you to tell me about them now, but I really would like to talk about what you were thinking."

She searched his face as if she could find answers there. While she wanted to believe him, honestly, she just wasn't sure she could trust him.

"What?" he asked, his voice filled with frustration. "What did I say wrong now?"

"Nothing. I'll put together some material and set up a meeting."

His jaw tightened, then relaxed. "Callie, I don't want to be the asshole brother. You're my sister and I want you to be happy here. I want us to get along. I don't know why we got off on the wrong foot, but I'd really like to know if you think we can change that now."

Okay, that was honest, she thought, a little surprised he was willing to put it all out there. Maybe she should return the favor.

"I thought you were judging me."

He frowned. "What do you mean?"

"I thought you were judging me about having been in prison, that you were waiting for me to steal the family silver."

"I don't think there *is* any family silver."

"You know what I mean."

"I do." He motioned to the chair again. "Can you please sit down?"

"Sure."

She plopped into the chair. He surprised her by taking the one next to her rather than returning to his desk.

"I was judging you," he admitted. "I

didn't know what to expect. I guess I had some caricature in my mind. I'm sorry."

"Me, too. I'm not a bad person, Malcolm."

"I know. When it comes to Keira you're a much better sibling than I am." He leaned back against the chair. "Parenting sucks and I'm always getting it wrong."

"You're not doing so bad."

"I've left Keira to take care of herself. I didn't get her into counseling." His gaze met hers. "I didn't know she was scared of her bedroom and sleeping in the closet. I didn't know about the nightmares and the screaming."

Callie felt herself flush. "That's getting better. She hardly ever has nightmares anymore and she's sleeping in her bed more and more."

"See? You know that and I don't. It's not that I don't care about her. It's just . . ."

She waited, wondering what he was going to say.

"I'm not very good with people," he admitted. "In high school, I was all about learning and getting into college. I hardly had any friends. Santiago really helped loosen me up."

She did her best not to react to hearing Santiago's name. Just thinking about him made her feel all fluttery inside — which was incredibly stupid. She was very aware that she was living on borrowed time with him. The second he found out about her past, he was going to dump her and run for the hills.

"You were good for him, too," she said, trying to sound casual instead of giddy. "That's what friendship is about. Helping each other."

"I'd like us to be friends."

"Me, too." The words were automatic and it took her a second to realize she meant them. "Look, we have something in common."

"More than that. We're related by blood." Something she still had trouble processing. "I know almost nothing about our father. What I have heard isn't great. My mom never said much and I know she loved me, but I'm sure getting pregnant and then having to be a single mom totally messed up her life."

She thought about how Keira had been abandoned by her mother, her own tough circumstances. She wasn't sure what had gone on between Malcolm and Jerry, but she sensed they hadn't been close.

"Is there anything positive you can tell me about our father?" she asked.

He thought for a second. "He was really

good with women."

Callie started to laugh. Malcolm joined in and for that moment she thought everything was going to be okay.

"What time is it?" Noah asked for the fifth time in less than five minutes. "I don't want to miss it."

Santiago shook his head. "Noah, we're not going to miss it."

"But what if we do?"

"Do you want to run ahead and meet us there?"

"Yes."

Noah took off at a run but before Santiago could tell him to slow down, the boy began to walk. Okay — it was a fast walk, but still.

"He does this every time," Emma said, looking at her brother. "We never miss the demonstration."

"I know, but he's a worrier."

Santiago brought his niece and nephew to Chihuly Garden and Glass a couple of times a year. They loved the beautiful glass, the incredible colors and ways the displays were set up. While Emma enjoyed all of it, Noah's favorite part was the glassblowing dem-onstration at the end.

They walked more sedately, pausing to study favorite pieces. As they moved into a room with a magnificent glass ceiling, Emma moved close.

"Uncle Santiago, can I talk to you about something?"

He figured he was on safe ground. Hanna and her daughter were close. From all he'd heard, Emma had lots of friends and did great in school. "Sure. What?"

She thought for a second. "I guess it's not a question. Not really. Mom and Dad are fighting all the time and I don't know what to do."

He put his arm around her and pulled her close. "I'm sorry you know about that."

She wrinkled her nose. "Everyone knows about that. They get really loud sometimes. Dad doesn't like that Mom went back to college to become a nurse. I don't get that. She's really smart and she's worked so hard. Shouldn't he be proud of her?"

Santiago realized he was in way over his head with this conversation, but there was no escaping it now.

"You're right. She's done so well for herself. We're all proud of her. She's going to be a great nurse."

Emma looked at him. "What about Dad? Why is he so mad all the time?"

"That's kind of complicated," he admitted. "When your parents first got married, your mom stayed home with you and your brother. That's how things were for a long time. Now everything is different." He brightened. "Remember when you and your family moved into the house? You were scared because you thought you'd miss your old school and your friends there, but it worked out all right. This is like that."

She considered his words. "You're saying Dad doesn't like change."

"I'm saying change is usually difficult and a little scary. At least at first."

There was no way he was going to talk about how Paulo felt threatened by his wife's change in circumstance. Santiago would guess his brother was feeling left behind. Yes, the extra money would be nice, but at what price? What if Hanna started expecting more of her husband?

They continued walking through the displays and finally reached the open area. A crowd had started to collect for the demonstration. Emma grabbed his arm to keep him from joining Noah.

"Are my mom and dad going to get a divorce?"

Santiago stared into her beautiful eyes. He wanted to tell her everything would be fine, that of course her parents would stay together. Only he didn't know for sure and this was one problem he couldn't fix for them. They were going to have to do that themselves.

"I don't know," he admitted. "I don't think so, but it's not up to me. What I am sure of is they both love you and your brother. No matter what, they'll take care of you, as I will and your grandmother, too."

"That doesn't make me feel a lot better," she admitted. "But I get it. I hope they can work things out. A couple of my friends went through a divorce and it sucks."

"I know, kid. I know."

Malcolm waited for his sister in her room. Keira was due home from her friend's house by four and as far as he knew, she was always on time. He sat on the floor with Lizzy. The cat was growing fast — she'd nearly doubled in size since she'd been rescued. She was a friendly, playful bundle of fur. When she started to climb his shirt, he pulled her free, then held her against his chest. She curled up in his hands and purred, rubbing her head against his chin.

This was nice, he thought in some surprise. He'd never had pets growing up and hadn't ever seen the point to have one as an adult. But Lizzy was a good kitten. Maybe he should think about getting a dog or something.

Before the thought fully formed, he pushed it away. Right — when would he take care of a dog? The last thing he needed was to be responsible for one more life.

He continued to pet Lizzy. The kitten eventually fell asleep clearly oblivious to his very uncomfortable position supporting her. He lowered her to the carpet where she mewed a protest before giving his hand a quick lick, then falling back asleep.

"What are you doing here?"

He looked up and saw Keira in the doorway to her room. "Waiting for you. Lizzy was keeping me company." He stayed where he was. "I almost never see you these days and I wanted to see how you were doing."

Her expression stayed wary as she walked into her room. She wore jeans, a long-sleeved T-shirt and colorful tennis shoes. When she'd first arrived, she'd been underweight, but today she looked less gaunt and more relaxed.

Keira tossed her jacket on her bed, then sank down on the carpet a few feet away. "What did you want to talk about?" she asked cautiously. "Did I do something wrong?"

"Not that I know about. Did you?"

She flashed him a smile. "No. I'm actually

a really good kid. You should be grateful. I could be acting out in all kinds of ways. Stealing, breaking things, hoarding food."

All things he'd never thought about. "We are lucky. Thank you for that."

"You're welcome. By the way, I should have chores. I'm nearly thirteen and you need to be teaching me responsibility."

Something else he'd never thought of. "You're right. Do you want to come up with a list of chores or should I?"

"I can do it. I already take care of Lizzy. Carmen checks on me, but I do the work." She looked at him out of the corner of her eye. "You know, there are a lot of books on parenting. You might want to read one or two of them so you know what you're supposed to do. When I'm a teenager, things are going to be really rough. I'll be talking back and borrowing the car and staying out late."

"I can't wait," he murmured, thinking he probably *should* read up on what it was like to raise a teenage girl, although whatever any expert had to say was likely to scare the crap out of him.

"I'll have the chore list to you by the end of the week," she said. "Then we'll talk about my allowance."

"You already get an allowance."

"For doing nothing. I'm going to be doing a lot more. You should pay for that."

"I thought you were learning about responsibility. Isn't your payment a life lesson?"

She rolled her eyes. "Seriously? I don't think so. I'm a kid. I don't want life lessons. I want cash."

"Maybe we can work out a deal where you have both."

She grinned. "Maybe, but I won't like it."

"Fair enough. How's school?"

"Fine. I'm caught up with my assignments, I'm making friends." She looked at him. "All things you already know because you have to be talking to my school counselor and I know you saw my therapist."

She was an unexpected combination of child and adult, he thought. "I want to know what you think."

She stroked the sleeping kitten. "I think you should be nicer to Callie."

That surprised him. "What do you mean?"

"I hear you guys fighting sometimes. You should try to get along with her better. She's really nice and fun and she spends a lot of time with me, unlike some people."

Not a comparison he wanted. "Callie and I have different views of things."

"Maybe, but hers are right."

"You don't know what we were talking about." Although if she was referring to Callie's suggestions about adding to the company's catalog, he might have been too quick rejecting her ideas.

"I know Callie," Keira told him. "I know she works hard and that she's honest and does what she says she's going to do, although I guess that's kind of the same thing. I trust her."

The last comment seemed more pointed than the others. Had Callie told Keira about her past? He didn't know how to ask without betraying a confidence. He would have to speak to Callie about it directly.

"I don't distrust her," he said.

"That's not the same thing." Keira's eyes narrowed. "You need to be nicer."

"I'm trying."

"Try harder. You can be mean to me if you want, but not to her."

His sister's words slammed into him like a sledgehammer as the truth revealed itself. Keira trusted Callie. She wanted to spend time with her. He had no doubt that on Keira's phone, Callie would be listed under her name. The word *asshole* would never be mentioned when it came to her.

How had Callie done it? How had she cracked the code when Malcolm couldn't come close? For the first time in a long time, he felt lost, alone and inadequate. He'd always assumed he was just like everyone else — that he would get married and have a family. That he would be a decent father one day. Only being around Keira was making him think there was something wrong with him.

He cleared his throat. "How about if I'm not mean to either of you?" he said, trying to keep his voice casual so she wouldn't know how her words had hurt him. "And we'll keep working on being a family."

For a second he thought she was going to say that she and Callie already were a family — that he was the only outlier. Instead she nodded.

"I'd like that," she told him.

"Me, too."

The only problem was he had no idea how to make that all happen.

CHAPTER TWENTY-ONE

Callie had just stepped off the line for her afternoon break when her phone rang. She reached for it only to frown at the unfamiliar number. Keira and Santiago were pretty much the only people who called her. Grandfather Alberto had recently decided he needed to join "you young people today" and had bought a phone that allowed him to text, which meant that was all he did, multiple times a day.

"Hello?"

"Callie? It's Hanna, Santiago's sister-in-law. Do you have a second?" Hanna sounded frantic.

"Of course. What's wrong?"

"It's Noah. The school just called and he's sick. He's throwing up and they think he has a fever." Her voice thickened with tears. "I'm in Olympia with Emma's class on a field trip. I don't have any way to get back for at least a couple of hours. I can't get anyone on the phone. Not Paulo, or my brother-in-law, or my mother-in-law. I know it's a lot to ask but is there any way you could go pick him up and take him home? Just until my mom or Paulo can get there to be with him, then I'll get home as fast as I can."

Callie's stomach knotted and she felt like she was going to throw up, as well. Of course she wanted to get Noah — she was happy to help out. But what she didn't know was what Hanna would think if she knew the truth about her past. If she did, would she be willing to have Callie pick up her son?

"Callie, I'm desperate."

"Of course I'll do it. Tell me where his school is and I'll be right there."

Hanna gave her the name and the address, along with the safe phrase that would allow Noah to be released into her care.

"They'll need to see ID," Hanna told her.

"Not a problem." Callie didn't have a driver's license, but she did have a state-issued ID. "I'll call you as soon as I have him, then again when he's settled."

"You don't know how much I appreciate this. I'll owe you forever."

Callie hoped that meant the other woman would be forgiving when she found out the truth. A problem for later, she told herself as she searched out her supervisor.

Vern, a barrel-chested guy in his fifties, listened while she explained that she had to go help a friend.

"I'm happy to stay late and make up any time I miss," Callie said. "I know I'm new and it's asking a lot, but —"

Vern adjusted his baseball cap. "Don't sweat it, Callie. I have kids. Four girls, if you can believe it. I know all about them getting sick. Go help your friend, then make up the time. It's all good."

"Thank you."

She hurried out and requested a car. Two minutes later, it pulled up in front of the warehouse.

They drove north. Callie tried to pay attention — her driving instructor wanted her to learn her way around the city — but she got mentally lost as soon as they exited the freeway.

When the driver pulled up in front of the school, she hurried inside. After showing her ID, she said, "Mariners rule." The receptionist grinned at her.

"They do, but my computer tells me that's the secret phrase, so you're good to go. Let me have the nurse bring Noah out to you."

The ten-year-old was pale, shaking and

smelled of vomit. When he saw Callie, he started to cry.

"I want to go home."

"Of course you do. Come on, let's get you there right now."

She led him back to the car and held him all the drive. He stopped crying after a few minutes, then moaned. Callie made a quick call to Hanna to let her know she was on her way with Noah.

"My stomach hurts," Noah said. "I'm going to throw up again."

The driver met her gaze in the rearview mirror. Callie pointed to the street.

"Right here, then third house on the left. Hang on, Noah, we're nearly there."

She got him out of the car where he promptly threw up on the lawn. When he could walk again, they made their way up the front steps. Noah gave her the code to open the door and they went into the house.

She let him lead the way to his bedroom. Once there, she pulled back the covers, then got out his pajamas.

"I'm going to step out of the room," she told the boy. "You get changed. I'll take your clothes to the laundry while you get into bed."

More tears filled his eyes. "Don't go, Callie."

"I'm going to be right in the hallway. I'll talk to you the whole time." No way she was staying in the room while he got undressed. Her crime had nothing to do with children, but she didn't want any misunderstandings.

She knew she was probably overreacting, but she couldn't help herself. Everything about the situation made her uncomfortable. She barely knew these people and there was no way they would understand.

She stepped into the hallway. "Where does your mom keep the thermometer?" she asked through the closed door.

"In the hallway closet."

"Great. I'll get it and we can see what's going on."

They talked for another minute then Noah said he was changed. She went back into the room and got him into bed.

His face was flushed and his skin was clammy. The kid obviously had a fever, so a bug rather than food poisoning, she thought. Maybe some kind of stomach flu.

She found the thermometer. It was the kind she could run across his forehead. His temperature was 101. She knew that was higher than normal but wasn't sure if it was just a little bad or if it was very, very bad.

"Your mom said there was ginger ale in

the refrigerator. Why don't I get a little and we'll see if you can sip that? It might make you feel better."

Noah nodded listlessly.

Callie grabbed the clothes and hurried out of the room. She put his things on the washer before heading downstairs to the kitchen where she found the soda and poured some over ice. She was shaking a little herself, but her reaction had nothing to do with being sick — instead she was terrified that Noah was worse off than she realized. When that was added to her general worry, it was not a happy combination.

She got back in time for Noah to throw up again. He managed to avoid himself but totally got the sheets. He started to cry again.

She got him out of bed and onto the window seat, then wrapped his comforter around him. He huddled there while she changed the sheets. She got him back into bed and handed him the drink. He took a sip. They both waited for a second, then he took a second one.

"That's really good," he said. "But I'll drink slow."

"I think that's smart. Let me get rid of the sheets. I'll be right back."

"Don't be long."

"I won't. I promise."

She ran downstairs, dumped the sheets on the washer, then hurried back only to find Noah had set the glass on his nightstand and was now asleep. She watched him for a few seconds before backing out of the room. She would wait at the top of the stairs — that way she could hear him if he woke up.

What seemed like hours later but was probably less than twenty minutes, the front door opened and Santiago's mother raced into the house. Callie went downstairs to greet her.

"How is he?" Enriqua asked.

"Sleeping. I checked on him five minutes ago and he's still asleep. He's thrown up twice since I picked him up. Once outside and again in his bed. I changed the sheets and put the dirty ones on the washer."

Callie wrung her hands together. "When I picked him up at school, I used the safe word, then we took an Uber here because I don't have my license yet. You can verify the trip with the driver. When we got here, Noah changed into his pajamas while I waited out in the hall. I wasn't in his room with him at all."

She knew she was talking too fast, but she couldn't seem to stop herself. Her eyes began to burn.

"I took his temperature and it's 101. I don't know how bad that is."

"It's not too high," Enriqua assured her. "We'll monitor him. I'm sure he'll bounce back quickly. You're the one I'm worried about. What's wrong, Callie? You seem upset."

"I know. I'm sorry it was me. I mean I want to help but it shouldn't have been me."

Santiago's mother shook her head. "Why would you say that? Callie, what's going on?"

"Nothing. It's not anything, except it's everything and I never wanted you to know or not like me anymore. Not that I'm saying you like me now, it's just your family is so nice and Santiago is, well, you know what he's like and I didn't mean . . ."

Enriqua's eyes were kind as she touched Callie's arm. "I have no idea what you're talking about."

Callie swallowed against the rising bile in her throat. "I'm a convicted felon. I served nearly six years in Oklahoma." Callie quickly explained the circumstances and how she'd moved to Texas when she got out and was allowed to leave the state.

"I never did anything like that again. I'm not a bad person. I just want to start over and be normal."

Enriqua's expression was impossible to read. "How long have you been out?" she asked.

"Three years." She felt tears in her eyes.

No! She didn't cry — she couldn't be weak. She couldn't. Only suddenly she couldn't stop them.

Without thinking, she turned and ran. Ran from the wonderful woman in front of her, ran from the house, ran from what could have been with Santiago. She ran until she couldn't take another step, then she sat on the curb and gave in to the tears.

Callie worked an extra hour to make up for some of the time she'd been gone. Vern had told her to make up the second hour tomorrow. She would have argued but she was so exhausted, she could barely function. She took the bus home and once in the house, she went upstairs.

It was Tuesday so Keira was eating out with Malcolm before he took her to her therapy session. Carmen had taken Grandfather Alberto to a dinner with some old friends of his. She had the house to herself — something for which she could be grateful.

After checking on Lizzy, who was sleeping in the center of Keira's bed, Callie retreated to her own room where she stood for several minutes, trying to decide what to do. No, that wasn't true. She was trying to figure out if Santiago knew yet or not. Because it was just a matter of time until his mother told him. Until she told the whole family.

She twisted her fingers together and tried to ignore her growing sense of dread as she admitted she was going to lose them all. Not that she knew Hanna and the kids all that well, but still, she'd liked them. And his mother was so warm and friendly and she always made Callie feel special. What would Paulo do? Would he tell everyone at the warehouse? What would people say when they found out the truth about her?

She thought of her work friends and how much she enjoyed their company. What would change? Would she be forced to quit? Only she was Malcolm's sister and according to the lawyer, part owner of the business, so could she be fired?

All the thoughts and questions swirled in her head, making her feel dizzy. But no matter how much she worried and writhed and fought emotion, one key issue kept rising to the surface.

What would happen when Santiago found out?

She hadn't wanted to go out with him,

hadn't believed he was real. Only she had given in and he was and he'd won her over with his sexy brand of seduction. When she saw him, her heart was all happy and her body went on alert and sometimes, just sometimes, she allowed herself to think that maybe she was getting a second chance at a decent life. That maybe things could work out. Only now it was all lost and she had no one but herself to blame. If she'd been honest from the beginning, she wouldn't be sweating this now.

Which all sounded so great and mature but didn't do anything to help her figure out what to do next.

Her phone buzzed to alert her to a text. Panic chilled her, making her want to run and hide, but she forced herself to pick up the phone and read the screen.

Can we talk?

The text was from Santiago. Her shoulders slumped as she thought about the best way to answer him.

He obviously knew — otherwise why would he be asking that? He was always about saying hi and being flirty or making plans. No guy with nothing on his mind wanted to talk.

I don't think that's a good idea.

Cowardly, she thought, but right now she was in self-preservation mode.

I'm at your front door.

She sighed. Of course he was. Because that was her life.

Instead of replying, she went downstairs and opened the front door. Sure enough, Santiago stood there, looking all tall and handsome in his perfect suit. For once, he wasn't smiling — instead he looked concerned.

"Are you all right?" he asked, stunning her with the question.

"What do you mean?"

He stepped inside and she closed the door.

"I talked to my mom and she said I needed to speak to you. She wouldn't tell me why. I know Noah was sick, I got Hanna's message too late to help. He's doing better, by the way. His fever has dropped a little. So what's up?"

He sounded so caring, she thought sadly. So worried about her. Why hadn't Enriqua simply told him the truth instead of forcing Callie to do it? Or maybe this was his mother's way of punishing her.

No, Callie thought. That didn't feel right. Regardless, she was totally and completely screwed.

"I have something to tell you," she said. "I'm going to say a bunch of stuff and I want you to be quiet until I'm done. I mean that — no questions, nothing. Just listen. Then you can ask whatever you want or leave or call me names. But until I'm done, you have to just listen."

He tilted his head. "Callie, there's nothing you could say that would make me want to call you names."

"You think that now." She drew in a breath and tried to brace herself, then began to explain about her past. She told him about her high school boyfriend and the prank that had turned into a horrifying, life-changing event. She didn't go into detail, but she didn't gloss over the important parts, either.

"Malcolm knows," she said as she wrapped things up. "Keira, and Grandfather Alberto. No one else. I asked Malcolm not to tell anyone. I didn't want to be judged by my past. You probably think I don't deserve that."

He'd watched her attentively the whole time, his dark eyes giving nothing away. She didn't know if he wanted to spit on her or hug her. Okay, the hugging was unlikely, but she honestly had no idea what he was thinking.

"It's been three years," she added, trying not to sound desperate. "Three years of doing the right thing, of being the person I'm supposed to be. And while I know I'm okay, there are still restrictions. For the rest of my life, I will be a convicted felon." She dropped her gaze to the floor. "I probably should have told you before. And I felt awful about Hanna and her not knowing."

She raised her gaze. "But I was really careful with Noah and I took care of him and . . ."

She had nothing else to say, she thought sadly. There weren't any words to convince him that she was worthy and while in time she would get her mad on and convince herself that if he didn't see that she deserved to be judged on who she was today and not on her eighteen-year-old self, then he wasn't someone she wanted in her life.

But that time wasn't now and at this minute, she felt sick to her stomach as the realization she was going to lose him forever sank in.

"That's all," she said. "I'm done."

"That's a lot." He rubbed his face. "I wasn't expecting anything like that. I don't know what to say." His mouth straightened. "Don't take this wrong, but I need some time to process all this. Is that okay?"

No. No, it wasn't. Only she couldn't say that. So she nodded and walked to the door. He walked out without saying a word and he didn't once look back.

Callie crossed the foyer and sat on the bottom stair. She wrapped her arms around herself and began to rock back and forth. No tears, she promised herself. Not now. She was going to be strong. She was going to hold it all together.

She had no idea how long she sat there, breathing and telling herself she would get through it. She was in the middle of trying to convince herself she had to eat something when someone knocked on the door. She was stunned to find Santiago standing there.

"Okay," he said, looking at her. "I've thought about it." He smiled. "I'm in."

"Wh-what?"

He walked into the house and shut the door. After cupping her face in his hands, he kissed her. "I'm in. You screwed up and you paid a hell of a price. But I've seen how you are with the people around you. I hear how Malcolm talks about you and your relationship with Keira. Before I came over here, my mom confused the hell out of me by telling me everyone deserves a second chance. Now I know what she was talking about."

He kissed her again, his lips lingering on hers.

Disbelief made it difficult for her to feel anything. Then the warmth of his mouth cut through the fog and she became intensely aware of the man and his nearness. She wanted to throw herself at him, hanging on so tight she never had to let go. Instead she stepped back. She had to be sure.

"You're perfectly fine with my past? You can know about it and let it go?"

"Yes."

"Are you ever going to throw it in my face?"

"Nope. Not my style."

"What about your family? Are they going to be okay with this?"

"My mom is. I'm sure Hanna and Paulo will feel the same way. I don't think the kids need to know." He smiled. "You were involved with robbing a liquor store, not a child pornography ring. There's a huge difference. A dozen kids I know stole stuff in high school. You got caught and you paid a big price. I'm sorry for that, but it's done and you've moved on. I'm ready to do the same."

He was too good to be true, she thought, dazed by everything that had happened. She didn't know what to think, what to believe. All she could hang on to was the fact that it wasn't over with Santiago.

She threw herself at him. He caught her and held her tight.

"Thank you," she whispered.

He touched the bottom of her chin, forcing her to look up at him.

"Callie, you're special to me. I wish you could believe that."

"I'm trying."

"Good. Now do you want to get some dinner?"

Just like that, she thought in amazement. Things were back to normal.

"I'd love to. Let me get changed. I only need a few minutes."

"I'll wait down here. Oh, and later I want to talk to you about the charity gala we're going to in a few weeks. The company is one of the big sponsors." He winked. "I'll be in a tux, so you'll want to brace yourself."

She grinned. "To withstand all that manly goodness?"

"I am pretty impressive."

Tears threatened again. She blinked them

away before raising herself up on her toes and kissing him.

"You are most impressive. That's what I tell all my friends. We talk about you and then we swoon."

He chuckled. "I get that a lot."

She was still laughing as she raced up the stairs. Yet more weight was lifted from her shoulders. Normal, it seemed, might finally be possible.

CHAPTER TWENTY-TWO

Santiago walked into Malcolm's office around ten. His friend and boss was on the computer. Santiago sat in one of the visitor chairs and waited until Malcolm had saved his work.

Malcolm finished typing, then turned to him. "What's up?"

"I thought we could talk for a second."

Malcolm glanced toward the open door. "Need that closed?"

"Good idea."

Santiago shut it, then returned to his seat. He thought about all that had happened the previous day — how Noah had gotten sick and Callie had pitched in only to find herself needing to confess the truth about her past.

He'd been shocked — who wouldn't be — but he realized the knowledge didn't change anything. He'd seen her around enough people to have a sense of who she was inside. Everybody screwed up — the difference was she'd been forced to pay in a huge way. And she had. She wasn't angry or bitter or jaded. Instead she'd learned and moved on.

"You didn't tell me about Callie's past."

Malcolm's gaze flickered slightly but otherwise he didn't give anything away. "She asked me not to. How did you find out?"

"She told me."

"And?"

"I thought about it for a few minutes, but it doesn't matter to me. I accept her for who she is. What about you? Is what happened before the reason you were so reluctant to accept her?"

Malcolm leaned back in his chair. "Partially. Maybe. I'm not sure. Keira was different. She's a kid, but Callie is a grown woman with a life and a future. I guess I was suspicious and reluctant to trust her."

"And now?"

"She's growing on me."

"Me, too."

Santiago told Malcolm what had happened the previous day and how the truth had come out.

"What did your mom say?" Malcolm asked.

"That everyone deserves a second

chance."

Malcolm grinned. "That sounds like her. Did you tell Hanna and Paulo?"

Santiago hesitated. "My mom is going to. Hanna has a right to know, because of the kids, but I don't think she'll care. I'm more concerned about Paulo." He had a feeling he couldn't fully define.

"You think he'll tell people at the warehouse?"

"I don't know. Maybe. It's just something. I guess I don't have a choice. Mom isn't going to ask Hanna to keep secrets from her husband." Not only was it not right, they were already having problems. He didn't want to contribute to that. "I'll talk to Callie before I do anything. Oh, and I asked Callie to the gala."

"You expect me to have a problem with that?"

"Just checking."

"She's my sister, Santiago. There's no problem."

Santiago grinned. "About time you started thinking like that."

Callie logged into Keira's school's website and went to the section for parents. She and Malcolm had agreed she would take care of checking on things like assignments and

415

ongoing projects while Malcolm handled the therapy end of things.

She scrolled through the notes from the various teachers and read the entries. They were all variations on a theme.

Keira is doing much better in class. She's more outgoing and frequently volunteers answers rather than being asked. She talked to me about our outreach program for students transferring in.

"All good news," Callie murmured quietly, trying to remember the last time her sister had screamed in her sleep. It had been at least a couple of weeks, maybe longer. Keira was finally starting to feel at home.

Callie could relate to her difficulties in finding her way. She was twice Keira's age and there were times she wasn't sure what to make of her new circumstances. Santiago's acceptance of her past still left her breathless. She enjoyed her work and the people she met there and she was starting to think about crazy things, like maybe going on to get her bachelor's degree. Not that she would ever compete with Malcolm but she thought maybe that if she really did own a significant part of the company, she should get a business degree so she could understand more than the basket assembly line.

She returned her attention to the computer screen and noticed an alert. When she clicked on it, there was a request to confirm Keira's personal information including contact info. Callie followed the link and confirmed the phone numbers and the address. She was about to log off the page when she saw a date that drove her to her feet.

"What? How could I not know this?"

She double-checked, then thought about all the times Keira had mentioned being "almost thirteen." No wonder. Her birthday was in two weeks. What if she hadn't seen the information? Did Malcolm know his sister's birthday? Did anyone?

She logged out of the program, then went to find her brother. He was just walking out of his bedroom when she entered his study.

"I need to talk to you," she said. "It's about Keira."

"I'm having dinner with Delaney. Let me text her that I'm going to be a few minutes late."

Callie had the strangest urge to hug him. A few weeks ago he would have said he didn't have time right now and that they could speak later. They'd all come a long way.

"This will only take a second. Keira's

birthday is in two weeks. She's going to be thirteen."

His frown confirmed he hadn't known, either.

"We are so getting a family calendar," she told him. "We're going to put on all the birthdays and any other big events. We act like we're roommates, not family."

"You're right and that's a good idea. So what should we do for Keira's birthday? Have a party?"

"Let me ask her," Callie said. "I don't want to do too much or too little. She always has a clear idea of what she wants in any given situation." She smiled. "I'm hoping she wants a party. That would be fun to plan."

"How can I help?"

She smiled at him. "Let me talk to Keira and I'll let you know. While I appreciate the thought, I'm not sure a party for a girl turning thirteen is going to be exactly your area of expertise."

"I'd still like to be involved."

"Good for you. Okay, I'm off to talk to Keira. Tell Delaney hi for me."

"I will."

Callie went back down the hall and knocked on Keira's open door, then walked in the room.

"It's me."

"I'm here."

Callie walked into the playroom and found Keira sprawled on the sofa, her schoolbooks scattered on the floor.

"I have two quizzes this week," she said with a dramatic sigh. "My life is pain."

Callie scooped up Lizzy and sat in one of the chairs. "I'm sure that's true. Let me distract you with a question. It's your birthday in a couple of weeks."

Keira sat up. "That's not a question."

"See how smart you are?" Callie stroked the purring kitten. "I didn't know it was your birthday until just now. I'm glad I found out because I wouldn't want to have missed it."

Keira's eyes were hopeful, but her body language warned she was still wary. "Okay, again no question."

Callie gentled her voice. "I think a party would be fun. What do you think?"

Keira relaxed. "Really? A party for me?"

"You seem to be the birthday girl."

"I know but I've never had a party."

A simple sentence that cut Callie to her heart. She wanted to ask how that was possible. Surely her mother had . . . only Keira's mother had never bothered.

"Then it's past time," Callie told her. "I

need you to think about how many friends you want to have and what kind of party. Maybe a sleepover?"

"No, I don't think so. I'm not ready for that."

"Then how about something in the afternoon followed by a family dinner?"

Keira beamed at her. "That sounds perfect. I love it. Yes, let's do that. I have five friends I'd like to invite. So there will be six of us. That's enough for this year. Maybe next year I'll have a sleepover."

"It's a date. Do you want to talk about what kind of party? I mean like a theme?"

Keira wrinkled her nose. "Surprise me. I trust you to make it right."

Callie wondered if that was the real reason Keira didn't want to brainstorm her own party, or was she afraid that if she asked for too much it would all be taken away? She thought about the preteen sleeping in her closet because the room was too big and how she was terrified of being abandoned yet again.

"I have a million ideas," Callie said confidently. "You'll see. It's going to be fabulous. You and your friends will be talking about it for weeks."

She stood and was surprised when Keira

jumped to her feet and ran over to hug her tight.

"Thank you," her sister whispered fiercely. "For all of it."

"I haven't done anything yet."

"I know, but you will."

Saturday morning Delaney practically danced to the front door. She pulled it open and laughed.

"I'm ridiculously excited," she admitted as Callie entered. "And I have no idea why."

"Parties are fun. Plus, it's Keira, so what's not to be excited about?"

Delaney wondered if there was more to it for her. She was caught up in some weird space-time continuum where some days seem to last forever and others just sped by. She was confused, unsettled and way too emotional. When Malcolm had mentioned Keira's upcoming birthday and the fact that Callie was planning a party, she'd had to get involved.

"Thanks for letting me help," Delaney said as they walked into her living room. "I'll do anything. Seriously. I can blow up balloons or run errands. I just want to be a part of this."

"I appreciate the offer," Callie told her as they sat at the sofa. She looked around the room. "This is really a nice place. Have you lived here long?"

"A few years now."

Callie's eyes widened in surprise. "Oh. I thought maybe . . ." Her voice trailed off. "It is really nice."

Delaney didn't bother pointing out Callie was repeating herself, nor did she try to justify why her condo looked as if she'd just moved in. There were a thousand reasons, none of them easy to deal with.

"I'm sorry," Callie said, looking at her. "It's just you're such a vibrant, alive person. Your home doesn't reflect that."

Vibrant and alive? Delaney had never thought of herself that way. Or maybe she had once, but not anymore.

"Time got away from me," she admitted. "I always meant to do more. Or something." She shook her head. "Okay, let's ignore the sterile white walls and focus on what's important. Keira's party." She thought for a second. "I've never planned a party for a thirteen-year-old and I have no idea where to start."

"That's okay. I did a lot of research. I love Pinterest. There are so many great ideas, plus I used to work for a caterer, so I've seen what works and what doesn't. I hope it's okay, but I have some notes."

"Let's see them."

Callie pulled several folders out of her backpack and opened the first one.

"I think we should start with the theme. I went round and round, playing with several ideas and I settled on jewelry."

Delaney had no idea how that would work as a theme, but she was hardly an expert. "What does that mean?"

Callie laid out several pictures. "We'll do the traditional 'official teenager' cake. I think that's pretty much required. I found a woman online who makes beautiful, inexpensive jewelry and she does home classes. She'll use glass beads and braided thread, so it's not too expensive. The goody bag can be filled with the usual lip gloss and stuff but also some jewelry-making supplies."

She showed Delaney several pictures of cute goody bags.

"I'm thinking if Keira and her friends *do* something together, it will help form a bond between them. That they'll feel closer and have something they've shared together. You know, to cement the friendship."

"Wow. You've really thought about this," Delaney said, studying the various pictures. "It's a brilliant idea. And hey, don't worry about the cost. Malcolm will be happy to write a check for his baby sister."

She didn't mention the guilt that drove him, but knew it would be a part of why he would agree. He was really working the program when it came to his sister. She admired that about him, among other things. Everyone was moving forward, she thought wistfully. Everyone had a direction and a goal.

"We've got to be careful with the food," Callie continued. "Nothing too greasy because of the jewelry."

"Right. We don't want to ruin the supplies."

They brainstormed different food ideas then finalized the decorations. Keira had provided them with her guest list, so it was easy to go online and design a fun invitation. Three hours later they had the party planned and the tasks divided.

As Callie packed up her papers, she glanced at Delaney. "Did Malcolm tell you I'd been in prison?"

Delaney was sure she hadn't heard correctly. "I'm sorry, what?"

Callie smiled. "Prison. And I can tell by your face that the answer is no. I swear, he annoys me all the time, but he's very good at keeping a secret. Everyone else knows, so I thought you'd want to, as well."

Delaney hoped she didn't look as shocked as she felt. "No one likes to be the last to know," she said, trying for a light tone.

"It's okay," Callie told her. "Most people are surprised." She explained how she'd robbed a liquor store with her boyfriend and the consequences of her actions.

"I was living in Houston when the lawyer found me," she said. "She swabbed my cheek and now I'm here."

"But you're so . . ." Delaney pressed her lips together, not sure what she was supposed to say. "Normal" certainly wasn't very polite.

"On the outside, I do look like everyone else," Callie said. "On the inside, I'm a little more shattered. I wish I could go back and change what I did, but I can't. I can only move forward and learn from my mistakes." She paused. "Keira knows, so you don't have to worry about saying anything."

Delaney still had trouble wrapping her mind around the information. "Thank you for trusting me. I won't say anything to anyone."

"Thanks, but I'm starting to wonder if it's worth keeping a secret. I haven't decided, but maybe I should make some big announcement on social media."

"Let me know how that goes."

Callie laughed and collected her things. "I'll text you later about the cake," she said. "If there are options, I'll want your opinion."

"You've got it."

Delaney walked her to the door, then turned back to the now-empty condo. She still had homework to do and grocery shopping. Her bathroom needed a good scrub. It wasn't as if she wasn't busy. Even so, she lingered in her tiny foyer, staring at her boring living room and thinking about Callie.

For someone who had gone through something awful, Callie was so upbeat. She could have been angry or bitter or resentful, but she wasn't. She accepted responsibility for what she'd done and then moved on. Everyone, it seemed, had moved on.

Delaney sank to the floor and wondered what on earth she was doing. Was she really going to be a doctor? Yes, the medical personnel who had helped her dad had been amazing, but really? A doctor? She'd barely gotten through a frog dissection. Plus, she'd loved her work at Boeing. She'd liked the people and the company. She'd dreamed of moving up the corporate ladder. She'd only quit because . . . because . . .

Because of Tim, she thought, leaning her head against the wall and closing her eyes.

Because he'd never been happy with her choices and she felt guilty. He'd thought she should care more about them than getting ahead. He'd thought she should be happy just being his wife and living close to where they'd grown up. He'd never understood why she'd wanted more and she'd never understood why he hadn't. They'd been at an impasse and the wedding had been getting closer and closer and she'd felt trapped and then he'd been killed.

She didn't remember much about those early days. She supposed she'd been in shock from the trauma. There had been so much to deal with and her time had been dominated by the terror that she might lose her father, as well. It had been weeks before they'd known he was going to make it, and every single day she'd waited, someone from her old neighborhood had been there for her. She'd never had to deal with any of it alone.

Everyone had talked about Tim and how much he'd loved her. They'd talked about her dad. They were her extended family and what they'd never realized was that her dreams had started to take her beyond the confines of their street and that Tim had never approved of that.

Was she the one who was wrong or was

427

he? She couldn't ever figure that out. Even now, he was the voice in her head, telling her to be . . . less.

No, she thought. That wasn't right or fair. Not less, just other than who she was. To be how she'd been before. To be right for him. Somehow everyone had moved on but her and she didn't know if that was because she wasn't allowed to or if she simply wasn't capable. One thing she knew for sure — as long as he was the voice in her head, she was stuck with one foot in the past. Until that changed, she simply couldn't move forward.

She opened her eyes and tried to fight against the familiar sense of dread. She was lost and confused and scared and angry and sad, all at the same time. She wanted to stand up and scream or maybe just run. If she could start over where no one knew her, things would be easier.

She forced herself to her feet and looked at her living room. The white walls, the bland furniture.

"Dammit, no!"

She grabbed her purse and headed out.

Delaney returned an hour later with a can of pale sage-colored paint, brushes, rollers and a tarp. She shoved her sofa to the center of the room, moved tables and lamps, then taped off the baseboard and ceiling. One wall, she told herself. She would paint one wall. *Then* she would get on with the rest of what she had to do.

She used a brush to do the edging, then pressed the roller to the wall in a big W pattern and nearly gasped as the color came to life. It was darker than she'd expected, but still pretty. Indecision and fear tried to take hold, but she kept painting. Her heart raced, her stomach twisted, but she kept moving her arm up and down, filling the paint when she needed to.

She worked straight through, stopping only to drink some water. When the job was done, she stepped back and looked at the fresh color.

It was beautiful, she thought in surprise. She liked it a lot. This was good — she was moving on. But as she stood there, the wall got blurry and seemed to shift a little. It was only then she realized she was crying and, honest to God, she had no idea why.

CHAPTER TWENTY-THREE

Malcolm looked at the sample Callie had made, then at the six acrylic tumblers on the table in front of them. The project was simple enough — use different colors of nail polish to put dots on the clear material to make the glasses more festive. Easy enough, he thought, reminding himself he had an MBA. There was no way he should be intimidated by a simple craft project.

"Just start," Callie said, her voice filled with humor. "Otherwise, you'll psych yourself out."

"I'm fine," he told her, then opened the first bottle. He dabbed polish on a piece of white paper, realized there was too much polish, then scraped the brush against the side of the bottle and tried again. When he had figured out how much polish he needed on the brush, he lined up the glasses and applied eight dots of Aphrodite's Pink Nightie to each glass.

"Who comes up with these color names?" he asked.

"It's OPI. They're known for great polish and fun names." She pointed to the half dozen bottles on the kitchen table. "Those are from the classics collection."

"If you say so."

They'd taken over the kitchen and given Keira orders not to even think about peeking. While he decorated glasses, Callie was putting together photographs into a collage in the shape of 13. The finished project would be big enough to hang on the wall.

Callie and Delaney had handled all the details of the party, invitations had been sent out and five girls had accepted. Malcolm didn't know if that was a good number or not, but both Callie and Keira were pleased, so he was going to assume all was well.

He finished the first color and picked up the next bottle. Chick Flick Cherry. Obviously fashion wasn't his thing.

"You're looking fierce," Callie said.

"I don't want to mess up." He carefully applied eight dots to each of the glasses. "And I'm intense, not fierce."

"If you say so."

"There's a difference."

She laughed. "So you seem determined to

have me realize."

"Fierce can be scary. Intense is more positive."

"You sound like a self-help book."

"I'm sure we both need to read more of them."

He spoke without thinking then braced himself for some kind of backlash. When there was only silence, he glanced over at Callie and found her studying him.

"I get you thinking I need help, but you're willing to admit it for yourself?"

He reached for the next bottle. "*Do You Lilac It?* That's cute, and yes, I could probably use a lifetime of therapy. It's not going to happen, but I'm trying to do better. Reach out to the people I care about, pay more attention to Keira. Not assume that people who come to me with interesting ideas don't know what they're talking about."

"If that last one is about me, don't sweat it. It was just an idea and you're running a huge company. I should have done some research first. It's not the idea that changes the world, it's the execution."

He motioned to all the party supplies filling the counters. "You are creative and you have a vision. I'm the one putting nail polish dots on glasses."

"If you do a good job, I'm going to let you glue fake gemstones onto plastic flatware. If you can handle that small task, then and only then will you be allowed to glue the ornaments on the little jewelry boxes that will serve as the goody bags."

"If only that could be true."

She grinned. "Goals are important."

He liked this, he thought. Just hanging out with Callie. She was funny and smart and as he'd said — she was highly creative.

"At the risk of having you take away the flatware reward, do you ever think about going to college?"

She glued the last picture on the collage, then stepped back to study the effect.

"Sometimes. I was able to take a couple of classes toward my AA while I was incarcerated. I'd always hoped to keep going with my degree, but my short-term goal was to save enough money to buy a condo."

"You didn't like renting?"

She sprayed some kind of clear coat onto the collage, then capped the can. "When you get an apartment, there's an application. One of the boxes you have to check is whether or not you're a felon. Imagine how many people want you in their building after you check yes. I found rooms to rent. The applications were simpler and when I said I paid in cash, I was usually given a chance."

He kept his attention on the task at hand, not sure what to say. In the back of his mind, he thought he'd read something about how hard it was for felons to return to regular life, but until he'd met Callie, he hadn't thought about it.

"Is Washington State easier for you than Texas?" he asked.

"It's less restrictive. There are still things I can't do, but none of them affect me personally."

He glanced at her. "You own a third of this house, Callie. You don't have to worry about paying rent. If you want to work, go ahead, but if you want to think about going back to college, you should. I'd be happy to help you with the application. Oh, and tuition qualifies as an expense you can pull out of the trust, so you wouldn't have to work to pay for it."

She walked over to the stack of bags by the entrance to the kitchen and grabbed two of them, along with a small wooden crate about two feet square.

"I still have trouble believing any of what you're saying. Not because you're saying it," she added quickly. "I mean the part about having money and a home. It's new to me."

"I know, but it's all true. You're family." A word he was becoming more comfortable with, he thought. "I wish I could have met your mom."

"Me, too. If she were still alive . . ." Her voice trailed off. "I would have liked her to know I wasn't still screwed up."

"You were never screwed up. You made a mistake. There's a big difference."

She set a half dozen stuffed dogs on the counter. They were cute and fluffy and made absolutely no sense.

"I thought the theme was jewelry," he said. "Where do the stuffed dogs fit in?"

"They don't. They're going to be a surprise parting gift. They'll be in the crate by the door when the girls leave. I'll make a sign that says 'Adopt a dog.' "

"Nice."

"I hope Keira thinks so."

He capped the last bottle of polish. "I'm done with these. Have I earned my way into gluing?"

"You have."

They both moved to the other side of the large kitchen table. Callie had already set out the plastic forks, knives and spoons, along with a glue gun and bowls filled with plastic gemstones.

She pointed to the pile of plastic flatware.

"Start at the bottom. Blue, yellow, pink, clear. Don't burn yourself. Glue burns hurt."

"Don't all burns hurt?"

She slapped his arm. "You can be so annoying."

"No way. You adore me."

"Maybe. A little. On a good day."

An unexpected warmth seemed to fill his chest. It took him a second to realize it was affection for the blue-eyed blonde who was his sister. Somehow he'd gone from dislike to ambivalence to something a more self-actualized man might be willing to admit was very close to love.

Damn — how had that happened?

Without considering there might be consequences, he pulled Callie close to him. For a second, she resisted his embrace. Her arms hung stiffly at her side. Then she relaxed a little and hugged him back.

They stayed like that for two, maybe three seconds before pulling apart. Malcolm felt foolish and uncomfortable, which kind of matched his sister's expression.

"Awkward," she murmured.

"But nice."

She glanced at him. Her mouth turned up in a smile. "Yes, nice."

"We'll keep practicing until we get it right."

"I'd like that."

"Me, too."

Delaney arrived at The Grill a few minutes before her lunch date. She started to give her name to the hostess only to spot Chelsea waving at her from a table in the back.

"I got here early," Chelsea said with a laugh as they greeted each other. "Thanks for meeting me. It's been forever since we've seen each other."

"I know. Time is slipping by."

Delaney took a seat across from her friend. When Chelsea had texted her a couple of days ago, she'd actually hesitated before agreeing to the lunch. She was still fighting a sense of unease — not with anything in particular, but maybe with everything. But now, as she started to relax, she wondered if staying isolated was only exacerbating the problem.

Chelsea leaned forward and lowered her voice. "I say let's be wild and have a glass of wine with lunch."

"I think that's an excellent plan. How did you get the day free?"

"Isaac's cousins are visiting. The ones that live in Virginia." She tucked a strand of dark hair behind her ear. "It's so sad how much they wanted kids, but she can't have them or something and adopting is a nightmare because of his cancer. Anyway, they want to be with our kids 24/7 and hey, I'm not going to say no. We've always talked about sending them back East for a few weeks in the summer. We're seriously considering it with the two older ones. We'll see. This visit is a trial run."

"I can't believe they're that old already." Delaney remembered when her friend had first been pregnant. She did the math in her head and realized Chelsea's oldest had to be close to nine.

"It seems like only yesterday that we were in high school," Delaney admitted.

"Tell me about it." Chelsea motioned to the restaurant. "Remember when my mom would bring us here for special occasions? But it had to be extra special, like getting As or something." She sighed. "Then, when we were teenagers, we would walk through the store and pretend we could afford to buy all the pretty clothes. Good times."

"They were."

Their server stopped by the table. They each ordered a glass of chardonnay.

"I'll have the Shrimp and Crab Louis," Chelsea said.

"The BLT salad for me."

"This is nice," Chelsea said. "Remember when it was the four of us? You and Tim and me and Isaac? That was the best."

"It was a long time ago."

"Was it? Sometimes it feels like Tim was here just yesterday. Do you ever get that feeling?"

Delaney told herself Chelsea didn't mean anything by her comment, that there wasn't a hidden message saying it was too soon to have her own life. But the words made her uncomfortable. They were familiar, as was the sense of being trapped. So many of her friends and neighbors had talked about him being such a huge part of her life. She'd been told over and over again that she could never find anyone like him.

Delaney got that they'd been in pain, too, and she had missed Tim desperately. It was just, with him gone like that, she'd started to realize how stuck she'd felt.

"It's been eighteen months," Delaney said. "That's a long time."

"I know, but you started dating him in high school." Chelsea sighed. "I guess it's different for you. You had other things to distract you."

"You mean like my dad? That was so hard."

She shook her head. "I meant your job and your other life. Isaac and the kids are all I have. If I lost one of them, I would never get over it. I'd never be able to move on."

Delaney held in the need to snap that Chelsea had no idea what she would or wouldn't do. That she'd never suffered on that level. She told herself that she wasn't being judged, no matter how it felt.

"You're strong," Delaney said lightly. "But I hope you never have to lose anyone you care about."

Chelsea shot her a look Delaney couldn't read.

"How's school?" her friend asked.

"Difficult. Good. I'm wondering if I'm doing the right thing. I'm less excited about being a doctor than I'd expected. I miss working for Boeing."

"So go back to it."

"I'm not sure it's that simple." Would they take her back? She would have lost whatever momentum she'd had in her career, but maybe she could make that up.

"So you're still not willing to be one of us," Chelsea said, her tone light but her gaze sharp.

"What do you mean?"

"You're not talking about finding someone

and getting married, then popping out a few kids."

"Just five minutes ago you said I should feel like Tim is still with me."

"No, I didn't. Why would you say that?"

"Because that's how it sounded to me. Like everyone wants me to stay in the past."

"You can do whatever you want," Chelsea told her. "You always have."

"What does that mean?"

"Just that you've changed so much."

"Me? What about you?"

"I'm who I've always been. The rest of us stayed in the neighborhood, got married and had a family. Not you. You had to go get your fancy degree, then a fancy job. Look at the car you drive. For that much money, I could add two bedrooms onto my house."

Delaney didn't understand what was happening. "Why does my car have anything to do with your house?"

"You're different. Our dreams were never good enough for you."

Their server returned with their glasses of wine. Delaney ignored hers while Chelsea took a big swallow.

"You always looked down on me for having kids so young," she continued. "You treated me like I was stupid."

"That is so unfair." Delaney noticed people looking at them and consciously lowered her voice. "It's also not true. I never judged you. I wanted something different but that doesn't mean I didn't respect you or your choices. You're the one who pulled away. You're the one who stopped being my friend when I didn't want what you wanted. You could talk for hours about being pregnant or having a newborn but you had no interest in me. You didn't want to hear about my work or any of it."

"You didn't love him anymore," Chelsea said loudly. "We could all see it. You stopped loving him and you were going to marry him anyway."

Heat seared Delaney's face and humiliation held her immobile. She tried to speak, tried to breathe, but she couldn't. Several patrons looked at her, then glanced away.

"He was a great guy," Chelsea said, leaning toward her, her brown eyes bright with anger. "He loved you with everything he had, but it wasn't enough. Not for you. And you know what's ironic, because hey, even without going to college, I can still use ironic in a sentence. What's ironic is all the time you wondered if he was good enough for you, we all knew it was the other way around. You weren't good enough for him."

442

She tossed her napkin on the table and stood. "Go to hell, Delaney."

With that she turned and walked out. Their server walked up with two salads on huge plates.

"Shall I box these up?" she asked.

CHAPTER TWENTY-FOUR

Malcolm watched the last of the partygoers head out the door. The afternoon had been a success. He'd stayed in the kitchen and out of the way through the event, but he'd been close enough to hear that everyone got along and that the theme had been a hit.

"You and Callie outdid yourselves," he told Delaney. "Thank you for all your help."

She gave him a smile that didn't reach her eyes. She'd been quiet ever since she'd arrived and he'd had the feeling something had happened.

For at least the third time he asked, "Are you all right?"

"I didn't want to say anything before, but I've had a headache all day. I guess I thought it would go away, but it hasn't. Would it be all right if I gave Keira my regrets and ducked out of the family dinner?"

"Of course," he said automatically, even

as his mind flashed back to all the excuses Rachel had given him throughout their relationship. There was always something going on, something she had to be doing. At the time he'd believed her. It was only when he caught her in bed with his father that he'd realized how much she'd been lying to him.

Delaney wasn't Rachel, he reminded himself. She was open and honest and he had no reason not to trust her. He'd avoided entanglements since the breakup, isolating himself too much. Someone wonderful had caught his attention and he wasn't going to blow it by acting like a jerk. His issues were his business, not hers.

"Let me drive you home. Carmen can follow in your car. It will only take a few minutes."

For a second he thought she was going to cry, but instead she moved toward him. He automatically pulled her close.

"Thank you," she whispered. "You're very good to me. I'm not sure I deserve it."

He lightly kissed her. "Of course you do. I'm sorry about the headache. I wish you'd said something before."

"I didn't want to take away from the party. And while I appreciate the offer to drive, I'm okay." She squeezed his arms before stepping back. "I'll go have a word with the birthday girl, then slip out." She paused by the door. "Call me in the morning?"

"You call me," he said. "I wouldn't want to wake you if you're sleeping in."

"Thank you, Malcolm. I'll talk to you tomorrow."

She headed upstairs for a few minutes. When she returned, she got her coat off a bench in the pantry, then walked out. He escorted her to the front door, kissed her again, then watched her leave. Something was wrong — he was sure of it. While he wanted to run after her and insist she tell him what it was, the more sensible section of his brain said to give her time. When she was ready to talk, she would.

The decision made but not fully accepted, he joined Callie in the living room where the presents from the family were piled high on the coffee table as they prepared for round two.

"Is Carmen still sulking?" Callie asked, her voice teasing.

"She gave me a stern talking-to," he admitted, thinking of how the housekeeper had scolded him for arranging for dinner to be brought in. "She explained that next time I was to *ask* before hiring a caterer."

He had a sudden thought that the women

446

in his life were starting to confuse the hell out of him. "I was only trying to help. You and she made all the food for the party. I thought she might like a break."

"I know your heart is in the right place, but she wants to be a part of Keira's birthday celebration."

"She is a part of it. She made the cake."

Callie flashed him a look that said he was incredibly stupid, then smiled. "If you say so."

"Women," he muttered.

"Men," she said, mocking his tone. "Do you think they're sleeping together?"

Malcolm stared at her. "If you're trying to distract me, you're doing a good job. Do I think who is sleeping with whom?"

"Grandfather Alberto and Carmen. Keira thinks they are and she knows stuff."

Mercifully, his mind went blank because those were not images he wanted to remember. "No. Just no. And we're not asking."

"I wouldn't ask. I just wondered. Carmen's a lot younger, but our grandfather is still a vital, handsome man. It would be nice to think people still had sex at that age. You know, for when we're older."

"He's your grandfather. Grandparent sex is inherently uncomfortable to think about."

She grinned. "Technically he *is* my grandfather, but I haven't known him long enough to feel the family connection. To me he's just a lovely older man who may or may not be doing the wild thing with his housekeeper and best friend. You, on the other hand, are now overwhelmed with a vague icky feeling. My work here is done."

"You're not a nice person."

Callie laughed. "That may be true. Now help me get the drinks. Everyone will be ready in a few minutes."

They went into the kitchen where the caterer and her staff were already at work. Keira had gone upstairs to put away the birthday presents her friends had given her and Carmen was with . . . Malcolm winced. Carmen was with his grandfather. Were they more than friends? Did he want to know?

He carried a bottle of wine and four glasses into the living room, along with Keira's favorite Lavender Dry Sparkling Soda. Callie brought in a tray with mini quiches on them.

"I'm not sure Keira ate much at the party. There was so much going on. I know I'm starving." She offered him the tray.

He took a mushroom cheese quiche, then set the tray next to the drinks.

Keira raced into the room. "That was the

best party ever," she told him. "I had a great time."

"I'm glad. Thirteen is an important birthday."

"I know. In three years I get to drive."

"Not something we're going to talk about tonight," Grandfather Alberto said as he and Carmen walked into the living room. "I want you to wait to grow up."

"I'm not sure I can help it," Keira said, rushing to him.

Malcolm did his best not to overmonitor his grandfather. So what if he was —

He silently swore at Callie for saying something. Worse, he knew she'd done it on purpose — just to mess with him. They'd gotten to know each other well enough for him to see she had a wicked sense of humor and could certainly hold her own. She was fierce when necessary and she cared deeply about Keira.

He knew she was seeing Santiago and he hoped that went well. Funny how when they'd first gone out, he'd been worried about Santiago getting involved with her. As time went on, he found himself more and more concerned about Callie instead.

"We'd better get started," Grandfather Alberto said. "You have a big pile of presents to get through and then we'll have dinner."

Carmen glared at Malcolm. "Yes, I saw the caterer is here."

"I'm sorry," Malcolm told her. "I will never hire a caterer again without talking to you."

Keira laughed. "You're in big trouble."

"Tell me about it."

Keira looked at the pile of presents. "That's a lot," she said, her smile fading a little. "Where do you want me to start?"

"With mine," Grandfather Alberto said, pointing to a huge box leaning against the coffee table. "I picked it out myself."

Keira knelt next to the box and began to tear at the paper. Malcolm had no idea what it was until she sat back and grinned at her grandfather.

"For real?"

Malcolm stared at the picture of a guitar on the box. His heart sank. That was going to be noisy and he was only a hallway from Keira's room.

Callie leaned close. "Stop looking so stricken. It's electric and there are headphones."

"You're starting to scare me with your ability to read me."

"I should hope so." She sipped her wine.

The next present was a gift certificate for lessons. Keira ran over to her grandfather.

"This is exactly what I was hoping for."

What? Keira wanted to learn to play the guitar? Why didn't he know that? She never talked about it. Or had she and had he not listened?

The present reveal continued. Lizzy — no doubt with help from Callie or Carmen — had given Keira a subscription to *Teen Vogue,* with a request for cuddling while Keira read the magazine. Carmen's gifts included some weird kind of floppy curler that one could sleep in, along with a stack of books and certificates to teach Keira how to make tamales, spaghetti sauce from scratch and pie crust. She reached for his presents next.

She studied the box then looked at him. "Textbooks?" she asked, shaking a large box. "Nope. Not heavy enough."

She ripped the paper and stared at the picture of the girly, pink sleeping bag. He'd been inspired by her new friendships and had figured sleepovers were just around the corner. He'd gone online to find the pinkest sleeping bag he could find. But as Keira stared at the box, her face fell.

She turned to him. "How could you?" Her voice shook and tears spilled down her cheeks. She jumped to her feet. "So when you throw me out, I'll have a place to sleep?"

The accusation was so unexpected and stunning, he couldn't think of how to respond. "What? No. Keira, it's for sleepovers." He fought embarrassment and shame, although he knew he hadn't done anything wrong.

"I got you games and slumber party *Mad Libs,* as well. For your friends."

Callie leaned over and squeezed his arm. "Keira, honey, you need to calm down."

She was crying harder now, barely able to catch her breath. "You don't get to tell me what to do. None of you do. I hate you all. I hate you!"

The last words were a scream. The tears turned into sobs as she ran out of the room. When she was gone, no one said anything for a long time.

Carmen sighed. "She's overtired, Malcolm. She doesn't mean it."

He was less sure. "I bought her games," he repeated.

His grandfather looked at him. "She knows. She'll pull herself together and be fine. You'll see."

"I'll go after her," Callie said as she stood. "I think we need to just hug it out."

Malcolm excused himself as well, but instead of following Callie, he went into his study and closed the door. He felt sick and confused. He had no idea what had gone wrong or how to fix it. He reached for his phone to call Delaney only to remember she wasn't feeling well.

"Hell in a handbasket," he muttered to himself. "Hell in a handbasket."

About nine that night Callie stepped into the hallway and drew in a breath. The meltdown was over and Keira was asleep, Lizzy curled up next to her. Callie felt exhausted and wanted nothing more than to crawl into bed and pull the covers over her head, but she still had one more thing to do.

Carmen had checked in earlier to get an update, and Callie had asked her to tell Grandfather Alberto Keira was feeling better, which left only Malcolm.

She walked the few steps to his half-open door, knocked once and then entered. Malcolm was at his computer. He looked up at her and motioned to a chair.

"Someone is stealing at work," he said. "It's been going on for a few months now. Santiago and I can't figure out how they're doing it."

Stealing? "What department?"

"Dry soup and drink mixes."

"I'm there now." She didn't mean to

453

sound defensive, but that was how it came out anyway.

"It started happening long before you got here, Callie, and even if it hadn't, I still wouldn't think it was you."

"Thanks."

She sat down across from him and leaned back against the chair. "I'm exhausted."

"I'll bet. How is she?"

"Sleeping." She straightened and looked at him. "She feels awful."

"That makes two of us."

"Are you mad at her?"

"No. Hurt. Baffled. I don't know what I did wrong."

"Nothing. You did nothing wrong, Malcolm. It was all too much for her. Her first party, then the big family dinner. All the presents, us, she was overwhelmed. She's still a kid and she doesn't have a lot of coping skills. She held it together for as long as she could and then things kind of exploded."

"At me." He pressed his lips together. "Sorry. I realize she's the one we're talking about."

"But you got the brunt of it, I know. It's hard. On the bright side, she thinks it's safe to yell at you, so that's progress."

He raised his eyebrows. "How is that progress?"

She smiled. "Keira trusts you enough to be mad at you. She made you the focus of her meltdown."

"Or it could mean I'm the one who matters the least."

"You need to look on the bright side."

"You do it for me."

She felt bad for him. She knew things had been rocky with Keira, but Malcolm was trying.

"She's going to apologize to you in the morning," she told him, then paused. "There are going to be ups and downs. She's had a tough time."

"I know that. I just wish I knew she was adjusting. I want her to be happy. I want her to feel safe. This is her home and we're her family."

"It would really help if you told her that when you see her."

"I will. Thanks for taking care of her."

"It's easy. She's my sister."

And Malcolm was her brother. Why was connecting with Keira so natural, and bonding with him was more challenging? She thought maybe age had something to do with it. Keira was a kid and Malcolm was a grown man who could be intimidating.

His gaze sharpened. "How are you adjusting?"

She smiled. "I'm doing okay and I promise not to cry if you give me a present on my birthday."

"Even if it's a sleeping bag?"

"Malcolm, no. It was a really thoughtful gift."

"Apparently not." He drew in a breath. "Are you happy at work?"

"I am. The people are great." She wrinkled her nose. "There is a huge difference between the basket department and where I am now. There everything was computerized. The dry goods area is so primitive."

"A remodel is coming. We'll be able to mechanize much of the work and keep tighter controls on the inventory." He tapped his laptop. "It will be harder for people to steal, which might be why the thefts have increased. They're doing their best while they still can." He shook his head. "Sorry. I didn't mean to get into that. We were talking about you. Have you thought any more about college?"

She laughed. "We talked two days ago. It takes me longer than that to do my research." She paused as she wrestled with the truth. "I'm going to download an application. I do want to get a degree. I have an opportunity here and I want to take advantage of that."

What she really meant was according to the lawyer, a third of the company was hers. One day she would like to be higher up the food chain. Malcolm would always run the firm — he'd been a part of things for years — but she would like to be involved. She wanted to be confident and educated and successful.

"Let me know how I can help."

"Thank you. I will." She started to stand, then flopped back in the chair. "Okay, I have a question."

Malcolm waited.

She shifted her weight. "There's some gala charity thing," she said in a rush. "Santiago invited me and I said yes, only I don't know anything about it and I looked online and it's really fancy and kind of scares me so maybe I should tell him I've changed my mind."

He made a couple of clucking noises.

"Not fair!" she protested. "Come on. I'm not like you. I didn't grow up in this house. I'm just some kid from —"

"A perfectly normal upbringing," he said. "Your mom was great, you've told me so yourself. There's no reason you can't fit in and have a great time."

She thought about the pictures she'd seen online. "Do you know what those women are wearing?" she demanded. "Fancy dresses and stuff. There's *dancing*. Like real dancing."

His mouth twitched. "And you don't know how?"

She felt herself getting angry and even though she knew it was a self-protective mechanism, she still wanted to yell at him. Instead she forced herself to speak calmly. "It wasn't a required class in prison, so no. I don't know how to dance."

"I appreciate your restraint."

"What are you talking about?"

He winked. "I was sure you were going to throw something at me."

"I wanted to." She slumped in her seat. "I'd like to go and I'm scared. There. I said it."

"It's just a fancy dinner with a bunch of people who care about a cause."

"Rich people."

"They still pee every single day. Sometimes more than once." He leaned toward her. "Santiago will take care of you."

He was right about that, she thought. Santiago would be there for her. "There's still the dancing. Can I take lessons or something?"

"I'm sure you can, but you don't need to. Santiago does a very basic box step. I've seen him."

"For a second I thought you were going to say you've danced with him."

He ignored that and stood, then walked over and held out his hand. She stared at him in confusion, then shook her head. "No. No, no, no. You are not teaching me to dance."

He pulled her to her feet. "You are all attitude with absolutely no backbone. It's not hard. This will take ten minutes. We'll practice a couple of times and you'll be fine."

He led her out into the hallway. "Basic box step," he repeated. "Whoever invented dancing hated women so I step forward and you step back." He thought for a second. "There are maybe six steps."

He moved next to her. "Watch my feet. I'm doing the man part, so you'll be going in reverse."

"In high heels," she muttered. "Okay, show me."

He walked through the steps a couple of times. She watched intently, then stepped in front of him.

"On four," he said, before counting. He took a step forward, she moved back, concentrating on what they were doing.

"My right, your left." His voice was steady.

Callie felt stiff and awkward and she stepped on his foot twice but the third time through it was easier. By the fifth, she was ready for music.

He found a song on his phone and set it on a nearby windowsill, then they began to dance in the wide hallway.

"See," he said after a few minutes. "Not so hard." He kissed her forehead. "You'll do great. And if something bad happens, give me the high sign and I'll spill my drink as a distraction."

She wanted to say something snarky back to him, or maybe just thank him, but she couldn't talk. At least not without bursting into tears, and no one wanted that. Malcolm had endured enough trauma for one day.

She gave him her best smile, willed herself to be strong. "I appreciate the lesson."

"You're welcome. We'll practice again in a couple of days."

She nodded and retreated to her room. Once there, she sat on the edge of her bed. From all she'd heard, her biological father had been a thoughtless jerk who used and abandoned women. Callie should hate him. Only she couldn't. If it wasn't for him, she wouldn't have Malcolm as her brother and she was starting to think having him around was worth a whole lot.

Delaney tried to act normal as she sat through Sunday brunch with her dad and Beryl, but it was difficult. She was still tired and conflicted and upset and confused and a host of other emotions she couldn't begin to name. Her fight with Chelsea — because she didn't know what else to call it — haunted her. Sometimes she blamed her friend entirely and sometimes she admitted she was just as responsible.

"Delaney, are you all right?" Beryl asked as they washed dishes. "You've been quiet all day."

Delaney glanced toward the family room where her father was watching a baseball game.

"I'm tired and maybe a little out of sorts."

"Is college too difficult? You've already done it once, I'm not sure why you have to go back." Beryl smiled at her. "I do admire your drive, however. A doctor. That's a long road."

"I don't know if I want to do that any-more," Delaney admitted, rinsing plates before putting them in the dishwasher. "I thought I did, but now I'm not sure. You're right — it's a very long commitment and if

I'm not sure . . ."

She pressed her lips together. "I just don't know what to do. Chelsea said —" She stopped herself. She couldn't be completely honest about that!

"I'm so glad you two are spending time together again," Beryl told her warmly. "You used to be good friends. I'd worried you'd had a falling-out."

"We didn't. Not exactly. It's just our lives are so different. She's married with kids and I'm, well, I'm on another path."

"If only Tim hadn't died." Beryl's voice thickened. "Of course that would have changed everything. I miss him so much. I know you do, as well."

"Of course."

Her answer was automatic but was it true? Tim had been a huge part of her life. For years she'd been half of a couple and everyone had assumed they would always be together. Even her, at least at first.

Chelsea's stinging words echoed. Had everyone really known she hadn't been in love with him anymore? Had he? She didn't want to think that, didn't want him to have guessed she wasn't sure.

"I would have had grandchildren by now," Beryl mused. "I always wanted grandchildren."

Delaney felt her control slipping. "I sometimes think no one wants me to move on," she blurted. "We always talk about Tim."

"Why wouldn't we? He was important to both of us. Delaney, honey, I don't understand."

She knew she had to be careful. Beryl was one of the sweetest people Delaney knew, and she was engaged to Phil. This was one relationship Delaney couldn't walk away from. She was going to have to —

The truth smacked her upside the head, leaving her dazed. No, she told herself, even as she wondered. She didn't walk away from relationships. She didn't! She had a lot of friends and she'd been with Tim forever and there were others.

Only there weren't. She hadn't bothered to stay in touch with her work friends after the shooting. They'd reached out over and over again, wanting to help and be with her as she dealt with the aftermath of the awful nightmare. Even when she'd gone back to work, she hadn't been the same. She'd pushed them so far away, they'd stopped trying to get closer.

She'd done the same with Chelsea, avoiding her, not returning her calls until they weren't really friends anymore. When she looked back on her life, she saw a pattern of leaving people behind, just as she'd been left all those years ago when the pretend moms had gone back to their homes, leaving her behind.

"Delaney, honey, what's wrong?"

"Nothing." She felt the heavy brunch sitting uneasily in her stomach. "I suddenly don't feel well. I need to go."

"Of course. You head home. I'll tell your dad." Beryl hugged her. "If there's anything I can do, you'll let me know, won't you?"

"Yes. Thank you. I'm sorry. I'll be in touch when I feel better."

Delaney hurried out of the house and to her car. She felt trapped and exposed and had a desperate need to go to ground. She drove to her condo as quickly as she could, parked, then raced into her apartment and locked the door behind her. Then she sank onto the floor and pulled her knees to her chest.

What was wrong with her? Why was she feeling all these uncomfortable emotions? She didn't want to think she was a bad person, but she couldn't seem to escape that uncomfortable truth. No, not bad, she thought. Shallow. Uncaring. She wasn't evil, but apparently she tossed the people in her life aside whenever things got tough. *Just the way she'd tossed her career aside.*

Delaney leaned back against the door and closed her eyes. Had she done that? Thrown away her career? She'd wanted to do something different. Had needed to make a change. But why? She allowed her mind to slip back to that horrible time. Her father was finally coming home from months in the hospital and rehab, she was exhausted and could barely function. Tim had been gone almost three months and she was still trying to accept the fact that she would never see him again.

She remembered feeling so much sadness over what had happened and relief that she still had her dad. Everyone on their street had been so supportive, which she'd appreciated, but she'd also felt . . . trapped.

Trapped by their kindness and expectations. Trapped by how everyone always talked about Tim. She'd needed to escape, only there'd been nowhere to go.

What was it Chelsea had said? That Delaney had wanted different dreams. That was true. She'd always wanted to escape the small world that was their neighborhood. She'd wanted to be successful and have an exciting career and she'd been willing to do the work to get it.

Chelsea hadn't understood, nor had Tim. He fought her every step of the way. Because of her, they'd delayed getting married and he'd resented that while she'd felt guilty.

She knew that somehow those elements of her past were all tied up together. Her friends from childhood, her decision to have a career, being good at her job, disappointing Tim and finally her fear that she really didn't love him anymore.

Chelsea had screamed that at her, Delaney thought, wincing. Had she been right? Did everyone know? Had Tim known?

She hoped not. She didn't want him to have thought that she didn't love him. Only she wasn't sure she still had. They'd become different people and the truth was, if he wasn't making her happy, she doubted he was very excited about being with her.

So why had they stayed together? Habit? Expectation? Maybe they'd both been stuck. Maybe they'd both been overwhelmed by it all. But weeks from getting married hadn't seemed like the time to discuss the problems in their relationship. A stupid decision, she thought now, but one she'd believed in at the time. Then disaster had struck and she'd been hanging on by a thread and then she'd tried to go back to her old life and she hadn't felt right there either and now here she was. Working part-time in a coffee kiosk and going to college for a degree she was pretty sure she didn't want.

"I'm a mess," she whispered, opening her eyes. "A complete and total mess." Information that was interesting but not particularly helpful. If she wasn't going to be a doctor then why was she studying biology? And if she didn't want a different degree, then shouldn't she get off her ass and use the one she had?

She only had questions and not a single answer. There was nowhere to go, no one to talk to. She was completely and totally alone and the sucky part was, she had only herself to blame.

CHAPTER TWENTY-FIVE

Malcolm waited until Sunday afternoon to seek out Keira. Since the outburst the previous night, she'd kept to her room. Carmen had said she'd been down early for breakfast, but then had retreated upstairs. Malcolm wasn't sure if she needed the alone time or if she was scared to face the rest of the family.

A little after three he knocked on her door. There was a second of silence before he heard the soft, "Come in."

He found Keira on the floor by her bed. There were no books around, no TV on, no music playing. Just her, Lizzy and a feather cat toy.

When Keira looked up at him, he saw shadows under her eyes. She was pale and her mouth trembled. He had no idea what she was thinking or feeling, but her sadness and remorse were so clearly visible, he couldn't think of anything to say and he had no idea what to do.

He was incredibly bad at this, he thought grimly. And the last man on the planet who should ever have a family. He swore silently before telling himself any action was better than simply standing and staring at her.

He dropped next to her on the rug and put his arm around her. Keira startled him by throwing herself at him and bursting into tears.

"I'm sorry," she sobbed, hanging on with more strength than he would have imagined. "I'm sorry."

"Shh. There's nothing to be sorry about."

He picked her up and set her on his lap, then eased her head onto his shoulder. She hung on as if she would never let go and he did the same. After a few minutes, when the tears had lessened and her breathing was more normal, he freed one hand and stroked her head.

"It's our fault," he told her. "We should have thought about the day more. A party like that is a big deal and it takes a lot of emotional energy. You're still finding your way around here. We should have moved the family dinner to tonight, giving you a chance to recharge. It's not you, Keira. Even good things can be too much."

"Callie said that, too," Keira admitted

with a sniff. "She apologized, just like you."

The tears began again and he had no idea why. He wished Callie was here instead of him. He wished his mother had lived longer because she was the best person he'd ever known. He wished his father hadn't been such an asshole because that would have helped. His father who had never once bothered to even sit down and talk to his own son.

"I'm really bad at this," he admitted. "I'm sorry about that, too."

She raised her head and sniffed. "You mean being a brother?"

"Yes."

"You're not bad at it. Just, you know, inexperienced." She shifted off his lap onto the floor and brushed the tears from her face. "You should practice more."

"Yes, I should." He leaned toward her. "Keira, I don't want you to be scared anymore. I want you to be happy and feel safe and excited about your life."

She glanced down, then back at him. "I do sometimes. Not feel scared, I mean. And the other stuff. I'm getting better."

"You don't need to get better. There's nothing wrong with you."

"But I'm in therapy."

"So you have someone to talk to who is

safe for you. So you can learn coping skills you might have missed out on because of all you've been through." He struggled to find the right analogy. "It's like painting a couple of walls in the house rather than tearing the whole thing down and starting over."

She tilted her head. "Am I the paint or the wall or the house?"

"You're the house and the therapy is the paint and okay, maybe it wasn't the best way to explain what I meant, but I hope you —"

She flung herself at him again. He held on to her because he didn't have anything else. Hopefully it was enough.

When she released him and sat back down, she drew in a breath.

"I really am sorry about yesterday. The sleeping bag was a really nice idea."

"I'm glad you're okay with it. Do you want to try the family dinner again? There are more presents to open and I'm sure Carmen would be happy to fix something special for dinner. All the while telling me that she could have done that in the first place, but no, I had to go hire a caterer and if that ever happens again, she is going to be very angry with me."

Keira giggled. "She would probably slap you."

"She'd try and I'd have to let her, which I would not like. So do-over?"

She nodded. "Yes, please." Her expression shifted from happy to stricken. "Did you guys eat my cake?"

"No one touched your cake. It's still there, in all its glory."

"Whew, because that would have been horrible." She scrambled to her feet. "Come on, Malcolm. We have to go tell everybody there's going to be a party tonight!"

Delaney spent the next week avoiding both her life and the people in it. She went through the motions, showing up to her job, going to class, texting with Malcolm. She'd put him off for a couple of days only to realize she missed him desperately. She'd invited him over for basically a booty call and he'd obliged with great enthusiasm. What was there not to like? But by the weekend, she'd figured out that avoiding wasn't going to fix the problem. Not that she'd defined the problem exactly but it was on her to-do list, right there at the top.

At eleven on Saturday morning, Callie arrived for their shopping adventure. She'd begged for help finding a dress for the upcoming charity gala.

"I come bearing addresses of consignment stores," Callie said as she walked into the condo. "I am not paying retail for a dress I'm going to wear once in my life."

Callie's natural energy and upbeat personality lifted Delaney's spirits. She laughed for the first time in what felt like ages.

"You do realize that you're kind of an heiress, right?"

Callie rolled her eyes. "Oh, please. I work on a factory line pouring tablespoons of secret spice mix into plastic bags, then sealing them."

"You're the one who wanted to work."

"I know and it was the right decision. I would go crazy cooped up in that big house. I need to be out doing something." She studied Delaney. "How are you feeling? Malcolm said you caught a bug."

Which was what she'd told him when he'd asked about her spending so many evenings at home, Delaney thought, ignoring the guilt. She hadn't been sick from anything but trying to figure out her life. Going to work and to class had taken every ounce of energy she had.

"I'm getting my strength back," she lied. "Okay, the gala. Let me show you what kind of dress we're going to be looking for, then we will start our consignment store bonanza."

She led the way into the bedroom and walked to the larger of the two closets. As she reached for the door handle, she mentally braced herself to step into her former existence. She flipped on the light and took a breath, then allowed herself to breathe in the happy sight of suits and shells and dresses and dozens of shoes.

"Holy crap." Callie stared at the neatly arranged racks. "What is all this? You have a secret life I knew nothing about."

"I used to be in corporate finance."

"Like Santiago?" Callie groaned. "Everyone I know is so smart and successful. I know it should be inspiring, but it's a little intimidating."

"I work part-time as a barista and I'm taking two classes at college. I'm hardly an inspiration to anyone."

"You're wrong. You wanted to change your life and you did. That's amazing."

It was less amazing when you knew that she wasn't sure she'd made the right decision, Delaney thought glumly.

"Dress," she said pointedly. "Let's look at those to give you some ideas. Although honestly all you have to do is flash a little something-something and you'll do fine."

She wrinkled her nose. "I'd offer to let you borrow one of mine, but you're what, twenty pounds lighter, two inches shorter and yet you have bigger boobs. Why do I like you?"

Callie laughed. "Well, when you put it like that, I have to feel special."

Delaney walked over to the dress section of the closet. "Okay, here's one of my favorites. I wore this two years ago to the Seattle Humane Society's Tuxes and Tails event." She held up the St. John velvet cold shoulder gown.

Callie touched the fabric, then studied how the straps would drape across the upper arm. "That's really lovely. So a long dress?"

"You'll see all lengths, but most will be long. The guys have it easy. They only have to wear a tux."

She got out a second dress that still had its tags. Deep green sequins covered the knit column style. The V-neck was flattering and the straps were wide enough that she could easily wear a regular bra.

"Oh, that's beautiful," Callie breathed. "Have you ever worn it before?"

Delaney waved the tags. "Not even once. I need like five kinds of shapewear to make it work, but maybe I'll try it for the gala."

"You should. With your red hair and green eyes, you'll be stunning. Seriously. Okay — I sort of have an idea of what I'll be looking for. I really appreciate you going with me. I would be nervous on my own. I'm still nervous about the whole evening, but I figure it will be a good life experience for me."

"Don't be nervous. You'll do fine. Malcolm and I are at the same table and you'll be with Santiago."

Callie looked away. "Yes, that will be great."

Delaney's radar went on alert. "What's wrong? Are you two fighting?"

"No! It's fine. Everything is . . ." Callie put her hands on her hips. "Actually it's not. I can't figure him out. He acts like he's crazy about me."

"How is that bad?"

"It's not. It's wonderful except he won't, I mean we haven't . . ." She closed her eyes, then opened them. "We kiss. That's it. Kissing. He doesn't even try to take things further and I don't get it. From everything he's told me he was a total skank with women, so why not me?"

Delaney did her best to look serious even as she desperately wanted to laugh. "You're mad because you're not getting any?"

"It's been nearly a decade. I think I've earned the right to be moody."

"Oh, right. Good point. So ask him. Or rip off your shirt. Either way, he'll figure it out."

Callie sighed. "I'm not really the rip-my-shirt-off type. I guess I'll have to talk to him and that totally sucks." She brightened. "Maybe I can find a really slutty dress that will make me impossible to resist."

"You absolutely will be."

They drove to the first consignment store. Delaney scanned the layout, then headed directly to the back where the evening gowns were.

"Don't worry about length," she said as she began to flip through the dresses. "I know a great tailor who can work miracles in very little time."

She checked sizes and pulled out several dresses, studying them before handing some to Callie and putting the others back. Ten minutes later, she ushered Callie into the dressing room with firm instructions to come out in every one.

"You're not the decision-maker here," Delaney informed her. "I'm the expert."

"You're kind of bossy."

"Tell me about it."

While Callie changed into the first dress,

Delaney wandered the store. She was having fun, she thought in surprise. Her dark mood had lifted. Maybe she should have gotten out of the house sooner. She still didn't have answers to her questions, but for now, that was okay.

Callie came out in a fairly traditional strapless black dress that hugged every curve.

"I feel like the top is going to fall down," Callie said, tugging at the bodice. "I'd need a strapless bra, I guess. I don't know."

Delaney eyed her critically. "It's okay, but not special. Next."

"You're just like Keira," Callie told her. "You should have seen her when we went shopping. She made her decision in about two seconds and what I thought didn't matter."

Delaney grinned. "I knew I liked that girl."

Callie tried on every dress Delaney had picked for her. There were a couple of maybes but not *the one.* They went to the second store and repeated the process. On the third dress, Delaney smiled at her friend.

"That's it."

The "it" was a strapless gown that was fitted to midthigh before flaring out slightly. The wrapped fabric hugged every curve, but the effect was softened by an overlay of mesh dotted with black flower petals. The fit was perfect and with the right shoes, the hem only had to come up a couple of inches.

Delaney circled her. "You'll need a great strapless bra. I have the name of someone in the lingerie department at Nordstrom. She'll get you fitted."

Callie looked at herself in the mirror. "It's not very sexy. I mean it's not low cut or anything."

"Trust me," Delaney told her. "You are stunning. How do you feel?"

"I don't know. It's not really me."

Delaney had a feeling Callie wouldn't be comfortable in any fancy dress. Given what she knew about her friend's past, she doubted Callie had ever worn one before.

Callie looked at the tag and yelped. "Oh my God! This dress is six hundred dollars. That's used."

Delaney grinned. "Honey, it's a Carmen Marc Valvo couture gown. It would have cost over three thousand new."

"For a dress? One dress?"

"You want to look the part."

"But for that I could go to a department store and buy something new." She looked at herself in the mirror. "It is really pretty."

"It is."

"But six hundred dollars."

"Are you going to faint? Do you need to breathe into a paper bag?"

"Very funny. All right. I'll take it. But don't tell anyone how much I spent."

"I cross my heart."

Callie smiled at her. "Thank you, Delaney. You're so sweet to me. I really appreciate it."

"You're easy to be friends with."

Callie returned to the dressing room. Delaney looked out the window as she waited and thought about the other friends she'd had — the ones she'd let slip away. She was still trying to figure out why. Guilt, maybe? Her payment for having what she wanted? She wasn't sure if she had a clue, but what she did know was that she was desperately unhappy with how things were and she wanted to change. As it was her life, it was all up to her. But how, and more importantly, did she actually have the courage and strength to do it?

Santiago didn't like being nervous — it was an unfamiliar state of being and one he didn't generally permit. But as he rode the elevator up to his place, Callie at his side, he had to admit, there was general unease going on.

It was her, he admitted if only to himself.

Being around her always made him happy and he wanted things to work out. Maybe a little too much, which meant worrying they wouldn't, which created a crazy cycle of wanting desperately to be with her, then being nervous when he was. Life had been a lot easier when he'd cared less about the women he was with. But this was a whole new ball game. This was Callie.

She laughed as the doors opened on his floor. "I think that's the longest elevator ride I've ever taken."

"We should go to the Space Needle. You take an elevator up to the observation deck where, if the weather's good, you can see forever. This was only thirty-eight stories or about four hundred feet. The observation deck is at five hundred and twenty feet."

"You are filled with unexpected information, aren't you?"

"It's a gift."

He led the way to his front door, then opened it and let her go first.

He'd tidied up before he left. The cleaning service had been by that week, so every surface gleamed. He'd already prepped dinner. Appetizers were ready to go into the oven, the salad only needed dressing and his mother's famous potato casserole would bake after he pulled the appetizers out. He was going to panfry the salmon, something he'd done dozens of times. It was an easy entrée he often made for himself and he hoped Callie would like it.

He waited in the foyer as she explored the condo's open floor plan. The unit was on the corner, so he had a 180-degree view of Puget Sound. There was a beautiful sunset on the horizon, ferryboats heading to and from the dock, and a massive container ship heading out to sea. He couldn't have asked for a more perfect moment.

Callie looked around the big living room with its leather sectional and matching club chairs. The tables were all glass and chrome, the art bold, colorful abstracts. He'd left the integrated sound system on and jazz played in the background.

An area in the corner was raised slightly. He'd put the dining room table there. It, too, was glass and chrome. He'd used pale linens, bought fresh flowers for the table and had set a high-end chardonnay on ice. He'd done his best to impress at every turn yet couldn't shake the feeling he'd somehow done it all wrong.

"You hate it," he said as Callie crossed to the window to study the view.

"What? No. I'm overwhelmed. Your place is beautiful. Very modern with clean lines.

The view is incredible." She smiled. "Did you order the sunset just for me?"

"I did."

"Must be nice to have that much power. I'm not sure I could handle the responsibility."

He chuckled. "You get used to it."

He crossed to her and stood behind her, his arms around her waist. She leaned back against him.

They touched from chest to thigh, but it was the middle part that got his attention. Her ass nestled right up against his dick and he liked it. A lot.

No, he told himself firmly. No way. He was not going there with Callie — not for a while yet. He wanted them to get to know each other better. He wanted things solid and for their time together to be special. Sex was easy — it was relationships that were a bitch.

"How long have you lived here?" she asked.

"A couple of years."

"You bought the houses for your mom and your brother and his family first, didn't you?"

"Why would you ask that?"

She turned in his arms and smiled up at him. "Because you have a hero complex.

Not in a bad way, I don't think. More that you have to take care of everyone around you. So family first."

He thought she might be complimenting him, but he wasn't sure. A lot of women he'd dated had complained about how much he was there for his family.

"Two houses on an oversize lot don't come on the market very often. When I saw those, it made sense to buy them first."

She put her hands on his chest. Heat burned down to his groin. He had to use all of his considerable willpower to keep himself from reacting physically to her touch.

"Uh-huh." She raised herself on tiptoe and lightly kissed his mouth. "You're a softy."

"I'm not sure I like that. Can't I have a superhero name?"

"King Softy? Super Softy?"

He winced. "We're moving in the wrong direction." As his control snapped and blood rushed to his groin, he took a step back so she wouldn't feel his sudden erection. He needed distance and a distraction.

"I have appetizers. Let's get them in the oven."

"Let's."

They went into the kitchen. Callie prowled around, checking out the various stainless steel appliances and reading labels in his small wine cellar.

"It's like something out of a magazine," she said as she slid onto one of the stools at the island. "I didn't know people really lived like this." She smiled at him. "I say that very aware of the irony. I mean, look where I live."

"It's a family home."

"It's the size of an airplane hangar. Still, there's a warmth there. And the yard is huge."

"It would be a great place to raise kids."

Her eyes widened. "I never thought of that, but sure."

He slid the cookie sheet into the oven and set the timer, then collected ingredients for martinis.

"Vodka okay?" he asked.

"Um, sure."

There was something in her tone that alerted him to a problem. "You don't like martinis? I can make something else. What would make you happy?"

She flushed as her gaze slipped from his. She seemed to collect herself after a second. Her shoulders squared and her chin went up.

"I've never had a martini," she admitted. "I don't know if I like them or not."

He swore silently. He was an ass. Of course she hadn't — when would she have had the chance? She'd gone to prison when she'd been eighteen and got out three years ago. Since then she'd been scrambling to keep her head above water. There hadn't been extra money for things like martinis.

He walked around the island, spun the stool until she was facing him, then cupped her face in his hands and kissed her. He moved deliberately, brushing her mouth with his before running his tongue along her bottom lip. She parted insistently, inviting him to the party. Her hands settled on his waist.

He gave himself a full twenty seconds to enjoy the lushness of her mouth before carefully, deliberately releasing her. His dick throbbed like a son of a bitch. Relief would have to wait, he told himself. Until he was alone.

"Your past made you what you are today," he told her. "I'm more and more impressed every time I'm with you. I do forget that there must be a lot of things that are new to you. I hope you know I'm not put off by that. In fact, I want to share as much as I can with you."

Her eyes got big and her mouth trembled

slightly. "Will it be shaken or stirred?" she asked.

He grinned and walked around to continue making the drinks. "True aficionados will tell you shaking the martini bruises it and it is always preferable to stir the liquor in the ice."

"And you?"

"No pain, no gain."

She laughed, then leaned forward to watch what he did.

"How are the driving lessons going?" he asked.

"Really well. I'm getting more confident. I'll be taking my test soon. I just need a few more hours of practice."

"I'd be happy to take you out."

"Yeah, that's not happening. I know what you drive. Your Escalade is the size of a building and the little convertible costs as much as a building. I'm okay with my small, sensible training car."

"You seem a little obsessed with buildings."

"Maybe it's because of the one I'm in."

He finished shaking the drinks and filled two glasses, then handed her one. "Tell me what you think."

She took a sip. "Oh, it's not what I thought. It's really clean and a lot of liquor."

"We'll just have one."

"I like it." She raised her glass. "This is good practice for when we go to the gala. I don't want to be obviously out of place."

"Why would you be?"

"I'm a small-town girl from Oklahoma. Events like these aren't part of my regular routine."

He was pleased she'd talked about herself in that way rather than defining herself by her incarceration. She was so much more than the mistake she'd made.

"Now if it were a potluck on the line at work, I'd be one of the gang," she said with a smile.

"Still liking your job?"

"Yes." She hesitated. "I've made my decision."

"About?"

"Going to college. Malcolm's helping me with the application. I hope I get into the University of Washington. It's a great school." She glanced at him out of the corner of her eyes. "I could wear a Huskies jersey for you sometime."

He didn't think she was trying to be provocative, but her teasing words hit him hard, all the same. A jersey and nothing else, he thought, trying to keep his breathing even.

"I'll stay where I am at the company until I start school, but if I get in, I'm going to go full-time."

"Smart and beautiful. How'd I get so lucky?"

"I think you always get lucky. This is not a unique experience, but thank you for the compliment."

They went into the living room. He set their glasses on the coffee table, sat down and pulled her onto his lap. She snuggled into him, cuddling close before raising her mouth to his.

Just five minutes, he told himself. He could stand it for five minutes and then he was going to stop.

Everything went according to plan right up until Callie unexpectedly shifted so she was straddling him. The heat from her center enveloped his erection, making it tough to breathe. Or not start ripping off clothing. Or bury himself so deep he would never find his way back.

"What's with the kissing?" she asked.

"What do you mean? Don't you like it?"

"I like it fine. I like it a lot. But that's all we do." Her gaze was pointed. "Kiss. There's plenty more we could be doing. You seem to like me and find me attractive, so what's the problem?"

She was so damned direct — how was he supposed to resist her? Still, he had to. Their future depended on it.

He carefully moved her onto the sofa, then stood and put some distance between them. He'd thought they might have to have this conversation but he'd never imagined she would be the one insisting they talk about it.

He cleared his throat. "There have been a lot of women in my past," he began.

"Yes, I know. You keep rubbing that in."

"I'm not rubbing it in. I'm trying to be honest."

"I honestly wish you'd stop talking and have your way with me." She stood and put her hands on her hips. "What? *What?* Is there a medical condition? Do you secretly play for the other team? What is it?"

"I want it to be special."

She snorted. "What does that mean? Are we waiting for an eclipse?"

"No, although that would be really cool." He tried to figure out how to articulate what he was feeling. "You're the princess," he finally admitted. "You need to be won."

She muttered something that sounded a lot like, "What I need is to get laid." She glared at him. "A princess? Are you serious?"

"Totally."

"And you want to win me?"

"Yes." He held his hands out, palms up. "Callie, there have been a lot of —"

Her gaze narrowed.

"I mean, I've had plenty of short-term relationships in my time. This is different. *You're* different. I want to do the right thing." He lowered his voice. "You have no idea how much I want you, but not before we know each other better. When it's right. When I've won you."

"For real?"

"I swear on my mother's beating heart."

"That's a serious swear."

"I'm a serious guy. You okay?"

She nodded.

"Are we okay?"

Instead of answering, she walked toward him. He pulled her close and held on. He was going to make this work, he promised himself. He had to — she was the one.

CHAPTER TWENTY-SIX

Callie told herself she *had* to stop smiling. She'd been grinning like a fool since she woke up that morning and probably looked ridiculous. Only it was difficult not to be happy after her evening with Santiago.

The man was incredible. Yes, he was smart and kind and honorable and all that was really important. In fact, a case could be made that those were much more important qualities than the one she was focused on. Only all she could think was he thought she was special.

Her! Special! Who knew that was possible? The waiting-to-have-sex thing was a bit frustrating but the reason was so incredibly sweet and lovely and how was she supposed to ever resist him?

Not that she was going to, she thought, smiling again. Just his kisses were driving her crazy. In a way, he was an unexpected miracle. Not only had she been given a chance at a new life, she'd met a wonderful man who thought she was practically a princess.

She turned her attention back to her work and carefully sealed the small plastic bag filled with a proprietary blend of spices until the light turned green. She tossed it into the bin with the 47 million she'd already made that morning. Okay, maybe not that many, but a lot. The dry goods department was nowhere near as interesting as the basket group. Automation had yet to hit the section, so giant vats were filled with spices measured out by hand. Once everything was mixed together, the results were measured into bins with built-in pour spouts. From there the mixture went into big funnels that released a predetermined amount into tiny plastic bags. The bags were sealed by hand to be put into soup mixes later.

From what Callie had learned, the entire division was due for an overhaul in a few months. Everyone was excited about the changes. Despite the upcoming automation, no jobs would be lost. Employees would be sent to other departments to fill in there.

Callie reached for a bag only to realize she'd run out. She slid off her stool and headed for the storage area where both supplies and finished product were kept. As she opened the huge doors, she hesitated. She still wasn't sure how to find her way through the maze of stacked boxes, bins and crates.

She looked at the numbering system on the shelving units, then up at the map on the wall.

"Row E, section five," she said to herself. "Row E, section five."

She found the correct row, but couldn't find anything close to supplies. Had she read the map wrong? She looked over the boxes, then shook her head. They were all filled with dried soup and pasta kits. She stepped back and realized that information was written on the side of the boxes, along with the codes that said when they'd been manufactured.

She started to turn away, then looked back to study the coding. It didn't make sense. She translated the numbers in her head twice more and came up with the same piece of information. Two entire days of work were gone. Last Monday and Tuesday were right where they should be, with the Friday boxes pushed up against them. But there were none from Wednesday and Thursday.

She walked up and down the rows, wondering if the boxes had been put in the wrong place. They had to have been. But when she checked the handwritten logs at the end of each aisle, the boxes on the forms matched the boxes on the rows.

Malcolm had talked about someone stealing from the company, right in this department, and she had a bad feeling she'd just found proof.

She walked back to the map, realized she needed to be two rows over, then found her supplies. But instead of returning to her station, she went in search of her supervisor.

He wasn't around, but she spotted Paulo and headed toward him. He smiled when he saw her.

"Hey, Callie. How's it going?"

"I can't find Brandon. Do you know where he is?"

"He had a doctor's appointment. You look worried. Can I help?"

"I hope so. I hope I'm wrong and if I am, I'm sorry I bothered you." She took a breath. "I think there's missing inventory." She explained about the two days she couldn't find.

Paulo watched her intently, then groaned. "We've been having a lot of problems with theft lately. I thought we'd put in enough inventory checks, but obviously not. Thanks for letting me know. I'll go double-check, then report it up the chain of command.

Once we have our remodel, everything will be on computer. Then this won't be able to happen."

"Sorry to add to your workload."

He grinned. "It's why they pay me the big bucks."

She headed back to her workstation and began filling small bags with spice blend. Doing the right thing felt good. That was a lesson she would carry with her always. The consequences for anything else weren't worth it.

The hotel ballroom looked like something out of a movie, Callie thought as she and Santiago walked around the displays for the silent auction. Twinkling lights, beautifully dressed people, with both laughter and music as delightful background noise.

She'd spent the afternoon getting ready. Keira had insisted they go to Nordstrom for makeup, so Callie had dutifully braved the Clinique counter to get advice on what she should buy. She'd stayed for a lesson, then had duplicated the effort as she'd gotten ready. She'd left her hair in hot rollers for nearly an hour and then had sprayed the resulting curls with half a can of hairspray. With luck they would last several hours.

In her fancy dress and wearing a strapless

bra with the power to support far more than she had, she felt confident and pretty and almost tall. Having Santiago give her surreptitious looks of approval only added to the specialness of the night.

Once they'd arrived, they'd swung by one of the bars in the room to get a drink. Now they surveyed the grouping of tables with cute signs above them. Each section of tables had a charming name like Whiffen Walk.

"Here's how the night goes down," Santiago said, putting his free hand on her waist. "We start with the cocktail hour and the silent auction. I have an app on my phone and we bid on anything we want. Items are usually grouped together. Wine packages, experiences, dining out, travel. There are more special items in what's called a Super Silent."

He winked at her. "Sports tickets, artwork. We could get you a picture of dogs playing poker."

"Could we, because that would be the best." She looked around at all the tables. "There's a lot here. We'll never get through it all." Not that she would be bidding on anything. "I thought there would be a live auction. I've never seen one."

"Oh, there is. It's during dinner. Those

items are the really exclusive. Dinner for twelve on a private yacht or a week in Bali. That kind of thing."

Callie wasn't sure she could put together a dinner for twelve. Did she even know that many people? But even as she thought the question, she realized she did — at least these days. Back in Houston she'd been on her own but since moving to Seattle, everything had changed. She had family and friends and, well, a really hunky boyfriend.

He drew her close. "Come on. Let's go spend money for charity."

Callie had no idea what to expect from the silent auction. They spent a few minutes in the wine section. Santiago bid on a couple of cases, then handed her his phone.

"You do the next one." He showed her how the app worked. "You put in the amount of your bid here and the maximum you're willing to bid. The app will automatically increase your bid every time someone else bids on your item. You'll get a notification when that happens and if you end up being outbid."

She studied the screen. "What's that for?"

"It's the 'buy it now' button. If you really want something, there's a purchase price that's usually double the actual value." He smiled. "For those who are impatient or unwilling to take the risk."

"How often do you use the 'buy it now' button?"

"Me?" He chuckled. "A lot."

"Figures."

They wandered through the various sections, then Santiago took her to the Super Silent area.

There were bottles of wine that looked a lot like the wine they'd seen before, but based on the opening bid obviously weren't. Someone had donated a sapphire and diamond pin. There was a bronze sculpture of a mother and baby penguin, a suite for a Mariners game and a couple of travel packages.

"See anything you like?" he asked.

She looked at the sculpture. The opening bid was twenty-five hundred dollars. "Ah, not really."

"It's for sick children, Callie. I'm prepared to be generous. What's appealing?"

Her gaze settled on a brochure for a hotel up in the mountains. The pictures were beautiful with lots of trees. The package included three nights in a luxury suite, breakfast, one dinner and a couples' massage. She'd never heard of the resort but according to the brochure, Whistler, British

Columbia, was only a few hours away by car.

She handed him the brochure. "You said it had to be special the first time. Does this count?"

He looked from the pictures to her, then grabbed his phone and punched the "buy it now" button.

She laughed. "So that was a yes?"

"You're killing me, you know that, right?"

"I wasn't sure but it's good to know."

Their gazes locked. She felt her attraction to him all the way to her toes. When she was around him she felt cared for, adored and safe. He was good and funny and smart and kind. She had no idea why she'd been so blessed, but Santiago was a true miracle in her life and she planned to hold on to him for as long as she could.

"Delaney? Is that you?"

Delaney saw a tall blonde woman hurrying toward her. "Emilie-Louise! I can't believe it."

The two women embraced. Emilie-Louise took her hands and stepped back a couple of feet. "Look at you. You're just as beautiful as ever. Don't you get older?" She released her hands and sighed. "I'm such a horrible friend. I'm sorry. I've been meaning to get in touch, but time got away from me. How are you? How is everything?"

Delaney and Emilie-Louise had worked together at Boeing. They'd been hired within a few months of each other and had often worked together on projects. Delaney's climb had been a little faster but she would guess Emilie-Louise had passed her by now.

"I'll go find our table," Malcolm whispered in her ear. "And leave you to have a little time with your friend."

She gave him a grateful smile, then turned back to Emilie-Louise. "Everything is good."

"We miss you. I know you went through so much. You're back in college, right? I think that's what I heard."

Delaney nodded. "What about you? How are you doing?"

Emilie-Louise held out her left hand. "I'm getting married in a few months. Oh, you have to come to the wedding. And I want us to get together for lunch. I mean that."

They talked for a few more minutes before Delaney excused herself to go find Malcolm. She'd run into more people than she'd expected. Old friends and people she'd worked with. Everyone had been so pleased to see her. None had looked at her as if she'd emotionally abandoned them. They'd all said they missed her and were sorry they weren't seeing more of her but there hadn't been blame and more than one friend had claimed responsibility for the lack of contact.

While she appreciated the support, she was left more confused than ever. Had she been the one to cut herself off or had it simply been circumstances? Had she retreated after Tim had died and her father had been shot because she'd needed to preserve her resources or had she been hiding?

This was not the time or place to figure that out but when she had some time to herself, she needed to think on the problem.

She made her way to a table by the stage. As Malcolm's company was a major sponsor of the event, they had prime seating. She spotted Callie and Santiago together — they made a handsome couple and Callie looked amazing in her dress.

Malcolm saw her and moved toward her. When he reached her, he put his arms around her and lightly kissed her.

"You're a fun date," he said. "And the most beautiful woman in the room. How did I get so lucky?"

"I have no idea. How did you?"

He smiled and pulled her close. Being next to him felt good. Right. He was the only thing that made sense in an increasingly confusing world.

"You know a lot of people here," he said, holding out her chair.

"From my previous life." She looked around the room. "Sometimes I miss it."

Sometimes she wondered if she'd made the right choice to leave it.

"You could go back."

"I could." She leaned close. "But I'd rather spend tonight thinking about being with you."

He smiled at her. "See? I'm the luckiest guy ever."

"I can't believe you didn't take a picture of Delaney," Keira grumbled late Sunday morning as she and Malcolm walked along the waterfront. "I wanted to see her dress."

"Sorry. I didn't think of it. For the record, she was beautiful."

More than beautiful, he thought, remembering the kick in the gut the first time he'd seen her. Stunning. Incredible. Everything he'd ever wanted.

The last thought had him stumbling on the perfectly level curb. Did he mean that? Was he finally ready to trust again, and if so, was she the one? He thought maybe she was.

They walked into a bakery and stood in line. Keira admired everything in the case before turning to him.

"I want coffee."

"No," he said mildly.

"I'm thirteen now. I should be allowed coffee. Besides, you're not the boss of me."

He raised his eyebrows. She sighed.

"Okay, maybe you *are* the boss of me but you don't have to act like it all the time."

"Fine. Have you had coffee before?"

"Once, with Angelina."

"Did you like it?"

"No, but everybody drinks it all the time. I live in Seattle now. I have to join in."

"You want a drink you know you don't like? Okay, kid, you're on."

"While you're in a good mood, I want to say that Callie's nearly done with her driver's training. She's taking her test in a couple of weeks."

"I know. And?"

"And you should buy her a car."

"You're very free with other people's money."

She rolled her eyes at him. "You're rich and she's your sister. You like her and she needs a car. Besides, when does anyone ever get to be that much of a hero except in the movies?"

"You might have a point."

"Might, smight. You know I do."

He grinned at her. "Yes, you do."

It was a great idea and he was sorry he hadn't thought of it himself. The kid had game.

They reached the front of the line.

"I'll have a mocha," Keira said confidently. "With extra whip. And one of the egg and sausage sandwiches. And a chocolate croissant." She looked at Malcolm out of the corner of her eye, as if not sure the order was all right.

"I'll have the same food," he told the woman at the cash register. "But make my coffee a regular latte."

They found a table by the window. Keira sat across from him. After a couple of seconds, she said, "How do you know if you like someone? Like a boy. I guess a girl for you. And if you like them, then what? I'm not sure I get the whole dating thing. I mean why do it? I'm not sure I like boys yet. They can be mean sometimes. My therapist says that being mean isn't just for boys and that I should be careful and at the same time give people a chance."

She shifted in her seat. "I kind of know

505

what she's saying but when you think about it, it really doesn't make sense. One of my foster sisters was raped by our foster brother. I wasn't there when it happened, but it scared me and I know not all boys do that, but some do."

Just when he thought things were going well, life jumped up to kick him in the ass, he thought grimly. He honest to God had no idea what to say or do.

"Did you talk about what happened with your therapist?" he asked.

"Yeah. It was right before you came and got me, so I wasn't sad to leave that house. And it didn't happen to me, but I don't know. There's this guy at school I think is cute and sometimes he smiles at me. I like that, but the rest of it, I'm not so sure. Sex sounds really stupid."

"It can be, which is why it's a good idea to wait. Back to your foster sister." He paused while a server delivered their breakfast. "What happened to the boy?"

"The police came and he was taken away. I don't know anything else. I left a few days later. Everyone was upset, though, and there was a lot of crying."

He was so out of his depth and completely the wrong person to be having this conversation. Only Keira needed to talk to someone and for reasons he would never understand, she'd chosen him.

"Keira, a good guy won't hurt you," he began.

"How do you know the difference?"

"Sometimes it's hard to tell, so you have to listen to your gut. If you're uncomfortable, pay attention to that. As for dating and sex, that's a long way off. I think this is something we should continue to talk about over time."

She bit into her sandwich and nodded. "That's what my therapist said, too."

"How would you feel about taking up some kind of martial arts? So you'd be able to beat the crap out of anyone who tried to hurt you."

Her eyes widened. "That would be so cool. Could I do that?"

"Sure. Let me do some research. I'll find a class and you can get started."

The sport would give her confidence, he thought. And she would know she could handle some handsy asshole who tried to take advantage of her.

"How about if I took the class with you?" he asked.

She grinned. "I double-dog dare you to do that. Let's ask Callie to come, too. It will be all of us."

"You're on."

"Yay!" She took a sip of her coffee and wrinkled her nose. "That is so gross."

"Want a hot chocolate?"

She sighed. "Yes, please. I'm sorry I wasted your money ordering this. Thank you for not making me drink it anyway."

"You have life lessons to learn. Liking or not liking coffee isn't one of them."

She laughed and got up. He handed her five dollars, then called her name. She turned back to him.

He held out his arms and she threw herself against him. He held her close.

"I promise I will do my very best to always take care of you," he whispered. "For always. I swear."

Her thin arms tightened around him. "I know. I love you, Malcolm."

Her words caught him off guard. His throat tightened and it was a second before he could speak.

"I love you, too, Keira."

CHAPTER TWENTY-SEVEN

Sunday brunch at her dad's house was better this week than the last time Delaney had been there. Conversation flowed easily, the food was delicious and she found her tension was dissipated. Probably the result of a wonderful evening, she thought.

The gala had raised nearly four million dollars for local children's charities including two that supported hospitalized kids and their families. She and Malcolm had had a great time. They'd danced and laughed and enjoyed each other's company. Later, at her place, when he'd made love to her, she'd felt a connection that had helped soothe the rough edges of her soul.

After the brunch dishes had been washed, Beryl excused herself to go shopping with a friend, leaving Delaney with her father. Delaney half suspected Beryl's absence had been arranged in advance, which meant Phil had something to talk about. She sat on the sofa next to his wheelchair and waited. It didn't take long.

Her father shook his head. "I'm worried about you, baby girl. Something's going on and I don't know what it is."

Her good mood evaporated. She tried to hang on to the feelings, but they faded as if they'd never been and she was left uneasy and empty.

"Dad, I'm okay. I'm wrestling with a few things, but I'll figure it out."

"Like whether or not you want to be a naturopath?"

"What? How do you know that?"

He squeezed her hand. "Delaney, I raised you. Of course I know what you're thinking. I'm sorry you've had to go through so much since the shooting. Losing Tim, me. Everything's different. You loved your old job — I never understood why you felt the need to leave it."

"I was too exhausted," she admitted, remembering that time. "I didn't have anything left. I felt as if I needed to change."

There had been more. A gnawing restlessness that had never left her. A need to help or run or something . . .

"Do you think you made a mistake?" he asked. "Leaving finance?"

"Maybe."

"You could go back."

"No. It's too late."

"It's only been a few months. I'm sure you could find something at Boeing. Or maybe another company." He grinned. "Beryl loves shopping on Amazon. Go work there so we can use your employee discount."

She tried to smile and failed. "Dad, it's not that easy."

"Sure it is. You're the one making it hard." He studied her for a few seconds. "I know you still miss Tim, but you've got to let him go, Delaney. You can't live in the past."

Something burned hot and dark inside of her. Like a collapsing star, she felt pulled into something she couldn't define.

She wasn't going to say anything, she promised herself. She was going to nod and listen and —

"I don't," she said before she could stop herself. "I don't miss him. I wasn't even sure I wanted to marry him. I felt trapped and alone even before he was killed. It was awful, Dad. To fit in, to be like everyone I grew up with, was really hard. I'd been with Tim forever. How could I not be with him? But I wasn't sure. That's why I kept putting off the wedding. I couldn't let go, but I couldn't surrender to what was happening."

She turned away as tears slipped down her cheeks. "I know that makes me awful. I just didn't know how to tell anyone I didn't want to be with him. Not him, not you, not anyone."

Her father squeezed her hand again. "I'm sorry you feel that way."

"Right," she said bitterly. "Because I'm supposed to mourn Tim forever. I'm never allowed to move on or have a life or anything." She stood and glared at him. "That's what's wrong, Dad. That's why I can't decide. I don't know who I am or who I get to be, because it sure as hell isn't my decision."

"That's a lot of energy." Her father's tone was mild. "How long have you been wanting to say that to someone?"

"What?"

"Delaney, you feel how you feel. I'm sorry you felt trapped with Tim. I wish you'd said something before. He loved you but he wouldn't have wanted to marry you knowing you didn't feel the same way. As for the neighborhood, they would have gotten over it. They would have forgiven you."

"You don't know that."

"Yeah, I do. I've known these people over thirty years. They would have figured out a way to be okay with the information." He studied her. "The problem isn't them, it's you. You're defining yourself by what you assume everyone else thinks. You say you weren't in love with Tim anymore, but the truth is you've never recovered from what happened. You've been going through the motions of having a new life, but you're as trapped now as you were six weeks before your wedding. You can't decide if you're willing to be your own person or if you're going to live by everyone else's rules. What do you want, Delaney? What would make you happy?"

She sank to the floor and covered her face with her hands. "I don't know," she admitted for the first time in nearly two years. "I really don't know."

Callie stared at her phone. No, she thought. Absolutely not. She wished she could throw the stupid thing across the room, but it wasn't the phone's fault. She read the text again.

How about a long weekend in August?

August? It was nearly June. August? Santiago intended them to wait over two more months? Was he insane?

Callie stomped her foot before grabbing

her pillow and screaming into it. Stupid, stupid man. She was not waiting until August to have sex.

She looked at her bedside clock. It was just after five. Keira and Malcolm had gone out to an early dinner before Keira's therapy session and Grandfather Alberto was playing bridge with his friends. No one was going to be upset if she had a little evening out herself.

August is an interesting idea. I have to go. Are you going to be home later?

Heading there now for a quiet evening. Text me when you can.

Promise.

She would do more than text, she thought as she crossed to her closet. She would show up in person and explain that she was done waiting. They were going to have sex and they were going to do it now. They could also do it in August and many times between now and then, but the whole "You're so special, I have to wait" crap had gone on long enough.

She studied her still meager but growing wardrobe. She didn't know what she was

514

supposed to wear to seduce a man. Not a dress — that was too . . . something. Jeans, she thought. Tight jeans and a cute sweater.

She got out her tightest pair of skinny jeans and a pretty V-neck sweater that she usually wore over a shirt because it was cut so low. Her trip to buy a strapless bra for her fancy gala dress had also yielded other new bras and panties. She'd gone wild and had purchased a sexy black bra and matching thong for this very reason.

She showered and then dressed. She didn't bother with makeup beyond mascara — less to smudge that way. She pulled on her faux Uggs so she could take them off easily and left a note for Keira, saying she was with Santiago and might be late, then called for a car.

She got out in front of Santiago's condo building, walked into the entryway and pushed the button to buzz his unit, then waited.

"Yes?"

"Hi. It's Callie. Can I come up?"

There was a moment of surprised silence followed by delighted laughter. "You're here? How did I get so lucky? I'll meet you at the elevator."

The knot of nerves in her stomach lessened a little. At least he was happy she'd shown up. Now if only she could convince him to put out.

She rode the elevator to his floor. As promised, he was waiting for her in the hallway, leaning against the wall, looking all sexy and masculine. Her girl bits did a little dance while her heart seemed to get a little fluttery.

"You're the best surprise of the day," he said, cupping her face and kissing her. "What's going on?"

"I wanted to talk to you."

He followed her into his condo and shut the door. She turned to face him. He'd taken off his suit jacket and tie but was still wearing his dress shirt. She was momentarily distracted by the thought of unbuttoning said shirt, then reminded herself they weren't at that part yet. He needed to say yes first.

"Look, we've been going out for a couple of months now. I like you and you seem to like me. I appreciate that you think I'm special. It's wonderful and great and makes you even more irresistible, but you have some crazy idea about us or me or maybe yourself. I'm not sure and I no longer care."

She moved a little closer and put her hands on his chest. "The last time I had sex was my eighteenth birthday. I am not interested in waiting until August for that to happen again. Yes, I very much want a romantic weekend away with you. I think it will be fun, but I'm wondering why you have all these rules. I'm a real person, not a fantasy, and if you can't understand that, then we have a bigger problem here and I think we should deal with it. If you have a genuine reason, then I want to know what it is, otherwise, put up or shut up."

She'd started out strong, but was shaking by the time she was done. What if she'd misjudged the entire situation? What if he'd been trying to tell her he wasn't interested in her that way and she'd totally missed the point? What if this was just a game and totally broke her?

He kept his gaze on her face and didn't speak for several very long seconds. Then he drew in a breath.

"I'm sorry. You're right about all of it. I have this weird idea in my head — that because you're so amazing, I have to do things differently. I want a different outcome, but I never meant to make you feel I didn't want you or that you were just a fantasy. I just didn't want to screw up."

He kissed her lightly. "You on birth control?"

"The shot. I started two weeks ago. I also

left a note for Keira telling her I would be home late."

He smiled. "A lady with a plan. I like that." The smile faded. "Tell me about before. The other guys."

"What? Why would you want to know that?" This was not the time to grill her about her past.

He took her hand and drew her down the hall to the master bedroom. "One guy, one time is different than five guys over three years. I want to know if I'm dealing with an experienced woman who's ready to ride me hard or a born-again virgin who needs to be wooed."

"Oh." She felt herself flushing. "One guy, two times. Both were pretty fast and awful."

He released her and walked to the bed. After pulling back the comforter and sheet, he faced her.

"Born-again virgin it is."

He removed condoms from the nightstand, then began to unbutton his shirt. Sunset was still a couple of hours away so there was plenty of light to see everything, even without him turning on a lamp.

He tossed the shirt over the back of a chair in the corner, then sat down and took off his shoes and socks. He stood and dropped his pants, leaving only his low-cut briefs in place.

His body was amazing, she thought as her breath caught in her throat. Honed muscles, broad shoulders and long legs. He worked out and it showed. He'd been an athlete and that showed even more. Her stomach clenched, her breasts began to ache and she felt a heavy kind of swelling deep inside.

She wanted him. She was totally terrified, but she wanted him.

He took her hands in his, then placed them on his bare chest. His skin was warm as she touched him.

"Here's how it's going to go," he told her, putting his hands on her shoulders. "This is all about you. It's been long enough and I've had enough fantasies that I just need about two minutes at the end."

One corner of his mouth turned up. "I want to impress you with my staying power, but the first time, it's not going to happen." He brushed her hair back, then kissed her. "If you don't like something I'm doing, tell me. If you want me to do something different, tell me. More, less, harder, softer. I'm really good at taking directions. Eventually I'll know your body better than you do, but for now, I'm going to need help."

His words made her shiver and she had

no idea why. What he described made sense on an intellectual level and she knew she wanted to be with him, but she wasn't sure what was going to happen next. Everything about this was so different than the awkward fumbling in the back of her teenage boyfriend's car.

"Okay," she whispered before stepping out of her boots.

He pulled her close and held her tight. Their bodies touched everywhere. The hug felt good — safe and arousing at the same time. She ran her hands up and down his back, enjoying the feel of bare skin. He had so many muscles, she thought absently, aware of his hands mimicking her own. Up and down, up and down, lingering where she lingered.

Wondering if she was imagining things, she moved lower, cupping his butt. He did the same, then squeezed the curves, causing her to arch against him. Her belly came in contact with his erection. The length and thickness stunned her. No way that was going to fit.

She was still mulling over the possibilities when he grabbed her hand and led her to the bed.

"I do my best work lying down," he murmured, urging her to stretch out on the mattress.

She did as he asked, not sure how all this was going to work. He was almost naked and she was fully clothed. Wasn't there something wrong with this picture?

Santiago settled next to her and smiled at her. "You're so beautiful," he said right before he kissed her.

His mouth claimed her with an intensity that stole her breath. His tongue slipped inside and teased her own, circling, dancing, arousing. She angled toward him and wrapped her arms around him. The kissing she understood and liked. She didn't have any questions about doing this — it was the rest of it that was vaguely confusing.

Not that she was a virgin, but it had been such a long time and those couple of times had been so disappointing.

He kissed her over and over again, as if he had all the time in the world. She was aware of hands moving over her body. Her back, her hip, across her stomach, the outside of her thigh. He touched *safe* places, which was nice, but wasn't at all what she was looking for. Despite his request for information there was no way she could tell him to get on with it. At least not out loud. Still, she silently urged him to keep moving, stretching lower or higher, to her breasts or between her legs. She ached and needed in ways she never had before. She was restless and warm and melting from the inside out.

He unbuttoned her jeans and slowly, so slowly, undid the zipper. As he peeled down her jeans, two of his fingers lightly grazed the top of her thigh and brushed against her feminine mound before drifting away. She felt the jolt to her toes, then up to the top of her head. Goose bumps broke out everywhere as a keen sense of desperation overwhelmed her.

They had to keep going. He had to be inside of her. She wanted that sense of release, of perfection, and she wanted it now. Hunger burned so hot and bright, she found herself needing to take control.

She opened her eyes and said, "You're going too slow."

He looked at her. "Excuse me?"

"You're going too slow. I'm not afraid of you or what you're going to do." She motioned vaguely toward his groin. "Okay, that intimidates me a little but I'll deal. Santiago, *please.* Let's move this along."

"But I'm seducing you."

"Seduce faster."

One corner of his mouth turned up. "You are a complicated woman."

"Not really."

"You'll tell me to slow down if I —"

She made a low growl in the back of her throat. "This would be exactly what I was talking about. Just do it."

"Do it? Do it? I don't just do it. I —"

She sat up and pulled off her sweater, then reached behind her and unfastened her bra. She tossed it to the floor and flopped back on the bed.

She was about to ask if she was making herself clear when she realized everything was different. Gone was the gentle, teasing guy who had taken things incredibly slow. In his place was a man who wanted his woman. She saw the fire in his dark eyes and the tension in his body. His moved with a purpose that left his intentions in no doubt, shifting so he was kneeling beside her. With one easy, experienced move, he tugged off her thong, then moved between her thighs.

She was about to say that maybe this was a bit *too* fast but before she could, she realized he wasn't going to push inside of her. Instead he leaned over and licked her left nipple.

The feel of his warm, wet tongue against her tight, sensitive skin was explosive. Her breath caught, her body went on alert and she lost all sense of control. Just one touch and she was his. All of her. As long as he kept doing that, he could take whatever he wanted.

He licked her nipple a few times before sucking it into his mouth. The deep, pulling sensation had her trembling in a matter of seconds. Heat poured through her, collecting between her thighs.

He moved to her right breast and put his hand on her left. The combination of fingers and tongue and sucking and rubbing cleared her mind of anything but what she was feeling — and what she was feeling was amazing. Wanting was everywhere. Deep desire that made her want to part her legs and expose every inch of herself to him. She wanted to beg and scream and demand and be. Just be.

He moved from breast to breast, pulling harder, lightly using his teeth on her nipples. The swelling between her legs became painful with its intensity. Her breathing grew faster, her body was restless. When he finally began to kiss his way down her belly, she nearly sang her relief.

She drew her thighs apart and raised her hips slightly. Without thinking, she reached down and parted herself for him. She was wet and oh, so ready. She needed him to —

At the first swipe of his tongue, she knew she was going to die. The pleasure was so sharp, so bright, so intense, she couldn't possibly survive the onslaught. But she hung on as he explored all of her before settling over the very center of her.

The steady rhythm of him circling her was the best kind of torture. With each movement of his tongue against her clit, she grew more and more aroused. Every muscle tensed as her entire body focused on that spot of ready nerves.

She dug her heels into the bed and tried to keep breathing even as heat burned through her. She felt everything — his tongue, his breath, her skin, the steady pressure. In the distance was the promise of her release. She strained toward it, wanting that sensation, that moment of perfection when everything was as it should be. Her body wept as she got closer and closer until finally it was there.

Her orgasm claimed all of her. She knew she cried out and shuddered and possibly begged. It went on and on in the most perfect moment ever. She came and came and came until there was nothing left and she was simply a vessel gloriously emptied.

Santiago sat back on his heels and stared at her. He didn't say anything for a long time, then he swore under his breath. "You about killed me. That was unbelievable. I didn't think I would be able to hold out. If you'd been touching me, I would have lost it in a second."

She smiled. "Now you can."

He stood and pulled off his briefs. His erection sprang free. That, she thought with a lot less worry, was going to be interesting.

He grabbed a condom and opened it, then slid it on. "So here's the thing. You're kind of petite and I'm a big guy and this is your first time in a long time, so it might be easier if you're on top."

She sat up. "I've never been on top before. I'm not sure what to do."

He grinned. "You're not going to have to do much. Just go up and down maybe three times and I'll be done. Not my proudest moment, but I'm being realistic. I just think you'll feel more comfortable if you have control."

Before she might have been embarrassed to try but not anymore. The man had practically taken her to the stars — at this point she would try anything he suggested.

He got back into bed and stretched out on his back. She straddled him, then he helped her so she settled onto his erection. He was huge, she thought as her body stretched to accommodate him. She went slowly until he was fully inside of her.

"Get used to me," he said.

She felt herself loosening up a little and gave a little wiggle. He groaned, then put his hands on her hips and guided her up and down, before hissing out a breath.

"Okay," he said, his teeth clenched. "Just like that. You okay with it?"

The movement was easy. Even more fun, it felt really good. She liked how he filled her and the way certain parts of her were rubbed and bumped and aroused.

"Stay forward," he told her, obviously struggling for control. "If you sit up, you might be uncomfortable. We'll try that later."

"Okay. You ready?"

"Almost. Give me a second."

She thought he was going to try to distract himself or something, but instead he moved his hand against his belly, slipping between where their bodies touched. She felt his thumb start to rub against her still-sensitive center and caught her breath.

He grinned. "Good. I was hoping you could come again. Wait until you're close, then start moving."

"What if I get distracted and forget?"

"I'll remind you."

She smiled, then closed her eyes as he continued to rub against her. The upward pressure was different — deeper or maybe harder — she wasn't sure. She shifted a little, pulsing her hips in time with his movements. Her breathing quickened as the familiar heat returned and her body began to focus on the promise of another release.

He quickened his pace and she moaned. Like that, she thought and instinctively began to move her hips. She went up and then down. As he filled her, rubbing against every inch of her, the sensation intensified. It was amazing and wonderful and she wanted more.

She rocked again and again, never wanting all the sensations to end. Without thinking, she straightened, giving him a better angle on her clit and at the same time taking all of him all the way in.

It was like touching pure energy, she thought as the heat built on the inevitable journey. She rose up, tightened her muscles as much as she could, then pushed down hard.

Her orgasm exploded into pulsing fiery light. She continued to ride him, wanting to feel all of it, even as he grabbed her hips and hung on to her. She came, calling out his name, forcing him over the edge, then collapsing on him.

"And you wanted to wait until August," she gasped. "Stupid man."

He began to laugh and she joined in. As he drew her next to him and hung on as if he would never let go, she realized that sometime in the past few weeks, she'd given her heart to this man. After all she'd been through, she was happy to know she'd healed enough to fall in love. Life really was a miracle.

CHAPTER TWENTY-EIGHT

"Are you listening to me?" Paulo asked in frustration as they stood in the warehouse. "This is about work. You should care."

"I care." Sort of, Santiago thought with a grin. He did care about work but after last night it was hard to think about anything but Callie. Their time together had been incredible. *She* had been incredible.

"We caught the guy stealing," his brother said. "There were a half dozen boxes in his truck. He says he was set up, but who admits they're guilty even when they're caught?"

"You're right. Good work, Paulo."

His brother stared at him. "What's going on with you? There's something. I can tell."

"Nothing I want to talk about."

Not with anyone. Callie was too special. He wanted to keep what had happened to himself. Not just that they were now lovers, but what it all meant. He'd known one day he was going to find the right woman and he had. She was perfect and he was going to do everything in his power to not screw up.

"You've always been weird, man," his brother said. "But this is bad, even for you."

"I can live with that."

It had been a great week, Callie thought, treating herself to an Uber ride home from her driving test. Her first night with Santiago, followed by a second and a third. She'd taken last night off so she could catch up on sleep before her driving test today. Which she'd passed.

She pulled out her temporary license to stare at it again. The picture was grainy and not her best, but who cared — she had her license!

Until coming to Seattle, she'd pretty much given up on second chances, but here she was getting a do-over. She'd been blessed and she knew it.

The driver pulled into the driveway. Callie collected her backpack, thanked him and got out, only to stumble to a stop at the edge of the circular drive.

Right in front of the steps was a car she'd never seen before. It was blue and beautiful and there was a huge red bow on the front windshield. Even as she struggled to comprehend what it meant, her heart knew. It just knew.

The front door opened and Keira burst out.

"You're here! You're here! You passed, didn't you? I know you did." She raced over and hugged her. Malcolm, Carmen and Grandfather Alberto followed.

Callie tried to catch her breath. "You bought me a car?"

Malcolm shrugged. "Your grandfather, Keira and I bought it together. For you."

"I picked the color," Keira told her. "It's called Lapis Blue Pearl. Isn't it pretty? And the interior is brown and it has lots of safety features Malcolm can tell you about, but I picked the color."

Her grandfather pulled her close, then passed her to Malcolm. Seconds later, Keira joined them and Callie found herself enveloped in a group hug that had her chest tightening to the point where she couldn't breathe.

"I don't understand," she whispered as her eyes burned. Happy tears, she thought. When was the last time she'd had happy tears?

"It's a car," Carmen said with a laugh. "How can you not understand?"

"But . . ." It was too much. It was a wonderful gift. They'd thought about her and planned for her and she just had never thought anything like that would ever happen again.

"Thank you," she whispered.

Carmen and Grandfather Alberto went back inside. Malcolm had Callie sit in the front seat while he sat on the passenger side and Keira leaned over from the back.

"We'll take this slow," he told her, handing her the keys. "This is a Subaru Outback with all-wheel drive. You'll be safe in all the rain we get around here."

"And the snow," Keira said. "We get snow sometimes and with all the hills, it's really slippery. Tell her about the lane change thingies. It's so cool."

"You have a blind spot indicator. If you put on your signal to change lanes and there's a car in the way, you'll hear a beep. If you start to drift out of your lane, you'll be notified. There are a lot of safety features you can read about." He winked. "I paid for the first year's insurance. After that, you're on your own."

She had a car. That was hard enough to grasp, but even more important, she had a family. She looked at Keira's freckles, exactly like her own, and the smile she and

Malcolm shared and wished desperately that her mother was still with her.

"I don't know how to thank you," she admitted. "This is wonderful."

"Let's go get mani-pedis," Keira suggested. "That would be really fun."

Malcolm shook his head. "Not for me."

"Have you ever had a mani-pedi?" Keira asked. "You might like it a lot."

"I'm willing to take the risk of missing out."

"You're scared."

"Not that I'll admit to you, munchkin."

Malcolm explained the rest of the features of the car to Callie. Eventually Keira went inside to hang out with Lizzy until it was mani-pedi time. Malcolm insisted on accompanying Callie on her first drive and made her promise to let him know when she needed gas. He was going to show her how to fill the tank herself.

Later, as the nail technician applied bright green polish to her toes, Callie reached for her sister's hand. Keira squeezed her fingers and laughed at her own purple polish.

"Thank you," Callie whispered, acknowledging all the gifts she'd been given. Her family, Santiago and the promise of a new future. Finally, finally, everything was going to be just fine.

■ ■ ■ ■

Delaney half expected Chelsea not to show. She'd texted her friend and invited her over for coffee. Chelsea had taken two days to get back to her, but in the end, she'd agreed. Delaney's doorbell rang right at three o'clock on Saturday afternoon.

She felt more than a little apprehensive as she answered the door. They stared at each other for a couple of seconds before Chelsea walked in.

"I can't remember the last time I was at your place. It doesn't look all that different."

"I painted a couple of walls," Delaney said. "Otherwise, it's the same."

They went into the living room and sat across from each other. Their gazes met, then skittered away. Delaney knew she had to make the first move, only she didn't know what that was.

"I'm sorry," she began. "About us not being close anymore. I never meant to drift away. I'm still not sure what exactly happened. For some reason every time there's a life change for me, I think I cut people off. I don't know why. Guilt maybe? Fear of being judged. I don't want to be that person, yet here I am."

Chelsea looked at her. "I'm sorry, too. I could have tried harder to stay in touch. It's just I was so jealous and angry."

"What?"

"Oh, come on. You were always the smartest of all of us. You're pretty and funny. You could have been anything or married anyone. You wanted a big, fancy career and you made it happen. I got married at nineteen and popped out a couple of babies. Even a stray cat can do that."

"I'm not sure cats are allowed to get married."

Chelsea smiled. "You know what I mean. I'm sorry about what I said about you not being good enough. That was about my insecurities, not anything you did."

"But you have Isaac and the kids."

"Sometimes I want to put on a suit and go to an office. Sometimes I want to be more than somebody's wife and mother."

Things Delaney had never considered. "Sometimes I want somebody to love me," she admitted. "Tim wasn't right for me. Not for a long time."

"I know. I could see that. What I didn't understand is why you didn't let him go."

"I don't have an answer to that." It was something Delaney had been wrestling with.

Why hadn't she just moved on? "I think maybe he was my only connection to the past. Without him, I didn't have an anchor. When I moved out of the neighborhood, I left everyone behind. He kept me grounded."

"He also got in the way of what you wanted." Chelsea looked a little chagrined. "He talked to me some. I know he wasn't very supportive of what you wanted. I was selfish enough to be glad at least your relationship wasn't perfect."

Delaney wondered what else her fiancé had said, then told herself it didn't matter. Not now. He was gone and she was doing her best to figure out her life.

"Nothing about me is perfect," Delaney said, trying to sound like she wasn't breaking apart inside.

"Oh, I don't know. My mom always held you up as an example of what I was supposed to be. Every time we went somewhere without you, that's all I heard."

Chelsea's words sparked a memory — of Delaney standing on the sidewalk, watching her friend and her family drive away. It wasn't that they were moving or anything that dramatic, it was just that they were going somewhere together and Delaney was being left behind.

Memories flashed through her mind, each a mini vignette of the same moment. Her being left behind. Sometimes it was a trip to the mall or for a vacation. She remembered the painful truth so clearly — she wasn't really a part of their family. Yes, she'd had her father, but he'd worked long hours, supporting her and maybe burying his grief. Only Tim had been a constant.

"Do you think I couldn't let Tim go because he was so faithful?" she asked. "Because I knew he would always be there? That I could count on him, no matter what?"

"I'm not sure you would have been able to get rid of him if you'd tried," Chelsea teased. "Once he chose you, that was it."

Maybe that was the point, Delaney thought. She'd struck out on her own to follow the career path she'd chosen, but there had been a price. She'd gone against all she knew back in the neighborhood. She'd wanted a different kind of life and maybe, for once, she'd wanted to be the one leaving them behind.

The same thing had happened at work. She'd fit in and had had great friends, but she'd felt torn between her old life, and Tim, and her new life. So when Tim had died and she'd felt lost, she'd once again left her friends behind. For once, she hadn't been the one standing on the sidewalk, all alone.

"I don't know if we could have been happy," she admitted.

Chelsea sighed. "I don't think you would have been. You were always so sure about what you wanted. So driven. Remember in high school how we would go out late on school nights and you never would because you wanted to study for a test? And when you were in college, you hustled to get good grades. I know what I said before, but don't let my envy take away what you accomplished. You did good. You should be proud."

"Then why did I leave it?"

"Damned if I know."

Delaney smiled. "That makes two of us. Maybe it was guilt — I didn't deserve it anymore."

Chelsea leaned toward her. "Maybe you were overwhelmed. You'd lost your fiancé, your dad was paralyzed and you didn't have anyone else to share the burden. We all pitched in, but you were the one there every day. Maybe you just needed a break from your life. Like taking the summer off or something."

"I quit my job. I dissected a frog. I've

ruined everything."

"Don't you think that's a little dramatic? You might have made some poor choices, but now you can make better ones."

Delaney's head hurt from too much thinking. "Can we start over? Can we be friends again? I miss you and I hope you miss me."

"I do miss you and yes, I want to be friends, too."

They set up a time to go to lunch and promised to stay in touch regularly. By the time Chelsea left to pick up her kids from her mother-in-law's, Delaney was feeling better. But the second she was alone, the doubts returned.

How could she have messed up her life so much and so fast? She knew she didn't want to finish her college classes, but if not that, then what? Could she get another job in finance and if she applied, what was she supposed to say about what had happened? Her mind went round and round like a hamster on a wheel and she didn't know how to make it stop.

Around five, Malcolm called.

"Hey," he said when she answered. "I was thinking about our dinner tonight. I have reservations at that Mexican place we like, but was thinking it might be nice to stay in with takeout. What do you think?"

"I think that sounds great," she said, wiping away tears and grateful he couldn't see them. "I'd love a quiet evening in."

"You okay? You sound upset."

She supposed she shouldn't be surprised Malcolm knew her that well. "I'm tired and need a good hug."

"I have a few good hugs to spare."

"Then you should bring them along. Want me to call in a take-out order at the Mexican place?"

"Thank you. I'll grab a bottle of wine and be there in an hour."

"I can't wait."

She hung up, then pressed the phone to her chest. She was still lost and confused and unsure, but when she was with Malcolm, all that went away. She would give herself a few days to sit with her revelation, then she would make some decisions. This time she would be thoughtful and sensible, considering all sides. She wouldn't do anything rash and she absolutely would not do anything without remembering that every choice had consequences.

Callie had always known reality was a bitch, but she'd hoped that truth wouldn't have followed her here. Like everyone else who worked in the warehouse, she'd been told that the thief had been caught with boxes of product in the trunk of his car. He'd claimed innocence, and opinions were mixed as to whether or not he was telling the truth.

Callie hadn't known the guy well enough to form an opinion so she'd stayed out of the discussion, but two days later, she would have sworn inventory was missing. Just to be sure she wasn't imagining things, she'd noted the sequential box numbers herself and had kept the list in her locker. This morning, over a dozen were missing. She confirmed that they weren't on the inventory sheet anymore. It was as if they'd never existed.

"Hey, Callie."

She jumped and spun around, then breathed a sigh of relief when she saw Paulo. "You scared me," she admitted with a nervous laugh.

He raised his eyebrows. "What are you doing in here?"

"Nothing." She realized how stupid that sounded. "Actually I was checking on the inventory. I know you already caught the guy, but I'm not so sure. The last time I brought a box in, I did some checking."

"Who told you to do that?"

"No one." She couldn't tell if he was mad or simply curious. "I wrote down the inventory as it was yesterday and came back today to check." She pulled the paper out of her pocket and showed him. "See how all the boxes between 102 and 117 are gone? They're not on the inventory sheet, either. It's like they were never packed." She glanced at her list. "I can't remember exactly but I think most of them had really high-end stuff in them. The expensive cocoa and the upscale soups."

"You know there's going to be a new system in place in a couple of months. Everything will be computerized."

"I know, but someone is still stealing. I think they got the wrong guy."

Paulo's gaze was steady. "You're right. They did. But you're not going to say anything, are you? Just like you're not going to tell anyone about this conversation. Especially your brother."

Callie's mouth went dry. She felt sick to her stomach and more than a little scared. Paulo was nowhere near as big as his brother, but he was still taller and stronger than her and there was something in his eyes that warned her he wasn't kidding about any of this.

"See, I know all about you," he continued. "Who you are and that you served time. I also know you've kept that information from your friends here. So you're going to keep quiet. In fact, you're going to help me. If you don't, I'll tell all your new friends who you are. Worse, I'll pin the whole thing on you. You like my brother, don't you? He's not going to appreciate his girlfriend stealing from the company he loves. He trusts you now but he won't when I'm done with him."

His smile was cold. "Who are they going to believe? A trusted employee of more than a decade, the brother of a senior executive, or a convicted felon? Besides, I know you hate Malcolm. Think of this as a way to screw your brother. It's a win-win."

She couldn't stop shaking. She was going to be sick. Hate Malcolm? Why would he —

That time she'd been so mad, she thought bitterly. He'd overheard her saying horrible things. But that had been a long time ago and she and Malcolm had a different relationship now. Not that Paulo would want to hear that.

"I can't," she breathed. "I won't."

"You think you have a choice?" He winked at her. "It turns out, I know someone in accounting who would be more than happy to make it look like the thefts took place when you were working. Too bad it would only be your second offense. Three strikes and all that."

She really was going to throw up. Or pass out. Or scream. This couldn't be happening. "What do you want me to do?"

"Keep your mouth shut for now. Next week you can help me with a little something."

"You want me to steal for you?"

"Sure. Then you'll be as guilty as me."

Guilty, she thought grimly. She would always be guilty. She thought about how great her life was now, how she had a family and friends and Santiago. She couldn't lose any of it — not and still have faith in herself. Not and still have hope.

Defeat tasted bitter on her tongue. She hung her head and nodded slowly. "Just tell me what you want."

His slow smile returned. "I knew you'd see it my way. You do what I say and no one has to know — not even Santiago."

As soon as her shift ended, Callie drove directly home. Once there, she locked herself in her room. A hot shower did nothing to make her feel better. The sense of being trapped grew and grew until she wanted to scream. What was she going to do? She couldn't go to Santiago. Paulo was his

545

brother and she was worried there was a better than ever chance he wouldn't believe her. Even if he did, he would hate her for exposing his brother as the thief. There was only one person she could trust and even that was an iffy situation.

She dressed but didn't bother drying her hair. After telling herself she was doing the right thing, she went down the hall to Malcolm's room and knocked on the half-open door.

"Come in."

She stepped into her brother's study and found him reading on the sofa by his desk. He'd already changed from a suit to jeans. He looked up and smiled at her.

"Hey. What's up?"

She carefully closed the door behind her and walked toward him. "I have to tell you something and I don't want you to interrupt me until I'm done."

His welcoming expression shifted to worry. "All right," he said slowly. "What is it?"

She told him everything, explaining what she'd noticed missing that morning and how Paulo had found her.

"I swear, I never stole anything," she added quickly, forcing herself to keep looking at him when all she wanted to do was run away. "I wouldn't. You have to believe me. But it's Paulo and I didn't know what else to do. I can't tell Santiago. If he believes me, then I've hurt him and his family and if he doesn't believe me, then he's hurt me."

Malcolm stood and put his hands on her shoulders. "It's okay. You can stop explaining, Callie. I know you didn't do anything wrong."

"You do?"

"Sure. Maybe I didn't trust you when you first arrived, but I do now. You could have taken the money and run. You could have lived off your trust fund. You could have not given a damn about anyone but yourself. But I know you now and I believe you."

The impossibly heavy weight she'd been carrying lifted. She drew in a full breath for the first time in hours. "Thank you. We need to come up with a plan. Or maybe you do because I've been so frantic, I haven't been able to think straight. And I don't know what to do about Santiago. He's important to me and we're sleeping together and —"

Malcolm groaned and moved away.

"What?" she asked.

"Please don't tell me you're sleeping with my best friend. I'm not surprised, but I don't need details."

Despite everything, she laughed. "Then I

won't share any except to say he's really —"

"Stop!"

She held up both hands. "I'm done, I swear."

He swore. "You can be a pain."

"So can you."

"We need a plan."

"That's what I said."

"How do you feel about going under-cover?"

CHAPTER TWENTY-NINE

Delaney knew that taking out her frustrations on her bedroom wall rather than a living person was probably a good idea. She just hoped she didn't regret the outcome.

"You look unsure," Callie told her.

"A little. I've never been the DIY type before, but I'm learning."

She'd already painted her bedroom a pretty teal color. Now she was going to use two different glazes to sponge paint one of the walls. Callie had volunteered to help. They'd practiced on poster board she'd bought so their sponging techniques were similar.

Her furniture was pushed to one side and draped, she had all the supplies, and Callie was here to help. There was no reason to hesitate. She poured the glaze into two small paint trays, then handed one to Callie.

"Let's do this."

"I'm ready."

Delaney pressed the sea sponge against the wall a few times, then stepped back to study the result.

"I really like this," she admitted.

"Progress."

Delaney went back to work. "Speaking of progress, how are things with you and Santiago?"

"They're, ah, good."

"You didn't sound very sure."

"No. It's fine. We're fine. He's a great guy who treats me well and who loves his family. What's not to like?"

Delaney glanced at her friend. "Are you all right?"

Callie nodded. "I'm fine. There's some work drama that's bothering me, but it's no big deal. You get too many people in a confined space and it all goes to hell."

"Tell me about it. You should hear some of the storeroom fights at my job."

"When are you done with the quarter at school?"

"I take my finals next week."

Callie turned to her. "Are you kidding? We're painting the Saturday before finals?"

"Yes. It's clearing my head. Besides, I've been studying a lot. I'll do fine."

She'd decided to finish her classes because it was the right thing to do, but she hadn't sent her application to Bastyr. Her future was still uncertain, but one thing she knew for sure — she was not going to be a naturopath. A career like that required passion and she didn't have it in her.

"What do you take next?" Callie asked as she pulled the step stool over and climbed up to reach close to the ceiling. "More math?"

"No. I'm not taking any more classes. At least not now. I'm trying to figure out what to do with my life. It feels like everything is suddenly different."

"I know that one," Callie said. "How is it different for you?"

"I'm so confused. I've been thinking about my past all the time."

"You mean when you were little? I thought you grew up on a great street with all kinds of people who cared about you."

"I did. I was well taken care of. But it was only my dad and me and he was gone a lot. Sometimes I felt left behind. I don't know — I'm not making any sense. It's just sometimes I wonder if I never got the message that it was okay to take the next step, you know? Grow up and move on. I physically left, but in so many ways I was tied to the same place."

"Because you were engaged to Tim?"

Delaney nodded. "He kept trying to draw me back and I wanted to be free. Only not free enough to actually separate. I think I always had one foot in each camp, so to speak, and when I lost him, I think I was sort of cut adrift. I didn't know what to do."

Callie nodded. "You were devastated. Of course you were confused. Delaney, it's okay not to know what to do next. Take your time before you decide to figure out what's right for you."

"I miss my job at Boeing."

"Have you talked to anyone there about going back?"

"I couldn't."

"Why not?"

She didn't want to admit failure. Or what if they said no? Or what if she no longer had her fast-track status?

"I'm scared."

Callie surprised her by smiling. "We're all scared. Some of us are just better at faking it." She nodded toward the big closet. "If you'd truly let go of your former career, you wouldn't have kept the clothes. They are a physical reminder of who and what you used to be. You loved what you used to do. Most people don't ever love their job. You should embrace the blessing and do what-ever it takes to feel that way again."

"Sound advice," Delaney murmured. "But?"

"I think I'm afraid I'm not allowed to be happy."

"That's just sad."

"I know, but what if it's true?"

"It isn't. The only person keeping you from being happy is yourself."

"How can you be sure?"

Callie got off the step stool and moved to another section of wall. "Being incarcerated isn't easy. People cope in different ways. I don't know what it's like for men, but the women form close bonds. Some are intimate, some aren't. The ones who make it, the ones who figure out how to get through, have a goal — something they can look forward to. But it's more than that. They also have an internal peace. When your joy comes from within, no one can take it from you."

She shrugged. "I never got there. I was counting the days until my release. I was scared and depressed. There's no way to explain what it's like to be physically locked in a room. You can't get out until someone lets you out. You have to find a way to cope or you go crazy."

She took a breath and reminded herself that was behind her. She was out and she was somewhere so much better.

"I got my GED, earned a few college credits, did my job and kept my head down. But those women who surrendered to the moment, who found their own joy, I always admired them. And what they taught me was that happy comes from inside of us. Circumstances can make it more difficult but the ultimate decision is ours."

She glanced at Delaney. "If you're not happy, it's all on you. If you want to find your way, be your own compass." She smiled. "Pick your favorite cliché. They're annoying but they're also mostly telling the truth."

Delaney had always assumed the power came from outside of her. At least she had lately. Not before, she thought wistfully, remembering her determination to make it through college. How she'd worked the program, saving every penny to buy the perfect interview suit. She'd known what she'd wanted and she'd gone for it. She'd been clear on her future.

Except for Tim. She'd loved him and had always only been with him. On the one hand Tim had said he would move with her, if she got a promotion that required that. On the other hand, he'd wanted her to stay home and have babies. Which meant what

— that he was as complicated as everyone else?

"I can't imagine being responsible for my own happiness," she admitted. "I've been drifting so long, just letting things happen."

"Maybe it's time to pick a destination."

Delaney nodded slowly. Callie made a lot of sense. The only question was where did she want to go?

"You up to this?" Malcolm asked.

"I'm shaking," Callie admitted. She was more than shaking, but that seemed to be the most polite sensation to admit to, at least out loud.

"You'll be fine," Tom, the newly hired private detective, told her as he checked the sound from the microphone that had been clipped to her bra.

Just like on TV, she thought, trying to find humor in the situation, or at least not disaster. Because in her gut, she knew this was going to go badly.

Malcolm had hired Tom, who'd consulted with the Seattle Police Department. In less than three days, the so-called sting had been arranged. All Callie had to do was wait for Paulo to contact her so she could help him and thereby catch it all on a recording.

That was certainly enough to send her

screaming into the night, but it wasn't the absolute worst bit — no, that was saved for her fears about her relationship with Santiago.

They'd just gotten to the good part, she thought wistfully. They were together and having sex and he was so wonderful and he cared about her and made her laugh and she was almost, maybe, totally sure she was falling in love with him, and now this. How was that fair? Paulo was his brother. Santiago was not going to take kindly to hearing about the thefts, and knowing Callie had been a part of taking his brother down, well, she had no idea what was going to happen, but it wasn't going to be good.

Nearly as upsetting was how this was going to affect the rest of the family. What about Hanna and the kids, and Santiago's mom? Would they blame her, too? Would they understand? She knew she was doing the right thing, but wished it didn't feel so perilous. She was terrified she was going to lose so much that mattered.

As the waiting was awful, she was grateful when Paulo took only a couple of days to set up a time for her to help him steal the product. They were meeting at the warehouse at eight on Monday night.

"We'll be in the building," Tom told her.

"Listening to everything. If you feel you're in danger or that he's going to hurt you, yell the safe word and we'll come running."

She nodded, thinking her screaming *African violet* was supposed to confuse Paulo and in that second, she was to run. Assuming she wasn't staring down the barrel of a gun.

No, she told herself. He wasn't going to shoot her. His plan was about money, not violence. At least she hoped it was.

Tom checked her microphone again. The tiny battery pack was tucked between her breasts so if Paulo patted her down, he was unlikely to feel anything.

"You okay?" Malcolm asked. "I'm worried about you."

She gave him a fake smile she was pretty sure fooled no one and said, "I want to do this. I have to stand up to my past — otherwise it's always going to loom over me." Her smile turned genuine. "Looming is your job."

He hugged her. "I want you to stay safe."

"I will. I know a few moves from our new karate classes. Besides, Paulo doesn't want me, he wants product to sell. We'll get him and then this will be over."

There would be consequences, but she would face them later.

Malcolm and Tom left at seven so they could get in place. Callie followed at seven thirty. She left her car parked right by the main entrance where it could easily be seen. She waited by the door, watching for Paulo, only to jump when the door opened from the inside.

"Right on time," he said, motioning for her to step inside. "You alone?"

She pointed to her car. "You're welcome to check it out. I swear, I don't have anyone stashed in the trunk."

His dark eyes narrowed. "For someone in your position, you have a lot of attitude."

"I'm operating on adrenaline right now."

He led the way to the storage area. There were three big carts right outside.

"Stack the boxes on the carts," he told her. "I want your fingerprints on every one of them."

Her sense of dread grew by the second. Thank goodness she'd gone to Malcolm — otherwise she would have been terrified she really was being set up to take the blame for all the thefts.

She carried dozens of boxes — they were bulky, but not heavy. Still, by the tenth trip, she was starting to breathe heavily. At least the physical activity had burned off her nerves. She was working too hard to be shaking.

"I need to take a break," she said, putting down a box and wiping her face. "You know, you could help."

"I could, but I won't."

She studied him. "You don't like me, do you?"

"I don't care about you, Callie. You're a symptom, not the problem."

"What's the problem?"

"Trying to get me to talk about it? Going to psychoanalyze me?"

"I wouldn't begin to try that, but I am curious. You have so much, Paulo. Your family, a good job. Why are you doing this?"

His expression sharpened. "I have so much? You mean my brother has everything. He always did. He's bigger, stronger, faster. Do you know he could have played pro ball and he walked away from it? Who does that? Asshole. I would have taken the contract in a second. But not Santiago. He went and got his MBA, then worked for a hedge fund."

"I don't understand. You're angry because he's successful?" Not that she wanted to know any of this, but her gut — trained over several years of incarceration — told her while he was talking, she was safe.

"I'm angry because he never had to work

for anything. It was all handed to him."

Callie knew that wasn't true. She remembered what Santiago had told her about his struggles with his schoolwork and how he'd always assumed he was dumb. How he'd practiced hard, done the drills, stayed in shape and had peed blood after games in college. He'd more than paid the price for anything he'd achieved.

"Do you know what he does now?" he asked bitterly. "He *helps*. My brother takes care of his family."

"Why is that bad?"

"I don't want him taking care of me. He bought our house. Hanna's graduating from nursing school and my brother wants to send us to Hawaii. It's demeaning. Always the hero."

He was interrupted when the buzzer at the warehouse door went off. Callie jumped.

"What's that?"

"Relax. It's my buddy. We have to get this stuff out of here." He looked around. "Hell, we should just take it all and make it look like a break-in."

"What about the security cameras and the alarm system?"

Paulo's look was pitying. "All taken care of." He eyed her. "I think we will take it all and then leave enough evidence that points to you. How about that? Only you'd tell if it were that big, wouldn't you? Which leaves me with an interesting dilemma."

Callie didn't know what made a person cross the line from stealing to something more violent and she really didn't want to find out. She was pretty sure Paulo wouldn't hurt her, but she was less confident about his friend.

"There's a batch of expensive cocoa in the vat," she said to distract him. "That has to be worth a lot."

He turned in that direction. "You're right. My clients really like it. I've been making a whole lot more than you'd think selling this stuff. I have an online store and everything." His smile turned sly. "And it's all mine. Hanna has no clue. Now get back to work."

She turned to the boxes and picked up the next one. She'd barely set it on the cart when nearly a half dozen police officers rushed in, their guns pointed at Paulo.

"Hands in the air! Don't make any sudden moves."

Paulo swung toward her. "You bitch! You set me up."

Malcolm appeared and stepped between her and Paulo. "No, she didn't. I did." He put his arm around her. "You okay?"

"I will be."

"You'll pay for this," Paulo screamed as he was handcuffed. "You'll be sorry. Santiago is never going to forgive you. I'm family and you're just some piece of ass. Worse, he needs to be the hero and you've shown him he's nothing but a mark. You'll see. You're going to be ruined. Everyone is going to know."

He was still yelling when he was led away.

Malcolm pulled her close. "They got his accomplice. Tom is already looking for the website. We'll get access to all his bank records, then figure out where the money is. Insurance will cover the losses. You did good. Thank you."

She stepped back and tried to smile, only to realize she was shaking again. Not just because of the adrenaline, but because she was afraid Paulo was right — Santiago valued family above all and she'd just ripped his apart.

Santiago drove to the warehouse, not sure what could be happening on a Monday night that required his attention, but Malcolm had texted to ask him to stop by.

He pulled into the parking lot and got out of his SUV only to realize there were several police cars right by the warehouse. The main doors were open and the lights were on inside.

"Well, hell," he muttered. He and Malcolm had both suspected the so-called thief had been set up, but they hadn't been sure. Malcolm had mentioned he was working on something. Apparently he'd figured out who was doing what and had called in the authorities. But why hadn't he told Santiago?

He hurried inside but came to an abrupt stop as he saw his brother being led away in handcuffs.

"What is going on?" he demanded.

The cops ignored him and Paulo didn't look at him or say anything. Santiago started to follow, but stopped when he saw Callie and Malcolm. Malcolm made sense but Callie?

She saw him and went pale. For a second, he thought she was going to run, but why? And what about his brother?

"Tell me what the hell is happening," he demanded as he approached. "Why is Paulo being arrested? What have you been doing here? Dammit, Malcolm, if you're screwing with my family . . ."

"It was Paulo," Malcolm told him. "He was the one stealing from us. He set up the whole thing and wanted one last score before we computerized the rest of the warehouse."

Santiago stared at him. "No way. He wouldn't do that."

"He did it."

"You made a mistake."

Callie looked at him. "It was him," she said quietly. "He blackmailed me into helping him because he knew about my past and he wanted to pin the whole thing on me. He said he messed with the alarm and the security system. He said he could get into the accounting programs, so you'll want to check that."

He didn't believe her. He couldn't. "You're lying."

Malcolm stepped between them. "She was wearing a wire, Santiago. We all heard him."

He couldn't believe it. "Not my brother. I got him this job. He's family. He would never . . ." He glared at Callie as anger burned hot and bright. "What did you do to him?"

"Me? I didn't do anything. He threatened me. I went to Malcolm right away. And if you're going to ask why I didn't tell you, this is the exact reason." She swallowed. "I knew when it came to your family, you would side with them regardless and I was right."

She took a step toward him and met his gaze. "You're wrong about me and you're wrong about your brother. I didn't do anything, but you can't see that, can you? It can't possibly be Paulo. He's one of you and I'm just that piece of ass."

He flinched. "I never said that. You're not being fair."

"Me? What about you? You're accusing me of setting him up. Of making this happen. What else am I supposed to think?"

She was making sense, only he couldn't seem to believe her. Someone had to be to blame and it couldn't be his brother.

"He's family. I have to stand with my family. He's the one who —"

She took a step back. "Matters. He's the one who matters. You're right. It was never going to be me, was it? Because for all you said, all you promised, in the end, I'm just the girlfriend and they're your family." She looked at Malcolm. "I'll be waiting outside."

"You don't have to. I'll take you home right now."

He took Callie's hand and pushed past Santiago. Together they walked out of the warehouse.

Santiago stood staring after them. He should go talk to her, he thought. Tell her . . .

Tell her what? That it was okay? It wasn't. What she'd done couldn't be forgiven. She was right — family was family and she was just . . .

He sucked in a breath, not sure how to define exactly who she was. Not that it mattered. He had bigger problems than her walking out on him.

CHAPTER THIRTY

Callie spent Tuesday morning with the Alberto's Alfresco attorney, giving her statement to the police. Once the paperwork was signed, she went back to the warehouse to start her shift. While parking, she realized she hadn't bothered to tell her supervisor that she would be in late. As she considered her options, hysterical laughter, brought on by exhaustion, threatened. She supposed she could simply tell him she was part owner and that she was giving herself an excused tardy. That would go over really well.

She hadn't slept at all the previous night. Of course she was upset about what had happened with Paulo but what really got her was her conversation with Santiago.

She'd believed him, had trusted him and in the end, he'd betrayed her. He hadn't even once thought about the situation from her point of view. When push had come to shove, he'd walked away from her. She'd been busy falling in love with him and he hadn't cared about her at all.

She was still trying to reconcile herself to that ugly truth and she had a feeling there was plenty more pain to come.

She walked into the warehouse and went to clock in. On her way to the locker room, she spotted Frankie. Her friend stared at her before hurrying over.

"Is it true?" Frankie demanded, her gaze sharp, her tone edgy.

"Is what true?"

"All of it? That you're not who you said. That you're Malcolm Carlesso's sister and really rich and that you were in prison and that you had Paulo arrested."

Callie came to a stop and emotions flooded her. Shame, fear, anger and regret all blended into a stomach-churning mixture that left her barely able to stay upright.

"Is it true?" Frankie demanded. "Is that why you were here? To spy on us? To report back to your brother on all of us? I thought we were friends. I looked out for you."

Callie wanted to scream. This was so like the conversation she'd had with Santiago the previous night, only this time *she* was the bad guy.

"It's not like that," she began, wanting to

explain so Frankie understood. "I wasn't spying."

Frankie's eyes went cold. "So it is true. You lied about everything, didn't you?"

"I —"

Before she could say anything else, Frankie walked away. Callie stood in the center of the hallway, aware of people walking past her, watching her, whispering about her, judging her.

She wanted to yell that it wasn't her fault — that *she'd* done the right thing. Paulo had been the one stealing, not her. Only she had a bad feeling Frankie's accusations didn't have very much to do with Paulo. Instead they were about Callie — what she'd told them and what she'd concealed.

She saw Beverly, one of her work friends, and moved toward her. Beverly shook her head.

"No way. Don't even think about it. You lied and I don't forgive that."

Callie felt the awfulness of the situation and didn't know how to fix it. She wanted to call out that she was the reason they had a new lever in the basket department and she'd been the one to get Malcolm to change the leave exchange policy, but she knew that wouldn't matter. As much as she

569

felt betrayed by Santiago, they felt betrayed by her.

She left and drove home. She climbed up to the second floor and walked into her bedroom. She looked at the pretty decorations, the elegant furniture, then crossed to her closet.

She didn't belong here. She'd never belonged here, she'd only been fooling herself. She was some kid from nowhere, an ex-con who couldn't help screwing up no matter what. She would never fit in, never be comfortable anywhere. Certainly not here.

She grabbed the battered suitcases she'd brought with her when she'd flown to Seattle and tossed them on the bed. After opening one of them, she began dumping in the contents of her dresser, then pulled clothes from the closet. Only they didn't fit. The first suitcase overflowed and there was no way she was going to get it closed.

Fine! She would leave everything. Just leave it all. She would get in her car and drive. She had money. Not just the trust, but her paychecks. Except for clothes and the gifts she'd bought Keira and their mani-pedi dates, she hadn't spent much. She could drive until she found somewhere that made sense. Or maybe just a place where she could get lost and —

"What are you doing?"

She spun and saw Keira staring at her from the doorway to her room.

"What are you doing home?" Callie asked, surprised to see her sister. "It's barely noon."

"It's the last week of school. We only have half days." Keira's eyes were wide and filled with fear. "You're leaving, aren't you?"

Callie felt the stab of the question all the way to her heart. "I have to," she whispered. "I can't explain it, but I have to. I'm sorry."

Keira began to cry. "You said you loved me. You said we'd always be together."

"I know, but —"

"No!" Keira's voice was a scream. "No! You're not leaving me. You can't. I need you. I know where there's more luggage. I'm coming with you. You have to take me with you. You can't leave me behind. Callie, you can't. You promised."

The teenager's pain and fear were tangible forces in the room. They grew and filled every corner, sucking out all the air and burning all they touched. When Keira sank to the floor and started to sob into her hands, Callie realized she'd damaged someone she'd promised to always care for. Until this second, she hadn't realized the awesome power of love and trust.

"I'm sorry," she said, hurrying over to her sister and sitting next to her on the carpet. "I'm sorry. I'm so sorry." She pulled Keira close. "I was wrong. I was so wrong. Oh, Keira, please, please forgive me. I won't leave you. I swear I won't. Not ever. Even when you want to move out and be on your own, I won't let you or I'll go with you. You'll be sick of me. I'm sorry. I love you. I love you so much."

Callie rocked her as they both cried. Pain was everywhere, but so was the dawning realization that she'd brought all of this on herself. She'd been the one to insist no one know who she really was. She was the one who had concealed her past. If she hadn't done that, Paulo couldn't have used it against her and Santiago wouldn't have been mad and broken her heart.

She knew that it was better she know where she stood with him now — the more time they spent together, the harder it would be for her to get over him, but still, it hurt so much.

"You okay?"

Callie looked up and saw Malcolm walking into her bedroom. He glanced from them to the suitcases.

"Tough morning?" he asked, joining them on the floor.

"You have no idea."

He put his arms around them both. "Tell me what happened."

Keira sniffed. "Callie was going to leave and I said I had to go with her, but then she said she wasn't leaving, which is really good because you would have had to come, too, and what about Grandfather Alberto? He needs us and we need him. You adults make things really complicated."

Callie flopped back onto the carpet and stared at the ceiling. "I'm an idiot."

"You're not." Keira patted her arm. "You're really smart about a lot of stuff. You just have to stop running as a way to deal with your problems. It's better to face them and find solutions. Problems don't go away. They're like that stain in the rug that keeps popping up. You have to find out what's underneath."

Callie turned to Malcolm. "You're the one who put her into therapy. I blame you for the insights."

Keira grinned. "It's great, isn't it?"

Despite everything, Callie smiled. "Yes, it is."

Malcolm stayed with Keira until he knew she was all right. Around four o'clock she was picked up by a friend and her mom for an early movie followed by a sleepover. She'd assured him, to quote her, "57 million times" that she was okay and promised to text him on the hour.

One problem down, a dozen others to deal with.

He returned to Callie's room and found her putting away her clothes. She motioned to the mess on the bed.

"I might have overreacted," she admitted, then told him what had happened at work.

"It's my fault," she concluded. "I'm the one who lied about everything. I should have come clean from the start."

He motioned for her to join him in her sitting room. "I'm going to fire him."

She flinched. "You can't. What happened between us is between us. It's not about work."

"Has he called you?"

She dropped her chin to her chest. "No."

Anger burned inside of him. He'd trusted his friend with his sister, and Santiago had hurt her. "I'm going to fire him," he repeated.

"Do you think that will make me feel better?"

"It might brighten my mood." He sighed. "I'm sorry, Callie."

"Me, too. He's being a dick. I'm not willing to say he *is* a dick. I haven't decided yet." She tried to smile. "I'll be okay. I just need some time."

"What do you want to do?"

She thought for a second. "I'm going to quit my job. It's too hard being there. I should hear on my fall application at UW in the next week or so. In the meantime, I checked with the closest community college and I can register for a couple of summer classes. There were a couple of culinary classes that looked interesting."

"Is that what you want?"

She hesitated just long enough for him to know she was thinking about Santiago. "I want to move on with my life. No more hiding, no more lies. I am who I am. Some people will be fine with it and some won't. I'll have to deal with that, but I'll be doing it honestly."

"That's totally your call."

She looked at him. "I'm interested in food development. I'm thinking I'll major in management, go heavy on the science and marketing classes, and take it from there." This time the smile was genuine. "I want to be a part of things for real — not just working at the company because I'm family."

He wasn't the least bit surprised. He'd known Callie long enough to have a good sense of her character. She would want to earn her place, not be given anything. He thought maybe they had that in common.

He'd been doing a lot of thinking since the arrest last night. About what had happened to her, and how she had changed him. Not just Callie . . . Delaney, too. Watching Santiago screw up things with Callie had made him wonder what mistakes he was making. Was he holding back because of what had happened with Rachel or was he moving forward? Delaney was amazing — she deserved his best and he wanted to give it to her.

"Do you like living here?" he asked.

She blinked. "There's a subject change. Do you mean in the house or in Seattle?"

"Both."

"Moving out so you can start a new life with Delaney?"

He hadn't been able to articulate what he was feeling but as soon as Callie said it, he realized she was right. That was exactly what he wanted.

"What would you think about that?"

She grinned. "You're thirty-four. That's kind of old to be living with your grandfather."

"Not answering the question."

"I know. Okay, so truth. I like Seattle and

I love this house and if you're asking how I feel about staying here with Keira, I'm happy to be with her for as long as she needs me. Maybe just a little longer than that so I can be annoying."

"I'd still be close and I'd honor my commitments."

"I know. You've grown, little grasshopper."

"You'd have to deal with Grandfather Alberto more than I would."

"He's sweet, plus Carmen is here. Do you think they're sleeping together?"

He winced. "Stop asking me that."

She grinned. "Keira brings them up every now and then. Should one of us mention that we know and they can stop hiding?"

"Go ahead. I'll lead from behind."

She grinned. "You're a coward."

"About some things, yes. Happily so."

"Then we have a plan. You're going to move out on your own while I take over this gorgeous house and decorate it in crimson and cream."

"Why would you do that?"

"Oklahoma crimson and Oklahoma cream. For the University of Oklahoma? How can you not know that?"

"It is astonishing. You'll have to take that up with Carmen. I'm not sure she wants Sooners memorabilia in the dining room."

"You can't possibly know that."

"I can guess. Plus you're going to be a Husky. University of Washington — Go Dawgs." He leaned toward her. "You okay?"

Her smile disappeared as if it had never been. "No. My whole body hurts. I miss him, but I have to figure out how to deal with that. They say time heals. I hope they're not lying."

He thought about how much he would like to gut punch his friend, then how he'd felt after he'd found Rachel with his father.

"I know you don't think it now, but you will start to feel better. The process is slow and takes a long time, but you'll get there."

"Thanks. I'll get through it. I'm tough."

She was. Tougher than she knew.

Hanna brushed away tears. "I'm fine," she said, sniffing as she spoke. "Or I will be."

Santiago knew she was lying but wasn't sure calling her on it would help either of them. He was still having trouble wrapping his mind around what had happened. He couldn't imagine what Hanna was going through. She'd just found out her husband had committed a felony — that he'd been stealing from his employer for months, maybe longer — and she'd never had a clue.

"Have you been to see him?" he asked.

"No. What am I supposed to say? He did this himself. He ruined everything."

They sat at her kitchen table. The kids were at summer camp and Hanna hadn't started her new nursing job yet. Santiago knew that she'd been planning on taking the kids to visit her folks for a week before she and Paulo were to take a few days just for themselves.

"Are you ready for me to bail him out?" he asked.

"No. I'm not." She looked at him. "Does that make me a horrible person?"

"You couldn't be a horrible person."

"But I am." Her mouth trembled. "I want him punished. I'm so angry at him. All these years I stood by him. What else has he done? Where's the money from all the stuff he stole? There has to be thousands of dollars. Where is it?"

A good question, Santiago thought, and one that hadn't been answered. The forensic accountants had barely started with Paulo's accounts. Hanna had given permission for them to go over everything, but based on the lack of excess cash in any of their accounts, Paulo must have stashed it somewhere else. Or spent it, but on what?

"He lied," she said, her voice shaking. "I can't get over that. I've worked my ass off and he's done this to our family. I don't think I can stay with him."

"Don't make any rash decisions," he told her, aware of the ironic nature of his advice. Right now he was the king of rash decisions. "Think things through."

"I have. I've thought about it a lot even before this happened. He's different now. He used to be determined and driven. Now he's angry all the time. Bitter. He blames you for being successful, as if because of that, he couldn't be successful, too. He won't try. What he doesn't see is that you worked hard for everything you had. He was never willing to put in the effort."

Santiago wondered how much of that was his fault. Had he given his brother too much, not made him work for things? Was the problem a character flaw, circumstances or both?

"Whatever you need, I'll be here for you and the kids," he told her. "Mom will, too. You're family."

"Thanks. I appreciate that." She sucked in a breath. "Okay, I've kept you way too long. You need to get back to work. Thanks for stopping by."

"You're welcome. And if you want me to take the kids this weekend, just say the word."

"You should run that by Callie," she chided. "It's her weekend, too."

"She'd be okay with it," he said, telling himself it wasn't exactly a lie. At this point he didn't think she gave a damn about him. Not that he blamed her. "Let me know what you'd like to do."

"I will."

He walked to his car and got inside. Halfway down the street, he pulled over, mostly because he didn't know where to go or what to do. A case could be made it was a weekday — he should be at the office. But he hadn't gone to the office since Paulo was arrested. He hadn't wanted to see anyone — mostly Malcolm.

Humiliation burned hot and bright. *His* brother, he thought grimly. His own brother had been the thief. Paulo had set up an innocent man, blackmailed another employee into helping, and Santiago had no idea how long it had all been going on. Weeks? Months? Longer?

He still couldn't wrap his mind around what he'd learned, mostly because every time he got close to accepting it, he had to deal with what he'd said and done to Callie.

He'd rejected her for being used by his brother. She hadn't done anything wrong, but he'd totally gone off on her. He didn't know why or what it meant beyond the fact that he was a total asshole. Him! The guy who was always the hero.

His phone buzzed. He pulled it out and glanced at the screen.

Warehouse. Now.

The text came from Malcolm's phone. Santiago thought about ignoring it, then told himself he might as well face whatever it was. He would deal and then figure out his next move.

He drove to the warehouse and parked, then walked inside. Malcolm was waiting for him. His friend raised his eyebrows when he saw Santiago's jeans and T-shirt.

"Casual Friday?"

Santiago flipped him off. "What do you want?"

"Later we'll talk about your attitude but for now, you need to see something."

Santiago followed him through the warehouse. "Why aren't you pissed at me about Callie?"

"Trust me, I am. I'm trying to decide if I want to beat you up with a two-by-four or just fire you."

Malcolm spoke so casually it took Santiago a second to realize his friend wasn't kidding.

"About time you stood up for her," he grumbled.

"Why wouldn't I? She's my sister."

"You didn't think that before."

"Now I know better." Malcolm looked at him. His blue eyes were cold and determined. "When this is over, you and I are having a talk."

"Anytime, anywhere."

They walked into the large lunchroom. Santiago stumbled to a stop when he saw Callie at the front of the room with about thirty employees gathered around to listen. Pain and longing and feelings he didn't dare define twisted together inside of him. She was so beautiful, he thought sadly. So funny and smart and easy to be with. She was . . . perfect and he was just the jerk who'd blown it all. Not just with her but with his brother and who knew where else. He wasn't a hero — he was a disaster. He'd ruined everything.

Callie began to speak. "Thank you for coming to the department meeting," she said, her voice strong, her gaze steady. "I know it was mandatory, but I appreciate it all the same. There have been a lot of rumors going around and I thought it would be better for everyone to clear them up."

She hesitated. "Let me start with a few facts. First, I am Malcolm Carlesso's half sister. I found that out a few months ago and moved to Seattle. The decision not to tell anyone was mine."

He heard a few gasps and some murmurs. Callie ignored the interruptions and kept talking.

"Some of you have also been talking about my past, wondering if I really am a convicted felon. The answer to that question is also yes."

The gasps were louder this time. She ignored them and went on to briefly outline her past.

"I didn't want people judging me based on a few facts they might or might not understand. But that was a mistake. I got trapped in the lies and they weakened me. They allowed Paulo to try to use me. Hiding from who you are never works."

She gave a slight smile. "Some of you are going to think worse of me now and some of you are going to think better of me. Either way, I'm the same person." She seemed to search the audience. "To my friends, I'm sorry I lied. I was afraid. I should have trusted you more."

One woman broke free and ran toward Callie. Santiago recognized Frankie as she hugged Callie.

"I'm sorry, too. I was upset with some stuff with Levi. You were so good to me." Frankie put her arm around Callie and turned to the audience. "She's the one who got the leave policy changed. She made it possible for me to be with my boy when he's having treatments."

Callie ducked her head. "Anyone would have done that for you."

"It wasn't anyone. It was you."

Santiago turned and walked away. He felt sick and angry and sad and confused, all at the same time. He had to do something — he just didn't know what.

He heard footsteps behind him, then Malcolm caught up and grabbed his arm.

"Where are you going?"

"I don't know."

Malcolm stared at him. "You were wrong. You hurt her and I can't let that go. Neither should you." He shook him. "You don't always get to be the hero, Santiago. You don't always get to save the day. Sometimes you just have to let life happen and then pick up the pieces. That doesn't make you wrong or bad — it makes you human. Paulo made his own choices and he has to live with them. You're going to have to do the same. You want to have to deal with everything with or without Callie?"

"I hurt her."

"Yes, you were a total idiot. So what? You just going to walk away because you made a mistake? You're one of the hardest-working people I know. Why would you give up so easily now?"

Santiago looked away. "She was my princess and I let her down."

Malcolm swore. "Get over yourself. What the hell is that? Callie's not a princess — she's a woman. Love her or don't love her, but don't be some dramatic shit who doesn't take responsibility. Jesus, Santiago. I expected a whole lot better of you."

CHAPTER THIRTY-ONE

"I can't believe Callie stood up to everyone she worked with. And went undercover!" Delaney picked up her glass of wine, then put it down. "I haven't talked to her in maybe five days. How could all this have happened?"

"It's been a busy week."

Delaney sensed there were parts of the story Malcolm wasn't telling and wondered what else had happened. She would text Callie in the morning to see if she wanted to get together and talk.

"What a scary experience. She's impressive in so many ways. You're lucky to have her in your life."

"I am."

They were in her small dining room, eating the takeout he'd brought over. For the first time in a long time, she felt comfortable in her skin. It had taken facing some demons from her past, but she was making changes.

Callie's comments about her being responsible for her own happiness had resonated. Delaney was starting to see she'd allowed herself to get caught between two worlds, never truly committing to one. She hadn't completely decided what she wanted to do next, but she'd talked to a few former work friends and was networking to find out about finance jobs that might interest her.

"You'll have to check out the sponge painting in the bedroom," she said, her voice teasing. "I think it came out really great. I'm going to tackle the bathroom next."

"More sponge painting?"

"No, just a different color. I can't believe how long I lived here without doing anything to fix up the place. I guess I was never sure how things were going to turn out. Tim and I had always talked about using this place as a rental after we got married."

A plan she hadn't been comfortable with, she realized now. While she didn't plan on living in her condo forever, she hadn't wanted to move back to the old neighborhood.

"You'd have no trouble finding someone to rent this," he said. "Great location, good floor plan and there's parking."

She smiled. "Parking is always a plus."

"Callie and I were talking about our family home." He put down his fork.

Delaney thought about the beautiful house. "Oh, no. You're not going to sell it, are you? I know it's big and it's probably expensive to maintain, but it's a wonderful house. Plus, Keira needs to know she has roots." She winced. "I'm sorry. I'm doing all the talking. What did you two decide?"

"That it's probably time for me to move out. Callie wants to live there with Keira, but I'm thinking I'm ready to be on my own again."

She laughed. "It's not like you're living in the basement. You've stayed to be with your grandfather."

"And because of Rachel."

Yes, that, she thought, remembering what he'd told her. Those memories would have been an open wound for a long time. Whatever her problems with Tim, neither of them had cheated on the other.

He leaned toward her. "I've always been a cautious person. Keira would tell you I have a stick up my ass."

She tried not to smile. "She does have a way with words."

"She does and I love that about her. I want to do the right thing, whether it's with business or the people in my life. Rachel's betrayal has made it difficult for me to trust."

"Rachel's but not your father's?"

"His actions surprised me less. I've dated some, but you're the first person I've been involved with in a long time."

"I can say the same about you. We've had a pretty drama-free relationship," she told him. "That's nice."

"It is. So back to me moving out on my own, I've been looking at a couple of houses."

"Want a woman's opinion?" she asked, her voice teasing.

"I would because I've found something I really like. It's an older place, built in the early 1900s. There's a view of Lake Washington and a big backyard. Most of it has been remodeled and a big master suite was added on." His gaze intensified.

"Delaney, I know it's probably too soon, but I would very much like you to come see the house and let me know what you think. I want to know if it's someplace you see yourself living." One corner of his mouth turned up. "What I'm trying to say is I'm falling in love with you and I'm hoping we have a future together."

They were words to warm any woman's

heart — any woman who wasn't her, she thought as the walls seemed to close in on her. Yes, he was a terrific guy and he made her happy, but a house? Love? What was next — a proposal?

She wasn't ready. She'd barely figured out she didn't want to be a naturopath. She hadn't made peace with the past enough to let it go, she didn't know what she wanted to do, career wise. What if she found a great job in Atlanta or New York? Malcolm was tied to Seattle — he always would be. She didn't know enough about herself to be able to decide if he was the right man to marry.

Her whole body went cold, as if she'd been plunged in icy water. Her chest tightened and she felt a pounding behind her eyes.

"No," she said, coming to her feet. "No! I won't be trapped again, not by anyone. I don't know what I want. I don't know my next step. I can't, Malcolm. I just can't. Not a house, not marriage, not any of it. I'm not ready to love anyone. I don't even know what that is anymore. Did I love Tim? I was going to marry him and I just don't know. Not who I am or where I belong or what I want. I don't want to be trapped. I have to decide for myself and I just can't do this now. I'm sorry."

She pointed to the door. "I need you to go."

For a second she saw the shock in his eyes, and the hurt, but then it was gone. Instead she stared at the polite expression of a stranger.

"Of course. I hope you're feeling better soon. Good night."

With that, he left. She stood where she was, her arms wrapped around her chest, her heart thundering so hard, she thought it might break against a rib.

Horror swept over her, causing her to sink back into her chair. What had she done? What had she lost by rejecting him? She held in a sob, telling herself she needed to be sure. This time she was going to be completely sure about who she was and what she wanted, no matter what. If she didn't do that, she wouldn't have learned anything at all.

Callie sat in the kitchen with Grandfather Alberto. Dinner was done and Keira had gone upstairs to start on her homework. For reasons that were totally confusing to Callie, the thirteen-year-old had asked to go to a math and science camp for the summer. Not just that, but there was homework and tests. When Callie had teased her about it,

Keira had pointed out Callie was taking summer school at the community college, so they weren't that different.

"Your granddaughters are strange," she said as she smiled at her grandfather. "We're both in school over the summer."

"You make me proud."

"Thank you. I'm excited to get my degree, then join the company. I think Malcolm and I will be a good team." He would always have more experience than her, but she thought maybe she would bring a gut instinct to the job. Besides, thinking about that was way better than missing Santiago, which she still did. Every. Single. Day.

He hadn't called, hadn't texted. She'd thought she'd seen him at the warehouse yesterday when she'd confessed all to her coworkers, but by the time she'd finished, he'd been gone, so maybe she'd imagined the whole thing.

Love sucked, she thought, wishing she could forget him, or at least not miss him so much. She didn't want to wish she'd never met him because being with him had been so much more than she'd ever imagined a relationship could be. She wanted to tell him that he was punishing her for something that wasn't her fault, but what was the point? He already knew that. She could love him but she couldn't make him love her back.

She looked at her grandfather. He was still healthy and vital but he didn't have a lot of years left.

"Are you in love with Carmen?"

Grandfather Alberto sipped his brandy. "I have no idea what you're talking about."

"Okay, but Keira says you two are an item. If that's true, then you should marry her. Or at least tell us so you can stop sneaking around. No one is going to disapprove. We all love her and we love you. Actually you make a cute couple. You've been alone a long time. Having someone to love is pretty wonderful, Grandfather. Don't miss out on a chance to experience that one last time."

"I'm too old for her."

"Oh, please. If that were the case, she wouldn't still be with you." She stood and kissed his cheek. "Just think about it."

She passed Carmen as she walked out of the kitchen. With a little luck, at least someone would be happy in love, she thought wistfully.

She was halfway up the stairs when she heard the garage door open, then close. She turned and saw Malcolm crossing the foyer. She knew he'd been out with Delaney and it was barely eight. Why was he home —

She took one look at his drawn face and groaned. "No," she said sympathetically. "What happened? Are you okay?"

"I'm fine." He gave her a tight smile. "Seriously, I'm okay."

"Did you two have a fight?"

"Why would you ask that?"

"You were on a date and now you're home early. Something happened." She briefly hoped that it had been something as simple as a headache or unexpected rescheduling, but the tightness in her chest told her otherwise.

For a second she thought Malcolm was going to blow her off and tell her everything was fine. She sensed the battle within him, then the all-is-well facade shattered and she saw the anguish in his eyes.

"I told her I was falling in love with her and she said she didn't want to be trapped." One shoulder rose and lowered. "So much for a happily-ever-after ending." He cleared his throat. "I was so sure she was the one. I started looking at houses." He shook his head. "No. Not looking. I found one. A great house on the lake. It was perfect and now it will be perfect for someone else."

She hurried down the stairs and wrapped her arms around him. "I'm sorry, Malcolm.

I thought you and Delaney were doing great."

"So did I. We were both wrong."

She knew about his past, how he'd always been so careful with his heart. He didn't trust easily but once you were in, it was forever. Didn't Delaney understand that? Didn't she know what she'd given up by turning Malcolm away?

Either she had no idea or she knew and didn't care. Callie wasn't sure which was worse.

She stepped back and pointed down the hall. "Media room. Now."

"I'd rather be alone."

"I'm sure that's true, but your wishes aren't that important right now. Media room, Malcolm. I'm serious."

For a second she thought he was going to defy her, but instead he nodded once and walked down the hall. Callie raced upstairs and burst into Keira's room.

"Delaney dumped Malcolm. We have to do something."

Keira slammed her book shut and jumped to her feet. "What happened?"

"I'm not sure of the details, but he feels awful."

Keira's gaze saw more than it should. "You feel awful, too. Maybe we're all just

596

unlucky in love."

"I'm sure that's not it. Come on."

Keira scooped up Lizzy and followed Callie downstairs into the kitchen. Grandfather Alberto and Carmen were nowhere to be seen. Callie hoped they were making future plans — someone should find a life partner in this family and why not her grandfather?

"Ice cream," Keira said, opening the freezer. "With chocolate sauce."

"Cognac," Callie said, heading for the wet bar across from the butler's pantry.

"Cookies. Carmen and I made them this afternoon."

Callie smiled as she set everything on one of the infamous trays always in use. Together they carried everything into the media room.

Malcolm sat on the huge sectional. He looked up when they entered.

"I'm not sure what you have planned, but I'm fine."

"Uh-huh. We'll be the judge of that," Callie told him.

She set the tray on the coffee table and poured two large servings of cognac. Keira searched through the DVD collection, then pulled out one and waved it over her head.

"*The Princess Diaries*. It's kind of old, but

it's about finding where you belong. Something we can all relate to."

Callie touched his glass with hers. "I swear, I want to be her when I grow up."

"Me, too." He smiled. "Thank you for this."

"You're welcome. We're going to deal with our heartaches the way God intended — with liquor, sugar, a movie and people we love."

He surprised her by leaning close and kissing her forehead. "I love you, Callie."

The unexpected admission filled her eyes with tears. "I love you, too, Malcolm."

"Sibling love rocks but romantic love seriously sucks."

"That it does, and yet we will try again."

"We will."

He clinked glasses with her. Keira put in the DVD, then raced over to the sofa and sat on Malcolm's other side. She reached for the remote and started the movie.

As the opening credits began, she picked up her bowl of ice cream, then snuggled close to him. She rested her legs on top of his while Lizzy meandered over and began to knead his lap.

Callie leaned against his other side and closed her eyes. Yes, she hurt. She had a feeling she was going to hurt for a long time.

While she wanted to say that believing in Santiago was a mistake, she wasn't sure if that was true. Things hadn't worked out between them, but that didn't mean she hadn't learned a lot. She would be more open with the next guy — less guarded and insecure. She would be a bit more careful with her heart, but if she wanted to find someone special, she had to be willing to take a chance. Santiago had allowed her to learn she was capable of loving a man and wasn't that a great thing to know?

She hadn't been looking for a family, but she'd found one all the same. She had friends, a sense of purpose and a great future. The lack of one stupid man wasn't going to get her down. She would give herself tonight to pout and whine and miss him and in the morning, she would start over. Yes, there would still be pain — there was a Santiago-sized hole in her heart — but eventually she would heal and, between now and then, she was going to keep moving forward.

Delaney told herself to let the suit be her shield of bravery and confidence. She was good at what she did and her nine months out of the job market wasn't going to kill her. She had a good reason — the death of her fiancé and her father's surgery and rehabilitation would have rattled anyone. She'd taken some time, had healed and was now moving on.

All of which sounded great in her head but she was slightly less sure about how they would play in an interview.

She hadn't meant the job search to go so quickly — in fact she'd barely started. But her networking had paid off when a former colleague had told her about three suppliers to Boeing who had recently merged. They were looking for a new CFO who had experience in aerospace manufacturing. After a phone interview, Delaney had been brought in for a full day of meetings. So far they'd gone well and she was excited about what the company wanted to do. She'd enjoyed the technical talk and had been familiar with all their software. Now she had to get through the HR interview, which would probably be the most difficult of the day.

Neal, a handsome man in his late forties, looked over her paperwork. "You come highly recommended."

"Thank you. I really enjoyed working for Boeing and would be excited to get back into aerospace."

"You quit your job because of family issues?"

Delaney sensed the pitfalls about to come and deliberately relaxed her body language. She had the education and the experience they were looking for. She was the best they would find and if they couldn't see that, then they were going to lose their chance at her.

"My father was with the Seattle Police Department. He and my fiancé were shot in the line of duty. Tim was killed and my father was left permanently disabled. He spent several months in the hospital. He's much better now, although he uses a wheelchair."

Neal went pale. "Oh my God! I thought you were going to say you got a divorce or something. I'm so sorry. What a nightmare. No wonder you needed a little time to work through things."

"I did," she said, relaxing for real. "I was so busy handling everything that I didn't have time to process the pain and loss. I kept pushing that off but there's no avoiding the mourning process. Eventually it catches up to all of us. I quit to figure out my next act, so to speak. I played with a few different career directions only to realize I genuinely loved what I'd been doing before. So here I am, excited about my next opportunity."

As Neal asked a few more questions, Delaney realized that was exactly what had happened. She'd put off having to deal with her emotions. She'd been constantly running just fast enough that they couldn't catch her — first with getting her dad settled, then by wanting to be a naturopath, then going back to college. She was always so busy, she didn't have time to think or mourn or heal.

It wasn't until she'd accepted how unhappy she'd become that she'd finally stopped to face what she'd been avoiding: her past, her failing relationship with Tim, her drifting friendships. She'd needed to work through all that before she could understand what she wanted from her life. And in the middle of all that, she'd met Malcolm.

She forced her attention back to the interview. It lasted another thirty minutes. From there she went on to speak with the president of the company. The day ended with wine and appetizers with the entire management team. Delaney got back in her car close to seven.

She'd just been on a ten-hour interview and if she had to guess, she would say it had gone really, really well. They were going to make her a job offer — she could feel it. Which meant one part of her life was in order, but what about the rest of it?

CHAPTER THIRTY-TWO

Callie had to admit, as she left class, that for all the sucky rain in the winter and spring, summer in Seattle was amazingly beautiful. The sky was bright blue and the temperature a perfect seventy-two degrees.

She felt good. Her culinary classes were going well — the shorter sessions were a little intense, but she appreciated that she didn't have a whole lot of time to miss Santiago. She and Malcolm were closer than they'd ever been, which was unexpected and pretty wonderful. Keira was making new friends and discovering an interest in science. Grandfather Alberto and Carmen had taken off for two weeks in San Diego. There hadn't been an announcement about their relationship, but Callie figured them traveling together was a kind of statement. Now if only she could bitch-slap some sense into Delaney, all would be well. Or almost well, because hey, Santiago.

She was about ten feet from her car when a very familiar, tall, broad-shouldered man wearing a bright red cape stepped out from between an SUV and a minivan. She blinked twice to make sure she wasn't seeing things, then couldn't decide if she was happy to see him or just a little scared.

"You're wearing a cape," she said.

"I know. Can we talk?"

"You're wearing a cape."

Santiago smiled. "You're not going to let that go, are you?"

"It worries me."

He unfastened the cape and balled it up in his hands. Once he was back to himself, she was able to breathe in the sight of him and let the pain of missing him wash over her.

He looked good. Handsome, a little tired, maybe, but so much the man she'd wanted in her life.

"I was making a point," he said. "With the cape. I've been thinking a lot and it's kind of my thing to always be the hero. Especially when it comes to my family. I always want to take care of them, be the good guy, solve all the problems."

With deeds or money, she thought. Whatever it took, he would be there, trying to fix what was broken. As far as flaws went, it wasn't a bad one — unless you got between him and those he loved.

She'd wanted to be one of them, she thought wistfully. One of the loved.

"But I can't," he continued. "I'm not a guy in a cape — I'm just a regular person. I have flaws and loving my family a little too much is one of them."

He put the cape on the hood of her car and took a step toward her. "You were right to do what you did about Paulo because you're the kind of person who does the right thing. I know that and I admire it about you, but in that moment all I could see was my brother in trouble."

"You lashed out," she whispered.

"I did and you got caught in the cross fire. I blamed myself for what he did. I was humiliated and ashamed and you were a part of that and I was totally and completely wrong."

Wrong was good, wasn't it? Okay, not being wrong, but admitting it. It meant — well, it had to mean *something.*

"There's no excuse for what I did." He nodded at the cape. "That's to explain, but not to make it right. I screwed up." He looked at her. "I'm going to screw up again, Callie. I'm kind of controlling and a little overbearing and I'm going to make mistakes and get it wrong and I'm going to hurt you. There's no way I can't. But here's what I want you to know — I'll never stop trying to get it right. I won't give up, not on you or us. If you're willing to take a chance on me."

She heard the words and loved what he said, but needed him to be more clear. "What does that mean?"

He smiled. "You're my princess."

Her heart sank. "No," she told him sadly. "I'm not. Or if I am, I don't want to be. A princess isn't real. I don't want to be put on a pedestal. I want to be a partner. I want to share my life with someone who loves me and sees me as special, but not other than. I want to be part of a team, not be worshipped."

He reached for her hands. "Callie, when I say you're my princess, I mean you're the one I've been waiting for all my life. I want us to make each other stronger and better. I want us to have a life together." One corner of his mouth turned up. "I'm not interested in worshipping you, except maybe in bed. I'm clear on your flaws. You're moody and you don't trust very easily and you get caught up in the little things, but that's okay. I think we could make a great team."

The smile faded. "Callie, I'm in love with you."

She wanted to believe him but she wasn't sure. What if he hurt her again? What if it wasn't real?

And there it was, she realized in a moment of total clarity. She was being handed everything she'd ever wanted. All she had to do was have enough faith in herself to reach out and take it. Yes, she was scared and yes, she'd made mistakes in the past, but everyone had. Her punishment had been harsher, but so what? She'd survived. More than that, she was thriving. She could take a chance on the man she loved or she would live with regrets for the rest of her life. It was, to quote Keira, a no-brainer.

"Keira," she said quickly. "Malcolm is going to be moving out so I'll be staying with Keira and Grandfather Alberto. I can't leave them."

He leaned in and kissed her. "I know."

"I mean I'm going to be the main caretaker or guardian or whatever. You have to accept that."

He kissed her again. "Callie, with my hero complex do you really think it's going to bother me to help raise Keira?"

She smiled. "I hadn't thought of it that way, but you're right. And we may have

Lizzy when Keira goes off to college. I doubt they'll let a cat in the dorm room."

"It's fine." He cupped her face and kissed her a third time. "I love you. It would be really great if you said something back."

She looked into his eyes. "Something like I'll love you forever and when we make love, maybe you should wear the cape?"

"Something like that would be perfect." His smile faded. "I really do love you."

"I believe you."

"I'm sorry about what happened with Paulo."

"Me, too. I should have warned you."

"No. You did everything right. And when you screw up, I promise to be just as gracious."

"Me? As if."

"You know it's going to happen." He touched her face. "Want to go to my place?"

"Very much."

"Want to marry me?"

Her breath caught. "Yes."

"Good. That wasn't official, by the way. The real proposal will be in the next day or so. There will be champagne and a huge diamond ring."

She laughed and wrapped her arms around him. Santiago couldn't help himself. He was always going to make things bigger than life.

"Don't forget rose petals," she teased. "There should be rose petals."

"Great idea. Depending on where I propose, I'll bet I could get some swans in the background. Or we could save them for the wedding."

She sighed. "Let's do both."

The house was charming. Delaney had walked through it twice, admiring the built-ins and the views from nearly every window. There was a big yard, lots of bedrooms and the newly added master bedroom was to die for.

Finding the listing hadn't been that hard, given the description she had. The price had made her teeth hurt, but with her new job and Malcolm's fortune, they could afford it. As long as he understood they were buying it together. Assuming he still wanted to have anything to do with her.

She'd taken the last week to get her head where it needed to be. The job offer had come through and she was starting on Monday. She'd cleared the air with Beryl and her dad, and had seen Chelsea for a great girls' night out. She was journaling and healing and figuring out all the times when she'd been so scared of stepping wrong that she hadn't made a single move.

She realized now she'd spent her whole life caught between two worlds. The wonderful women in her neighborhood had totally been there . . . right up until they'd gone back to their own families. She'd grown up with the feeling of being forever left behind. Maybe because of that or maybe because of who she was, she'd never learned when to hang on and when to let go.

With perfect hindsight, she knew she should have broken up with Tim years ago. He'd been so clear on what he wanted and she hadn't been that. She wrestled with guilt and hoped that she hadn't messed him up or made him unhappy.

She was less sure about her job at Boeing. She had loved it, but she was so excited about her new opportunity. Maybe it was okay if there were detours along the way.

She walked back through the main floor of the house and imagined what it would look like if she and Malcolm ever lived here. There would be a room for Keira, of course, and a big table in the dining room for when they had their families over. She wanted to get pregnant fairly quickly, assuming he was interested in that much of a commitment. She hoped he was. The first test of that would be whether or not he showed up.

She'd texted him and asked him to meet her at the house. If he didn't show, she would have her answer.

"Please be here," she whispered to herself, then walked to the front porch to wait.

At exactly two, he turned into the drive-way. Relief was sweet and happy and for the first time in days, she felt herself believing in what could be. When he got out of his car and their eyes met, she felt her love for him grow until it filled every part of her. She raced toward him, needing to hold him and touch him and tell him everything.

"Malcolm!"

She threw herself at him and he caught her, then held on so tight, she thought he might never let go.

They stood like that for a long time, hugging, holding, breathing. Finally she drew back enough to look up into his eyes.

"I've missed you so much," she said, talking quickly so she could get it all out and they could move on to the good part. "I'm sorry for what happened before. I needed to work some things out. My past messed me up a little, or maybe a lot, but whichever, I had to figure it all out."

She smiled at him. "I have a new job. I'm the CFO of a Boeing supplier. It's really exciting and I'm beyond thrilled. I've talked to my dad and to Beryl and I know now I should never have stayed engaged to Tim as long as I did. I was so scared to get it wrong. I needed to be free but at the same time I didn't think that was allowed. Then there was the shooting and everything changed."

She searched his gaze, but had no idea what he was thinking. Which meant she was going to have to be brave all on her own.

"Going back to college wasn't right for me. Or the doctor thing. I'd already found my passion. I don't know if I was punishing myself or if I just needed a break. Regardless, I've come through it. I'm better and stronger now. A lot of that is because I found you."

She smiled. "You're a really good guy, Malcolm. You're exactly who I want in my life. I wasn't ready before, but I am now. If you still want me."

No, she told herself. That was the weasel thing to say. Not if he still wanted her. "If you still love me," she amended. "Because I am very much in love with you."

He studied her before speaking. "I do still love you, Delaney. I always will, but I need you to be sure."

"I know and I am. I want you. I want this house. I want us." She curled her toes in her shoes. "I want us to have a family and

613

grow old together. I love you, Malcolm."

The carefully neutral mask fell away and she saw into the soul of a man who'd just been given the moon and the stars. He grabbed her and swung her around, his laughter echoing in the afternoon. When he set her down, he kissed her with a fiery passion that left her weak.

"I've missed you so much," he told her.

"I've missed you, too. I'm sorry I had to get my act together, but it's done now and we can move forward."

He put his arm around her. "About this house."

"We should so buy it, despite the insane price. But I want to pay for it, too. I want us to be partners in everything."

"Even a mortgage?"

"Especially a mortgage." She grinned at him. "As it happens, I'm very good with numbers."

"You're very good at a lot of things."

"I know. Cool, huh?"

"You have no idea."

EPILOGUE

"You're so calm," Delaney said as Callie sat by the vanity set up in the temporary bride's room.

The makeup artist hired for the event finished applying blush. Callie waited until she was done before opening her eyes and smiling at her friend.

"There's nothing for me to worry about. Santiago has it all under control."

One of the advantages of falling for a guy who always wanted to be the hero was he had no problem taking care of details. Once she and Santiago had picked their wedding planner, he'd coordinated most of their wedding with her, leaving Callie free to focus on her classes at the university and taking care of Keira. She, Delaney and Keira had gone together to buy her wedding dress and the attendant dresses. Callie had given her thoughts on the menu and had picked the flowers for her bouquet, but otherwise, Santiago was in charge — with a little help from his mom and Hanna.

Emma raced into the bride's room, Keira at her heels.

"Everyone's arriving," Emma announced, grinning with excitement. "There are so many cars. And the swans are in the lake."

Yes, swans, Callie thought with a secret smile. Because they made him happy and he made her happy.

Their quiet wedding had grown from family and close friends to something a whole lot bigger. Santiago had hired out a local winery and brought in a caterer. They'd agreed on a fall harvest theme and, of course, swans. The wedding colors were burgundy, soft green and blush.

Luis, Santiago's youngest brother, had flown in for the wedding. Paulo's lawyer had eventually worked out a deal on his charges. He'd pled guilty and was serving time, so would not be attending. Hanna had filed for divorce and was picking up the pieces of her life.

Santiago had changed the family trust so the house was in Hanna's name only. Callie suspected he'd put aside some money for Paulo to be given to him when he'd served his time. She hoped Paulo would accept the gesture in the spirit it had been given, but with him, she wasn't sure.

Not thoughts for today, she thought, looking at her soon-to-be sister-in-law. Delaney and Malcolm were engaged and getting married on Valentine's Day. They'd already moved into their new house and were working hard on decorating it. Keira joked about her two families, but Callie knew she appreciated that both sets of adults wanted as much time with her as possible.

Santiago had listed his condo a few days before the wedding. He would move into the big, old house on the lake when they were back from their honeymoon. Malcolm's old rooms had been renovated into a master suite.

Her wedding day hairdresser sprayed her updo one last time, then Callie got up to finish dressing.

Keira and Emma had on junior bridesmaid dresses done in soft green. They were knee length, with cap sleeves and lace over the bodice. Delaney and Hanna had the grown-up version of the same dress, but in burgundy.

Her own gown, also with a lace bodice, was a little surprise for her husband-to-be. Strapless and fitted to the waist, the dress had a full skirt that billowed and swayed with every step. It was a classic princess dress. One she thought he would appreciate.

Delaney helped her into the petticoats, then she and Hanna held up the dress so Callie could shimmy into it before they took turns fastening the thirty-six buttons.

When she was ready, the wedding planner got everyone into place. Grandfather Alberto, tall and handsome in his black tuxedo, smiled as he joined her.

"You are as beautiful as your grandmother was the day I married her. I hope you will be as happy." He reached into his jacket pocket.

"Something old," he said, handing her a diamond choker. "Something blue." He pointed to the small sapphire on the clasp.

Callie stared at the stunning piece. She had no idea how many carats or who was the designer, but she recognized quality workmanship. The rows of diamonds nearly blinded her and the tiny sapphire was in the shape of a heart.

"Grandfather," she breathed. "I couldn't possibly . . ."

"Of course you could, child. You're family."

He moved behind her and fastened the choker, then kissed her cheek. "I'm so proud of you."

The wedding planner opened the door to the bride's room. "It's time," she said. "Are you ready?"

Callie blinked back tears and nodded. She and her grandfather moved into position, just out of sight of their guests. She listened for the music to change to the wedding march and just for a moment, sent all her love and gratitude to her mother, wherever she might be.

So much had changed, Callie thought as she and her grandfather started down the aisle. Friends, family, a home and a man who loved her more than anything in the world. She'd been blessed in ways she couldn't have imagined ever happening.

A few months ago she'd been utterly alone in the world and now she had enough love and support to last a lifetime. Her gaze settled on Santiago. He looked stunned. When their eyes met, he took a half step toward her, then stopped himself. She smiled. He would always do that, she thought happily. Always be willing to step first, to be there, to support her and love her. And she would be there for him.

There would be rough patches, but they would get through them. Fifty years from now, they would look back on this day and be grateful for all of it. Especially the love.

WHEN WE FOUND HOME

SUGGESTED MENU:

Shrimp with Lemon Linguine (recipe
follows)
Salad with vinegar and olive oil
Triple Chocolate Biscotti Brownies (recipe
follows) with vanilla ice cream

SHRIMP WITH LEMON LINGUINE

1 lb dry linguine, cooked according to package directions
2 tbsp olive oil
1 lb shrimp, peeled, deveined and thawed (if frozen)
Juice and zest of two lemons, in separate bowls
1/2 cup half-and-half or heavy cream
1/2 cup shredded Parmesan cheese
Salt and pepper to taste

Cook the linguine according to package directions. While pasta is cooking, heat olive oil in heavy-bottomed pan with deep sides over medium heat. Add shrimp and lemon zest. Cook until shrimp is opaque, about 2-3 minutes, flipping halfway through but otherwise not stirring. Stir in lemon juice and half-and-half. Scrape up the browned bits from the shrimp. Continue cooking until slightly thickened. Add noodles and cheese. Toss. Season with salt and pepper.

TRIPLE CHOCOLATE BISCOTTI BROWNIES

Italian biscotti is traditionally baked twice to remove all the moisture, but Grandfather Alberto Americanized these delicious treats by baking them only once. You might even call them half-baked. They are 100 percent delicious!

2 cups flour
1 cup cocoa powder (optional: dark chocolate cocoa powder)
1 tsp salt
1 tsp baking soda
1/4 cup butter, room temperature
2 cups brown sugar
1/4 cup granulated sugar
1 tbsp vanilla
1 tbsp chocolate liqueur or brewed coffee
3 large eggs, one at a time
1 cup dark chocolate chips

Preheat oven to 325 degrees.

Sift together the flour, cocoa, salt and baking soda. In a separate bowl, cream the butter and sugars until well mixed. Add the vanilla and liqueur or coffee. Mix well, scraping bowl. Add one egg at a time, mixing well between additions. Add the dry ingredients and mix gently just until incorporated. It's okay if the batter is a little lumpy. Fold in the chocolate chips.

Line two baking sheets with parchment paper. Form four long, narrow loaves, two on each sheet. Bake until slightly cracked on top, about 25-30 minutes. Remove from oven, cool and cut into brownies.

ABOUT THE AUTHOR

#1 *New York Times* bestselling author **Susan Mallery** writes heartwarming, humorous novels about the relationships that define our lives — family, friendship, romance. She's known for putting nuanced characters in emotional situations that surprise readers to laughter. Beloved by millions, her books have been translated into 28 languages. Susan lives in Washington with her husband and pets. Visit her at SusanMallery.com.

The employees of Thorndike Press hope you have enjoyed this Large Print book. All our Thorndike, Wheeler, and Kennebec Large Print titles are designed for easy reading, and all our books are made to last. Other Thorndike Press Large Print books are available at your library, through selected bookstores, or directly from us.

For information about titles, please call:
(800) 223-1244

or visit our website at:
gale.com/thorndike

To share your comments, please write:
Publisher
Thorndike Press
10 Water St., Suite 310
Waterville, ME 04901